Th  to
the

"You aren't a Tiger. Who are you working for?"

An evil smile curled the lips of the man on the ground. "You will never know," he spit.

"What have you got planned for America?" Bolan asked. He could see that the man's time was growing short. He'd bleed out in a few minutes. "What's Subing going to pull off in the States?"

"That...I *will*...you," the dying terrorist said, "because you...will never find him in time." He paused, then breathed out one faint and final word. "Nuke."

Charlie Latham looked at Bolan. "Oh, hell."

Don Pendleton's Mack Bolan®

False Front

A GOLD EAGLE BOOK FROM
WORLDWIDE®

TORONTO • NEW YORK • LONDON
AMSTERDAM • PARIS • SYDNEY • HAMBURG
STOCKHOLM • ATHENS • TOKYO • MILAN
MADRID • WARSAW • BUDAPEST • AUCKLAND

First edition March 2005

ISBN 0-373-61504-3

Special thanks and acknowledgment to
Jerry VanCook for his contribution to this work.

FALSE FRONT

Printed in U.S.A.

Whatever deceives seems to exercise
a kind of magical enchantment.
—Plato,
The Republic, III, c.350 B.C.

There are two kinds of evil in this world—the kind
that's planned, reveled in and enjoyed, and the kind
to which men who are otherwise good fall prey
during weak moments. Many have been the victim
of the latter. My mission is to obliterate the former.
—Mack Bolan

PROLOGUE

The smell was what he noticed first, a blend of old and new.
At one time there had been cattle in the building and the scent
of manure still lingered. Hay had been stored in the second-
floor loft but it had molded away, leaving only its stench.

The scents of rotted wood and unwashed human bodies,
however, were current. Old and new, the numerous odors
combined to produce a smell far more nauseating than any one
could have generated by itself and, as he stepped into the barn,
the foul mixture hit Candido Subing like a baseball bat between the eyes.

Subing stopped just inside the door. One odor was separate from the others and seemed to rise alone above them. And
it filled the air like a hanging corpse.

Fear.

Subing had caught the man following him off guard with
his sudden stop and his fellow freedom fighter slammed
into his back, the hard lens of the video camera the man carried cracking into his spine. Subing sent an angry glance
over his shoulder, then turned his attention back to the six
hostages huddled in the corner farthest from the door of the

barn. Four men and two women were seated in the mud, their backs against the wall. Their hands were bound in front of them by a rope that traveled around their waists before dropping to secure their ankles. Makeshift hoods, which had once held grain for the animals who had inhabited the barn, covered each prisoner from the top of the head to the shoulders.

Subing felt his face twist into a sneer. The people beneath the hoods were worse than mere infidels. They were *Christian* missionaries, sent from the Great Satan America to infiltrate the Philippines and to snatch his people from the one true god, Allah, and his prophet.

Subing waded through the muddy floor to the cowering figures. He had no need to remove the hoods to know what lay in each prisoner's eyes. Terror in some. Acceptance of their fate in others. But at least *some* hope still left in most of them.

And outright defiance in one.

Subing stopped in front of the seated captives. He had seen their faces earlier in the day when the hoods had been removed. As soon as their eyes had adjusted to the unaccustomed light, one of the women and two of the men had wept. Two other missionaries—a husband and wife—had closed their eyes and he'd seen their lips move silently as they'd offered up some infidel prayer. But none had dared to meet his eyes. At least, none but one. And that man still mocked him. Subing stared at that man now, his eyes filled with hatred.

Before he killed them—and he *would* kill them all, regardless of whether or not the Filipino and American authorities agreed to the demands he had put forth to them—he would force them each to denounce their false savior. He continued to stare at the hood over the face of the defiant one.

He would denounce his false doctrine this very day.

Subing narrowed his eyes, savoring this moment. The man

who defied him sat between the two women. Worden was his name. The Reverend James A. Worden.

Subing waved the cameraman to his position in front of the hostages and the man began to unfold the legs of his tripod. Like the other hostages, Worden had been given many opportunities to renounce his false religion and embrace Islam. But he had refused and his refusal had kept the other, weaker-willed missionaries stalwart in their own faith. Two of the men, he suspected, would have denounced Jesus Christ as their savior had it not been for Worden's strength. The husband and wife he couldn't be sure about. They appeared to have some personal strength of their own. But at least their refusals had come fearfully, which meant that time might eventually wear them down. Worden, on the other hand, refused to convert with apparent joy in his heart. And as Subing stared at the ragged, mud-encrusted clothes and equally filthy hood that enshrouded the recalcitrant man, he knew that beneath the cloth James A. Worden was still smiling the same smile he always had on his face when his hood came off. And that knowledge infuriated him.

Candido Subing's hand fell to the barong sheathed in the carved wooden scabbard at his side. In his mind he saw himself draw the short sword and bring its razor-edge down across the back of James Worden's neck. Would he finally see fear in the American's eyes as his head left his body and rolled across the ground? Would he see pain? Horror?

He didn't know. But he was about to find out.

Subing sloshed his black combat boots two more steps forward in the mud and halted between the hostages and the video camera. The prisoners shifted uncomfortably, sensing his presence near them. Standing guard were ten of his fellow Tigers. He moved a step closer to the group, then turned his attention toward Reynaldo Taboada. The man was a new-

comer to the Tigers, but he showed potential. Catching the
man's eye, he said, "Remove the hoods."

Taboada looked hesitant for a moment, but Subing suspected the new man was merely nervous because of his presence. Subing's duties took him away from this operation often
and he had met Taboada only a few times before. In any case,
after a moment's delay, the man walked along the line jerking the dirty feed sacks from the heads of the prisoners.

All twelve of the infidels's eyes blinked furiously as the unaccustomed light hit them. A few more tears rolled down
three of the faces as they stared at the mud in front of them.
The husband and wife team leaned closer to each other and
began, once more, to pray.

But the Reverend James A. Worden turned his eyes immediately upward to Subing, and the same infuriating smile the
Tigers's leader had known would be there beamed out at him.

"Jesus loves you," Worden said from his spot in the mud. "He
will forgive you for all of this. All you have to do is ask Him."

One of the guards stepped in to bring the stock of his AK-47
down on Worden's shoulder and a loud crunching sound echoed
off the rafters. Worden winced and, for a moment, the smile disappeared. But a second later it was back and Subing felt an almost uncontrollable urge to behead the man immediately.

It took all of his self-control to turn toward the cameraman
instead. He saw that the video was now ready, clasped his
hands behind his back and turned full toward the lens. The
cameraman nodded. Subing nodded back. He heard the click
as the start button was depressed. "We have done our best,"
he said into the camera. "To reach an agreement with your
leaders in America. For ten months now we have spared you,
and we have not asked so very much in return. We have asked
only that the United States release our brother patriots they
keep captive and remove all troops from the Philippine Islands

and the Mideast." He paused, turning sideways now and addressing the missionaries themselves. "Our pleas have fallen on deaf ears. Your President does not care about you—he does not care if you live or die." Pausing dramatically he said, "Or perhaps he does not believe we are serious."

Turning once more to the camera, he scowled into the lens. "If the American President does not care about his people, there is little I can do. But if he does not believe I will carry through with my promises…" He let his voice trail off, took a deep breath, then said, "Then I must prove to him that I will."

Twisting slightly, Subing nodded to two of the guards. They moved in next to the Reverend James Worden and hauled the man to his feet, dragging his bound legs through the mud to a spot directly in front of the video camera. One of the guards kicked Worden's legs out from under him and the missionary fell facedown into the soggy earth. The other guard knelt, grabbed the man by the back of his hair and jerked him up to his hands and knees.

Worden's mud-splattered face looked directly into the camera. And smiled.

Again pure rage and hatred rushed through Candido Subing's body like a disease. He yearned to kill the insolent infidel *now*, without further delay. But he had carefully scripted his next moves to make the most lasting impression possible on the news agencies to which copies of the video would be sent. Improvisation would be counterproductive. He wanted the American people to see what he was about to do and to know that it had been done with little, if any, emotion.

America had become a nation of cowards who coddled the weak and took pride in being victims. His killing without emotion would frighten them far more than anger.

So, biting back the indignation in his breast, Subing gave the camera his own smile. He forced himself to speak calmly.

"I am giving this man—this American Reverend James A. Worden—one final chance to renounce his false belief and embrace the true faith." As he spoke, he pulled the barong from its scabbard. Then, raising it to his eyes, he glanced at the inscription on the blade: there is no god but Allah.

"James Worden," Subing said, looking down at the still-smiling face beneath him, "I ask you now to repeat after me." After a short pause he said, "There is only one god."

To Subing's surprise, the smiling face below him said, "There is only one god."

"And Mohammed is his prophet," Subing said.

"And Jesus Christ is His son," Worden said.

Anger and hatred shot once more though Subing's veins. And this time he couldn't hold it back. Grasping the barong with both hands, he brought it up over his head, then down toward the back of the Reverend James A. Worden's neck.

A geyser of blood shot out from the severed arteries to the brain, spotting the camera lens with crimson dots. Worden's body stayed frozen on all fours for a second, then collapsed into the mud.

Subing saw the cameraman frantically wipe at the lens with a rag as he stooped forward to retrieve the bloody mass of flesh and bone from the ground. Grasping it by the tufts of hair at the front hairline, he held it up to the camera. Vanished now were his hopes of showing no emotion and he screamed, "America must release our brethren! American must remove all soldiers from our islands and all Muslim nations!" With a dramatic sweep of his free hand he indicated the shocked hostages behind him. "Or I will kill each and every one of them! Allah be praised!"

As Subing had ordered him to do, the cameraman panned the faces of the missionaries, pausing long enough to register each one's dismay and horror before moving on to the next. Then he pressed the stop button and ended the recording.

Subing realized he had been holding his breath since speaking and finally let it out with a sigh. But when he looked down at the head dangling from his fingers, the sight caused him to suck in another sudden breath and hold it.

Reverend James A. Worden might be dead, but the smile was still on his lips. And it looked wider and more peaceful than it ever had in life.

CHAPTER ONE

The plane in the distance grew smaller, gradually becoming a mere speck in the sky before vanishing from sight altogether. Mack Bolan was alone, but such was almost always the case with the man also known as the Executioner.

Bolan looked down as he free-fell through the sky. Below he could see the deep blue waters of the Sulu Sea. Farther east lay the island of Mindanao, in the Philippines. In a moment he would open his parachute, but it would still be some time before he reached land. The Executioner had chosen a HAHO—High Altitude High Opening—dive both to avoid detection and to give himself room to maneuver the treacherous winds just north of the Sulu Archipelago. If all went as planned, it would take him approximately twenty minutes to reach the arranged landing zone where two already-on-the-ground contacts would be waiting for him. One was a CIA agent who had been trying to infiltrate the Liberty Tigers for several weeks. The other was a retired Delta Force special operations soldier who was also an old friend of another counterterrorist operative who worked out of Stony Man Farm.

Wind whipped at his face as the Executioner free-fell to-

ward the white-capped waves below. Finally he grabbed the
ripcord with his right hand, jerked, and the chute shot out over
his head. Bolan watched as the canopy hit the end of the lines
and saw that there was a problem.

It hadn't opened.

As he continued to plummet, Bolan stared at the flat chute
that some jumpers called a "Roman Candle." Other parachut-
ists referred to them as "streamers." But no matter what you
called it, the bottom line was that the canopy had failed. It
looked like a long, limp dishrag or the tail on a child's homemade kite as it followed him down through the sky toward certain death.

The Executioner's jaw set tightly as he reviewed the pre-
jump equipment check in his memory. Everything had been
in place. Everything in order. Everything had checked out. So
why hadn't the canopy opened properly? He didn't know.
And probably never would.

Bolan continued to fall, forcing himself to stay calm, not
a particularly difficult task for a man who had lived a life such
as his. Remaining composed in the face of impending destruction had become second nature to him. He had stared into the
dark face of the Grim Reaper many times and each time the
man with the sickle had been the one to break eye contact and
back down. Bolan had too much experience under his gun belt
to be upset now.

To most men, the unopened chute would have been cause
for panic. But to the Executioner, a primary canopy malfunc-
tion seemed hardly more dangerous than a bee sting.

The irony of dying from something so minor, however, was
not lost on Bolan. A small grin broke at the corners of his lips
as he was reminded that warriors were still human and that
in addition to the extra dangers they faced they were still subject to all the hazards waiting to ensnare the normal man. Gen-

eral George S. Patton, Jr., had been killed in a car wreck. Colonel Rex Applegate had died of complications following an easily treated stroke. Bolan had known warriors who had succumbed to cancer and other terminal diseases. The truth was that warriors sometimes died like warriors. Other times they passed on in ways that seemed more befitting schoolteachers, accountants and stockbrokers.

Bolan spread both arms and legs to slow his fall. What had started out as a HAHO jump would now be turned into a midopener at best. He reached up to the harness at his left shoulder as, below, the whitecaps became more distinct. He could even make out several black spots that he assumed to be fishing boats. The island of Mindanao was still at least a mile in the distance.

Tugging the D-ring of the reserve chute, the Executioner glanced upward once more to see the streamer break free and fly off into space. That was the first step in the emergency procedure—to get the failed chute out of the way so it didn't entangle the emergency canopy. Bolan counted—one…two… three—then saw the second canopy shoot up and out, blossoming into a life-saving orb that suddenly slowed his descent.

The Executioner had remained tranquil throughout the minor emergency. Still, he breathed a sigh of relief as he began to steer his way toward the landing site. He had work to do and it was that work to which his mind now turned.

As he floated through the sky, Bolan's mind floated, as well—back to the telephone conversation he'd had only hours before with Hal Brognola, director of the Sensitive Operations Group at Stony Man Farm. The CIA had intercepted intelligence that a mammoth terrorist strike against the U.S. was imminent. Details as to exactly what, where, how and when were sketchy, but the chatter was that it would make September 11, 2001 seem like little more than a firecracker. What was clear was the "who." Candido "Candy" Subing and his terrorist group, the Liberty Tigers of the Philippines, were planning the attack. A Filipino Moro-Muslim terrorist organization, the Tigers, as they were commonly called, had achieved notoriety during the past year by kidnapping six American missionaries. Just the day before, the major news networks had all received a videotape of Subing brutally murdering one of the hostages. An edited version had been aired throughout most of the world. Al-Jazeera, of course, had shown the entire gruesome ordeal.

The waves and fishing boats below him, and even the land in the distance, became more distinct as the Executioner sailed to the ground. At the same time, other distinctions filled his mind. First and foremost was the fact that much of the intelligence the CIA had about Candy Subing and his Tigers didn't quite add up. Even before intercepting the intelligence from the CIA, Stony Man Farm had been monitoring the progress of a Filipino military force tasked with locating the hostages. But their attempt appeared halfhearted at best and so far their search had been unsuccessful.

Yes, Bolan thought, Candy Subing was a nasty little terrorist. But was he capable of any kind of major strike at the U.S.? Doubtful. The Liberty Tigers were simply too small and too limited financially to pull off such a thing. In the Executioner's estimation the group simply didn't have what it would take to carry out a large-scale strike on other side of the world. At least not without help. And there had been no mention of any of the other terrorist groups teaming up with them.

Finally over land, Bolan worked the toggles, steering the canopy. The failed primary chute had thrown him slightly off course, but not enough to worry him. He was still several miles north of Zamboanga, the southwestmost city on the island of Mindanao. He might not come down exactly where his ride was supposed to be waiting, but as long as he landed reasonably close, the men would easily spot him. If not, all Bolan needed to do was to make his way to the nearby main—and only—road that followed the coastline. His pickup would have no choice but to drive on it even if he gave up on finding him.

Bolan's mind turned back to the captive missionaries. While their location was still a mystery, the CIA had finally learned that Subing himself slipped in and out of a small village near Zamboanga to visit his uncle. They had notified the President that they were about to send in a team of covert operatives who would do their best to take the Tigers's leader alive, then pump him for information concerning both the hostages and the strike planned for America. If live capture proved impossible, Subing would be assassinated with the hope that the strike in the U.S. would end before it got off the ground.

Bolan shook his head as he dropped closer to the trees. The CIA plan had far too many ifs, ands and ors to suit the President. The Man in the White House had contacted Stony Man Farm and specifically told Brognola who he wanted on the job: the best. Mack Bolan. And he had ordered the CIA director to have only one agent link up with the Executioner—who would be going by the name Matt Cooper. The President had also made it clear who would be in charge, and it wasn't the CIA.

Bolan looked down on the coastal area of Mindanao. Unless he was mistaken, he could see some kind of vehicle parked to the side of the road. A figure was getting out of the driver's side and it looked as if he was wearing a hat.

THE MAN IN THE BATTERED straw cowboy hat pulled the Jeep Cherokee off the pitted asphalt, killed the engine and turned

to face the thick foliage that paralleled the road. He reached
into one of the pockets of his khaki cargo shorts and pulled
out a round tin of chewing tobacco. Dropping a pinch of the
finely cut substance under his bottom lip, he thought of mouth
cancer for a moment, then pushed the troublesome possibility from his mind. Tapping the lid back into place, he returned the tin to his pocket.

Charlie Latham stared at the sky, watching the black speck
he'd first spotted a few seconds earlier grow larger, finally dividing into two parts. As the dots continued to grow, he was
able to discern the outline of both man and parachute. A frown
creased his forehead as he sucked on the tobacco. He'd been
told the jumper—a man he should call Matt Cooper—would
have no trouble finding the clearing across the road. The guy
was an expert skydiver.

But as he watched the sky now, Latham had to wonder just
how accurate that evaluation had been. Considering the wind
direction and the parachutist's current positioning, it looked
as though Cooper would come down at least a mile north of
where he was supposed to land. And a glance at his watch
made him wonder about the other man who was supposed to
meet them here. A CIA agent named Reverte. Where the hell
was he?

Latham twisted the key in the Cherokee's ignition and the
engine roared to life. After a quick glance in his rearview mirror, he pulled back onto the pothole-pocked asphalt the people of Mindanao called a highway. He drove slowly; he had
plenty of time. Matt Cooper wouldn't find his feet on solid
ground for a good ten minutes or so.

Topping a rise, Latham saw another break in the trees,
twenty yards off the road. A glance upward told him Cooper
was maneuvering toward that spot to land. Latham lost sight
of the clearing as the road dipped down but when he reached

a point he guessed was directly across from it he pulled off the road and killed the engine again.

Latham glanced once more into the rearview mirror, this time to lift the weathered straw hat off his head. The leather sweat band came up off his scalp and he felt a quick rush of cool breeze roll over his closely cropped hair. It was a nice relief from the sultry Filipino heat and he almost dropped the hat onto the seat beside him. But the sun would beat down on his face and neck if he did, and besides, he was from Texas. The only time he'd ever felt right without a hat was when he wore a helmet. Football in high school. Then U.S. Army until a year or so ago.

Settling the hat back onto his head with a sigh, Latham reached into the back seat and grabbed a rusty two-dollar machete. He got out of the Jeep, crossed the road into the semi-thick vines of the coastal secondary jungle and lifted the long blade over his head.

A thin trickle of sweat ran down his cheek as he began slicing a path toward the clearing. The jungle canopy blocked his view of the sky, but he knew Cooper had to be nearing the site. It was the only open landing zone in the immediate area.

By the time he had cut himself into the clearing, Cooper was clearly visible in the sky. Latham was surprised to see that the chute beneath which the big man drifted was smaller than he would have expected for such a jump. In addition to the usual parachute gear, Cooper wore a huge backpack. Other equipment carriers were belted around his waist and strapped to his shoulders. Almost as quickly as his brain registered these details Latham was able to answer his earlier question as to why the man was so far off course. No, it wasn't due to a lack of expertise as he had originally guessed. In fact it appeared that Cooper might be even beyond expert. At least the man knew how to keep his head in the face of danger. His main chute hadn't opened and he was landing with the small reserve canopy. That was what had thrown him off course. He was loaded down like a pack mule and, considering the tricky winds through which he'd just come, the fact that he'd even survived with the small reserve chute gave him master-jumper status as far as Latham was concerned.

The Texan stepped out of the trees into the clearing and let the machete hang at the end of his arm. He suspected Cooper could see him by now. Even if he couldn't, the big American would know someone was down here waiting for him by the sunlight shining off the large silver belt buckle that held up Latham's shorts. As he continued to wait, the Texan chuckled silently at himself.

After retiring from the Army, the last ten years of which he'd been assigned to Delta Force, Charlie Latham had come to the Philippines to further pursue his life-long love affair with the Filipino martial arts. But he had brought a part of Texas with him and the unusual combination of clothing he wore was a pretty good indication of his bifurcated personality. The straw Stetson screamed *Texas!*, as did the Western belt and buckle. But the Philippines were just too hot for denim jeans and boots, so the rest of his attire consisted of a tank top, khaki cargo shorts and sandals. It was an unusual, eclectic image he projected, he knew, but he didn't care. He was an unusual man—a mixture of nineteenth-century gunfighter and twenty-first-century soldier with a little bit of Eastern mystic thrown in. He saw no reason his clothes shouldn't reflect that mix.

Latham's mind jerked back to the present as Cooper landed expertly on his feet, rolled to his side, then popped back up to a standing position. In his mind, he gave the man an A-plus on landing to go with the high grade he'd already earned in canopy steering. The Texan could see now that, beneath all the equipment, Cooper wore some kind of skintight blacksuit that had to be hotter than his aunt Betty's salsa. He grinned to himself as he walked forward.

He hoped the man had brought along some cooler rags. Finding anything to fit a guy his size in this land where a man who weighed 130 pounds and stood over 5' 4" in height was considered a giant wasn't going to be easy.

Cooper was already gathering up the chute by the time Latham reached him. He shifted the machete to his left hand and extended his right. Before he could speak, the big man turned his way and said, "You're Charlie Latham?"

Latham nodded as he shook the hand. "And you're Matt Cooper." The handshake was firm and confident without being overly hard. Latham was glad of that. He got the feeling that had this guy wanted to, he could have snapped off several of his fingers.

Bolan released his hand and frowned, his eyes scanning the area around and behind the Texan. "Where's the CIA man?" he asked.

Latham shrugged. "You got me. He hadn't shown up at your original landing site by the time I saw where you were heading and left."

Bolan nodded. "Something may have delayed him. We'll check the spot on the way back."

"Sounds good to me," Latham said. He reached to the ground and lifted two of the heavy equipment bags the parachutist had shrugged out of when he'd hit the ground. "Ready to do it?" he asked. "Sounds like it should be fairly easy."

Bolan hoisted the rest of his gear. "Yeah," he said. "To be honest, it sounds *too* easy." He let the Texan take the lead and followed the man along a recently cut path through the trees. Walking single file as they were wasn't conducive to conversation and both men lapsed into silence as they dodged branches and vines. Left to his own thoughts, the Executioner found himself questioning certain aspects of the mission once more.

He still hadn't gotten over the fact that there were parts of the CIA intelligence reports that didn't make a lot of sense. One of them was how easily Candy Subing could be located. If the man slipped in and out of Zamboanga all the time as the CIA believed, why hadn't the Filipino search force already grabbed him? Better yet, why hadn't they put a tail on him and followed him back to where the missionaries were being held? The CIA even had an address for Subing's uncle. So what, exactly, had this CIA man—Reverte was his name—been doing over the past few weeks? For that matter, where was the man now?

Reaching the Jeep Cherokee parked on the side of the road cut Bolan's thoughts off again as he and Latham tossed the equipment bags into the back. The Executioner shook his head. His mission sounded easy on the surface—capture Candido Subing, interrogate the man concerning both the hostages and the "big strike" the Tigers had planned in the U.S., free the hostages and take whatever action was called for in regard to the American strike.

Bolan found that he was grinding his teeth together as he contemplated the situation. If everything was all that cut and dried, somebody would have already done it.

With the Cherokee's tailgate still open, Bolan unzipped one of the ballistic nylon bags and pulled out a short-sleeved blue chambray shirt, a pair of khaki cargo pants and a plain white T-shirt. The blacksuit he had worn for the jump came off and the khakis went on. The Executioner felt a hard rectangular lump in one of the hip pockets, a micro-cassette recorder brought along for one simple reason—he didn't speak or understand any of the languages in the Philippines except English. Tagalog—sometimes referred to as Pilipino—was the

major tongue, but there were close to a hundred other lan
guages and dialects used throughout the islands. According
to what he'd been told, Latham was fluent in Tagalog and
could get by in a couple of the tribal tongues. Reverte was re
ported to have the same skills. But the Executioner could
foresee an eventuality in which something he suspected was
important might be said with neither one of them present. If
that happened, it would benefit him to be able to record it and
have the words translated later.

The white T-shirt came down over Bolan's head, then he
unclipped the TOPS Loner combat-utility knife that had been
fastened upside down on his blacksuit. Slipping the thick
four-and-one-half-inch blade into a Concealex inside-the
waistband sheath, he fastened it to his belt at the small of his
back. In his peripheral vision the Executioner saw Latham's
eyes widen slightly as he slid on the shoulder rig that carried
his sound suppressed 9 mm pistol.

The Texan squinted under the sun. "Beretta 92?" he asked.

Bolan adjusted the gun in its holster. "It's a 93-R."

"Ah, yeah," Latham said. "I see the front grip tucked under
there now. Three-round-burst selector, right?"

The Executioner nodded, snapping the belt retainers on
both sides into place. Under his right armpit the shoulder rig
carried a double magazine pouch, also of the form-fitted plas
tic known as Concealex.

Latham's eyes got even wider and his mouth dropped open
slightly when the Executioner pulled the mammoth .44 Desert
Eagle magnum from the same bag. It was already at home in
an inside-the-waistband holster of the same space-age plastic

"Far as I know," Latham said, "we're going after a man
not an elephant."

Bolan chuckled as he stuck the big pistol into his pants
and looped the retaining snap around his belt. "You remem

ber the legend of the Model 1911 .45 auto, don't you?" he
asked the Texan.

Latham nodded at the Executioner. "Oh, yeah," he said.
"Spanish-American War. Our troops kept shooting the Filipino Moros on Mindanao with their little bitty .38 Colts and
the Moros kept coming anyway, cutting us to shreds with
bolos, barongs, krises—any blade they could get their hands
on. Which led to the development of the bigger, harder-hit-
ting .45 ACP."

Bolan zipped up his bag, slammed the tailgate door and
walked around the Cherokee toward the passenger's side.
"Right," he said as he got into the vehicle. "And what island
are we on?"

"Mindanao," Latham said.

"And who are we looking for?"

"A Moro-Islamic terrorist named Candido Subing."
Latham slid behind the wheel.

Bolan tapped the big .44 beneath his shirt. "Well, this thing
hits even harder than a .45," he said.

Latham nodded, then reached across the Executioner and
opened the glove compartment. "Thanks for reminding me."
He pulled out a cocked-and-locked Browning Hi-Power with
a stainless-steel frame, blued slide and what looked like black
plastic and rubber grips. As he lifted the weapon and brought
it across to his belt, Bolan noticed a small ramp at the top of
the grip just behind the trigger guard. And as the gun moved
through the air, a tiny red dot raced across the dashboard in
front of the barrel.

"That 9 mm or .40?" Bolan asked as Latham jammed the
weapon into his shorts.

"It's a .40 S&W," Latham replied, grinning. "Remember
the Moros."

Latham reached into the glove compartment again and

pulled out a black nylon double magazine carrier, which he stuffed into one of his pockets. Bolan settled back in his seat as his contact pulled the Cherokee onto the road. He didn't need to ask about the red dot he'd seen dancing in front of the Browning. A laser site. And the ramp in the grip and lack of any exterior wiring on the pistol, meant the laser was one of Crimson Trace's new models for the Hi-Power. The laser beam shot out the front of the ramp when a button—activated by taking a normal grip on the weapon—was depressed. Wherever the red dot fell, the bullet followed as soon as the trigger was pulled.

Latham drove back to the spot where they had originally planned to meet. But there was still no sign of the CIA man. He turned to Bolan, but before he could speak the big man said, "Let's go on. We'll either hook up with him later or we won't."

The Texan nodded. "Undercover work never was my specialty," he said. "But I've done some. And if there's one thing I learned, it's that you can get delayed. You're always working on someone else's timetable."

"Maybe he'll have some decent intel when he shows up," Bolan said.

The two men fell into silence again as the Cherokee bounced over the bumps and cavities in the asphalt. Ahead, the outskirts of Zamboanga appeared and clusters of stilt houses—running from the shoreline well out over the sea above the water—began to sprout.

Latham was the first to speak again. "Hawk told me you weren't the most talkative guy around," he said as he twisted the wheel and turned the vehicle onto San Jose Road.

"I talk when I've got something to say," Bolan told him.

"That's not what I meant," Latham said as rural Mindanao continued to become more suburban. "What I meant was,

Hawk advised me not to ask you a lot of questions about yourself." He glanced at the Executioner then turned his eyes back to the road. "Like, what your real name is or where you're from or who you work for."

Bolan turned sideways in his seat. For a long moment he didn't answer. The connection between him and Latham had come through T. J. Hawkins of Phoenix Force—one of the counterterrorist teams working out of Stony Man Farm. Hawkins and Latham had been friends as kids growing up in Texas and by chance had become reacquainted when both had been assigned to Delta Force. Hawkins eventually resigned and later joined Phoenix Force. Latham had retired, too, becoming an American ex-patriot on Mindanao to study the martial arts.

Finally the Executioner said, "Did T.J. tell you who he worked for when he called?"

"Nope," said the man behind the wheel. "Sure didn't."

"But you asked?"

"Sure did."

"Well, I can't tell you, either," the Executioner said as he turned back toward the windshield. "Thanks for picking me up. I appreciate it. And while T.J. tells me you were as good as him when you were both with Delta Force—and I could use some backup while I'm here—I'll understand if you want to bail out. No hard feelings." He paused a second, then added, "I'm not sure I'd trust someone I just met on a deal like this."

A look of genuine surprise shot across Latham's face as they passed a large athletic field set well off the road. "Hawk's word about you is good enough for me," he said. "I'm in for the duration—or until you kick me out. To tell the truth, things get a little boring around here after a while. I mean, how long can you bang rattan sticks against each other and stab your training partner with rubber training knives before you'd kind

of like to get out and do something else for a while? " He
paused, took in a deep breath and let it out again. "Don't get
me wrong. I love what I'm doing. Kali, Arnis, Escrima—the
Philippines have the most practical martial arts in the world,
you ask me, and the best of the best is right here on Mindanao. But other than that, once you've been to Fort Pilar and
seen the Yakan Weaving Village, there's not a whole lot left
to do."

When Bolan didn't respond, Latham went on.

"Okay, look," the Texan said, lifting his hat off his head and
wiping a hand across his scalp. "Hawk was the best friend I
had when I was a kid. I could tell you stories about trouble we
got into that would curl your ears." He stopped, glanced at the
Executioner, then amended the statement. "Well, maybe not
your ears but most people's. And Hawk was the best trooper
to ever come out of Delta Force, too—don't listen to him
when he tells you I was just as good. I wasn't. Anyway, one
thing you could always count on out of Hawk was getting the
truth. Bottom line—if he says you're okay and I should work
with you and not ask questions, that's good enough for me."

The Cherokee passed Don Basillio Navarro Street, then
turned south on Alvarez. A few minutes later it turned east and
entered the city proper. Barely slowing the vehicle, Latham
guided them in and out of residential and business areas, past
houses, restaurants and bars. The streets were alive with activity. Children played happily in front of houses and older,
more sullen youths, gathered on street corners to glower as
they passed.

Bolan was reminded that Mindanao's cities, as well as its
hinterland, were hotbeds of crime. Robberies, rapes and mur-
ders of both tourists and natives were common, and kidnapping for ransom—especially of Americans—was almost the
national sport.

Pablo Lorenzo Street took them to Valderoza and they drove past Fort Pilar, which Latham had mentioned earlier. Bolan recalled that the fort had been founded by the Spaniards in the early seventeenth century, and conquered at various times by the Dutch, Moros, British and even the Japanese during World War II. Finally claimed by the Filipinos themselves, the fort now housed a marine museum and an ethnographic gallery that concentrated on the Badjao—or sea gypsies—who spent most of their lives on houseboats along the Sulu Archipelago.

Just past the fort they turned away from the city. According to the CIA, Subing's home was in Rio Hondo, a small village—almost a suburb—to the east.

The Jeep topped a rise in the road and in the distance they could see the spiral towers of a village mosque. The Texan snorted humorously and shook his head. "Rio Hondo," he said. "Sounds like a John Wayne movie, doesn't it?"

Bolan smiled as they drove toward the village. He had taken a liking to Charlie Latham and appreciated the man's unique way of viewing life. Latham was a straightforward type and, according to Hawkins, one heck of a fighter both with, and without, weapons. The Executioner hadn't seen any firsthand proof of it yet but he suspected he'd find out up close and personal before this mission ended. Until then Hawkins's word—which had given Latham confidence in Bolan—also meant the Executioner could trust the Texan when the going got tough.

The road rose and fell as they neared Rio Hondo and with each rise Bolan caught glimpses of the shoreline and water beyond. Several shallow-draft sailboats—*vintas*—moved gently back and forth along the coast. In them he could see tiny brown figures casting fishing nets over the sides. He was so occupied when he suddenly heard Latham say, "Uh-oh," in a calm voice.

The Executioner turned his attention back to the road. They had just rounded a curve and Latham was slamming on the brakes, barely coming to a halt before hitting an ancient, rusting Chevrolet parked in the lane in front of them. Blocking the oncoming lane—and preventing them from passing— stood an equally old Ford Fairlane with a huge dent in the front fender. Two men stood between the vehicles, their arms waving wildly as they shouted at each other. To the average tourist it would have appeared that they had just been involved in an accident and were attempting to assign the blame.

But Bolan was neither tourist nor average. And neither was Latham.

"Kidnappers," Latham said quickly as he pulled the Browning from his waistband. "Fake car accident. Standard ploy."

Bolan didn't need to be told. The Desert Eagle had come out of its holster the moment he'd seen the two cars. Now, as the two arguing men turned to face the Cherokee, he held the big .44 Magnum pistol just out of sight below the dashboard.

Both men wore dingy brown shirts, the tails untucked over baggy, tropical fabric slacks. They smiled as they began to casually walk forward as if to ask for assistance.

Then the shirttails came up and both men pulled pistols from their belts.

The Executioner twisted the door handle, threw open the door and leaped from the Cherokee. As he did, he saw a half dozen more men with AK-47s suddenly rush out of the jungle at the side of the road. The outbreak of automatic rifle fire behind him told Bolan that even more gunmen had appeared from the jungle on the other side of the road. As he dived below a burst of 7.62 mm rounds he wondered briefly if Latham had gotten out of the car. He hadn't heard the man's door open amid the explosions.

Bolan returned his attention to the men on his side of the

vehicle. Latham was either alive or he was dead. Either way, there was nothing the Executioner could do to help him at the moment.

Another volley of fire struck the Cherokee as Bolan hit the ground and curled his body into a shoulder roll. As he rolled he caught a flash sight of the six men in front of him, his brain registering the fact that they wore a mixture of camouflage and more traditional dress. He wondered briefly if kidnapping was really their objective. The ambush was taking on more of the aura of a well-thought-out terrorist op.

Maybe even an assassination. Did the Tigers know he was on the island?

The Executioner pushed the possibility to the back burner for the moment. Right now it made little difference who the men were or what they wanted. They meant to kill both him and Latham, and at this point the important thing was to make sure they didn't get it done.

Bullets struck the highway's shoulder to both of the Executioner's sides. Huge chunks of black asphalt, heated to softness by the hot Mindanao sun, ripped open as if tiny earthquakes had erupted. Bolan's brain raced at near-inhuman speed, analyzing, evaluating, taking in the details of the situation. He weighed the odds and calculated the percentages of every possible course of action as he rolled beneath the onslaught.

The bottom line was grim. He was outnumbered and outgunned. There were six men directly in front of him, and even if he could make it to the rear of the Cherokee some of them would still be angled for clear shots. But the rear of the vehicle was the nearest thing to cover available so it was toward that goal he would have to fight.

Bolan rolled again amid a shower of lead. The gunmen on Latham's side of the vehicle continued their assault, their rounds exploding from that direction.

The Executioner rolled up to one knee and lifted the Desert Eagle. The enemy had both superior manpower and firepower. He and Latham had superior thinking, superior thinking that could be turned into superior strategy. And both the thinking and the strategy would have to be *far* superior.

The Executioner pointed the barrel of the Desert Eagle at the man closest to the rear of the Cherokee. Heavyset and bareheaded, the would-be kidnapper wore what looked like faded blue gym shorts and sandals below a camouflage BDU blouse. A tap of the trigger sent a 240-grain semijacketed hollowpoint round exploding from the .44 Magnum pistol's barrel. It drilled through the third button in the stenciled leaf-pattern cammie shirt, snapped the man's spine in two, then blew on out of his back taking with it a hurricane of mangled muscle tissue, blood and splintered bone. The man himself went limp, collapsing to the ground like a dropped rag doll.

The soldier swung the Desert Eagle to his left, toward the next man closest to the rear of the Cherokee.

This man sported a stringy mustache and equally wispy growth of beard. Like the gunner who had fallen before him, he, too, would still have a direct line of fire at the back of the vehicle once Bolan reached it. Which meant he had to go next.

The Executioner squeezed the trigger once more and a second .44 Magnum hollowpoint round blasted from the barrel. It caught the attacker high in the chest, the velocity throwing him backward into a complete flip in the air. He came to rest on his belly, his chin caught on the ground, his face staring back at the Executioner. But the open eyes above the thin mustache saw nothing. Nor would they ever again.

Four more kidnappers remained on his side of the Cherokee and their return fire now zeroed in on Bolan's sides. He rolled to the ground again, angling toward the Cherokee's rear, the rounds exploding in his ears. One bullet cut through the sleeve of his blue chambray shirt, scorching the skin on his arm as it passed. The Executioner barely noticed it as he pulled the trigger, sending another pair of rounds into the blurry mass of camouflage that whirled past his eyes. As he continued to roll he caught another flash picture.

But this time the picture was of Charlie Latham. The Texan had indeed exited the Cherokee. Somehow he had even made it to cover beneath the vehicle.

Coming to a halt on his stomach, the Executioner extended the big .44, gripped in both hands. The four men still in front of him had expected him to rise to his knees and their auto-volleys raged high over his head. Bolan pulled the trigger back once more and watched a man wearing a mud-stained yellow T-shirt take the result between the eyes. The top of his head disintegrated from the nose up.

Three down, three to go. But that didn't count the attackers on Latham's side. Or the two men posing as auto accident victims to his front. In the back of his mind, as the front dealt with the more immediate crisis, the Executioner registered that the phony drivers seemed to have disappeared.

Bolan swung the .44 left again, letting the front sight fall onto a burly, bare-chested Filipino wearing nothing but camouflage pants. His long, straight black hair was tied back from his face with a white cloth. The white made a perfect target. The Executioner let the sight fall on the bright strip across the man's forehead then pulled the trigger. The would-be kidnapper lost the top half of his head the same way his friend had.

With four of the assailants on his side now down and out of the game, the Executioner rolled behind the Cherokee and came up onto his knees, his head just above the bumper. On Latham's side of the vehicle he saw two men firing at the Cherokee. One .44 Magnum round took out a clean-shaven kidnapper wearing blue jeans and a BDU blouse. A second after he'd pulled the trigger, the Executioner saw a faint red dot appear on the black T-shirt of another man. The sun was too bright for Latham's laser sight to be at its best, but at close range it could at least be seen. He heard a boom from beneath the car and the man in black went down.

Bolan smiled inwardly as he fought on. The red dot meant that both the Crimson Trace laser sight and Charlie Latham were still working.

Another massive Magnum round from the Desert Eagle took out a young Filipino with an acne-pocked face. Now, with both sides temporarily clear, the Executioner dropped the near-empty magazine from the Desert Eagle, jammed a fresh load between the grips and transferred the big gun to his left hand. As he drew the Beretta 93-R with his right, rounds continued to pepper the vehicle from the front.

Bolan took advantage of the short pause in the action to evaluate the situation as it now stood. He didn't know how many men Latham had been able to take out. He did know if Latham was still alive. The man might well be wounded but he had to find out the Texan's status before he went on. Latham's condition would have a major effect on his next moves.

The Executioner leaned down under the bumper. "Charlie!" he yelled over the cacophony. "You all right?"

"I'm not hit if that's what you mean!" Latham yelled from beneath the vehicle. "But 'all right' might be stretching it a bit. I've been—" Yet another barrage of rifle fire drowned out whatever else he had to say.

Bolan had ascertained Latham was unharmed, but that could change at any second. There were still two men with pistols in front of the Cherokee. Still a pair of AK-47s blasting away near the front on the Cherokee's passenger's side. To reexamine his battle plan, it was imperative that he find out exactly how many men were still in the fight.

Round after round continued to bombard the Cherokee. Jamming the Desert Eagle into his belt, the Executioner quickly unscrewed the sound suppressor from the Beretta. There were times when you needed a quiet weapon. Other times you wanted noise and confusion. This situation fell into the latter category.

Bolan's arm snaked around the rear bumper, firing a blind burst of three 9 mm rounds toward the two men still on the passenger's side. Then, without hesitation, he leaned the other way and triggered the Desert Eagle twice.

Then he stood.

In the fraction of a second during which he was forced to make himself a perfect target, the Executioner saw three bodies on the ground—one he remembered shooting himself, the others evidently fallen to Latham's Browning. Two other men stood near the corpses. They started to swing their AKs his way as the Executioner's eyes skirted to the other side of the vehicle.

The two men he had left standing on that side still fired away full-auto. More shots—slower, from pistols—came from behind the parked cars in front of the Cherokee.

Bolan nodded to himself. That had to be where the phony accident victims had taken cover.

Bolan hunkered down behind the Cherokee a half second ahead of a thunderstorm of 7.62 mm rounds that now sailed his way. Dropping to his belly, he saw Latham's shadowy form still under the car. The Texan turned to look at him as the Executioner squirmed beneath the bumper toward the right rear tire well. Latham lay on his back, the Browning Hi-Power aimed toward the passenger side of the vehicle. As the Executioner moved beneath the Jeep, his head passed within a foot of the Texan's.

Latham turned to face him in the shadows. "What I was

trying to say earlier, before we were so rudely interrupted,"
he said, "was that I've been better."

Bolan grinned as he moved in farther beneath the Cherokee. T. J. Hawkins had been right. Latham could definitely
keep his cool under fire.

When he'd come as close as he dared to the edge of the vehicle, the Executioner could see two sets of legs from the
knees down. Without hesitation, he extended both hands. The
man on the right caught a .44 Magnum round in the shin. The
man on the left took a 3-round burst of 9 mm rounds in an
ankle. Both men fell to the ground, screaming. Mercy rounds
from the Beretta ended their suffering.

The Executioner crawled backward again.

"How many left?" Latham whispered as he passed.

"Two to the right," Bolan whispered back. "And the two
guys faking the accident. Behind their cars."

"I hit one of them on my way down here to this hobbit
hole," Latham said, looking up at the Jeep's undercarriage.
"Don't think it killed him, though."

Bolan emerged from beneath the back bumper, his brain
taking in the fact that the quantity of return fire from the kidnappers had withered considerably. Part of that, he knew,
came from the fact that many of the riflemen had been killed.
But there was more to it than just that.

The kidnappers—if that's what they really were—had outnumbered the Executioner and Latham twelve to one when the
gunfight had begun. They'd planned on an easy snatch of two
unarmed foreigners if ransom was their game. Or an easy kill
if Subing had sent them to assassinate him. But now, regardless
of their motives, within sixty seconds or so, they had lost three-
quarters of their manpower. That had a way of playing on the
mind and they had to be wondering just what kind of men
they'd run into. Which, in turn, was causing them to hesitate.

Bolan leaned down beneath the bumper once more. "Roll out on the driver's side and cover me," he ordered Latham. "On three. One, two—"

The Executioner rose up as he said, "Three!" stepping out to the side of the Cherokee. The final two men who had emerged from the jungle on his side of the car had indeed been hesitating. But they had obviously made their decision.

They were one step away from returning to the brush when Bolan shot them with a double tap from the Desert Eagle.

In his peripheral vision, Bolan saw Latham standing next to the open driver's door. The Texan held his Browning in both hands, sending a slow but steady stream of .40-caliber hollowpoint rounds into the parked vehicles. At this distance, the laser sight was unusable in the bright sun, but Latham was proving he could shoot without it.

The Executioner turned away from the road, leaping over the body of a man he'd shot earlier and darting into the leaves and vines. Quickly, while the men behind the vehicles were concentrating on Latham, he made his away through the foliage until he had gone past the point where the cars were parked.

From there, it was easy.

The Executioner saw that Latham had indeed hit one of the men high in the arm. The man had ripped half his shirt off and tied it around the wound in an attempt to staunch the blood. But the makeshift bandage wasn't working; crimson fluid drained past his elbow and along the limp limb before splattering onto the asphalt.

Bolan flipped the Beretta selector switch to single shot. With plenty of time to use the sight, he lined the weapon up on the injured man and squeezed the trigger.

A lone 9 mm round streaked from the 93-R into the injured man's temple.

The other man behind the car whipped his face over his shoulder to stare at the Executioner in shock. The reality of what was happening suddenly spread across his face and he tried to turn farther, swinging his pistol around with him. He didn't make it.

A second 9 mm round entered his open mouth and blew out the back of his skull.

Suddenly what had sounded like a Chinatown fireworks factory exploding became as quiet as a graveyard. Bolan stepped out of the trees and walked forward. Quickly he stopped by each man he passed to be sure none of the bodies would suddenly rise from the grave to shoot again. All were dead.

The Executioner met Latham between the kidnappers's parked cars and the Cherokee. "We've got to clean this place up and hope one of the vehicles still works," he said, glancing over his shoulder to see the Ford Fairlaine resting on its rims, all four tires blown out. The Chevy had lost only one tire but water dripped from the punctured radiator. When he stepped forward, the distinct odor of gasoline filled the air. Turning back to the Cherokee, he saw that while the body was riddled with holes, all four tires were still intact. Bolan nodded at the vehicle. "See if it still starts," he ordered Latham. "And while you're there, grab my sound suppressor off the ground behind the rear bumper."

As the Texan walked toward the Cherokee, Bolan began to lift the bodies and drag them toward the jungle. Behind him, he heard Latham's car cough to life. Or at least a half life. Something beneath the hood had been hit and the timing was off. And a periodic ping meant the half life wouldn't be long, either.

The Executioner tossed another body into the brush, reached down and sent the AK-47 the man had wielded flying out of sight. In addition to no longer having any faith in the engine, the bullet-ridden Cherokee would be a mobile sign attracting attention they didn't need. It was time for another change in plans. He'd just have to hope this vehicle would get them out of the immediate vicinity and back into town where they could appropriate a more reliable and less conspicuous mode of transportation.

With the engine still choking and coughing, Latham joined the Executioner in hiding the bodies. When all but two of the attackers had been hidden, they pushed first the Ford, then the Chevy off the road onto the shoulders. Setting a body behind both steering wheels, they turned the dead eyes to face each other across the highway.

To anyone passing, it would look as if two drivers had met on the road and pulled off to have a quick conversation. At least it would look that way as long as no one noticed the pools of blood spotting the asphalt.

Bolan glanced at the mutilated autobody as he hurried to the Cherokee again. Latham's Jeep looked as if someone had methodically gone over it with an awl, punching holes every half inch into the body. He ducked inside as the Texan took his place behind the wheel again.

"This thing's gonna stand out in Rio Hondo like an ex-husband at the bride's second wedding," Latham said.

The Executioner shook his head. "Change in plans," he said. "Turn us back toward Zamboanga. We need some new wheels."

Latham immediately saw the wisdom in the order and didn't argue. He threw the Cherokee into drive, made a U-turn in the highway and started back toward the city. As soon as they were moving he stuck his tongue into his tobacco can. Twice.

Miraculously, there had been no traffic during the few minutes of the gunfight. But now, having gone less than a hundred yards, a rusty, primer-painted Datsun topped the hill, heading toward them. As the war-damaged Cherokee chugged on, Bolan adjusted the rearview mirror and watched the reaction of the elderly Filipino behind the wheel.

The old man passed the parked cars without giving either of the dead drivers a second look.

As they drove away from the scene, Latham frowned.

"You okay?" Bolan asked. The man had proved himself to be a more than adequate warrior, living up to what Hawkins had promised.

"Yeah, I'm okay," Latham said. "Just trying to remember something."

It was Bolan's turn to frown now. "What?" he asked.

"Whether or not I made my last auto insurance payment," the Texan said.

The Executioner's frown curled into a grin.

CHAPTER TWO

Bolan was faced with a problem: ditching the bullet-ridden Cherokee and finding a set of wheels that blended with the local atmosphere of Rio Hondo. He and Charlie Latham were going to look out of place as soon as they stepped out of any vehicle. He didn't need a stand-out car to announce their presence ahead of time adding to that problem.

Dusk fell over the island of Mindanao as Latham drove past Fort Pilar and Bolan pointed toward an intersecting road. He had studied a map during the flight to the Philippines and knew the road curved around the southeast corner of Zamboanga, eventually merging with General V. Alvarez Street and leading to the heart of the city. By the time they reached the downtown area twilight had become nighttime.

Beggars and gangs of youths began to appear on the streets as they drove. The Executioner was reminded that every city, in every country, in all of the world, had its share of "night people," men and women who were never seen when the sun was in the sky but emerged from robber's dens, crack houses and from under rocks as soon as darkness fell. Zamboanga seemed to have more than its share of such people.

But not all of the night people were evil, Bolan knew. Many were simply unfortunate.

The soldier pointed Latham into a left turn onto Lorenzo and more groups of shiftless teenaged boys appeared in front of the stores and other businesses lining both sides of the street. Angry black eyes set in berry-brown faces stared into the Cherokee as they passed. The Executioner could understand their anger. They had been born into a world of poverty and sorrow with little hope of ever escaping. But anger alone changed nothing. Anger put no food on the table. It purchased no medicine for the sick. It didn't change a dirt-floored house into one with tile or carpet. And now, the loathing in the black teenage eyes that watched the Cherokee pass changed to fury, which Bolan knew would produce tomorrow's terrorists if men like him didn't work for change.

Latham had finally had enough silence. "What are we looking for?"

Bolan started to answer, then stopped as the Buick Century Custom they'd been following for the past several blocks pulled over and parked on the street a half block ahead. "That," he told Latham, nodding toward the windshield. As the driver's door opened, the Executioner's eyes turned toward the sidewalk where yet another gang of teenagers leaned slothfully against the plate-glass window of a small café. As he watched, a dark-skinned man wearing a black-and-white checkered shirt stepped away from his cohorts and grinned at the car. The man was incredibly tall by Filipino standards— probably just under six feet. As he swaggered toward the Buick, the driver got out, walked to the sidewalk and handed the taller man a key ring.

"Pull in behind them," the Executioner said.

Latham followed orders as Bolan studied the man who had just driven up. Actually, calling him a man was stretching the term if not a complete misnomer. He was well under five feet tall and looked to be around thirteen. The taller man took the keys and slapped him on the back with his free hand. The child who had driven the Buick beamed as if he'd just become the new president of the Philippines.

"Well, *there's* a rough one to figure out," Latham said as he halted the Cherokee ten feet behind the Buick.

Bolan chuckled as he opened his door. Car theft was as common as kidnapping on Mindanao with older boys often using the younger ones to actually perpetrate the crimes. Just as in the United States, the younger the criminal, the more likely he would get a light sentence or get off altogether, if caught. Now, as the Executioner stepped out and up onto the curb he saw the tall man, the driver, and half a dozen other Filipino youths turn his way.

Although smiles appeared on many of the faces, the young men didn't look happy. Their expressions were more like what could be expected on the face of a wolf upon spying a particularly large sheep.

Bolan could hear low chatter among the men as he walked forward. Here and there, he heard a snicker as some of the younger ones pointed at him and spoke. Behind him, the Executioner heard Latham exit the Cherokee, the Texan's sandals flapping on the pavement with each step he took.

"Normally I'd say stopping to chat with these guys wasn't the smartest idea in the world," came the Texas drawl behind the Executioner. "Of course, it's all in your point of view, I guess. Compared to what we just finished doing, it pretty much pales by comparison."

The voices were clear now but in a dialect unfamiliar to the Executioner. Stopping five feet from the man in the checkered shirt, Bolan turned to Latham as the Texan fell in at his side. "You understand them?" he asked.

Latham shook his head. "They're Samal," he said. "One of the indigenous Manobo tribes. Got their own dialect."

"They speak Tagalog, too?" Bolan asked.

"I'd imagine," Latham said. He pulled out his can of tobacco, opened it, snaked his tongue inside then stuffed the can back in his pocket. With a smile on his face, he looked at the young men in front of him and spit out a fast mouthful of the national language. Bolan caught only the word "Pilipino."

The man in the checkered shirt smirked, shrugged and held out his hands, palms up. The rest of the Filipino gangbangers laughed.

"I asked him to switch languages. He's acting like he doesn't understand me," Latham said.

"But he does," Bolan said.

"Hell, yes, he does. He's just got to screw with us a little to save face in front of his boys." He sighed quietly. "It's all part of the game." Pausing again, he turned slightly toward Bolan. "You *do* realize that they won't be able to resist trying to rob a couple of Yanks like us, don't you?"

"That's what I'm counting on," Bolan said.

"Yeah, well...." Latham chuckled and shook his head in disbelief. "Okay, what do you want me to tell them next?"

Bolan looked the tall leader in the eye and grinned. "Tell him we'd like to trade cars with him. The Cherokee for the Buick he just stole."

"Oh, that'll go over big, I'm sure." Latham cut loose with another flurry of undecipherable words.

The man in the checkered shirt leaned to the side and looked at the bullet holes in the Cherokee. When he answered this time, he did so in Tagalog. Whatever he said brought riots of laughter from the others.

Bolan glanced to his side.

"It's a little hard to translate directly," Latham said. "But, loosely, he said the Cherokee has more holes in it than your father's prophylactic must have had."

The Executioner chuckled politely. But he was quickly growing weary of this whole game. Reaching into his pocket, he pulled out a large roll of paper money. "Tell him we'll throw in a few extra pesos to cover the holes."

The eyes of the tall leader fell on the money and his smile turned predatory again. Still staring at the Executioner's hand, he spoke again, pointing to the alley behind him.

"Do I need to translate that?" Latham asked. "He wants to go—"

"He wants to do the deal in the alley." Bolan shoved the money back into his pocket. "Tell him that's fine."

Latham spoke, then waved his hand toward the alley. The tall leader and the others fell in around Bolan and Latham, escorting them toward the dark opening between the buildings. The dialogue between the young men went back to the Samal dialect and with it came the return of the snickering. In the shadowy light from the overhead streetlight, Bolan could see that each and every one of them believed they had just met the two stupidest Americans who had ever been born. Now, they were leading the sheep to slaughter.

The Executioner walked calmly on as the tall man in the checkered shirt reached out with his left arm and took Bolan's, much as one might do to help an old lady across the street. He seemed to have no perception whatsoever that he has herding not a sheep but a *sheepdog*.

Twenty feet into the alley, the group halted. Dim light filtered in from the sidewalk and high above them on the roof to Bolan's right a spotlight brightened the barred-and-locked back door to the building. Still holding the Executioner's arm with one hand, a flash of silver suddenly appeared in the gang leader's other hand. What little light was available seemed to be drawn directly to the object, which sparkled brightly as it began to swing through the air accompanied by a series of clicks and snaps.

Bolan would have recognized the sounds even if he hadn't seen the knife. Although it had originated in the Philippine Islands, the balisong had become a worldwide weapon and various versions were now manufactured all over the planet. He was about to reach out to grab the gang leader's wrist when the man suddenly dropped his arm and stepped back.

The balisong began to dance through the air, making circles, squares and cutting figure eights. The man holding the knife stepped under the spotlight in front of the alley door. Amid a chorus of oohs and ahs of awe and delight from his young minions, he continued to open and close the wings of the butterfly knife.

"Want to just shoot 'em?" Latham whispered. "Of course it'd be sad to see so much worthless talent go to waste."

Bolan ignored him, watching silently as the leader finally finished, clamped the handles together in his fist and holding the balisong threateningly out in front of him.

"Does this mean the show's over?" Bolan asked.

He was a little surprised when the man in the checkered shirt nodded. "Unless you would like to become part of it," he said in overly dramatic, heavily accented English. The wolverine grin had returned to his face and, standing beneath the spotlight, he actually looked more like an actor on stage than a man with a knife in the middle of a robbery.

"Excellent grammar," Latham chimed in. "And here I was wasting all that time translating."

"We will take the money and *both* cars," said the man in the checkered shirt. "If you are lucky, we will let you two leave with your lives." He opened and closed the balisong one final time for effect. "Do you feel lucky, punk? Well, do you?"

"Oh, *man,*" Latham said. One hand shot up to his face to cover his eyes. "This is getting really embarrassing now." He turned to Bolan. "Everybody in the Philippines loves movies, but they get them pretty late."

Bolan had had enough of the whole Bruce-Lee-Dirty-Harry show. With one smooth movement he swept the tail of his chambray shirt back past the Desert Eagle, pulled the big .44 Magnum pistol from his belt and stepped forward. Using the heavy weapon as a club, he brought the barrel down across the wrist holding the balisong. A sharp, snapping, almost nauseating crack of bone filled the alleyway as the gleaming blade flew from the gang-banger's hand to clatter onto the ground.

The Executioner jammed the bore of the big .44 into the man's forehead. Out of the corner of his eye he could see that Latham had drawn his Browning. The red laser-dot moved back and forth from chest to chest as the Texan covered the rest of the gang.

Bolan turned to face the other men. "My turn on stage," he said.

Somewhere along the way the wolfish smile had disappeared and now the man in the checkered shirt looked like a boa constrictor with an elephant caught in his throat. He nodded slowly.

"Nothing fancy on my part," Bolan said. "Just give me the keys to the Buick. And move slowly. Very, very slowly." He pressed the Desert Eagle into the man's face a little harder to serve as an exclamation point at the end of the sentence.

The gangster got the message. His hand moved into the pocket of his dirty blue jeans with the speed of a stoned sloth. The key ring came out and he extended it timidly forward. Bolan took the keys with his free hand and dropped them into his pocket.

"Charlie, you got the keys to the Cherokee?"

He felt the Texan move in to his side. A second later Latham's hand dropped the keys into the breast pocket of the black-and-white checkered shirt.

"A wise businessman once told me that the best deals are the ones where both parties walk away happy," the Executioner said, still holding the .44 between the gang leader's eyebrows. "So. Are you happy?"

The man in the checkered shirt nodded slowly. The barrel of the Desert Eagle moved up to the man's hairline, down to the bridge of his nose, then up again.

"Good," Bolan said. "I'm happy, too." Quickly he stepped away from the leader and turned to the rest of the young men, waving them toward the wall as he and Latham backed out of the alley.

After transferring their possessions from the Cherokee, they were driving away from downtown Zamboanga with Bolan behind the wheel of the Buick Century Custom.

THE NIGHT HAD DARKENED even more by the time they returned to spot where they'd been attacked on the road. The Chevy and Ford still stood where they'd been left, the dead drivers appearing to be engaged in an across-the-road conversation. The moon had disappeared behind the clouds and Bolan drove on headlights alone.

Bolan let up on the accelerator, slowing the Buick as they entered the outskirts of Rio Hondo. Latham sat silently next to him as they drove past a long row of stilt houses built out from the shore over the water. According to intel, there were forty-six of the dwellings crammed so close together that they almost appeared to be one long structure. Candido Subing's uncle—Mario Subing—lived in one of the rickety shanties near the center. While neither Stony Man Farm nor the

CIA believed Mario was directly involved with the Tigers himself, the old man was perfectly willing to harbor his nephew. His was the twenty-first stilt house from the edge of town. Bolan counted the dilapidated dwellings as they passed.

Uncle Mario's place looked no different than any of the other raised dwellings as it blurred into the rest of the long row in the Buick's rearview mirror. The Executioner knew he'd have to count again when he returned later that night.

The rumor of the "big-time strike" in the U.S. floated through Bolan's mind again. And again, he couldn't see how such a small organization could pull off such an expensive enterprise. If there was such an operation in motion, the Tigers *had* to be linked up with some other group.

A half dozen elderly men in front of what appeared to be a café were the only ones who seemed to take notice of the Buick as they drove through the village. Bolan kept his eyes on the mosque to his left, finally turning off the asphalt highway and cutting back inland on a gravel road. Mentally he mapped the layout of the village for future reference, noting that behind the houses across the road from the stilt dwellings lay jungle and the most direct foot path between the mosque and Mario Subing's place would be to cut through the thick leaves and vines. The jungle would also provide even better cover than the darkness for much of their approach. There might even be a spot inside the trees where they could set up surveillance.

The Executioner passed a small brown man and woman holding hands as they walked away from the mosque. They stared at the Buick, an unfamiliar car in the small settlement. That was the primary drawback to his plan—the car. Even if the Rio Hondans didn't look inside the Buick and see the light-skinned men they were bound to take notice of any unknown vehicles that entered the village. The best plan was to find a parking place as close to the jungle as possible, then get out of the car and into the trees before they were spotted.

The Buick crunched over the gravel toward the towering sphere atop the mosque. If they were spotted, they'd do their best to pass themselves off as lost tourists. But that story was so thin it could have been anorexic. Latham had informed him that all of the tourist manuals and western government travel advisories discouraged visitors from visiting Rio Hondo during the day and just flat-out told them they'd be out of their minds to be in such an area after the sun went down. There was just too much crime. Visitors were encouraged to stick close to their lodgings from dusk until dawn.

Charlie Latham had to be thinking along the same lines because as the Executioner drove on he pulled the straw cowboy hat from his head and dropped it on the floor at his feet. Not knowing whether the mosque would be open when they arrived, they had nevertheless been aware of the fact that wearing shorts in the area would definitely be frowned on by Islamic leaders. So they had stopped along the road soon after acquiring the Buick and Latham now wore a faded pair of denim jeans he'd pulled out of the rear of the Cherokee. A well-worn pair of Nike running shoes had replaced his flipping and flopping sandals.

The gravel road led into a parking lot where several other vehicles already stood. Lights could be seen through the mosque windows. Bolan pulled the Buick quickly between two other cars, hoping they might serve as at least partial camouflage. Word that an unknown car was in Rio Hondo would travel fast enough. He didn't see any sense in hurrying it up any faster than he had to.

The Executioner cut the engine and killed the headlights. He estimated them to be roughly half a mile from the stilt houses.

Through an open door leading into the mosque Bolan could see several men kneeling in prayer. As he and Latham quietly exited the car, he saw the men rise to their feet and begin talking with one another. That meant that they'd be leaving in a few more minutes, returning to the parking lot to get into their vehicles and go home for the night.

Which, in turn, meant Bolan and Latham needed to hit the jungle even faster than he'd thought.

Bolan opened the car door and closed it quietly behind him, Latham doing the same on his side. Crouching slightly, the two men jogged away from the mosque. The Executioner's eyes swept left and right, but he saw no one looking back at him. As soon as they reached the trees they ducked inside, then turned to peer back out through the foliage.

The men who had been at their prayers were now leaving. Some of them took off on foot, others walked toward the parking lot. Two of the men stopped at the Buick, looking it up and down. Thought he was too far away to hear their words, the Executioner saw their lips moving and their arms waving up and down in animated conversation. He knew the news was about to spread throughout the village; how fast it went from house to house depended upon just how unique the sight of an unknown vehicle happened to be. But there was no reason to worry about that now. He would deal with whatever consequences the Buick brought when, and if, he encountered them.

Bolan motioned to Latham to follow, then took off through the jungle. The Texan had kept two rusty-but-shaving-sharp machetes in the Cherokee, which they now used to cut their way through the heavy growth toward the sea. Fifteen yards into the trees, they suddenly found themselves intersecting with a well-traveled footpath and halted in their tracks.

For a moment the Executioner considered taking the path,

for it no doubt led in the direction he was headed. But the fact that it was obviously often used warned him away. He didn't want to encounter any innocent Rio Hondans who might, regardless of their good intentions, tell the rest of the town that there were Yankees hiding in the leaves and vines.

Backing up, Bolan and Latham continued to cut their own route toward the highway.

The moon was still hidden in the sky when they finally reached the houses across the road from the stilt shacks. Peering through the leaves, Bolan could see the backsides of the crudely built sheds, chicken coops and shabby homes. Dropping their machetes, they darted from the jungle into the darkness, crouching as they made their way from building to building, stopping to check for curious eyes each time they reached new concealment.

It took twenty minutes to reach the rear of a splintering outdoor toilet the Executioner estimated to be halfway down the row of stilt houses across the road. Peering around the edge of the foul-smelling outhouse, he stared between two houses in front of him. The clouds had moved and by the dim light of a quarter moon he could just make out the shadowy stilt structures on the other side of the highway.

The Executioner stared at the ramshackle structures. He had decided that the best course of action was to wait on Subing, then tail him back to the hostages when he left his uncle's house. Of course there was no guarantee the terrorist leader would even show up this night and there was every chance in the world that as daybreak neared he and Latham would have to sneak back to their vehicle and find a place to hide out until tomorrow night. If that happened, he would give the plan one more night. And if Subing still failed to appear, he would interrogate the man's uncle.

It wasn't an idea the Executioner relished, Mario Subing

was reported to be an old man. But when he weighed one man against the lives of the hostages and all of the other innocents the Liberty Tigers would kill if allowed to go unchecked, a little fright put into the heart of an octogenarian didn't seem all that cruel.

Turning to Latham, he kept his voice low. "Stay here. There's no sense in both of us going."

"I don't mind—"

The Executioner shook his head. "I know you don't mind going. There's just no sense in both of us taking the chance of being seen. Two men hiding in the dark are twice as likely to be spotted as one."

Latham obviously didn't like the idea of staying back, but he was smart enough to see the logic behind the Executioner's order. He nodded in the darkness.

Bolan stole forward again, keeping low and thankful that they'd encountered none of the stray dogs he'd seen earlier. Barks and a few growls had sounded in the distance as they'd moved through the jungle but they had been the common sounds all dogs made at night, not the warning alerts wild canines sent their prey when they were on the hunt.

Reaching the side of the residence directly in front of the outhouse, the Executioner slid his back along the wall toward a window. Dim light flickered from the screenless, shutterless opening and when he reached it he dropped to his knees. Risking a quick glance over the windowsill, his eyes took in the candle flame dancing on the wooden table inside. Mosquito nets hung over moldy bare mattresses on the packed-earth floor. Six small children huddled in sleep on one of the threadbare beds. A man and a woman, looking far older than they could have possibly been if these children had come from their loins, sat listlessly at the table, staring silently off into space.

Bolan rose to his feet as soon as he'd passed the window and crept to the front corner of the house. Now the shoreline was more visible, and he saw that he was far past the center of the stilt village. Light—open candles and a few lanterns—glowed from some of the structures, glimmering off the water below. Others stilt houses stood in darkness, looking as dead as the faces of the man and woman the Executioner had just seen through the window.

Bolan started at the end and counted to twenty-one. A lantern hung from the porch of Mario Subing's house and through the window behind it he could see what looked like the silhouette of a man.

Turning back to where he'd left Latham, the Executioner ducked past the window and hurried back to the outhouse. Silently he pointed in the direction from which he'd just come, waited until he saw Latham's nod of acknowledgment, then crept back along the houses. A few seconds later he dropped to one knee again and looked out between the houses. Across the asphalt road he saw the same lantern. And the same silhouette still sat in the shadows at the window. But now Subing was looking outward into the darkness.

Waiting for his nephew? Maybe.

The Executioner turned back to Latham. "I'm going closer again," he whispered. "There may be another way into the house we can't see. Subing could slip in and out of the house and we'd never know."

Latham shrugged. "And I suppose you want me to stay here again," he said in a voice that made it clear he would prefer moving up with the Executioner.

"Right," the Executioner whispered. "Cover our rear and flanks." Without another word he turned away from the Texan and crept forward.

Another house; another side window in the same place. But

this window was dark. The Executioner dropped to all fours anyway, staying below the line of sight in case anyone inside might still be awake and watching. But the deep snores that drifted through the opening told him that wasn't the case. Passing the window, he stopped just short of the front of the house and dropped to one knee. Leaning against the splintered boards at his side, he settled in to study the stilt house across the road.

Not all of Rio Hondo was asleep yet and in the shadows and flickering lights of the mounted candles and lanterns the Executioner saw men, women and children moving back and forth between the structures that stood precariously above the water.

Three doors down from Mario's, the Executioner watched the walkway dip, bounce and creak under the weight of several children as they played back and forth along the ramps. Their area was better lit than most of the poverty-level stilt houses with both candles and lanterns hanging from wires suspended from the roofs. Laugher and an occasional scream met the Executioner's ears.

As soon as he was certain he'd not been seen, Bolan lowered himself into a sitting position, his back against the wall of the house. The snoring, punctuated by an occasional cough, continued to float through the window, reassuring him that the occupants had no knowledge of his presence a mere five feet or so from where they slept.

As he waited, Bolan's mind drifted back to the men who had exited the mosque and stopped to examine the Buick. Depending on exactly who they were, how they reacted and what else they might have to do tonight, they'd either pass the car off lightly or start asking questions. Worst-case scenario would be that they smelled trouble and would begin scouring the village for whoever had parked it. And in a town this small—even in the dark—it wouldn't take long for them to find Bolan and Latham.

The Executioner silently prayed that wouldn't happen. He had no desire to injure innocent men who would think they were simply protecting their town from outsiders. But there was little he could do to forestall that situation at this point. If it happened, it happened. As he had always done, he would deal with any specific trouble that came up when it came up.

THE MAN IN THE NEW custom-tailored Italian suit caught a glimpse of himself as he opened the glass door of the restaurant. The suit looked good on him, he decided. Made him look slimmer. Not that slim was anything he put much stock in. The fact was, he had grown up as a poor hungry child and slim had been unavoidable. He considered the corpulence he had achieved during the past twenty years as a sign of his success, and he *never* intended to be hungry again.

The maître d' in the black tuxedo greeted him as soon as he stepped inside. "Good evening, Mr. Mikelsson," he said with the broad grin of a man who knew he would receive a large tip before the night ended.

"Good evening to you, Hugo," Lars Mikelsson responded, following the maître d'.

As the man held his chair out for him, Mikelsson said, "I am expecting a few calls, Hugo. Please notify me immediately." Silently he hoped the calls would come between courses. Better yet, not until he had finished eating altogether.

"Of course, Mr. Mikelsson," Hugo replied, then hurried away.

Mikelsson had barely sipped the beer a waiter had automatically placed in front of him before Hugo reappeared.

"Sir, your call is here."

The fat man pushed himself laboriously up from the chair and followed Hugo through the tables to a short hallway, then into an office. Behind the desk sat the restaurant owner. He rose quickly to his feet without needing to be told, exiting the office with his employee. Mikelsson smiled to himself. The restaurant owner had been provided with a free, state-of-the-art, security system. It had been his payment for allowing the fat man to take certain calls in his office. And to ask no questions about them.

A red light was blinking on the telephone on the desk. The fat man in the new suit lifted the receiver and pressed the button next to it. "Yes?" he said into the phone.

"Nothing has changed, Mr. Mikelsson," said the voice on the other end, which he immediately recognized. "The union didn't accept the offer."

A slow boil of anger started in Mikelsson's belly. More and more, it seemed these days, his legitimate business enterprises such as the automobile and aircraft industries not only bored but irritated him. His mood wasn't helped by the fact that he was hungry. "Then let them wait," he said in carefully controlled words. "If they don't care to build automobiles for what I pay them, let them stay home in their pathetic little hovels. We will see who goes bankrupt first, them or me." Without waiting for an answer he slammed down the receiver. It rang again before Mikelsson could get up from his chair.

"Hello," Mikelsson said, sounding irritated.

"Mikelsson."

"Candido?"

"Yes," the voice on the other end said in Arabic.

"I assume you are in Israel, and all is well?" Mikelsson asked bluntly in the same language.

"All is well," Candido said. "Our martyr is ready to enter the synagogue."

Your martyr, not mine, you fool, Mikelsson thought. "Excellent. How far away are you?"

"Three blocks. You will be able to hear it," Subing stated.

"How long will it be?"

"One, maybe two minutes at most."

"Then I will wait," Mikelsson said, his pulse beginning to race. "I like hearing them." Seconds later he heard the explosion on the other end of the line.

"Did you hear it?" Subing asked excitedly.

"Yes."

"I will call you as soon as I return, so you will know where I am." Subing paused and the excitement returned to his voice. "In case everything is in place in America."

"I have told you," Mikelsson said, "the project in the United States is not yet ready. The ship will not even arrive until tomorrow."

"I will be ready," Subing said. "And, again, I will call you as soon as I return home."

The fat man hung up the phone, struggled to his feet and started out of the office, toward the buffet line. He smiled. "Yes, call me, little brown man," he said under his breath to himself. "But I will get word of your return to the Philippines and every other move you make, before you even reach a phone."

CHAPTER THREE

"I'd forgotten how much fun the jungle could be in the middle of the day," Charlie Latham said sarcastically. "Guess that's why the siesta was invented."

The Executioner glanced over his shoulder at the man behind him. They had been back on the jungle pathway for no more than five minutes but already sweat shot from every pore in their bodies to soak their clothes. Latham had produced a bandanna from somewhere on his person and tied it around his forehead as a sweatband. His straw cowboy hat now balanced atop the cloth high on his head, wobbling back and forth and threatening to topple off each time he took a swing with his machete.

The Executioner turned back, lashing out with his machete at a low-hanging vine before taking another step forward. He glanced at his watch to see that it was nearly 1300 hours.

They had fled into the jungle the night before to avoid being spotted by the residents of Rio Hondo. Once the Executioner felt they had gone deep enough that no one would follow their tracks, they had stopped to catch a few minutes' sleep among the foliage. It was the first time the Executioner had closed his eyes since arriving on Mindanao and it wasn't enough rest to bring him back into top form. But it was all he'd had, so it would have to do until another opportunity presented itself.

Upon awakening, he and Latham had found that the temperature has risen steadily. It now had to be somewhere between ninety and one hundred degrees with a humidity index that almost matched. They had returned to their parallel path, happy that only an occasional vine or limb had encroached upon them during the night. They walked quietly, swinging their machetes only when absolutely necessary, their ears cocked for anyone who might come down the regular shortcut from the mosque to the sea.

Considering the men who had so carefully looked over the Buick, Bolan suspected the men of the village were looking for whoever had left the car in the parking lot by now. At the very least, they would be curious.

The Executioner had just brought his arm back to slice through a thick green vine when he suddenly froze in place. Behind him, he heard Latham's foot fall a final time. Bolan had no need to hold up a hand for silence—Latham sensed the need for it just as he had.

For a moment the only sounds around them were the buzzing of insects and the sudden flutter of bird wings between them and the older path. The Executioner glanced overhead through a hole in the jungle canopy to see a rare Philippine eagle—known as the haribon—sail out of sight. More birds took wing as the noise continued to drift through the foliage between them and the native's shortcut.

As the sounds grew louder they became recognizable as voices, though the words could not be understood. The voices were low, muffled. They were the voices of men trying not to be heard, but not trying quite hard enough.

Bolan turned toward Latham.

The Texan silently mouthed the word Tagalog but shook his head, telling the Executioner he couldn't make out the conversation, either.

Bolan stared through the foliage as the voices continued, growing increasingly louder. They sounded as if they hadn't quite come parallel with the new path the two Americans had cut the day before. As they waited, the sound of feet trampling the underbrush began to accompany the voices. Then, as they apparently came abreast of Bolan and Latham, the words became more clear.

The Executioner turned back to Latham, but the Texan was holding up a hand for silence. He had twisted sideways, his other hand at the side of his face farthest from the native pathway. His index finger was stuck in his ear to block out all sound on that side. As the Executioner watched, the Texan nodded, frowning.

The words coming through the trees were discernable now and Bolan wished he could understand the language. What he did note, however, was one very distinct voice. One of the men spoke with a high, wheezing delivery as if he suffered from asthma or had some similar problem with his lungs.

Almost as soon as the voices had grown loud enough to hear, they began to decrease again. The men were moving past them now, slowly leaving audible range as they walked on toward the stilt houses and the sea. Their footsteps faded out first, then the words were gone again, too.

Latham looked at the Executioner. "They're looking for us, all right," he said. "Seems everybody in town wonders about the car."

"Could you tell how many there were?" Bolan asked.

Latham shrugged. "Three. Maybe four. One guy has trouble breathing."

"So I noticed," the Executioner said. "What else did you pick up?"

"Somebody—I don't think it was one of them—saw us drive into town yesterday." Latham had been holding his machete over his head, preparing to swing it when the first sounds of the search party had reached their ears. Now, realizing he still had the big blade frozen in the air he lowered it to his side with a short chuckle.

"That all?"

"All I could make out. Keep in mind I was getting all this in bits and pieces and I've added a little conjecture of my own. The conversation had been going on a long time, and we just caught some part in the middle."

The Executioner stared into the wall of green in front of him. Their situation was changing rapidly and his strategy would have to change with it. First, not only did they stand out among the natives of Mindanao, they were now being actively sought. Second, the Buick was burned. Even if the searchers had left no one to watch the car, and he and Latham could get to it without being seen, the vehicle was useless. It would be readily recognized regardless of where they went.

The Executioner took a deep breath and made a battlefield decision. They would hide out in the jungle the rest of the day, then stake out Mario Subing's house one more night. He was now more determined than ever that if the terrorist leader didn't show up, it would be time for another approach. But again, the only other avenue he could think of was to snatch Mario and take him some place for interrogation. He still didn't like that idea one bit. It would no doubt involve at least some amount of pain on the old man's part and even the thought of extricating information from an old man was repugnant to the Executioner.

"Well," Latham whispered, cutting into the Executioner's thought.

Bolan looked at him and saw the man staring at his forehead. "As my mama used to say, 'I can see the wheels a-turnin' behind them frown wrinkles.' When they quit, let me know what we're going to do next, okay?" He reached into his pocket and pulled out his can of chewing tobacco. This time, however, he reached in with his fingers, grabbed a pinch and stuck it under his lip.

The Executioner looked around him and saw that with a couple more machete chops he could open up a large enough area in which to lie down. His big blade flashed twice, then he dropped to his knees before rolling onto his side.

"I take it that means it's nap time," Latham said, cutting an area out for himself behind the Executioner. "Hope it's a little longer this time." He swung the machete forward side-armed, embedding it into the soft trunk of a tree and leaving it there.

Through half-closed eyelids, Bolan saw the man kneel, then lean forward on his stomach, bending his arm to use as a pillow on the side of his face. Moments later he was asleep.

AT FIRST Bolan thought he was dreaming. Then, as he suddenly snapped wide awake, he realized the voices were real. And at the same time, he realized they were the same voices he and Latham had heard from the jungle path earlier in the day.

He glanced at his watch. It had been less than two hours since they had dropped to the ground. He looked down at Latham, still sleeping peacefully. The Executioner considered wakening him, then just as quickly discarded the idea. Not only was there no sense in it, it could create a problem for what he was about to do.

Rising to a sitting position, Bolan pulled a small spiral notebook and pen from his pocket. Quickly he scribbled the words "Back soon. Stay here." on the top page, then quietly

tore it from the book. Working Latham's machete out of the
tree, he placed the note atop a bare patch of damp earth on
the ground, then drove the tip of the machete through it to hold
it in place.

A second later he disappeared into the trees toward the
more traveled pathway.

Bolan moved quickly but quietly, his senses on full alert.
He had seen the fatigue beginning to build in Charlie Latham
even before their first nap the night before. But there was another reason he hadn't brought the Texan along with him now.
While Latham had proved to be smart, quick and deadly as a
fighter, his jungle skills had been less than perfect. It was clear
that what T.J. had said about the man was true—he had come
to the Philippines for the martial arts training available, not the
jungle. Latham had made far more noise than Bolan had liked
during their earlier trip from the mosque to the stilt houses. It
hadn't mattered then; no one had been looking for them.

Now, it did matter. Someone *was* looking for them. And
the Executioner wasn't going to take the chance that a sudden cough or sneeze, or a footstep on a snapping dry branch
might give them away.

The voices grew louder as Bolan neared the path. He
slowed, staring at the ground before each step, taking shallow silent breaths, his ears cocked for any sign that he might
have been heard. In addition to seeing and hearing, the Executioner took full advantage of his other senses, as well.

And most of all that sixth sense men such as he developed
that some called instinct.

It took him close to five minutes to cover the fifty feet between where Latham slept and the jungle path. But when he
reached the open area, he could still hear the voices as they
made their way along the trail. Dropping down behind a clus-
ter of tangled vegetation three feet from the path, the Execu-

tioner pulled the tiny microcassette recorder from his pants, plugged in the directional mike and extended it through the leaves as far as he dared.

The voices grew louder. But none of the words made sense to the Executioner. He lay perfectly still, the lactic acid building in his outstretched arm, pleading with his brain to let him lower it.

Through the thick undergrowth Bolan watched as four men—three armed with machetes, the third carrying a pinute bolo short sword—strolled toward him. Their ongoing conversation met his ears, including the wheezing words of a man with asthma. It was obvious the group was no longer making even a halfhearted attempt to keep their voices down, which they had made earlier in the day.

Bolan let a grin creep over his face. They had walked this pathway once and not come across the strangers. They were tired of the search now and assumed that if they hadn't encountered anyone going toward the stilt houses, they wouldn't encounter anyone on the way back, either.

All of which worked in the Executioner's favor.

Bolan kept the mike pointed at the pathway as the men walked past. He continued to hold it in place until he could no longer hear their voices. Slowly he rose from his hiding spot, then stopped.

Should he follow the men on down the path back to the mosque? To get close enough on the path to record their words, he would have to take the chance of them spotting him. And if they did, they were likely to attack. The machetes and bolo had not been carried just for show.

No, the Executioner wouldn't follow. He had no intention of getting into a position where he had to kill innocent men simply trying to protect their village from strangers they probably assumed were as bad as terrorists, if not terrorists themselves. Besides, the chance that he'd record some important bit of information he hadn't already gotten on tape was small.

Bolan started back toward where he'd left Latham. He'd either gotten useful information or he hadn't. The risk of trying for more outweighed the potential return.

He had taken only a few steps through the undergrowth when he stopped in his tracks. Another sound—foreign and loudly conspicuous to the jungle—suddenly boomed through the branches and vines. Moving faster now, the Executioner hurried back toward Latham. The men on the path were out of hearing range for the noises he made as he ran. But he wasn't as sure about the long, booming, near ear-splitting cough-growls that broke the peace of the wilds.

The Executioner knew what the sounds were. And if the men searching for them heard it, they would recognize them, too.

Breaking out of the trees into the small clearing he and Latham had created a few hours earlier, Bolan saw the Texan on the ground. Latham had rolled from his stomach to his back in sleep, and now deafening snores thundered from his nose and mouth. Dropping to one knee next to the man, the Executioner grabbed his shoulder and shook him awake.

Latham returned to consciousness and his hand fell to the Browning in his belt.

Bolan held one finger to his lips and shook his head.

Latham caught on and relaxed.

The soldier let a good five minutes go by, listening, waiting to see if the search party had heard the Texan's snoring. Finally satisfied that they had not, he rose and pulled Latham to his feet.

"What's wrong?" the Texan whispered. He looked around, spotted the note stuck in the ground with the machete, then reached down and tore it from the blade.

"Old news," the Executioner whispered. "I'm back."

"Where'd you go?" Latham asked, yawning.

"The guys on the path came back. I went out to see if I could pick up more information."

Coming fully awake now, Latham's forehead wrinkled. "But you don't speak the language."

Bolan reached into his pocket and pulled out the recorder. "No," he said, "but you do."

"Aha," Latham said, throwing his head back slightly. Then he frowned and said, "But what was the problem when you woke me up? How come we had to freeze for so long? They hear you or something?"

The Executioner suppressed a grin. "Or something," he said.

"WELL, NOBODY ELSE ever accused me of snoring," Latham said defensively as he and Bolan cut yet another new route through the jungle toward the stilt houses along the sea.

Bolan didn't bother to answer. Night was falling quickly as it did in the jungle and the Executioner wanted to be within sight of the houses across the road from Mario Subing's before their surroundings turned ink-black. As to Latham's snoring, he had found it slightly amusing that this man—an accomplished fighter by anyone's standard and a good enough woodsman if not the best—had grown immediately sensitive when he'd been told he not only snored but did so in a way that threatened to rip leaves off their vines.

The Executioner came to the edge of the jungle and peered through the foliage. Ahead, he could see the rear of one of the inland shanties across the road from the stilt houses. He held up a hand, both to halt Latham and to signal for silence, then sat among the thick green growth to wait on darkness.

Latham dropped to a squatting position next to him.

Bolan rested his hand on his outstretched leg and felt the tiny microcassette recorder inside his front pocket. Latham had listened to the recording as they'd waited for the hot afternoon to become evening. But they had gained precious little information they hadn't already had. The Texan had, however, said that one thing was clear: it wasn't just the fact that they'd been seen driving into town that had alerted the villagers to potential trouble. They'd been tipped off by someone ahead of time that two men might be coming to the village and that they were trouble.

That, in itself, was worth the chance the Executioner had taken with the recorder. It also jibed with his suspicion that the men they had fought on the road the day before hadn't been random kidnappers. Someone knew he was on Mindanao, and that someone had alerted the Tigers.

Leaning back against the trunk of a tree, Bolan closed his eyes. He had also learned another valuable bit of intel by hiding near the path as the local men had passed—how they were armed. Although they would mistakenly view the Executioner as their enemy, he wasn't. And he had no wish to kill or even injure them. But if he had to deal with them somehow, he had been relived to see that their primary weapons appeared to be blades rather than firearms.

Latham, having dropped to the ground across from him, now crossed his legs on the ground. "You think they know who we are?" he asked Bolan in a low voice. "The locals, I mean."

"Probably not exactly who we are," Bolan whispered. "But if they were tipped off, then somebody knows that somebody new—from America—is looking for the hostages." He glanced overhead, squinting through the treetops into the quickly diminishing sunlight. Then, as an afterthought, he added, "At least I'm sure they don't know exactly who I am." He looked over at the other man now. "Exactly how well are you known on the island?"

Latham shrugged. "Around the gyms and martial-arts training halls folks know me as the 'big American.' I guess I kind of stand out."

"You didn't tell anybody about me coming, did you?"

"Of course not," Latham said. He rubbed the beard stubble on his face again. "I'm still wondering what happened to the CIA guy, too. If word's out on us, it may be on him, too. You suppose he's dead?"

Bolan shrugged. There was no way to know.

Latham pulled out his tobacco can. "They'll have men watching old Mario's house tonight," he said. "You can bet on it. We're going to have to be even more careful than we were last night."

"Or less careful."

Latham had been about to open the tobacco can but now he stopped and looked up at the Executioner. "Huh?"

Bolan didn't answer. For the past half hour, as they'd made their way back through the jungle toward the stilt houses, an idea had been forming in his head. It hadn't quite yet crystallized, but already it was beginning to look as though it had a better chance of succeeding than simply setting up on Mario Subing's house again.

With all the heat on them at the moment, Latham was right. The men of Rio Hondo would indeed be watching for them to make an appearance at the stilt houses. And while there had been no guarantee that Candido Subing would show up on any given night, there was practically a guarantee that he would not visit his uncle on this particular evening. The word was obviously out.

The Executioner finally looked at the Texan. "Let's just see how things go."

Latham still looked confused, but nodded as he packed his lower lip with the finely ground tobacco from the can.

The Executioner's eyes skirted the heavily wooded area

around them. Ten feet back into the jungle, he saw what he was looking for—a long branch, low to the ground, jutting out from the trunk of a tree. Rising slowly, he walked to the tree, raised his machete over his head and sliced the green limb away with one cut. With the branch on the ground now, he chopped both ends until he had a sturdy, relatively straight, three-foot stick roughly two inches in diameter.

Latham had watched silently, but as the Executioner turned he saw a light bulb flash on in the Texan's head. Latham smiled as he, too, rose to his feet, found a suitable limb and made his own short club. Both men sat.

Thirty minutes later the sun had finally gone down and Bolan and Latham found themselves in a darkness known only in the jungle.

The Executioner laid out his new plan.

"EVEN IF WE GET to the house without getting killed, you really think the old man is going to talk?" Latham whispered through the darkness to the man sitting across from him on the jungle floor.

The big shadowy form shrugged. "All I know is that everyone on Mindanao seems to know we're here. That means Candido Subing knows it, too, so he's not going to show up at Uncle Mario's again until we're out of the picture." He waited a second, then said, "If you think you have a better idea, I'm willing to listen to it."

Latham shook his head, then realized the movement might not be seen in the darkness. "Nope," he whispered. "Nothing better." He stared at the shadowy silhouette across from him. Latham knew the darkness would hide his eyes as he scrutinized Cooper with a mixture of respect and wonder. Slowly he shook his head. As a Delta Force soldier he had seen his share of action, but he had never worked with anyone even close to being like Cooper. His old friend T. J. Hawkins had told him this guy was the best, but that might well prove to be the understatement of Latham's lifetime.

The Texan pulled the straw hat from his head, then removed the bandanna he'd tied beneath it. The tobacco in his mouth had lost its flavor and he let it drop from his lip. Slowly and silently, he grasped the bandanna in both hands and wrung out the sweat. It was still damp when he retied it around his forehead and covered it once more with his hat.

Staring into the blackness, Latham knew they would be going soon, and he knew just as well that they would be attacked by armed villagers. Again, he looked at the man across from him, knowing Cooper couldn't see his stare. But this time he wondered if Cooper might not still know he was being scrutinized; might not simply feel it with whatever it was that made him so different. The guy did seem to have "powers far beyond those of mortal man" to quote the intros to the old "Superman" reruns he and Hawk had watched on TV when they were kids.

Latham chuckled silently. No, this guy wasn't Superman. He was flesh and blood, but he was something more, too. As a Texas schoolboy Latham had studied state history, and he was reminded now of a quotation that had stuck in his mind since those days. The words had been uttered enthusiastically by the English essayist and historian Thomas Carlyle speaking of James Bowie: "'By Hercules! The man was greater than Caesar or Cromwell—well—nay, nearly equal to Odin or Thor. The Texans ought to build him an altar!'"

Latham's gaze fell to the ground, but he continued to watch Cooper in his peripheral vision. Many altars in the form of statues and other memorials had been built for James Bowie in Texas, but Latham suspected that regardless of how deserving this man calling himself "Cooper" might be, he would never receive such honors. The wars the man fought were in the shadows. Clandestine. And Charlie Latham knew the man would never get credit for all he did for the world. At the same time he realized that, the Texan also realized that Cooper wouldn't care. He had probably never even given personal glory a passing thought.

"You ready?" he heard his companion whisper.

In the darkness he could see the improvised *baston*—a Filipino fighting stick—dangling from the end of the man's arm. Cooper's machete hung from the other hand and, though he couldn't see it in the darkness, Latham knew that it was held backward so that the blunt edge would be the striking side.

"I'm ready," Latham said. With his own stick in his left hand, he flipped his machete around, too. But a last moment of doubt made him say, "You still serious about this no guns thing?"

Bolan nodded. "Keep the firepower ready, just in case. But it's a last resort. Remember, these men think we're here to hurt them and their families. They aren't doing anything you or I wouldn't do."

"You realize we'd get better odds playing blackjack at the crookedest casino in Vegas, don't you?" Latham asked.

The tall silhouette nodded again, but said nothing.

Which, to Charlie Latham, said it all. Yes, they'd probably die trying to do what they were about to try to do. But it was the right thing to do, so they'd do it.

Bolan stepped past Latham into the open area behind the inland houses, leading the Texan to the back of a crudely constructed storage building behind one of the houses. Both men dropped to a knee to reevaluate the situation. They knew the villagers were out there somewhere. Watching. Waiting. Knowing they would come. Who knew what lies they had been told about what the Americans wanted to do to them and their families? But it didn't matter; the end result was the same. They erroneously viewed them as enemies and they would do their best to kill them both.

Scurrying out from behind the storage shed, the two Americans halted against the windowless back wall of the dilapidated dwelling directly across the roadway from Mario Subing's home. Bolan peered around the corner, looked back and nodded.

Latham took a deep breath then let it out. Cooper hoped to cross the street and mount the steps of the stilt house, unseen if possible, then interrogate Subing's uncle. With everyone looking for them already, Latham figured the chances of pulling that off were about a thousand to one. The fact was, had it been anyone else working with him, the Texan would have just flat refused to even try it.

Latham sighed. Of course the big man had a backup plan—for what it was worth. If they were spotted, they would do their best to snatch the old man and whisk him away somewhere before talking to him. To Latham, that, too, sounded like a terrific strategy for getting oneself killed and, again, he knew that if anyone whom he respected even half an ounce less than he did Matt Cooper had come up with the plan, he'd have told the idiot to go screw himself.

But Cooper had already proved he could pull off the "crazy" things in life. The worse the odds were against them, the better he seemed to perform. And now, Latham realized as they started around the side of the house, the big man would get a chance to prove himself again.

For they weren't even halfway to the front of the house when three of the village men stepped out with swords.

CHAPTER FOUR

Bolan saw the glint of steel in the moonlight as the man rounded the corner from the front of the house. As the blade rose over the Rio Hondan's head, he recognized the forked pommel and "crocodile" guard that characterized the Filipino sword known as the "kampilan."

Forty-four inches of razor-edged death came flashing toward the Executioner's head. He swung the machete across his body and steel met steel with a screech that sounded like a car wreck in the still night. The kampilan slid down the flat side of the machete and away from Bolan's body. Using the tree-limb *baston* he had fashioned earlier, he smashed the attacker in the side of the head.

The villager slid to the ground, unconscious.

Two more Rio Hondans stood immediately behind the first and Bolan stepped to the side to allow Latham room to fight. The larger of the two attackers stood to the left and Bolan took him, noting that the man had dressed in traditional Filipino fighting gear for the night's assault. A strip of red cloth—reminiscent of the Japanese kamikaze pilots of World War II—was tied around his forehead. Small but wiry arms extended from the vest he wore over his otherwise bare chest and in the man's hands were a pair of matching, leaf-shaped barongs.

The two-handed swordsman was skilled with his weapons and now he came at the Executioner with a double attack. Both short swords snapped over his head, then descended at forty-five-degree angles from opposite directions toward the sides of Bolan's neck.

The Executioner brought his machete up on one side, the *baston* on the other. The ping of steel against steel and the thud of steel against wood sounded simultaneously as he blocked both barongs. Taking a half step into the man in the vest, Bolan jammed the end of his stick between the eyes. By the time the villager hit the ground, his eyes had fluttered closed.

Glancing to his side, the Executioner saw that Latham had engaged his man and now blocked the wavy blade of a kris. Perhaps the most common of all the edged weapons of the Philippines, the twisting, snakelike double-edged blade could produce devastating wounds either cutting or thrusting. It was the latter tactic the villager chose now, and as Bolan moved on toward the front of the house he watched the Rio Hondan shove the serpentine weapon straight forward from his shoulder.

Latham stepped to the side and deftly guided the thrust past his body with his machete. His homemade *baston* came around in an arc to strike the villager on the temple.

The Executioner had just reached the front of the house when a Rio Hondan wearing what had originally been a white T-shirt stepped into his path from hiding. Countless washings in the brown waters of Mindanao streams had turned the shirt a dingy beige and the neck had been stretched out so far one side fell over his shoulder. The man carried a bolo knife in his right hand and he now brought it around in a sidearm assault.

Bolan blocked with the *baston*, stepped in and slapped the flat side of the machete against the man's cheek. A loud pop

broke the night but did little more than stun the villager. The
soldier knew that the force of the blow had been distributed
over too large an area to do serious injury and had hoped the
pain would provide compliance. Unfortunately it seemed only
to infuriate the man further and he brought the bolo back to
strike again.

The Executioner brought his *baston* down and around, arc-
ing it upward into his adversary's ribs. He pulled the machete
back again, altered his grip slightly, then struck again with the
thinner backside of the blade.

The blow caught the man on the side of the neck, shock-
ing the artery running up to his brain and cutting off the ox-
ygen. The villager fell like a steer under a slaughterhouse
hammer.

For a split second the front yard, the roadway and the area
around the stilt houses seemed deserted. Then what might
have been the hordes of Genghis Khan seemed to material-
ize out of nowhere. Bolan sprinted across the yard toward the
road, downing another man wearing a headband with his *baston,* one more with the blunt edge of the machete. A huge panabas—a cross between a sword and ax—flashed through the
air toward his head. The weapon was too heavy to block with
either *baston* or machete, so the Executioner brought them
both up together. An almost paralyzing electric shock ran
from his weapons down his forearms as the panabas made
contact. It stopped in midair, the attacker feeling the shock
even more than the Executioner. He showed his surprise with
the whites of his widened eyes.

Bolan recovered first. Lifting his stick up over his head, he
brought it down hard onto the man's collarbone. A sickening
snap met his ears as wood splintered bone. The panabas, and
the man who had wielded it, tumbled forward to the ground.

The Executioner saw Latham trading blows with an unusu-

ally large Filipino armed with a pair of golok swords. Used
for centuries by the Moros for jungle warfare, the man who
now flailed with them had been trained well. He had taken the
offensive, swinging hard and fast with both blades, giving the
appearance of twin airplane propellers flashing through the
air. Latham blocked, then blocked again. Then again and
again and again. But he was a half beat behind the man, which
kept him on the defense, unable to launch a counterattack.

Bolan knew that blocking only was the road to an early
death. Latham was good. But no matter how good a man was,
sooner or later, he missed a block.

Stepping in to the side, the Executioner brought the blunt
edge of the machete around in an arc against the back of the
big Filipino's neck. The Rio Hondan dropped to his knees,
then fell forward onto his face, unconscious. Latham's chest
heaved in and out with exertion, but he had the strength to
bring his machete up to his forehead in a smiling salute to the
Executioner.

Bolan turned back to the road and another villager stepped
in to face him. For a split second the man looked as if he held
a Fourth of July sparkler in each hand. Then, as the flashing
steel took better shape, the Executioner again recognized a
matched pair of bright stainless steel balisongs. The villager
appeared even more skilled in their use than the punk in Zamboanga from whom Bolan had appropriated the Buick.

Spreading and closing the wings of the butterfly knives,
then spreading and closing them again, the Rio Hondan made
the twin blades dance a graceful ballet through the air. And
as they danced they also sang, clicking, clacking and whir-
ring in the night and sending shafts of moonlight reflecting
off their surfaces in a colorful prism of death. But the balisong expert made one fatal mistake. He took too much time
showing off.

The Executioner stepped in and swung the *baston* overhead like a tennis racket, cracking it down first on the man's right wrist, then on his left. Both balisongs dropped to the ground. The man's lower lip dropped open almost that far in surprise. Bolan's third strike with the *baston* left the man lying on top of his fallen knives.

In the middle of the asphalt roadway now, the soldier was halted by three men. Each carried a klewang and each held the straight, single-edge blade with the widened point up and ready. But they had seen the unconscious men in the Executioner's wake and it had curbed some of their enthusiasm for battle. Each hesitated to be the next to hit the ground.

Bolan took advantage of their indecisiveness to initiate his own attack. Faking an overhand strike with the *baston,* he waited until the man's klewang came up to block, then cut the feint short, drawing it slightly back toward him before jabbing the blunt end into the man's face. The Executioner heard the crack of bone as the villager's nose broke. A half second later he brought the blunt edge of the machete straight up between the man's legs.

The villager had grunted with the broken nose. Now he screeched from the groin strike. As he bent in agony, the Executioner struck downward with the butt end of the stick, which extended below his fist. The short stub of wood cracked into the back of the man's skull. A punyo—the Filipinos called the technique—worked just as well on them as for them, ending the attacker's sounds of torment and sending him to sleep on the asphalt of the highway.

Turning his attention to the side, Bolan noticed that Latham had stepped up even with him to engage one of the two remaining attackers. As the Executioner feinted again with his *baston,* he saw the Texan crack his man across the jaw with the backside of his machete. Although it didn't break the skin, the long, thin striking area left an ugly red stripe across the top of the crumbled bone.

The third man had watched the men on both sides of him fall to the strangers and the sight brought out a desperate panic. With a shriek of terror, he abandoned all training he might have had and began to swing his klewang wildly back and forth.

Bolan had only to time the swings, then step in as the blade went past him. In one smooth motion he trapped the sword with his machete and, with the other hand, brought the *baston* down at a forty-five-degree angle against the frightened man's temple.

Although he could still hear townsmen running toward him in the darkness, there was no immediate threat. The Executioner took advantage of the break in the action to sprint across the asphalt to the sandy shore beneath the stilt houses. Behind him, he could hear Latham's feet beating the sand as he followed. "I'm...with you," the Texan panted.

The Executioner took the steps of Subing's house three at a time, the machete in one hand, the crudely fashioned *baston* in the other. Each time his foot hit the rotting wood the stairs screamed in agony, threatening to collapse beneath him. Halfway up the steps he saw a small dark figure step out of the house onto the porch.

Mario Subing aimed the pistol in his hands down the steps at the Executioner.

BOTH RACHAEL PARKS and her husband, John, believed strongly in prayer. Before accepting the mission assignment to the Philippines, they'd had a special time set aside each night when they prayed together. The both also did their best to offer up short individual appeals and supplications to God throughout the day. But there had been so much work to be done as soon as they'd arrived on Mindanao that too often they collapsed into bed at night and suddenly realized they hadn't spoken a word to the Lord all day.

"Yeah, but isn't there a proverb that says God loves busy hands?" Rachael remembered her husband saying one night when she'd pointed out that they'd forgotten to pray.

"Yes," she remembered saying back. "But there's a whole bunch of scripture that says He likes to talk to us, too." They had both laughed. Then they'd both prayed, because neither one of them were the type who fooled themselves into thinking a rapid-fire thank-you-God-for-another-day-and-enough-to-eat-amen was a real prayer.

Well, Rachael thought as she closed her eyes behind the hood, *I've got plenty of time to make up for lost prayers now.* The fact was that prayer, meditation and thinking was about all she or her husband had been able to do during the past several months.

Rachel shifted her mud-encrusted, water-soaked jeans beneath her and felt the chapped skin on the back of her thighs. Yes, for perhaps the first time in her life, she had all the time she wanted to pray. And though she had taken advantage of it, offering up prayers about her church, her husband, the other hostages, her family and herself, for some reason the words she found herself silently forming with her lips, over and over again, had nothing to do with her present situation. In fact, the words she caught herself saying most often were not even original on her part—they had been spoken by Jesus more than two thousand years earlier while he hung on the cross.

Father, forgive them. For they know not what they do.

Rachael opened her eyes beneath the hood. For weeks after their capture she had hated the terrorists who had taken them hostage. Then she had realized her hatred wasn't hurting the men who held them captive one bit. But it was eating her alive.

So she had prayed that God would remove the hatred from her soul and give her the strength to endure whatever happened. Then she had gone another step and prayed that the Lord would forgive Candido Subing and the other Tigers and that they would find salvation through Jesus Christ.

Rachael smiled as she remembered the sequence of events after the first such prayer. She'd said, "Amen" then felt obligated to add. "P.S. Lord, help me to someday mean it when I ask you I forgive them. Because right now I'd kind of like to see them rot away in Hell for all eternity."

No, Rachael thought as she sat in the mud as she had day after day after day, her hatred hadn't disappeared all at once. But somewhere along the line she had forgiven her captors. And now when she prayed for Candido Subing and the others she truly did mean it from the heart.

Rachael looked down and smiled. She still had things to be thankful for. Small things maybe, but gifts nonetheless. For one thing, she could tell it was daytime. The drawstring at her throat hadn't been tightened all the way and she could see the light on her chest. *Lord, I thank you for the light,* she said silently, and the new prayer made her realize how many of God's wonders she overlooked each day. God could make something good out of anything, no matter how evil its original intent might be at the hands of man. And one of the good things that had come out of their captivity was just that—she no longer took such things as the sun going up and coming down for granted.

There was some kind of rustling on the other side of the barn and Rachael's ears perked. A quick image of Jim Worden flew through her mind. In less than a heartbeat her mind's eye relived the horrifying death she had witnessed. She saw Jim kneeling on the ground, facing her and the others. He was smiling—he said something—she couldn't remember what at

the moment—then Candido Subing raised his sword and
Jim's head fell from his body. Seconds later his body fell forward while his head fell to the side. There was blood everywhere, but Jim was still smiling.

Rachael suddenly realized that she was crying just as she
had when the horrible death had actually occurred.

Rachael bit her lip with her teeth but the tears still flowed
down her cheeks. Did Jim's brutal death serve some higher
purpose that she couldn't understand? Rachael felt herself
begin to tremble. She felt as if she might be on the verge of
a breakdown. First the tears. Now she was shaking. She was
about to scream when she felt the hand on her shoulder.

As suddenly as it had come, the trembling stopped, her
eyes dried up and she felt the love of God within her once
more. The Lord had given her the sign she'd asked for through
her husband. John, sitting next to her, had somehow worked
a hand free and now it squeezed her shoulder reassuringly.

Rachael leaned her head to the side, resting her cheek
against the back of her husband's hand. It was God at work.
God answering their prayers. God giving her a blessing.

Rachael's cheek still rested on the hand when she heard the
rickety wooden door on the other side of the barn slide open.
She recognized the voice of Candido Subing shouting orders
to his men. She held her breath and knew the other missionaries were doing the same. Although it had been apparent
since the beginning that Subing was the leader, he was rarely
here in this hiding place. But when he did show up, things happened. And while all of those things had been bad so far,
Rachael knew that Subing would also be the one to tell them
if they were about to be released.

Boots sloshed through the mud toward the five missionaries. Rachael heard a sigh and then a moan as hoods were lifted
off faces. When the sack was jerked from her head she turned

in time to see Reynaldo Taboada pull the hood from John. She was glad it was Reynaldo. He seemed different than the others, not as mean. He never mistreated them for the fun of it like some of the guards did and there seemed something almost sad about the man.

"Thank you," Rachael whispered to John as soon as the terrorist had turned away.

"For what?" John asked, his face looking puzzled.

Before she could thank him for the hand on her shoulder Subing stepped forward to face his hostages. He was obviously about to speak to them; the last time he had done so had ended with the murder of Jim Worden. Rachael's eyes scanned the area behind him for any sign of video equipment. She saw none and that gave her hope that the horror might not be repeated.

Subing cleared his throat. "I understand," he said, "that in America there is a game in which someone says, 'I have both some good news and some bad.' First, I will give you the good news. America has sent new agents—CIA, I am sure—to look for you." He cackled sardonically, then spit into the mud. "Now. For the bad news. They will not find you. And the worst news of all for some of you…" He let his voice trail off to build tension. "Is that to make their hunt more difficult, I am going to separate you into three groups."

Rachael felt a chill go down her spine as she and her husband looked at each other, then back at Subing. Three groups. Five of them left. That would surely mean two hostages in two groups, one in the third. Surely, Subing would allow them to stay together. Even a man as misguided as he had to retain some compassion hidden deep within his soul.

The men of the Liberty Tigers trudged through the mud. Two of them grabbed Roger Ewton and dragged him toward the door. Two more lifted Kim Tate from where she sat next to Rachael, and then another two Tigers grabbed her and hauled her to her feet. Rachael suddenly realized that separating her from her husband was exactly what Subing planned to do.

"John!" Rachael screamed out, and heard him cry back, "Rachael! No!"

John tried to struggle to his feet, but a muddy boot kicked him in the face and he fell back to the ground. Rachael's husband rose again, this time getting as high as his knees before one of the men hit him with the wooden end of his gun in the side of the head.

The rough hands grasped Rachael's shoulders and pushed her toward the door. When she tried to turn back someone punched her in the stomach and she felt the air rush from her lungs. As she started to fall she cast a look over her shoulder and saw John trying to get up yet again, but with his ankles still bound and his hands tied to his waist it was futile.

Gasping for air, Rachael was dragged out of the barn into the bright sunlight. As soon as she caught her breath again she began to struggle. But her efforts were as ineffective as John's had been. The terrorists pulled, pushed and carried her toward two trucks parked just outside. Rachael doubled her efforts to strike the men with her elbows and even snapped her teeth at an arm that got too close.

"John!" she cried one final time as she was lifted into one of the trucks next to Kim Tate, and then the hood was pulled back down over her eyes.

It was only then, as she sat impotently listening to the truck engine start and feeling the wheels beneath her begin to roll, that the miraculousness of the sign God had given her earlier suddenly struck her. She had just watched John try three times to get to his feet and come after her. Three times he had been unable to do so, or to defend himself against the boots and rifle butts of the terrorists because his hands were still tied to his waist. Which meant he had *not* worked a hand free earlier as she'd thought, and it couldn't have been his hand comforting her by squeezing her shoulder.

But a hand had been there, warm and loving, just the same.

THE REVOLVER in the elderly man's hand looked like an ancient Spanish Star. The rifling, Bolan suspected, had been burned out before the Executioner was born. Or perhaps the old man at the top of the steps was simply a poor shot. Whatever the reason, although he was less than ten feet away, when the man Bolan assumed was Mario Subing pulled the trigger, the shot missed.

The antique wheel gun exploded almost in the Executioner's face. But the shot struck to his side, splintering the already rotten wood of the handrail above the steps and causing it to collapse in pieces over the staircase.

Bolan hadn't slowed at the sight of the revolver and now ducked his head as he continued to charge up the steps. Before the wrinkled, white-haired man on the landing could pull the trigger again, he thrust his head under the gun and into the man's chest.

The Executioner's force drove both men back through the doorway into the one-room stilt house; they dropped to the floor in a jumble of arms and legs. But old as he might be, frail as he might look, Mario Subing still managed to hold on to the gun as Bolan came down on top of him. And even after the Executioner had clamped the fingers of one hand so tight around his wrist that the dry old bone threatened to snap, he strained to maneuver the barrel back around at the big American.

Bolan didn't want to break Mario Subing's arm and he didn't want the old man to break it himself as he struggled. Relaxing his grip, he reached out with his other hand and caught the double-action revolver. Sliding his fingers behind the hammer, he clamped it to the frame to keep it from being cocked then ripped it from the aged fingers.

Mario Subing shrieked out a long stream of what the Executioner had to guess were choice Tagalog expletives.

Behind him, Bolan heard feet pounding up the stairs. He whirled on his knees to face the door, the revolver rising to shoulder height. But it was Latham who appeared on the landing outside, then ducked into the room. The Texan took it all in with a glance. "You okay?" he asked.

Bolan let his actions answer the question, leaping to his feet and pulling the old man up after him. His eyes scanned the room and he saw a thin dirty mattress covered by a mosquito net. A dilapidated wooden table and a three-legged chair were the only other two items in the stilt house.

No sooner had he let go of the old man than Subing reached behind his back and came out with a balisong knife. One wing of the knife was already open by the time the Executioner caught the old man's wrist again and wrenched the new weapon free. He had no sooner done that than Mario's other hand shot behind him and he produced a rusty K-bar fighting knife. As he took yet another weapon away from the screeching Filipino, the Executioner wondered what soldier or Marine had lost it during World War II.

Unarmed now, Mario Subing became a flurry of fists, elbows and feet. He looked like a tiny, aged dust devil as he bore into the Executioner.

Bolan had no desire to hurt the old man so he blocked, parried and dodged the first attack. But when he heard more voices gathering outside, he realized Subing was not to be subdued by anything other than brute force. Regretfully, the Executioner pulled back his fist and tapped the little man squarely on the chin. The whirlwind of arms and legs suddenly settled into place. Mario's eyes rolled back into his head and he fell into the Executioner's outstretched arms.

"More coming," Latham called from the doorway.

Bolan turned to face the doorway. Through the opening he could see at least a dozen men sprinting toward them on the potholed asphalt highway that ran through the town. Several old cars and pickups were also arriving. As soon as they parked, more men, armed with a variety of edged and impact weapons, leaped out. Among the vehicles, Bolan saw the Buick he and Latham had left in the parking lot at the mosque. He had the keys in his pocket, which meant the villagers had to have hot-wired it.

"Lay down some cover fire," the Executioner ordered. "Let them know we're serious but make sure you don't hit anybody."

As dedicated to the traditional Filipino martial arts as he might be, Latham looked more than happy enough to jam the *baston* through his belt and pull out a twenty-first-century weapon. Gripping the Browning Hi-Power in both hands, he extended the weapon through the doorway and let the red Crimson Trace laser dot fall onto an empty area of the asphalt highway. He opened fire, sending four loud but harmless rounds down from the stilt house. Chunks of the dry tarlike substance flew from the highway, one only three feet in front of the man in the lead of the pack. He stopped as suddenly as a sprinting dog hitting the end of his chain, then dived to the side of the roadway. The others behind him followed suit.

Latham didn't fire again but he kept the Browning aimed downward, the red dot dancing back and forth across the road, pausing now and then on a chest or face for effect.

In the silt house behind the Texan, Bolan hefted Mario over his shoulder in a fireman's carry, then moved to the door. "They'll speak Tagalog?" he asked Latham.

The Texan nodded. "Most of 'em will. At least some, anyway."

"Ask them if they can hear you."

Latham called out in Tagalog. Answers came back from behind the parked cars, houses, sheds and other available cover. "They hear me."

"Tell them we mean them no harm. Tell them we need Mario Subing's help and we'll release him unharmed when we're finished."

Again, Latham rattled off a string of words that were totally unintelligible to the Executioner. Again, several voices answered.

"They want to know why we want the old man," Latham said.

Bolan hesitated for a moment, thinking. There were several tacks he could take at this point. He decided on the direct one. "Tell them they know why," he said. "Tell them they know it's really the nephew we want and that they know Candido Subing is no good as well as we do. Tell them they have our word that Mario won't be hurt."

Latham shouted down at the men. This time, several sarcastic laughs accompanied the many responses to Latham's translation.

The Texan turned back into the room to face Bolan. "There were some colorful suggestions concerning what you and I could do, both to each other and to ourselves. But the bottom line was, they got word that we'd come to rob them."

"Ask them who told them that," the Executioner said.

Latham asked and the Executioner heard several muttered responses. None sounded like an answer and Latham confirmed that the general consensus of the words was "none of your business."

One of the hidden voices seemed to take charge, shouting out loudly.

Latham looked back at Bolan. "He wants to know why they should trust us when we say we won't hurt the old man."

With Mario still asleep over his shoulder, Bolan pulled out the Desert Eagle and stepped into the doorway. Flipping the off safety, he triggered the big .44 Magnum pistol three times into the air. As the thunder faded into the night, he looked at Latham and said, "Tell them *that's* why they should trust us. We had guns and we could have killed many of them. We didn't." He paused, then said, "Tell them to look around at one another. There may be some bruises, maybe even a broken bone or two. But we didn't seriously hurt anybody."

The Texan translated again. The area fell silent except for a few whispers that floated up over the sound of the waves lapping against the posts beneath the house. After a moment Bolan said, "Tell them again, Are any of them dead? Tell them I know they're all mighty warriors but don't they think we could have killed at least a few with our guns if we'd wanted to?"

Latham shouted the words in Tagalog. More whispering. Then a voice called out again. Bolan caught the name Subing several times.

Turning back into the room, Latham said, "They say they know Mario's nephew is a criminal. But he's never hurt them and the word they got about us is that we would." He paused. "They want to know what we'll do to Candido if we find him."

Bolan reached up with his free hand and rubbed his temple. Again he had to choose from several possible responses. And all were fraught with potential pitfalls. The village men had known it was Candido Subing he was after even before they had arrived in Rio Hondo. But the story had been twisted somehow—he didn't know how and doubted he ever would— to make it look as if Latham and he had come to do the Rio Hondans harm, as well. He wondered again who had told them and how whoever it was had known about their presence. But he wasn't going to find that out right now, either.

Latham pulled out his chewing tobacco and took what looked like a triple dip as Bolan further considered his response. Just how loyal to Candido Subing were the men below him? Did their loyalty to a fellow countryman outweigh their belief in good and evil? The men of this village would be no different than men the world over—there would be a few very good ones, a few very bad ones and most would fall somewhere in between. So the answer had to be no. The Executioner didn't think the majority would willingly shield a terrorist just because he was Filipino. But that wasn't all of the problem. They had it in their minds that he and Latham were the real criminals.

What he thought it all boiled down to was this: because Subing was Mario's nephew, the men of Rio Hondo had been willing to passively help the Liberty Tigers by looking the other way when he came to visit. But would they actively help the terrorists by trying to kill him and Latham? The Executioner's gut told him the answer was no. And it also told him to just tell these men the truth.

The Executioner's jaw set firmly and he felt his upper teeth grind against the lowers as he said, "Tell them one more time I mean none of them any harm, including Mario. Tell them when I find Candido Subing I intend to kill him and free the hostages."

Latham's eyebrows lowered slightly. "You're, uh, sure?" he said.

"I'm sure."

Latham shrugged, turned back to the men on the road below and spoke another couple of sentences.

The whispers among the men now became loud angry shouts. Bolan stared down at the shadowy figures. From what he could see, there was a division among them. Maybe some of them supported the terrorists, others didn't. Or maybe they were still just arguing over whether or not he and Latham could be trusted. There were an endless number of possibilities at this point and he didn't have time to have Latham translate all the words and decide.

As he had been forced to do so many times over the years, Bolan made his decision in less time than it takes most men to pick out a pair of socks. It was time to go. One way or another, they had to get Subing out of here.

The Executioner reached across his body and lifted old Mario's head by the hair, staring into his face. The man was still out and showed no signs of awakening soon. Good. He would be less trouble that way. At least one of Bolan's arms would be free to fight.

Letting the wrinkled face fall back onto his chest, Bolan looked out through the darkness to where the villagers had parked the Buick. He couldn't be certain but it looked empty. More than likely there were men hiding behind it, however, weapons ready.

Bolan holstered the Desert Eagle and leaned back into the room, retrieving the homemade *baston*, that had fallen from his hand during the wrestling match with Mario. Returning to the door, he turned to Latham. "Tell them we're coming down—"

The Texan twisted toward the men below and started to speak. Bolan tapped him on the arm with the *baston*. "Not yet," he said. "I'll tell you when."

"What are we doing?" Latham wondered.

"We're heading for the Buick. There's obviously a lot of disagreement down there, and we don't have time for them to hash it all out like a bunch of filibustering senators." He nodded down toward the car. "Besides, that's where our equipment is unless they've popped the trunk. And from here it doesn't look like they have."

Latham nodded his understanding.

"I want to get as close to the car as we can before the fighting starts," Bolan said. "Tell them we're tired of talking from up here. Tell them to show we can be trusted we're going to come down there."

As soon as the words were out of the Texan's mouth, the Executioner motioned for him to start down the steps. Bolan followed with the unconscious man still riding on his shoulder.

"Keep moving," Bolan said. "We've surprised them by suddenly coming down. We've got a couple of seconds before they figure it all out."

They reached the ground and were suddenly surrounded by men armed with sticks and blades. "Ask them who's in charge. That should create enough argument to get us a few more steps."

As they continued to move toward the Buick, Latham began a long-winded tirade in Tagalog, dramatically looking around with a puzzled look on his face.

"Don't run until I do," the Executioner instructed Latham. "Now tell them you want the *datu*."

Latham knew the word, of course, and now asked loudly that the village chieftain identify himself and come forward to speak with them. With each word, he and Bolan took another casual step in the direction of the Buick.

Closer now, the whispered arguments between the various men could be heard and the Executioner saw Latham frown. "We've got a problem," he said.

"Tell me," Bolan answered, taking another step toward the parked vehicle.

"I suspected it when we were still up there," the Texan said, glancing back over his shoulder to indicate the stilt house. "But I couldn't make out enough of their speech."

"We aren't in a position for a history lesson at the moment," the Executioner said, doing his best to hide the irritation in his voice. "Just tell me what the problem is." With Mario still over his shoulder, he inched another foot or so toward the vehicle. "Some argument over who the *datu* is?"

"No," said Latham. The Texan had a forced smile on his face and spoke to Bolan out of the corner of his mouth. "Not that at all."

As if to confirm his words, a middle-aged man stepped forward in front of them. The village chieftain wore faded blue jeans and tattered discount running shoes. But from the waist up he had dressed for battle. A Moro *pakil*—a jerkinlike shirt that served as body armor made from elephant hide and carabao horn—covered his chest. Atop his head sat a *kupya,* the wooden helmet worn by Bontoc Igorot warriors from the Luzon area.

"Then what *is* the problem?" Bolan demanded. They were now roughly twenty feet from the Buick. But at least forty men—men the Executioner had no desire to kill—still encircled them. And while the weapons in the villagers's hands might be primitive, they were still deadly.

"The problem is the men are divided," Latham said, the false smile still twisting his mouth. "Some of them hate Subing and want to let us go."

Bolan turned to look Latham in the eye. "And the rest?"

The Texan glanced at the ground, then looked back up to meet the Executioner's gaze. "They aren't in complete agreement, even among themselves," Latham said. "But the possibility of cutting our heads off and sticking them on top of poles at the city limits is being kicked around."

EACH TIME HE STEPPED OFF the plane in Tel Aviv, he not only began calling himself Thabit Ali, he actually felt as if that was his real name. Why? he wondered as he waited on his luggage to come around on the circular conveyor belt. Was it because the prophet had been Arabic? Because he spent so much time in Arabic lands? Or was it because, when he was in Israel, he was indeed in the land of the Jews, the enemies of God? It was, Candido Subing decided as he spotted his plain black suitcase on the conveyor, more than likely a combination of all these things.

Well, God be praised! He thought as he grabbed the handle of his bag. He had been born Filipino rather than true Arab. But his soul was Arab and God had given him a mission of honor to help his Arab people.

Subing hurried to the immigration line where his well-forged passport got little more than a cursory glance. He carried the suitcase toward the sign marked Immigration. Here, no one got only quick glances and he spent the next fifteen minutes watching the Israeli dogs go through every item in his bag. They opened his aftershave bottle and sniffed at the contents and checked the lining of every shirt, pair of pants and set of underwear he had packed. Subing stood by good-naturedly. He had nothing to fear; there was nothing incriminating in the bag. And knowing why he was here gave him patience with the Semite mongrels.

Because before he left again, a good many of them would be dead.

Subing retrieved his bag and walked out of the terminal to a long line of waiting taxicabs. He needed to find a cabdriver willing to leave Tel Aviv and many refused to do so. Walking to the nearest taxi, he bent slightly to the open window. "Ashkelon?" he asked.

The Jew behind the wheel was chewing an unlit cigar. He glanced quickly up, out of the window, then shook his head and turned his face back to the windshield as if Subing no longer existed.

Anger suddenly filled the Filipino's breast. It was so typical of the arrogant Jews. They complained about their treatment, not only during the World War II but throughout history, from the dawn of time. But give them their own country—let *them* be in charge—and they persecuted their enemies worse than any dictator the world had ever seen.

The Filipino controlled his anger, smiling and moving away. Now was not the time to cause a scene or to do anything that might attract undue attention. At the second cab he got lucky. The driver appeared to be Palestinian.

"Can you go to Ashkelon?" Subing asked in Arabic.

The driver nodded and hooked a thumb over his shoulder at the back seat. His face expressed no more emotion than the Jew's had, but Subing felt an instant kinship with the man. He opened the back door and got in, pulling his suitcase in after him and laying it on the seat. The driver pulled away.

The leader of the Liberty Tigers sat back against the seat and closed his eyes as they made their way out of Tel Aviv onto the highway that ran along the Mediterranean coast. He had used Ashkelon as a launching base several times during the past few weeks. It was where he met his men before giving them their final instructions, paying their families and sending them out on their missions. The Western world called them suicide or homicide bombers, but he knew what they really were. Martyrs. Martyrs for God.

Subing watched the beach as they drove on along the coast. It was probably time to change from Ashkelon to a new location. The Jews might be dogs but they were intelligent dogs and their Mossad agents and other police were as diligent as they came. He continued to watch the town as they drove into the night.

Ashkelon, he knew, had once been surrounded by castles built by the invading Christian swine during their damnable Crusades. Blanche Garde, Ibelin, Beth Gibelin—he was mildly surprised to find out he even remembered the castle names. But then much of his training had emphasized the ruthlessness of the Christian infidels throughout history so such facts, he supposed, were imprinted into his memory forever.

The moon cast its glow onto the sandy beaches to his side and the waves rolled into shore. Subing wondered what it would have been like to have lived during the days before the Jews had stolen this land. Ashkelon had once been the land of the Canaanite and later had become a Philistine city. The remnants of those great peoples—ancestors to many Arabs living today—could still be seen around the Gates of Ascalon where broken foundations and toppled columns marked the past glories of the people.

Then, of course, the Jews had come and spoiled it all. Finally they had been driven away. But then, with the help of their infidel friends the United States of America, they had returned.

The Filipino felt the bitterness swell within him as the scenery began to change. The sandy beaches grew fewer as hotels, restaurants, bars and other symbols of Western decadence began to appear. Ah, how the Jews *loved* their vices. The Jews and the Americans were a perfect match—a marriage made in Hell. He leaned forward and tapped the driver on the shoulder.

"In here?" the driver asked, looking toward a sign that read Holiday Inn. Subing nodded and the Palestinian twisted the wheel, taking them across the access road and into the parking lot in front of the huge hotel. They stopped at the front entrance.

"Please wait," Subing said, handing a wad of bills over the seat to the man.

"You are not staying?"

"No, not here," Subing said. "But I must speak to a business associate for a moment. I will be only a few minutes."

The driver nodded his understanding and Subing got out of the taxi, taking his black suitcase with him. He entered through the glass doors of the hotel, then crossed the lobby past gift shops, two restaurants and finally an American-style discotheque. Coarse music roared out the open door; an offense to God's ears, he was sure. He stopped only long enough to stick his head inside and the first thing he saw was a woman wearing a short skirt and low-cut blouse. She was dancing provocatively to the rhythm, and the sight of her sickened him. Yet, at the same time, her flesh aroused in him a fiery passion and he jerked his face away from her and hurried on down the hall. That doorway—it was like the gateway to Hell.

As he walked toward the elevator, Subing tried valiantly to erase the woman's vision from his mind. But the harder he tried, the deeper the sight seemed to stamp itself into his brain and he felt a stirring in his groin as he reached out and pressed the up button for the elevator.

The door opened immediately and Subing stepped back as an elderly woman weighted down with diamond rings and bracelets stepped out. She talked incessantly in English, in that annoying nasal twang so many American Jew women seemed to have, berating her husband's canary-yellow slacks and open-collared sport coat and telling him he should have worn a tie. The man listened passively and, for a moment, Subing felt sorry for him. If he had such a wife, the Filipino knew, he would have slit her throat long ago.

Subing punched the button for the seventh floor and waited as the car rose. The rear of the elevator was glass and through it he saw the hotel's atrium area and swimming pool. More infidels—nearly naked and almost begging for the wrath of God—swam or lounged around the pool on plastic chairs. Another woman—young, blonde and large breasted—caught his eyes and once again he had to force himself to turn away.

The doors rolled open again when the car reached the seventh floor and Subing hauled his suitcase out and down the hall. He came quickly to a T in the hallway and saw a sign telling him that rooms 701 through 732 lay to his right. Following the arrow, he found 714 roughly halfway down the first hall. He rapped on the door three times with his fist. Ten seconds later he saw the peephole darken as someone looked out into the hall. A moment later the door opened and a portly man with a full beard and thinning hair stepped back to let him in.

"*Salaam*," the man said as Subing entered the room.

"*Salaam*," Subing replied.

The Filipino saw what he had come for lying on the closest of the two twin beds in the room—a suitcase, identical in every outward detail, to the one he carried. Setting his own bag on the floor, he leaned over the bed and flipped the latches of the new case. The lid sprang open in his hands.

He looked down at the contents and smiled. Satisfied, he closed the lid and secured the latches. Turning back as he hoisted the case, he saw that the portly man now stood holding a large brown envelope.

"It is all there?" Subing asked. "All three contributions?"

"Yes," the man replied. "The money from Iraq arrived last night. The Palestinians left not ten minutes ago." He smiled. "But you know the Palestinians. They are always late with everything."

Subing stared the man in the eye. "They are in an occupied land," he said. "They must take special precautions."

"Of course," the portly man said quickly, the smile disappearing. "I meant only to make a joke."

"I am not a humorous man," Subing said as he took the envelope from him. "And the money from my friend from the north?"

"It has been here for several days."

The Filipino nodded. Without another word he left the room, found the same elevator still waiting and returned to the cab.

The driver stayed on the access road until they reached Subing's next stop, which was less than a mile away. Another large hotel, but locally owned and called the Garden of Eden. Subing settled with the driver, then walked into the lobby to the front desk. The desk clerk knew him.

"Ah," said the man behind the desk, smiling. "Mr. Ali. How good to see you again."

Yes, and I hope to kill you someday, Subing thought as he pulled out his reservation card. But the smile on his face betrayed no such feelings as he signed in, then took another elevator to his room. Inside, he saw yet another identical suitcase waiting for him on the bed. He flipped the latches and looked in to find exact reproductions of the clothing he had carried during his flight from Manila. He smiled again, this time genuinely. He had recently gotten word that the Israelis sometimes randomly picked visitors to be videotaped during luggage inspections. Then they compared the tapes to the contents of the suitcases they brought with them when leaving the country again. He doubted that had happened to him because he had seen no video equipment during his search. But it never hurt to be careful.

Lifting the suitcase he had picked up at the Holiday Inn, Subing made sure he had the key card to his room, then left. He walked back to the elevator, took it two floors higher to the ninth floor and knocked on the third door to his right.

This time the door was opened by an older woman in full Islamic dress. Her veil covered most of her face, but Subing could see the sharp black eyes above it. He entered the room and found a young man, eighteen to twenty, sitting in a chair by the table in front of the sliding-glass door. He jumped quickly to his feet as Subing entered and said, "God be praised!"

Subing nodded in agreement as he set the suitcase on the

bed. The boy stood around 5' 7" and couldn't have weighed more than 130 pounds. His hair was cut close to his head, and he had shaved the arms that extended from his round-necked polo shirt. He looked frightened.

"You are ready?" Subing asked.

The young man nodded.

He handed the brown envelope to the old woman. "You are the mother of a luminary," he said. "You, too, shall be remembered by God in Paradise."

The eyes above the veil looked humbly down at the carpet.

Subing opened the suitcase to reveal its contents. The boy looked down at it as if he were seeing a snake. But he walked forward. "God be praised," he said again, his voice trembling ever so slightly.

The Filipino helped the boy slide his arms into the vest. He showed the boy where the button was to detonate the combination of Semtex and dynamite packed into the many pockets and sewn into the lining. The boy's eyes flickered nervously and he nodded at each instruction. Finally he said the first words besides "Praise God" he had said since Subing entered. "When do I go?" he asked.

Subing looked at his watch. His return flight left in six hours. If they left now he could return to his room and catch a nap before departing. "Now," he said.

"Now?" the boy repeated, his voice cracking.

"Is there a better time to serve God than the present?" Subing asked pointedly.

The boy stood frozen for a moment. Then he shook his head and turned to look at his mother.

"Do you have a vehicle?" Subing asked.

The boy nodded. "My uncle sent us in his car."

"Then I will drive." Subing extended a hand toward the door, indicating that it was time to go.

The boy stopped long enough to hug his mother one final time, then walked purposefully to the door.

As Subing passed her, he saw tears in the eyes above the veil. The woman clutched the envelope of money to her breast.

The car was a ten-year-old Chevrolet and Subing took the keys from the boy as soon as he'd seated himself behind the wheel. He started the ignition and pulled out of the Garden of Eden onto the access road. The trip back to the Holiday Inn took less than three minutes and he circled the building, finally coming to a halt at the very rear of the parking lot.

"God be praised," Subing said as the boy got out of the cab.

The boy started to speak but something caught in his throat. He nodded instead.

"The discotheque is on the far side of the lobby," Subing said as the boy walked away.

The Filipino watched him disappear into the lobby and felt no sorrow for the boy. He was about to do the work of God and in only a few more seconds he would be with God in Paradise. He would have all of the rewards that had been promised.

No, Subing thought as he glanced at his watch, this was no occasion for sorrow. In fact, the only emotion he felt at the moment was envy. He would have liked to have been that boy walking into the disco himself.

But God had bigger things in mind for him. Much bigger. And he would just have to wait a little longer. His time would come and it would come soon now. And when it did he would show none of the fear and doubt that he'd seen in the boy's eyes. He would send far more infidels to Hell than this boy ever dreamed of.

Candido Subing glanced to his watch one more time. He knew he had made a deal with the devil—his fat friend from the North. But God would understand. The fat man was an infidel himself but he supplied weapons, explosives and money to Subing's martyrs and other Arab freedom fighters all over the world. Men like Subing had made the man rich. To show his appreciation, the Filipino would be given the grand prize in the businessman's collection. And with that prize Subing would not only gain Paradise, he would be remembered for all of eternity as the warrior of God who had killed more infidels than any other.

The explosion jerked Subing out of his reverie. It shook the building and he even felt the concussion rock the car. Across the parking lot, he saw flames begin to leap from the lobby area. He threw the car into drive.

Subing was back at the Garden of Eden by the time he heard the first sirens racing toward the Holiday Inn. Police, firefighters and ambulances.

Candido Subing grinned as he pulled into a parking space and killed the engine. He watched more flashing red lights go by and knew his turn was coming.

And it was coming soon.

CHAPTER FIVE

They had made it to within ten feet of the Buick when several of the villagers finally snapped to what was going on. No one said a word, but a dozen or so men moved in front of Bolan and Latham, cutting them off from the car.

Villagers were still arriving from other parts of the town. It seemed that every last man in Rio Hondo had turned out to look for the foreigners. The Executioner did a quick 360-degree scan. They were surrounded on three sides. Behind them was the sea.

Bearing a vast assortment of clubs, swords and knives, the men of Rio Hondo stared at the Executioner, awaiting the next development in the ongoing drama. Besides the various clubs and blades he had already encountered, here and there Bolan now saw other traditional Filipino weapons. Several of the men carried *buntot-pagi,* the semiflexible whips named after the tail of the stingray. One man—tall, burly, and extremely muscular—carried a curled latigo horsewhip in his left hand. In his right was a long dagger.

The problem hadn't changed. Bolan couldn't bring himself to kill innocent men who believed they were protecting their lives and those of their families. But the villagers could—and would—kill them.

Bolan glanced over the *datu's* head. The Buick was invisible now, the mob growing larger by the second as more villagers came jogging toward the stilt house. The Executioner scanned the men in front of him, studying each one individually and seeing in their faces the same divergence of purpose Latham had heard in their words. In a few of the men he saw pure, raw and unadulterated hatred, with the kill-lust beaming from their eyes. These were the men who either believed he and Latham had come to harm the village or who supported the efforts of the Tigers.

But in the eyes of other men Bolan saw sadness and even compassion. These would be the men who, while they would do whatever they had to do to protect themselves and their loved ones, had grown weary of fighting. They understood the horrors of terrorism and wished only to live out their lives in peace. They would sooner go back home than draw blood. But not if it turned out the Americans were a threat.

As Latham had indicated, there was also a third group of Rio Hondans, and this group represented at least three-quarters of the villagers who now encircled them. These were the men who were just flat confused. The Executioner suspected they didn't know where they stood or what position they should take concerning him and Latham. But he also suspected they held no loyalty toward Candido Subing and the Liberty Tigers, either.

Time seemed to stand still as the Americans eyed the Filipinos and the Filipinos stared back. Other than the waves lapping onto shore behind them, the only sound in the still Mindanaon night was the constant undercurrent of whispered bickering back and forth between the different factions. It reconfirmed Bolan's belief that they were divided and a plan began to form in his brain

The men with the kill-lust in their eyes didn't pose the greatest danger, Bolan knew. There were five, six at the most, and if the others didn't intervene he and Latham could fight their way past them to the Buick. No, the Executioner realized as the plan took further shape in his mind, it was the "undecided" group, the middle-of-the-road villagers, the ones who could go either way, who posed the threat. Like the vast majority of men all over the world, they had trouble making up their minds and taking a stand. But if the angry villagers could convince them the strangers should be put to death, they would go along with it like mindless cattle being herded into a pen.

And there were too many of them to fight. At least without resorting to firearms.

The man with the latigo was one of the angry ones and Bolan heard him raise his voice now, shouting in Tagalog. A few of the men who had remained neutral so far began to slowly nod. Bolan knew he had only a few seconds before this crowd of thinking individuals turned into a furious senseless mob. The put-their-heads-on-a-stick gang were always more convincing than their nonviolent counterparts.

Bolan looked down at the little *datu* again. "The men like this guy?" he asked Latham.

"Like him?" Latham asked, turning to look at the Executioner as if he were a two-headed alien. "Hell, I don't know if they *like* him or not," he said, his voice shaking slightly. "But who cares if—"

"Ask them," Bolan said, nodding out at the group.

"Ask them if they...*like* their *datu*?"

The Executioner nodded again.

Charlie Latham blew air out between his teeth in frustration. "Yeah, okay," he said. "I'll ask them if they *like* the little fellow. Anything else you want to know? Such as what kind of toothpaste they use, maybe?"

Bolan's sudden speaking had slowed the argument among the villagers for a second. But it picked back up again with the latigo-dagger man resuming his shouted appeals for killing them. "Ask them now," Bolan told Latham in a sterner voice. "Before it's too late."

Latham raised his voice, literally yelling the question to the villagers in Tagalog.

There was a sudden second of silence. Just as Latham had been, the men of Rio Hondo were dismayed at the strange question. But a second was all the Executioner had hoped for. Or needed.

Reaching out, Bolan grabbed the little *datu* by the shoulders, twirled him to face his men, then yanked him backward. A short stifled shriek escaped the Rio Hondo leader's lips. But it ended abruptly as Bolan wrapped an arm around his face and over his mouth. With his other hand, the Executioner drew the TOPS Loner and pressed the razor-edged steel into the *datu*'s throat.

A collective gasp shot from the villagers. They started forward.

"Stop!" Bolan shouted. He dug the blade in tighter against the throat of the man in his arms.

The villagers might not have spoken English, but they got the message. And they froze where they stood.

Latham was as surprised by the sudden action as anyone and it took him a good five seconds before he could speak. When his voice returned he said, "Well, maybe they *like* him and maybe they don't. But I'm pretty sure they aren't too crazy about you and me at the moment."

"Tell them to clear a path to the Buick," Bolan ordered, still gripping the little *datu* tightly. "Tell them as soon as we get the car started we'll let him go." He paused. "Tell them if they don't do exactly what we tell them to do, or if anyone tries to interfere, I'll cut his throat. Right now."

Latham spoke. Several of the men growled under their breath. Bolan lifted the *datu* into the air and kept the blade tight against his throat. A shallow wound opened beneath the keen razor edge and a drop of blood rolled down the *datu*'s neck to drip onto the asphalt roadway.

One of the villagers in the front of the throng held up both hands, palms out, signaling that they would offer no resistance. The man's barong was sheathed and held in place at his waist by a bright red sash. He wore an ornately embroidered black vest with no shirt underneath. Wiry muscles extended from the arm holes, shining in the moonlight with a light coat of sweat. Bolan remembered him as one of the men who, earlier, seemed to be screaming for their blood. But now his mood had changed. He looked to be in his early thirties and spoke quickly and clearly.

"He wants to know about Mario," Latham said.

"Tell him Mario goes with us," said the Executioner. "But I promised them before and I'll promise them again. He won't be hurt."

Latham translated, the men argued again for several seconds, then mumbled again. The man in the vest spoke loudly and clapped his hands for emphasis.

The bodies parted and a pathway opened. At the end of it stood the Buick.

Bolan kept the *datu* tightly in his grasp, the blade still in place as he followed Latham to the car. The Texan opened the door, tossed Mario Subing into the back seat, then got in behind the wheel. Bolan opened the passenger's door and rolled down the window. The men of Rio Hondo had followed them and now they crowded close.

"Tell them to back off," the Executioner said.

Latham translated.

Most of the men took a step backward. Bolan maneuvered

himself between the open door and the vehicle, glancing quickly inside to see that the steering column had been cracked and the car hot-wired. In one smooth motion he released the *datu,* pulled his arm back behind the window, then reached through the opening to wrap it around the short man's head once more. He was about to sit and close the door when a swoosh of air coming toward him caught his attention.

Instinctively, the Loner knife shot out to block the side of his head. A snapping sound pierced the night as leather met steel and Bolan turned to see the end of the latigo fall to the ground. The big man who had wielded the flexible weapon stepped back, the handle of his whip still extended in front of him, he stared at the severed leather in awe.

Quickly, the Executioner pulled his legs into the car and closed the door. He still held the *datu* around the head, the knife now returned to the man's throat. The *datu* stood awkwardly outside the car, bent backward at the waist. "Start slowly," Bolan ordered Latham, and the engine rumbled to life.

The men in front of the Buick stepped to the side as Latham threw the car into drive and gradually picked up speed. The *datu*'s feet pattered against the asphalt as he half ran and was half dragged beside the vehicle. "As soon as I let him go, floor it," Bolan said. He heard no response behind him but knew the Texan had heard him.

When they had reached what he guessed to be roughly fifteen to twenty miles per hour, Bolan pulled the Loner away from the *datu*'s throat and pulled both arms back into the car. The village leader fell away from the car and rolled as Latham leaned in on the accelerator and the Buick shot forward.

The Executioner turned in his seat to peer back through the darkness as they sped away from Rio Hondo. There was just enough light for him to see two men help the *datu* to his feet and begin dusting him off.

THEY WERE halfway back to Zamboanga when the Executioner heard Mario Subing stirring in the back seat. They rounded a curve and Bolan ordered Latham off the road onto the shoulder. The soldier got out of the front and into the back, pulling the still-groggy old man up to a seated position next to him. Latham took off again but as he did, the Executioner caught sight of a bedraggled pickup of indiscernible color rounding the curve behind them.

Bolan frowned. There had been no traffic coming through Rio Hondo when they'd left—he had checked as they'd driven away—which meant that the pickup had come from the village and that, in turn, had to mean one or more of the villagers had followed them.

The pickup slowed as soon as it came within sight of the Buick and as far as the Executioner was concerned that final detail turned his hypothesis into fact.

"Someone's following us," Latham said from the front seat.

"So I see," Bolan said. "Speed up."

Latham hit the accelerator and the Buick shot forward.

The pickup did the same.

"Slow down," Bolan said.

Latham tapped the brake pedal. The pickup followed suit.

"Okay," the Executioner said. "Speed up and then slam us to a halt."

In the rearview mirror the Executioner could see Latham grin as the Texan floored the gas, taking the Buick up to seventy on the ragged asphalt road. The pickup fell behind.

"*Too* fast, Charlie," Bolan said. "That bag of bolts wants to keep up with us. It just can't."

Latham let up on the pedal and the Buick dropped back to fifty miles an hour. The distance between them and the pickup narrowed.

"Now," Bolan said.

Latham stomped the brake and the tires squealed like a banshee from hell as the Buick began to fishtail down the road. The Texan rode the steering wheel expertly, turning it slightly in the direction of each skid. Behind them, the pickup screamed in agony as the driver tried to avoid running into the back of the Buick. Both of the truck's bald front tires blew at the same time and the vehicle shot off the road toward the bar ditch.

Latham brought the Buick to a halt. Bolan didn't need to tell him what to do next. The Texan slammed the gearshift into reverse and floored the accelerator again. The car shot backward, pulling even with the other vehicle just as the pickup rose out of the bar ditch and struck a tree at the edge of the jungle.

"Watch Mario," Bolan ordered Latham as he drew the Desert Eagle and leaped from the vehicle. A second later he was standing next to the driver's side of the pickup with the barrel of the big .44 jammed through the open window and into the jaw of the man behind the wheel.

Bolan recognized the driver immediately. He had been the villager at the forefront of the mob who had held up his hands—the man in the embroidered black vest with the barong sheathed through his red sash.

The villager's head had struck the steering wheel upon colliding with the fence. He was still leaning forward as the ancient pickup engine coughed, chugged and finally died.

"Slowly," the Executioner said. "Get out of the truck."

He got no response.

Bolan reached in with his free hand and grabbed the long hair at the back of the man's neck. He lifted the face away from the steering wheel and saw that the eyes were closed. A small abrasion in the center of the man's forehead bled slightly and the area was quickly swelling into a large goose egg. But he was still breathing.

The Executioner opened the door and pulled the man out onto the ground. Quickly frisking the unconscious man, he found a sat phone and a tiny Seecamp .32 pistol hidden in the red sash. Bolan frowned. The Seecamp .32s—roughly the size of a small .25 but with far more power—were made by a small, privately owned company in the U.S. They were held in high regard because of their size and the shops couldn't keep up with consumer demand. That meant they often sold for three times their factory retail price on the open market and such a gun didn't match the profile of a poor Rio Hondo villager.

Bolan eyed the piece again. Maybe the man had stolen it. But it still seemed unlikely that a gun like this would end up on Mindanao.

The Executioner dropped the little .32 into his pocket and checked further. He had just felt what appeared to be a billfold in one of the vest pockets when the villager began to regain consciousness.

As soon as the man's eyelids fluttered open, Bolan shoved the big .44 into the center of the swelling on his forehead. "Start talking, and talk *fast*," he said. As soon as the words came out of his mouth he knew they were useless. The likelihood of the man speaking English was minute and he turned back toward the Buick, about to call out for Latham to come translate.

But before he could speak the man on the ground said, "Hey, gimme a break, okay? Like, a second or two to collect my thoughts?" The accent that accompanied the words surprised Bolan as much as the words themselves. It hadn't been picked up in the Philippines. It was pure Brooklyn.

Bolan kept the Desert Eagle between the man's eyes as he took in this new development, trying to make sense of it. The man in the embroidered black vest shook his head back and forth several times, clearing out the cobwebs. "Man, have I got a konk!" he said as his hands rose slowly to rub his temples.

"You wanted a break, you've had it," Bolan said. "Now talk."

The man continued to rub his temples. "Vest,". he said. "Left pocket."

Bolan reached down and pulled out what he had earlier thought to be a billfold. It wasn't. What he found in his hands was a small black leather identification case. He flipped it open and, with one eye keeping watch on the ground, stared at the credentials inside. The picture looked like the same man, but with a shaved head and a more groomed mustache. Instead of the black vest and red sash the man in the picture wore a white shirt, conservative club tie and a dark gray pinstriped suit. The top of the card read Central Intelligence Agency and just below that United States of America.

The name beneath the picture was William Gerald Reverte.

"GO AHEAD," Reverte said. "Check it out. I want you to be comfortable working with me."

Bolan had his own sat phone pressed against his ear. "That's right," he said into the instrument. "Reverte, William Gerald. Check it out, will you, Bear?"

"Consider it done, big guy," said the voice of Aaron "The Bear" Kurtzman on the other end of the satellite connection. "That's what I'm here for. Just give me a second."

Bolan chuckled silently to himself. Asking Stony Man Farm's top computer genius to hack into the CIA personnel files was like asking a master jewel thief to shoplift a candy bar. The CIA knew they had a man linking up with someone working directly for the President, but the company knew nothing about the existence of Stony Man Farm itself, so Kurtzman's electronic wizardry would verify Reverte's ID with no questions asked. "Call me back when you've got it, Bear," the Executioner said.

"Will do."

The Executioner pressed the End button, dropped the phone back into his pocket and heard it tap against the steel of the .32-caliber Seecamp he had dropped there earlier. He had no reason to believe Reverte was anything other than what he claimed to be—the CIA operative who should have met them on the road outside of Zamboanga. And his story that he had been undercover with the villagers, learning a little more about Subing every day, and hadn't been able to break away at the appointed time made sense, as well.

Such things could happen. Undercover work never went according to schedule. And Reverte's CIA card also explained the pricey pistol the Executioner had found.

Leaving the Seecamp where it was, Bolan looked over to see that Latham still had both Mario Subing and the man in the black vest seated on the ground. The Executioner had put the Texan in charge of them both while he double-checked Reverte's story. Latham had positioned the two men in front of the Buick's headlights where he could see them. They both sat cross-legged with their hands clasped behind their heads. Latham trained the .40-caliber Browning Hi-Power back and forth between them, the red-dot laser dancing on, then off, then on and off again, as he pressed the button to remind them who was in charge.

Bolan glanced around at the trees, bushes and other shrubbery. They were off the highway now, hidden from passing traffic by the thick foliage. Almost as soon as Reverte had come around they had pushed the wrecked pickup out of sight into the jungle, thrown him into the back seat with Mario Subing, then taken the first side road into the trees they had come to. The Buick had bounced over the narrow path to a dead end clearing where the evidence of countless campers still covered the ground.

As he waited for the return call from Kurtzman, the Executioner walked to the trunk of the Buick, inserted the key and opened it. He breathed a silent sight of relief when he saw all of his gear exactly as he'd left it. He had worried that the village men of Rio Hondo might have pried open the trunk but that didn't appear to be the case.

Bolan unzipped one of the side pockets on a bulky ballistic nylon equipment case and pulled out a fistful of plastic restraints. Closing the trunk again, he walked back to where the two men still sat on the ground.

Mario Subing snarled at him as he approached and Bolan had to suppress a smile. The little man was like a tiny fighting rooster. He couldn't have weighed more than one hundred pounds, but he had fought the Executioner tooth and nail at the stilt house. He had started in again as soon as he'd awakened from the tap Bolan had given him on the chin, and it had taken Latham's Browning to quiet him. But as soon as he'd figured out that the man in the red sash and black vest—a man he had known and *trusted* back in the village—was playing for the other team he had gone straight for Reverte's throat.

Even now the red welts on Reverte's neck were visible in the Buick's headlights.

Stopping behind the elderly Filipino, the Executioner tightened a flexible cuff around both his hands, then secured them together with a third piece of the steel-reinforced plastic. Remembering the way the old man had used his feet, he did the same at the ankles. Mario Subing glared over his shoulder throughout the process, then muttered a long string of angry words in his native tongue.

Bolan glanced up at Latham for a translation.

The Texan just shrugged. "It's nothing you'd want your kids to hear."

"Hey, that isn't necessary!" Reverte said, holding his hands out to his sides theatrically, as Bolan turned to him with more of the plastic restraints. "In a minute you're going to find out I am who I say I am."

"Then in a minute," the Executioner said as he stepped in behind the man, "I'll cut you loose. Until then, put your hands behind your back." He was ninety percent certain that Kurtzman would call back and verify the ID, but there was still something about Reverte that bothered him. He couldn't put his finger on it but a shadow of doubt about the man still floated through his mind. He wrapped the plastic cuffs around the man's wrists and secured them the same way he had done with Mario.

Bolan had just finished when the sat phone begin to vibrate in his pocket. Pulling it out, he activated the device and said, "Go, Bear."

"Reverte, William Gerald," said the voice from the other side of the world. "Thirty-three years of age. Born in Queen's, New York, but grew up in Brooklyn."

"I could have told you that from listening to him talk," Bolan said.

"Okay, big guy," Kurtzman said. "But could you have told me he graduated from Northwestern University in Evanston with a B.A. in drama?"

The Executioner glanced at the man who had held his arms out for emphasis only a second earlier. Reverte had looked as if he were Caesar about to address the people of Rome from a balcony. "No, but it doesn't surprise me," he said into the phone.

"Yep," said Kurtzman. "And a year after that the CIA was so impressed with his acting they stole him away from a life of starvation between bit parts in soap operas." Kurtzman paused. "And I'll bet you didn't know he was the starting catcher on the NU baseball team his junior and senior years, either."

"We hadn't quite gotten to the tea party chitchat yet, Bear," the Executioner said dryly.

"Bottom line, Striker," Kurtzman said, using the Executioner's mission code name. "Looks like he checks out. CIA sent him over to infiltrate the Tigers. Last report I'm finding says he had made the acquaintance of Candy Subing's uncle. Let's see...his name is—"

"Mario," Bolan finished for him.

There was a pause, then a low laugh on the other end of the line. "You know him?"

"Fact of the matter is," the Executioner said, "he's kneeling in front of my vehicle at the moment all dressed up in plastic cuffs."

"Well, good, Striker. Glad to see you're taking your usual roundabout-low-key approach to life."

"Thanks, Bear," Bolan said. "Anything else I need to know?"

"Not unless you want Reverte's grade point average at Northwestern and his annual job evaluation ratings from the CIA," Kurtzman said.

"No, thanks." Bolan paused a moment. "Any more chatter on what this 'big deal' the Tigers are supposed to be planning in the U.S. might be?"

Kurtzman cleared his throat, then said, "No. We're checking every angle we can think of. Biological, chemical, food and water poisoning. Sky- and truck-jacking possibilities. Even nuclear. So far, the rumors are still out there but no one knows anything definite."

"They seem small-time to me," Bolan said. "Only way they could finance something big is to hook up with some money people."

"I'll let you know as soon as we find out anything," Kurtzman assured him.

"Thanks, Bear," the Executioner said, and disconnected.

Bolan reached into his pocket, pulled out the tiny See-camp pistol and dropped the phone back where it had been. He walked to the front of the car, withdrew the Loner, cut the restraints binding Reverte's wrists together and pulled the man to his feet. "You've got my apology," he said.

Reverte rubbed his wrists and grinned. "Hey, no problem. Can't be too careful in our line of work." He extended his hand and Bolan shook it. "I take it I passed the audition?"

By way of answer the Executioner handed him the .32 and his sat phone. Reverte took the tiny pistol and stashed it back in his sash. Something about the way he did it caught the Executioner's eye. Something in his unconscious mind, something mildly unsettling. But he couldn't put his finger on that any more than he could what bothered him about the man in general. "Tell me," Bolan said. "How'd you duke your way into the village?"

Reverte shrugged dramatically. "Usual way," he said. "Filipino cops busted a local boy. The folks at Langley stepped in and worked out a deal for him if he'd introduce me." He paused, turned slightly, and to Bolan he appeared to be consciously posing. "That was the closest we thought we could get to Candido without him getting suspicious—his uncle. Besides, we didn't have a snitch into the Tigers."

"You ever meet Candido when he came to visit?" Bolan asked.

"Nah, no way," Reverte said. "I wasn't in that deep yet." He glanced at the old man who was still on the ground. "Mario and I were just getting to know each other."

"What made you break cover and come after us?" Bolan asked.

"I didn't really break cover," Reverte said. "In fact, I probably helped it." He took a deep breath and rubbed his wrists again. Then one hand went to his throat where the welts Subing had left were still visible. "As soon as you guys took off I screamed out that I was going to kill you both and get Mario back, then grabbed the closest vehicle."

Bolan frowned. "So the men of Rio Hondo still don't know you're CIA?"

Reverte shook his head, then reached up and grasped the lapels of his vest with both hands. "None of them but this one," he said, glancing down at Mario. "Of course he was my link to his nephew, so that's screwed now. Not that it's all that big of a loss."

"Meaning?" the Executioner said.

"Meaning that I'd gotten to know the old man well enough to know I was wasting my time with him." He shook his head, again more like an actor on stage than a genuine human being. "He wasn't ever going to tell me anything about his nephew no matter how well I got to know him. That's one tough old bastard, as you've already seen. And I don't care what you do—stick bamboo chutes under his fingernails, burn his balls off with a cigarette lighter, whatever, he's not going to tell you dick, either."

Bolan looked away from Reverte, turning his attention to the grizzled old man in the headlights. Torture was hardly his style, but his gut level instincts told him that even if it was, Reverte was right—it wouldn't work. Reverte was right on Mario being tough, too.

The fact was, Bolan had to respect a brittle old man who would stand up and fight the way he did. Protecting a terrorist—even if it was your nephew—wasn't right. But he couldn't be sure old Mario was aware of all of Candido's crimes, either. Family members told each other *their* version of events, and those versions always seemed to justify their actions. As the old saying went, "one man's terrorist was another man's freedom fighter."

"So…" Reverte said, dragging out the word as if he wanted the audience in the back row to be sure to hear it. "That's why I followed you. I'd hit an impasse in Rio Hondo. I knew you'd be wasting your time with Mario, and I said to myself, 'Billy-boy, why not pool your remarkable talents with the genius already exhibited by the big dude with the big gun?'" He glanced toward Bolan's right hip where the Desert Eagle was again hidden by the tail of his shirt, then turned suddenly and quickly to Latham and added, "Not that you aren't an able performer yourself. No offense."

Bolan was quickly tiring of the CIA man's histrionics. When he looked to Latham, the Texan raised his eyebrows to indicate that he'd begun to find the man tedious, too. "No offense taken," he said, and the Executioner suspected the words came out of his mouth to shut Reverte up.

"So you *were* assigned to work with us," Bolan said.

"Sure was," the CIA agent said. "Sorry I missed the initial meet, but maybe it's just as well. I learned more from old Mario. Let's pool our resources to see if we can't come up with some constructive plan to find the hostages." He looked down yet again at the old man before adding, "And kill this son of a bitch's nephew while we're at it."

Bolan nodded. He'd give it a try because he'd promised Hal Brognola he'd work with the man. But if Reverte proved to be as full of BS as he seemed on the surface, he'd find himself packing for a return flight to Langley, fast. "Okay."

Reverte seemed not to sense the Executioner's hesitancy. "Now you know who I am, I gotta know about you," he said. He reached up and rubbed his neck again. "You aren't Company—they'd have told me. Military intel? NSA? Who?"

"Nothing you'd recognize," Bolan said.

Reverte raised his eyebrows and smiled sarcastically. As with all of his other facial expressions and body language, it seemed carefully calculated and overdone. "Top top secret, eh?" he said. "Big-time. For your eyes only. So secret even the CIA doesn't know about you? Tell me, you have one of those double-O licenses to kill? Report directly to the President himself?"

Bolan was already beginning to regret his decision to let the man come with them. "That's fairly close," he said.

The expression on Reverte's face seemed genuine for the first time as he frowned in puzzlement. Finally he said, "No, really. Who are you with?"

Bolan nodded toward Latham. "Him. That's all you need to know and all you're going to know. If you don't like it, we'll drop you off somewhere in Zamboanga."

Reverte remained silent for a moment then shrugged. "Okay. Whatever." He raised only one eyebrow this time as he pointed to Mario Subing with both hands palm up. "What do we do with him? We can't let him go back to Rio Hondo. I might need to go back sometime myself."

Bolan turned and stared into the dark trees, his jaw tightening. Reverte was right. They couldn't just let the old man go home to tell the other villagers all he now knew. The word would soon leak out to the Tigers. On the other hand, it was becoming increasingly more evident that Candido Subing and his men already had a pretty clear picture of Bolan's and Latham's movements. The Executioner no longer had any doubt that the men on the road the day before hadn't been kidnappers. They were members of the Tigers, sent to kill them. And the villagers had caught on to their presence fast, too.

Somehow, somebody was tipping them off.

"Want me to just kill him?" Reverte asked.

The Executioner turned to stare at the CIA man. Somewhere, hidden within the thick foliage but close, some nocturnal animal shook the brush as it moved about the night

"No," he said. "I don't want you to just kill an old man."
Reaching into his pocket, the Executioner pulled his sat phone
out again and tapped the redial button. A moment later the
voice of Stony Man mission controller Barbara Price said,
"Hello, Striker."

"Barb, get Jack ready and—"

"Wish you'd have said you needed him earlier," Price said.
"I just sent him to pick Phoenix Force up in Bosnia."

"How about Charlie?" Bolan asked. Charlie Mott was the
Farm's number-two pilot and plenty good enough for what the
Executioner needed him for now.

"Last I saw of him he was on his way upstairs to saw a few
logs," Price said. "He and Able Team were in the air most of
the night."

"Well," Bolan said, "wake him up. Tell him I need him here
and to contact me when he gets close."

"What have you got, Striker?"

"Nothing dramatic," Bolan said, then thought of Reverte's
antics and realized that wasn't entirely correct. "Just an old
man who needs to be put on ice for a few days so he can't talk
to anyone."

"Need me to send a blacksuit as guard?"

The Executioner glanced at the elderly Filipino still seated
on the ground, his face twisted into a mask of hatred. "Better
send two or three, Barb," he said.

"Anything else?" the mission controller asked.

"Some extra ammo and a few other things would help,"
Bolan said, then rattled off a short list of equipment. In his
mind, he watched Price jot it all down in shorthand.

"Okay. Now, I've got a request for *you*."

"What's that?"

"Be careful," Price said, and hung up.

The Executioner allowed himself a brief mental image of

his beautiful sometime love, then turned his attention back to the matter at hand. Hooking a thumb toward the car, he said, "Come on," and heard Reverte fall in behind him.

The Executioner stopped in front of Latham who was still guarding Mario Subing. "Charlie," he said, "I need to talk to you."

He nodded toward the trees, then looked at Reverte again. "You keep an eye on Mario."

Reverte pulled the little .32 caliber Seecamp from his sash and said, "My pleasure."

Latham still had his Browning in his hand. He shoved it into his belt and followed the Executioner to a spot in the trees just out of earshot. "What's up?" he said.

Bolan scratched the side of his face. "I don't know," he said. "Reverte checked out okay. But there's something about him that bothers me."

The Texan had the answer. "He's an asshole," he said simply.

"Not just that. Something else. Something else about him that doesn't quite add up."

"He wanted to kill the old man," he said under his breath. "We could always kill him."

"No," the Executioner said. "If he *does* have some other game going, I want to know what it is. And the best way to find out is to let him tag along. And give him enough rope to hang himself. Besides, it may be nothing more than the CIA having some agenda of their own."

"No kidding," the former Delta Force soldier said. "They may have something going that takes precedence over freeing the hostages. Innocent human life was never their top priority."

"I think we're better off taking him along where we can keep an eye on him," the Executioner said. "We'll watch him. And each other's back."

Latham pulled the hat off his head, then the bandanna, and

mopped his face. "Only problem with that is it means we'll have to *listen* to the mouthy son of a bitch," he said.

Bolan changed the subject. "We need a place somewhere close around here where a plane can land unnoticed."

"How big a plane?"

"Learjet," Bolan said.

"Hear tell there's a landing strip up near Panganuran," he said. "It'll land a small to medium plane."

Bolan frowned. "Government strip?"

Latham shook his head. "Hardly. Heroin out of Southeast Asia, so they say. Drop-off point and refueling stations goes the rumor." He tied the bandanna around his forehead again and replaced the hat. "Folks also say there's a tie-in to some of the local terrorists."

Bolan looked down into the face below the straw cowboy hat. "The Tigers?" he asked.

Latham shrugged. "Don't know. But we both know terrorists peddle dope for operating funds when they can. Besides the Tigers, the Moro Islamic Liberation Front and Jemmah Islamiah are strong in these parts. too."

The Executioner took a deep breath. Both the JI and MILF were fundamentalist Islamic fanatics like the Tigers. Sometimes they were all friends, other times enemies.

The Executioner would have been happy to set up on the landing site, wait on the drug plane to land and destroy both the drugs and the crew. But right now there were more pressing problems—human lives at stake—and he didn't want to get sidetracked onto a drug investigation which *might*, but wasn't very likely to, lead to his primary goal. "How much traffic does this place see?" the Executioner asked.

"I don't know." Latham shrugged. "Never been there myself. But it can't be like Kennedy International or anything."

"Any other place we could land our plane?"

"I assume you mean without anyone else knowing about it," Latham said, wiping sweat off his forehead beneath his hat brim. "Not unless you want to go all the way across the island to Baganga. There's a—"

"We don't have time for that," Bolan said, interrupting him. "Panganuran will have to do." He had intended to have Latham take Mario Subing to the meeting spot with the plane while he took whatever intel he could from Reverte and proceeded with the mission. But with the chance of facing drugrunners now, he would have to go with the Texan. It wasn't ideal, but he could use the drive north to glean whatever information Reverte had from the man. Then, after Charlie Mott had dropped off the new equipment and picked up Mario, Bolan, Latham and Reverte would resume the search for the hostages.

Returning to the Buick, Bolan glanced at Mario. "Get him into the back seat," he told Latham. "Reverte, you ride shotgun." He wanted Reverte where he could see him—at least until he figured out what it was that bothered him about the CIA man.

Since the Rio Hondans had cracked the steering column they no longer needed the key to start the car. Bolan slid in behind the wheel and fired it to life. Reverte got in next to him while Latham half carried a wiggling, spitting and Tagalog-cursing Mario Subing to the back seat.

A few minutes later they were back on the asphalt highway and headed toward Panganuran by way of Zamboanga.

CHAPTER SIX

Dawn had broken over the Philippines by the time the Buick reached the outskirts of Panganuran. Far in the distance, Bolan could see the tiny village at the end of the broken and chipped asphalt. He glanced into the rearview mirror to see Mario Subing. The old man's eyes were closed and his chin bounced lightly against his chest each time the Buick hit a bump or dropped into a pothole. But nothing so mild as that was going to awaken the old man; the events of the past few hours had finally taken their toll on his aged mind and body.

The Executioner looked back to the road but couldn't suppress a grin as he drove on. Regardless of how misguided Mario's efforts might be, he really did have to respect the old fighter. When Bolan had taken away his gun, he had fought back with a balisong. Then the soldier had taken the balisong and Mario had come at him with the rust-pitted Ka-bar. When that was taken away, too, the old man had used his fists. And when his limbs were finally bound tightly to his body, he had resorted to cursing and spitting. He had even tried to bite Charlie Latham in the back seat of the Buick before Reverte had offered his sash as a gag. Now the red sash was tied around Mario's mouth. After the gag had been applied old age had finally caught up to Mario and he'd drifted off to sleep.

Bolan glanced to his side and saw that Reverte's eyes were closed, as well. The CIA man was taking advantage of the driving time to catch a catnap.

As the village in the distance came closer, Latham leaned forward and rested an arm on the back of the front seat. "I've never seen this landing strip," he said, "but it's got to be close." He paused. In his peripheral vision the Executioner could see him studying the side of the road away from the sea. Which made sense—there wasn't enough land between the highway and the water for a landing strip, nor enough vegetation to hide it if there had been. The clandestine runway had to be set inland from the road.

"You're sure it's on this side of the village?" Bolan asked, nodding toward the windshield. "Not on the north?"

"I'm not sure of anything," Latham said, still frowning. "I've just heard there was a landing strip for the dopers around here." He continued to focus on the greenery as they drove on.

The Executioner rested his elbows in his lap and guided the Buick from the bottom of the steering wheel. He had made contact with Mott a half hour earlier and the Stony Man pilot had been approximately two hours out at the time. But Charlie Mott, too, had a vague memory of a landing strip somewhere in the area. He'd flown Phoenix Force, one of the counterterrorist teams working out of Stony Man Farm, over the island a few months back and had seen it from the air. The pilot had guessed at the time that it might be a site for drug planes.

So Latham half knew about it and Mott half remembered it. Bolan could only hope that the two halves equaled a whole and they'd all find a place for the Learjet to set down.

Had he not been looking for it, the Executioner knew he

would have missed the small indentation that suddenly appeared in the thick foliage. And at the same time he saw it, Latham shouted, "There!" The Texan still had an arm rested on the back of the seat between them and shot it out to point across Reverte's chest toward the jungle.

Bolan shifted his foot to the brake pedal, slowing the Buick and making a tight U-turn on the narrow roadway. He drove slowly back to the spot in question and stopped. Through the window he could see the tiny telltale signs of a hidden side road off the asphalt. The vegetation in the spot they'd noticed—wide enough to pull a car or even a truck through— was as least as thick and maybe thicker on either side of it. But here and there throughout the green were cleanly cut ends that had been made by machetes, the leaves and vines themselves were a slightly darker color, some even beginning to turn brown. Also scattered throughout the pile were tiny dirt clods, meaning that some of the plant life had been jerked from the ground before being used to camouflage the entrance to the road.

Reverte had awakened as they'd slowed and now the CIA man squinted along with Bolan and Latham. "Cute," he said, nodding his head vigorously. He crossed his arms and hugged his chest. "They keep the entrance covered by piling up debris. Easy enough to move it when they go in and out, and once it dies they cut more." He had stated the obvious and the words had come out sounding as if they were lines in a stage play.

Latham, Bolan knew, had taken a real dislike to the theatrical CIA agent. And the Texan wasn't particularly good at hiding his disinclination. "Why, thank you, Billy," he said in an equally spectacular voice. "I bet that *is* what they do."

Reverte either didn't catch Latham's sarcasm or chose to pretend he didn't. He just nodded.

Bolan halted the Buick across from the side road. "Why

don't you show us how easy it is to move it?" he said to the man next to him.

Reverte opened his door and got out, followed by Latham. Together, it took the two men less than thirty seconds to kick and slide the cut leaves and vines out of the way. As the hole opened, Bolan saw the dirt-and-gravel road behind it, and to the sides were scattered piles of dead brown plant life, which had served to hide the road in the past.

The Executioner kept an eye on Mario, still sleeping in the back seat, as he drove through the hole and stopped. Latham and Reverte piled the foliage back up over the entrance and returned to the car.

Bolan drove slowly now, both out of caution and necessity. The surface of the side road was even more rugged than the neglected asphalt highway and the Buick's tires bumped over exposed roots and rocks. Not knowing what to expect, the Executioner drew the Desert Eagle and rested it in his lap, guiding the vehicle with one hand. In the rearview mirror he caught a glimpse of Latham's Hi-Power coming out of his waistband, and next to him Reverte pulled his little .32.

Bolan looked at the tiny gun. "Is that all you have?" he asked.

"All I have with me," Reverte said. "I was undercover, remember?"

The Executioner ignored the man's sarcastic tone. He had to agree with Latham—Reverte was a royal pain in the neck to be around. But the man might still prove useful and Bolan wasn't quite ready to dump him just because he had a disagreeable personality. But something still bothered him about the CIA agent and the Executioner had just felt it again when the man got back in the car. Some strange thing he did, some mannerism—*something* at least, that nagged at the back of his mind because it didn't fit the man.

The one-lane road into the jungle twisted and turned. As

Bolan guided the vehicle around a sharp curve a gecko shot out from the jungle, stopped for a second to stare at the approaching metal monster, then darted on into the leaves on the other side. Through the open windows of the car Bolan could smell the strong odor of the durian fruits so populous on the island, and here and there through the thick foliage he spotted abacas, a hemp plant the Mindanaons used to make rope.

The curve straightened and the road suddenly dead-ended. Bolan took a firmer grip on the Desert Eagle as he saw what lay ahead. There, parked in the middle of the narrow path at the edge of the jungle, stood an old flatbed truck. His eyes scanned the road, then the thick vegetation around it. He could see no one, but that didn't mean they couldn't be hiding nearby.

The Executioner tapped the brakes and slowed the Buick almost to a halt, creeping forward until they were a hundred feet or so from the other vehicle. Crudely constructed homemade side panels rose from the sides of the truck bed and an equally rustic makeshift tailgate at the rear lay open. The cab's rear windshield had been broken and large shards of glass hung precariously from the corners.

Reverte started to speak, but Bolan held up a hand to silence him. He had watched the jungle ever since they'd left the highway but now he scrutinized every inch around the truck. His eyes finally fell on another stack of cut foliage.

Bolan squinted at the pile. It looked exactly like the one the drug runners had used to hide the entrance to the side road and he suspected behind this man-made mound he'd find a footpath that led to the landing strip. The old truck hadn't driven itself to this isolated spot.

The Executioner's jaw tightened. It looked as if he had picked the wrong time to make use of the landing strip. There was a drug shipment coming in. Today.

Bolan sat where he was, thinking, planning his next move. If there were drug runners close by their eyes—and the sights of their weapons—would be trained on the Buick right now. He knew that had the situation been reversed and it had been him hiding in the trees, he would wait until the driver killed the engine and the men got out of the car. There was no point in taking the chance that the driver might throw the vehicle into reverse and take off after the shooting started.

The Buick no longer needed a key to start it but Bolan had jammed it into the ignition just the same—mainly to keep track of the key for the trunk. He reached down to the remote control, which hung from the ring and tapped a button. Behind him, he heard a click as the trunk electronically unlocked. He left the keys where they were, the engine still running, as he grasped the door handle. "Stay here," he ordered the other two men, "and stay ready." Before they could reply he was out of the car.

The moment of truth was at hand, the Executioner knew as he closed the door behind him. If drug guards were stationed just inside the jungle to watch the truck, they would open fire any moment now. He would have little chance of returning that fire. The jungle was simply too thick and offered too many places to hide. But Bolan could see no practical way around the problem as he started for the trunk.

But no shots rang out as the Executioner moved. The only sounds continued to be the whizzing and clicking of insects and the fluttering of Sulu hornbills and other jungle birds in the trees. Most of all, Bolan *felt* no eyes on him from the bushes that surrounded them on all sides.

Opening the trunk, the Executioner blew air out through his nose at the irony of the situation. Although it would be a worthy war in itself, he hadn't come to the Philippines to fight drug lords. Now, however, some of them inadvertently stood in the way of his mission and he would have to confront them before he continued his search for Candy Subing and the American missionaries.

Reaching inside the trunk, the Executioner looked down at the bags that had hung from his body as he'd parachuted onto the island. Because of the air-entry he had been limited in what equipment he could bring and now wished he had arranged for more long guns upon his arrival. But he wasted no time considering what might have been.

Unzipping a black ballistic nylon bag, Bolan pulled out a .45-caliber Colt Combat Commander and a half dozen extra magazines. He stuffed the .45 into his belt and dropped the loaded mags into the pockets of his cargo pants. Opening a second bag, he eyed the Calico 950. The barrel had been modified to accept a sound suppressor and a 50-round drum magazine had been snapped in place at the top of the pistol. The grip was already attached to the shoulder harness, which would allow the machine pistol to hang under his right arm. The harness worked differently than most shoulder holsters in that it would allow the Calico to be carried on the strong side rather than cross-draw fashion. The weapon could even be fired without being removed from the sling. A 100-round replacement drum balanced the weight on the left side of the harness.

With the Beretta's shoulder holster beneath his blue chambray shirt, Bolan shrugged into the Calico rig, letting the strange-looking weapon and its backup drum hang over the shirt. Where he was going, there would be no need for concealment: drug runners making a pickup would be primed to kill anyone they didn't know—armed or not.

The Executioner closed the trunk with as little sound as he could, then rounded the car to the back seat and opened the door. Mario Subing had awakened, and the bound-and-gagged old man shook his head violently back and forth, his eyes shooting daggers. Bolan pulled him out of the car and stood him up, then turned to Latham. "Take him into the weeds," he said. "Far enough to be out of sight but stay close enough that you can hear me when I come back."

Latham nodded his understanding.

As he spoke, Bolan had pulled the Colt Commander and the extra .45-caliber magazines from his pockets. He extended the pistol to Reverte.

"Where are you going?" Reverte said as he took the pistol.

For a brief second the uneasy feeling came over the Executioner again. Whatever it was about Reverte that bothered him, the man had just done it again. The feeling stayed with him as he handed the man the extra magazines. "Somebody has to scout this out and find the landing strip," he said. "It's obvious we aren't alone."

Reverte nodded as he stuffed the .45 into his waistband. "I'll go with you," he said. He nodded toward Latham. "You can watch the old—"

"No," the Executioner said, stepping in slightly. "You'll with them."

Either Bolan's words, or his demeanor, or his size, or all of those factors suddenly drained every bit of thespian out of Reverte. The CIA man nodded sheepishly and stepped back.

"I'll whistle when I get back," Bolan said, reaching into the back seat of the Buick and retrieving one of the machetes. He turned away from the two men and walked toward the pile of cut debris. Behind him, he could hear the faint sounds of a minor scuffle as Latham and Reverte hauled the resistant old man into the trees.

Bolan stopped when he reached the pile of cut vines, leaves and limbs. Rather than move them out of the way he stepped into the jungle to the left, forced his way through the thick foliage for several feet, then cut back right again. As he had known he would, he found himself standing on a footpath. Narrow and rarely used, it was nevertheless evident that it had seen recent activity. Severed leaves, twigs and vines pointed the way forward and the fact that they were still green told Bolan they had been recently cut.

The Executioner dropped to one knee, examining the mud and vegetation on the ground. In many places the wild jungle growth had been flattened, and here and there in the damp earth were partial footprints. The footprints were of different sizes, shapes and sole treads. Several were identical except in size, however, and Bolan recognized the familiar pattern made by cheap Chinese-manufactured jungle boot soles. Scrutinizing the ground closer, Bolan counted eight different sets of feet, which meant that eight men—undoubtedly heavily armed—had come this way to help refuel the plane and probably pick up their own load of illicit drugs for distribution throughout the Philippines.

Rising to his feet, Bolan wrapped his fingers around the Calico's grip with grim determination. A plane was scheduled to arrive today. It would carry with it the same brain poison that had infected and destroyed the world. While stopping it was hardly his primary mission, the Executioner saw plainly that the plane's destruction would be necessary before Mott could land.

The Executioner started down the path. The men whose footprints he followed had walked along this same route no more than an hour or two earlier. And as they'd walked, they had chopped away at the vegetation that had grown back since their last visit.

Twenty yards into the jungle Bolan stopped again. On the ground he saw many footprints, some overlapping each other. Dropping down again, he noticed that some of the toes pointed forward but others faced the sides and rear. The men had stopped here. There were a few scattered cigarette butts. They had stood here, talking.

Bolan rose and walked on, his gaze still focused on the ground. It appeared that all of the men had continued forward along the path. He tracked their progress on until he came to a spot where they had stopped once again. Now his eyes fell on a flat rock half hidden by the growth at the side of the pathway.

Mud covered the top of the rock. Bolan reached down and ran a finger over the mud. It was still wet. Flipping the rock over, he found the opposite side to be relatively clean, which meant that the rock had been resting on the muddy side until the men had come along. Then a foot had caught the rock, turning it over.

Bolan's eyes searched the area until he found the oval depression. A smeared, sliding footprint in front of the shallow concavity told the rest of the story. One of the men had turned and caught the rock with his boot. The location where the rock had come to rest indicated that he had then left the path and headed out into the jungle itself. Why?

Bolan frowned. The answer was evident. At least one of the drug runners—maybe more—had hidden in the jungle to guard the path.

The soldier backed up several yards, then dropped to the ground again. Quickly he covered his face, hands and legs with mud, sticking clumps of wild grass and leaves into the mess to blur his outline. He didn't know exactly where the sentry had stationed himself, but the man couldn't be far. If Bolan directly followed the tracks leading off into the jungle, he risked being heard. Maybe even seen.

No, the Executioner thought as he rose, he would have to do this the hard way. He would have to track the man while maintaining a collateral course through the tangled flora.

A task, it turned out, that was far less trouble than he had first imagined.

Bolan had gone less than three yards when an out-of-place scent drifted his way. He froze in place, trying to identify it. It was a peculiar scent, one he had never smelled before. Then, almost at the same instant, he realized it wasn't one single odor that was out of place in the jungle, it was a combination. What filled his olfactory glands was the combined stench of cheap aftershave and marijuana smoke.

The Executioner grinned behind the mud covering his face. The man left to guard the footpath was close. And he was taking advantage of the downtime to get stoned.

Bolan moved at a snail's pace, creeping forward through the foliage. He could have used the machete a dozen times in the first dozen seconds, but he couldn't afford the noise. Instead he took his time, slowly bending limbs out of his way, then easing them back into place to keep them from whipping noisily through the air. It was time-consuming work, but with each inch he moved forward he was rewarded for his effort. For with each step the smell of marijuana and aftershave grew stronger.

Finally the Executioner caught a flash of bright blue through the greens, browns and blacks of the jungle foliage. He froze in place. The patch of blue moved.

Bolan risked another silent step forward, then stopped. He could see a faint trail of smoke now, rising from the patch of blue to disperse into the jungle canopy above. And what had been just a meaningless color now took on more definite shape. One more step and the Executioner looked through a hole in the dense plant life. In front of him, less than ten feet away, he saw that the patch of blue was a shirt, long-sleeved to protect the wearer's arms from mosquitos and other biting insects. The movement came each time the man brought the small clay pipe in his hand to his mouth for a toke.

Bolan watched the arm move again. The pipe rose up and out of sight behind the greenery, and the Executioner heard a long, sharp intake of breath as the man sucked the smoke into his lungs and held it. A good ten seconds later, the drug guard exhaled and continued to breathe heavily.

The Executioner moved one step closer, then stopped. Flipping the Calico's selector-safety to semiauto, he waited. When the arm moved up once more and he heard the intake of breath, he burst from cover.

Bolan suddenly found himself in a small open area the dope-smoker had cleared for his one-man party. The man was seated with his back against a tree. Behind him and to the side, the barrel of an AK-47 was visible on the grass-spotted ground. A large revolver hung from his belt, as did a machete in an OD green army surplus sheath.

The clay pipe still in his mouth, the man looked up at the Executioner. Between the hat and pipe, his eyes were streaked with broken red veins. But mixed in with the veins was a stare of stoned confusion. The emotion didn't last long.

Bolan squeezed the Calico's trigger and a quiet thumping sound exited the weapon. The 9 mm hollowpoint round shattered the clay pipe into a thousand pieces before passing through into the man's brain stem. The drug guard's arms fell to his sides but the rest of his body stayed in place, against the tree. A star-shaped hole in his forehead stared back at the Executioner like a third eye. His real eyes stared, too, but they saw nothing.

In death, the man against the tree voided both bladder and bowels, those odors now mixing with the aftershave and marijuana to produce an even more repugnant stench.

The soft thud of the suppressor had been the only sound. But eight men had entered the jungle to meet the plane, which meant there were still seven left. They might have decided to

leave more than one trail guard and that man might well have
been close enough to hear the noise. If so, the sound suppressor would have seemed as out of place to him in the jungle as
the aftershave had to the Executioner. Bolan waited, listening.

Two minutes later, when nothing had changed around him,
the Executioner cut quickly back to the site where he'd found
the overturned stone, then resumed tracking the men through
the jungle. He moved quickly but cautiously now, the sound-
suppressed Calico on full-auto, his eyes watching both the
path ahead and the prints below. He saw no sign of any other
men leaving the path, but suddenly a voice carried through the
trees, followed by a loud laugh.

Yet again, the Executioner stepped off of the pathway into
the cover of the jungle. Twenty yards later the foliage began
to thin. Finally he found himself at the edge of a clearing. Ten
yards past the spot where the trees stopped, he saw a steep
bank leading down to a creek bed. Stagnant water stood in
pools along the muddy basin.

The voices and laughter had grown louder as he'd neared
the area and now the Executioner could see the men responsible for both the noise and the footprints along the path.
Roughly a hundred yards away, on the other side of the creek
bed, a huge clearing had been chopped from the jungle. The
vegetation had not only been cleared away, but the dirt beneath it had been packed solid.

Bolan crept to a thick growth of shrubbery at the edge of
the clearing and dropped down behind it. He had found the
landing site. And he had found the heavily armed men who
were here to meet the plane. Only one thing troubled him.

Eight men had entered the jungle. One had been left behind
to guard the path and the Executioner had killed him. That
meant that there should now be seven men awaiting the plane.

But in the distance, the Executioner counted eight.

THE MEN'S BACKPACKS were empty. Bolan could tell because the limp nylon sides had caved in upon themselves where they'd been dropped in a pile at the edge of the landing strip. Ten feet from the pile the eight men sat cross-legged in a semi-circle on the ground. They were passing the time with some kind of card game until the plane arrived.

Bolan shifted his gaze to the other side of the runway and saw a large concrete slab. A round, waffle-topped, iron trap-door set in the center and he had no doubt as to what lay beneath. The fuel storage tank where the illicit aircraft filled up on their way to wherever.

Looking back to the men, the Executioner noticed rifles of various sorts lying on the ground. A variety of handguns were holstered on the men's hips or stuck in their waistbands. Like so many of the Filipinos he had encountered since this mission began, the men wore a combination of military camouflage and worn civilian clothing. One thing these men all had in common, however, was the fact that mud splattered their boots, pants and even their shirts.

Bolan's gaze roamed along the muddy creek bed that separated him from the men. Looking closer now, he could see the tracks where they had slid down the steep slope, then sloshed up the other bank to the landing strip. He watched silently as one of the drug runners shuffled the deck of cards and dealt to the others. A bottle of some kind made the rounds before and after each hand, and the laughter and conversation went on as the men continued their vigil. They obviously felt safe out here in the middle of the jungle; none of them appeared to have a care in the world.

The Executioner could understand why they felt so secure. They had left a man to guard the jungle path behind them and the steep walls on each side of the creek served as extra security. Anyone who overpowered or slipped past the guard would still have to go down the near-forty-five-degree angle in the slippery mud, cross the equally bemired creek bed, then claw his way up the other side before reaching the runway. Anyone who came after them would be in full view and within easy rifle range throughout the ordeal.

One of the men, bulky for a Filipino, suddenly leaned to his side and passed gas. The trumpet sound was greeted with a chorus of whoops and several loud phrases in Tagalog, which the Executioner took to be admonitions.

Bolan eyed the creek bed again. It was a death trap. Was there an easier way onto the landing strip? He doubted it. If there had been, the runners would have taken it themselves. Quickly he stuck his head out of the trees and scanned both directions. No, the creek bed ran on, eventually curving out of sight in both directions.

The Executioner glanced at his watch as he formulated his plan. Unless weather had slowed his progress somewhere over the Pacific, Mott would be landing here in less than fifteen minutes. Before that happened Bolan had eight drug runners to deal with.

The Executioner's teeth ground together and his jaw set firmly. He had no way of knowing when the drug plane was scheduled to arrive, but the men he saw in front of him now probably hadn't planned to arrive any earlier than they'd had to. Which meant their plane was probably coming in within an hour of Mott, maybe before, maybe after. If they were still sitting here playing cards when the Learjet touched down, they would immediately recognize that it wasn't their plane and shoot it to pieces.

Bolan didn't intend to allow that to happen. Pulling the sat phone from his pocket, he tapped in the number to Stony Man Farm and had Barbara Price patch him into the Learjet.

"Charlie," he said as soon as Mott had answered, "how far out are you?"

"Why are you whispering?" the pilot asked over the purr of the Learjet.

"Because I'm about a hundred yards away from eight guys who plan to kill you when you set down."

"Then keep whispering," Mott said with a chuckle. "I'm maybe five minutes out."

"Change course and stay in the air," the Executioner said. "I'll let you know when it's clear."

"You talked me into it, you silver-tongued devil," Mott said. "Be careful."

Bolan started to disconnect, then added, "You seen any other air traffic up there, Charlie?"

"Negative, big guy. But I'll keep a close eye on the screen. Is what I suspect is going on down there happening?"

Bolan nodded his head unconsciously. "If you suspect that we picked a very inopportune time for your arrival, then yes," the Executioner said. "You were right. This *is* a refueling station and drug drop-off point. And our schedules seem to be overlapping."

Bolan disconnected and dropped the sat phone back into his pocket. Again he gazed out from behind the bushes at the men playing cards. He hadn't exaggerated when he'd told Mott they were a hundred yards away. And looking again now he judged it as more like 120.

The Executioner took a deep breath, knowing what had to be done and how stacked the odds against him were. Then letting out the breath, he unsnapped the Calico's pistol grip freeing it from the sling. Rolling onto his belly at the side of the bushes, he extended the machine pistol with both hands and rested the bottom of the grip on the ground. Slowly, carefully, he lined up the front and rear sights.

At this range he would have to allow for bullet drop, so he aimed at a spot just over the head of the nearest drug runner. The man was facing away from him, and all the Executioner could see was long, dirty, unkempt hair hanging down over the back of a camouflage BDU blouse.

The Executioner flipped the fire selector to semiauto, took another breath, let half of it out and began to slowly squeeze back on the trigger. As had been the same with all successful target shooters since the invention of firearms, when the Calico's striker finally fell on the 9 mm primer, it came as a bit of a surprise.

The high-capacity machine pistol coughed once, quiet enough that the Executioner heard the metallic grind of the bolt working back to eject the spent casing and chamber another round. Above the white sights he saw the long hair part in the middle. Half of the drug runner's hair flipped up to one side, half to the other. It looked like two horses's tails flipping opposite directions in some strange choreographed circus performance.

A split second later residual blood sprayed out from the back of the man's head. But the exit wound was many times larger and as the 9 mm left the front of the man's skull it took with it a sea of blood and brain matter.

The long-haired man pitched forward and fell face-first into the center of the circle of men. Across from where he had sat Bolan now saw a card player who had been hidden by the camouflage blouse. The man was furiously trying to wipe blood and gore from his face, his hands working as he screamed at the top of his lungs.

Bolan swung the Calico slightly to the right. The drug runner seated next to the man in the camouflage seemed to have frozen in time. He held his cards with both hands just under his full beard but had turned to stare in awe at the gory sight that had fallen next to him. The soldier lined the sights up slightly high once more, pulled the trigger and a second 9 mm coughed quietly out of the Calico.

The Executioner's second round struck the bearded man in the temple and another mist of residual blood floated up from the entrance hole. It was followed by a trickle of red, which ran down the man's cheek into his beard. He still held his cards as he fell over the man in the BDU blouse.

The rest of the men suddenly lost all interest in the card game. Five of the remaining six leaped to their feet and grabbed at their rifles. The sixth man stayed where he was on the ground and continued to scream as he frantically tried to clear his face of his friend's blood.

The Executioner pulled the trigger again and dropped a drug runner wearing a khaki cloth-bucket hat as the man lifted an AK-47. Four of the men seized their weapons then suddenly realized they had no idea where the shots were coming from. Their heads looked as if they'd been mounted on swivels as they searched the jungle around them for their attacker.

But the man on the ground just kept on shrieking and clawing at his face.

Bolan took aim at a tall, shirtless man with an AK-47 who was staring across the runway toward the sunken fuel tank. The man provided another excellent profile target and the Executioner tightened his finger on the trigger. But a millisecond before the Calico went off, the bare-chested man took a slight step forward.

Although he couldn't see it, Bolan felt the round miss the second he pulled the trigger. The shirtless man confirmed Bolan's feeling, and the fact that he had felt the round go past him, by dropping his rifle and protectively grabbing his head with both hands.

The hands were still there when the Executioner corrected

his aim and drilled another round through both them and the man's skull.

Two of the three men still standing took off toward the jungle. Bolan dropped the one who stayed where he was with another 9 mm to the throat. He fell forward next to the blood-covered man still sitting on the ground and the screamer's shrill voice rose still. He jerked away from the fallen man, then went back to wiping his face.

Bolan shifted the Calico slightly on the ground and lined the sights up on the back of one of the men trying to flee. The drug runner wore tight black jeans and a matching black ragtop sweatshirt. The Executioner dropped him with one quiet 9 mm to the back of the head.

Muscular, sweat-covered arms extended from the second runner's royal-blue tank top, pumping with each step his green BDU-covered legs took. Bolan squeezed the trigger yet again and the bullet hit the runner dead center in the back. The running man's shoulder blades folded back as if they were trying to touch each other as the 9 mm hollowpoint round severed his spine.

Bolan swung the Calico back to the final man, still on the ground, still untouched except for the blood and brain matter that had flown from his friend's head. The man still screamed periodically as he rubbed furiously at his eyes, nose and ears. In between the blood-curdling screams he babbled incoherently.

The Executioner lined the sights up on his chest. One more shot would be all it took. One more shot and he could call Mott and tell him to set the plane down. The Stony Man pilot and the blacksuits could drop his supplies, take Mario Subing into custody and Bolan could be off after the hostages again.

The Calico's trigger was less than a pound of pressure away from firing when Bolan suddenly let up on the trigger. Lowering the weapon slightly, he stared out over the 50-round drum mag at the man still screeching on the ground.

The Executioner could never have put into words why he suddenly let up on the trigger. But something inside him— call it a sixth sense, or intuition, or just plain battle experience—told him to stop. The man on the ground hadn't even been hit, but he had behaved eccentrically since the first shot. He had rubbed at his face with the terror of the damned and Bolan couldn't keep from wondering what could cause a calloused drug runner to behave so strangely.

It took the Executioner another second to come up with a reason for the odd behavior and even then he couldn't be sure. But if what he suspected was true, it explained the man's overreaction to getting hit with a face full of blood.

Bolan got up slowly and stepped out of the jungle. He had noted the mud covering the men, which meant they had crossed the creek in front of him. But this man, he saw now, although drenched in blood from the middle of his chest to the top of his face, had no mud on him at all. He wore black-and-green jungle boots, ragged khaki work pants and a formerly yellow-and-now-blood-red shirt. His boots and pants showed dust and dirt. But they were dry.

The Executioner nodded as he walked forward. That was what he had noticed a second before pulling the trigger. That was what his unconscious mind had told him to investigate before killing the man. That was what had kept this man alive.

Bolan kept the Calico in front of him, ready, as he made his way down the steep creek bank, adding new mud to that with which he'd already covered himself for camouflage. No, he realized as he sloshed through the soggy creek bottom, eight minus one equaled seven. Always had and always would. This eighth—or ninth, actually—drug runner had not crossed the creek with the others, which meant he had to have come in through the jungle from some other direction.

Coming up out of the creek bed, the Executioner stopped ten feet from the man. "Freeze," he said. "Keep your hands away from your sides." He kept the Calico aimed at the man's chest.

The drug runner's eyes were shut tightly, like a fully awake toddler trying to convince his parents he was asleep. He obviously understood English because the hands that had pawed so fiercely at his face now rose above his head to his sides. As Bolan moved closer, he could see that much of the blood on his face was now gone. But the man had been crying and his face was still streaked with a combination of tears and blood that looked pink under the bright sun.

The Executioner stepped in and jerked a Government Model .45 from the drug runner's belt, then quickly patted him down. "Keep your arms out and drop to the ground on your front," he ordered. The man complied. He had stopped crying, but his back still jerked and heaved up and down with stifled silent sobs.

Bolan frowned as he flipped his sat phone open with his left hand, the Calico still trained on the crying man. Something more than mere capture was freaking this guy out. He suspected he knew what it was but he couldn't be sure. In any case, he'd find out soon enough. First, he needed to contact Charlie Mott.

The Executioner tapped the numbers into the sat phone and a few seconds later Barbara Price was again rerouting his call to the Learjet. The Executioner waited until he heard the pilot say, "Yeah?" and then said, "It's all clear down here now, Charlie. Come on down."

There were several seconds of silence during which all Bolan could hear was the crackling static on the line. Then Mott said, "I can do that if you really want me to, Striker. But before I do I think there's something you ought to know."

"Yeah?"

"Yeah," said Mott. "I've got a blip on my radar screen. Whoever it was your buddies down there were waiting for is here and getting ready to land."

CHAPTER SEVEN

Bolan looked up at the sky. The drug plane wasn't yet visible, but far in the distance he thought he heard the hum of an aircraft engine. "How long have I got, Charlie?" the Executioner said into the phone.

"Before they land or before they can see you?" Mott asked.

"See me," the Executioner replied. "How long before they can tell what we're doing on the ground here?"

"Two, maybe three minutes max," the pilot returned.

"Stand by," Bolan said, taking the phone away from his head. At his feet, the blood-soaked drug runner still sobbed. He tapped the man on the ground in the ribs with his foot. "Get up," he said.

The man didn't move except to continue his sobs.

"Get up, and shut up!" Bolan said, prodding him harder this time.

As the drug runner rose to his knees, then to his feet, Bolan continued to keep one eye and an ear cocked toward the sky. But he still registered no sign of the approaching plane.

Leaning down, he jabbed the drug runner in the back with the barrel. "We've got work to do," he said.

The man's eyelids were still tightly closed.

"Open your eyes," the Executioner ordered.

When the man didn't obey the order, Bolan flipped the Calico's selector to full-auto and fired a sudden burst of quietly burping 9 mms to the side of his feet. Even sound suppressed, the rounds made his point for him.

The drug runner shivered and shook but still wouldn't open his eyes.

"What's wrong with you?" Bolan demanded. If his suspicions were right, he might have to force the man to come to terms with the situation quickly. He didn't need some semicatatonic drug runner getting in his way during the next few minutes.

"HIV," the drug runner sobbed. "Juanito…he had…AIDS." The sentence brought about a whole new series of weeping and wrenching wails. But between the howls, he managed to get out, "I don't want it…in my…eyes!"

His suspicion confirmed, the Executioner said, "What's your name?"

"Reynaldo," the man panted.

"Reynaldo what?"

"Reynaldo Taboada."

"Well, Reynaldo Taboada," Bolan said. "It's too late to worry about getting Juanito's blood in your eyes." He paused, staring at the smeared blood and mucus all over the man's head. "You've already got it in your ears and nose. You're either eventually going to test positive or you aren't."

Taboada let out another gasp of horror and his chest heaved back and forth.

"So decide whether you want to live long enough to find out," Bolan said with another glance at the sky. "Decide whether you want to die sometime in the future or right now. Because if you don't open your eyes by the time I count to

three, I'm going to pull this trigger again and a half-dozen
9 mm hollowpoints are going to blow your head off." He
stopped talking, sucked in a breath, and said, "One."

Reynaldo's eyes remained closed. "You don't understa—"

"Two," the Executioner said.

"But—"

"Three!" Bolan shouted, and Reynaldo's eyelids shot up
like window blinds.

The distant purr of the aircraft was louder now above them.
Bolan looked up to see a tiny speck in the sky. If the pilot
looked down and saw the bodies sprawled across the landing
zone, he'd likely abort his landing and simply fly on.

The Executioner turned his attention back to Reynaldo. His
initial plan had been to have the blood-soaked drug runner
help him hide the bodies. But not only was there no longer
enough time to drag the dead men out of sight into the jungle, Reynaldo was still in a state of horror and all but useless.
The best the Executioner could hope for out of him was that
he did nothing.

"Okay," Bolan said. "Sit down on the ground for now. If
you move before I get back, I'll kill you. "

When Reynaldo didn't respond, the Executioner knocked
his feet out from under him with a sweep kick and turned toward the work at hand.

Snapping the Calico back onto the sling, Bolan let it hang
from his side as he hurried around the area. Grabbing the dead
men by the shoulders, he lifted them to sitting positions, back
to back. It wasn't the best of plans, but it was the best he could
come up with under the time restraint imposed by the descending drug plane. He left the long-haired man in the camouflage blouse for last. Avoiding the bloody head area, he
grabbed the corpse by the boots and jerked it into a reclining
position on its back, as if the man were taking a nap. Grab-

bing one of the empty backpacks, he rolled it up and shoved it under the man's head for a pillow.

Bolan walked back to Reynaldo. "Up," he ordered. When the bloody man had struggled to his feet, the Executioner went on. "Listen carefully," he said. "You can open your eyes or you can keep them closed. I don't care, and there's not much point in you caring, either, because if the damage has been done it's too late to worry about it now. But, either way, you're going to stand here with me like we're talking. And when I tell you to, you're going to turn your head toward the sky and smile as if you're as happy to see the plane as a kid catching Santa Claus halfway down the chimney. You got that?"

Reynaldo nodded his head. He chose to keep his eyes closed.

As the descending plane took shape in the sky, Bolan continued his instructions. "If there's shooting—and there will be—hit the ground and hope for the best." He paused. "You cooperate with me and you still stand a chance of walking away from all this alive."

A large lump went down the throat of the blood-covered drug runner. "I am already dead," he said.

"Maybe," the Executioner said. "And maybe not. But I promise you you'll die a lot sooner if you don't cooperate." Grabbing the Calico's pistol grip again, he shoved the barrel into the man's belly for emphasis. "Now. Move down the runway with me." He escorted the man to a spot roughly halfway down the landing strip and off to the side.

The plane engines were loud now as the aircraft made its final approach. Bolan turned away from the man in front of him toward the roar. "Look up at it," he ordered.

Reynaldo did as he was told, forcing his lips into a smile.

"Now wave," the Executioner said.

Reynaldo's arm shot up toward the sky and his hand flapped up and down.

Bolan identified the aircraft as a Payne Knight Twister SKT-125 with a 125-hp Lycoming engine. A version of the KT-85 with increased wing span, it was an ideal aircraft for the short, island-jumping drug runs it no doubt made. Even better, the Executioner knew that construction plans were available to amateur builders, which meant it would be built anonymously, leaving no paper trail should the owners be caught during illegal activities.

The Payne's wheels hit the hard-packed dirt and began to roll across the ground toward them. It shot past them to the side, slowing as it neared the end of the runway. Bolan turned toward it, and said, "Come on."

Bolan and Reynaldo began walking toward the end of the runway where the Payne was coming to a halt. The Executioner had chosen the spot where they had stood when the plane rolled past for several reasons. First, he knew it would still be moving quickly as it passed him, and a good enough look to recognize his Caucasian features was unlikely. Second, there were several "seated" dead men behind him. Rather than see them directly, the occupants of the Payne would view them in the aircraft's mirrors, which would make it less likely that they'd spot the blood covering the men or register the fact that nobody seemed to be moving.

As they moved closer to the Knight Twister, two men dropped down from the craft. The pilot stayed where he was and began to taxi the plane into a U-turn. He rolled the wheels toward the underground storage tank as the other two men began walking forward.

"Faster," Bolan said, increasing his pace as the two men angled toward the closest of the two bodies sitting on the ground. One of the men carried an M-16 A-2 at port arms. The other man's rifle looked like a Belgian-made FN-FAL. The Payne rolled to a stop at the refueling area.

Approximately twenty feet from the first pair of dead men sitting back-to-back, the drug runners from the plane both stopped in their tracks.

Bolan was close enough that he saw the sudden confusion come over both men's faces. The two seconds it took for their eyes to send the unexpected sight to their brains might have been a day. The additional second during which their brains made the determination that something was wrong could have been a week. And it took yet another second or so for the men to understand what it all meant and to react.

When they did, both the American and the Belgian rifle barrels rose toward Bolan and Reynaldo.

For the Executioner, however, four seconds to prepare had been as good as a year. The Calico was already gripped in both hands and stretched to the end of the sling. As the rifle barrels rose, he brought his weapon to eye level.

Suddenly the quiet clearing in the jungle was alive with the sound of gunfire.

HE WAS FAT, yes, he knew that. But he liked to think of himself more as simply *big.* He was a *big* man. He thought *big,* he brokered *big* deals. He did everything in a big way, so it was only natural that he would have big appetites. Not just for food and drink but for everything he enjoyed, as well.

The hotel room was elaborately decorated with turn-of-the-last-century furnishings. The beds, tables and nightstands were of ornately hand-carved wood which featured etchings of cherubs, gargoyles and other mystic beings. The curtains were of the finest silk and the lamps were more than just light fixtures. Their brass bases had been contrived by one of Europe's premier designers.

The fat man lay on his back, his head propped up on three pillows as the beautiful redheaded woman kissed him and rubbed her hands across his chest. Below his waist, barely visible above his massive belly, he could see the top of a blond head. Although her features were hidden behind his girth, he had watched her undress earlier and knew she was as attractive as the redhead, and she used all of her talents in an attempt to excite him.

So far, however, even her skilled hands and mouth hadn't been enough.

The fat man turned his eyes to the love seat across from the bed, focusing on the well-endowed brunette who sprawled provocatively across it. The woman was nude save for a black garter belt and fishnet stockings. Her bright red BOTOX-inflated lips smiled seductively at him as she rubbed both of her hands up and down her thighs. Then, closing her heavily made-up eyes, she let out a small moan.

The fat man felt an electrical charge of desire rush through his chest. But the charge ended there, refusing to drop farther down his body. He frowned, looking down at the top of the blond head once more. Nothing.

The sudden ringing of the telephone broke through the sounds of passion coming from the brunette in the chair and the fat man opened his eyes again.

The redhead stopped kissing his neck. "Shall I answer it?" she asked.

"Yes."

The redhead twisted toward the nightstand between the two hotel beds and lifted the receiver, holding it to his ear for him.

"What?" The fat man nearly spit the word into the receiver.

When no one spoke back to him, the fat man started to speak again. But before he could, he heard a dull explosion in the background and knew who it was on the line. As the explosion died down, he heard distant screams, then excited voices and the sounds of people running.

Finally a voice spoke on the other end of the line. "Did you like it?" Candido Subing asked in Arabic.

The fat man's anger mounted in his chest, but he forced himself to sound sincere when he said, "I am impressed." He, too, had spoken in Arabic, and he watched a surprised look come over the faces of the three women in the room. English, French, Spanish—even Russian wouldn't have shocked them. But something as foreign as Arabic did, and he found himself for some odd reason suddenly holding all three women in contempt for their unworldliness.

Turning his attention back to the phone call, he said, "Now, before you ask what I know you are about to ask, the ship is in port. It must be cleared by U.S. Customs. Then things will fall into place quickly."

"Allah be praised," Subing said quickly.

"Yes, well," said the fat man, "I'm sure Allah will be very proud of you."

"It will leave for America soon, then?" Subing asked anxiously.

"Within a few days," Mikelsson said. "Until then, carry on with both the projects in Israel and your missionaries in the islands." He glanced across the room at the brunette in the garter belt. Both the redhead and blonde had joined her on the love seat and were paying more attention to one another now than they were to him. He watched them and his chest filled with lust again, but his body continued to refuse response. "Now," he said into the phone. "I have many other responsibilities to which I must attend. Do you need anything else?"

"Yes," the Arab replied. "We are in need of more of your…" He hesitated, then, in a hushed, conspiratorial voice, breathed the Arabic word for *material*. "Other martyrs are ready to sacrifice themselves for the jihad."

Mikelsson pictured Candido Subing standing at the phone,

excitedly shifting his weight from one foot to the other. He caught himself chuckling. Subing so loved the cloak-and-dagger aspects of this business, and insisted on using euphemisms for things such as explosives even though all lines they used were as secure as the American Pentagon. How he loved pretending to be Arabic, too. In truth, he was a Filipino Moro, and no more Arabic than Mikelsson himself. The fat man laughed inwardly again and ripples of fat rolled up and down his belly. "More *material*," he said, doing his best to keep the sarcasm out of his voice, "should be in port at Haifa, even as we speak."

"Yes, I am aware of the Haifa shipment," Subing said. "But I was out of the country when it arrived. It was seized by Israeli authorities."

The fat man let out a short sigh. "These things happen," he said. "It is one of the hazards of doing business. But rest assured it cannot be traced to you or anyone else." He paused a second, then added, "And I'll have more sent your way tonight. Expect a man who calls himself Jabbar to contact you."

"When?" Subing asked. His voice was anxious, determined and irritating. But he was the perfect person for the fat man to have in the place he had him.

"Tonight, I said. Now, if there is nothing else…"

Irritated, he hung up. For a moment he stared off into space, shaking his head. Finding men crazy enough to become suicide bombers was easy. But finding men that crazy who still had enough sense to follow directions was almost impossible. Candido Subing was a rare man, indeed. But sometimes Subing walked a thin line between sanity and insanity. The fat man felt better, remembering he had one of his own men keeping an eye out for the little terrorist. And it had been a rare stroke of luck that had put that man so close to the American agents searching for the missionaries.

The brunette was halfway to the bed when the phone rang again.

The fat man cursed loudly in another language he suspected the women wouldn't understand and his pudgy hand grabbed the receiver. "What now?" he nearly shouted into the instrument. He had expected it to be another needless call from Subing, but the voice on the other end of the line this time spoke in English. "We have a problem."

All desire for sex drained from the fat man as he realized who it was on the other end of the line. He glanced up at the three women. Suspecting that at least one of them might speak English, he waved them back to the love seat across the room. Twisting as best he could onto his side, he turned his head away from them and whispered, "What are you talking about?"

"The ship has been red-flagged."

The fat man tried to sit up but again his abdominal muscles cramped. "Wait a moment," he said into the phone, then dropped the receiver onto the sheet next to him. Using both arms, he struggled to a sitting position, then lifted the receiver once more. "Of course it was red-flagged," Mikelsson said. "You red-flagged it yourself, so it would be passed to you for a full inspection." He took a deep breath and felt his heart racing. "So where is the problem?"

The voice spoke rapidly. "My supervisor is on board. A surprise visit."

The fat man breathed a loud sigh of relief. "Is that all?"

"Well…yes," said the voice on the other end. "But—"

The fat man chuckled to himself as he felt his confidence return. What was happening was obvious. The American Customs man he had bought was campaigning for more money. He had been paid to find several items of nonlethal contraband—some fireworks for which no tariff had been paid, a

FALSE FRONT   157

case of prescription drugs not yet certified by the FDA and a half ounce of marijuana in the purser's cabin. The sort of thing that might be found on any ship given close enough scrutiny. But he was to ignore a certain television box that would be in a stack of five hundred real televisions in one of the cargo holds.

"But the—"

"You are a clever man," Mikelsson said. "I am sure you can find a way to keep your supervisor busy." He paused for a moment, wondering if he should just offer the man more money now or make him beg for it. In a rare mood of generosity, he said, "I will double the amount of money in your wire transfer for your trouble."

"Thank you, sir. You can depend on me."

"Is there anything else?" the fat man asked into the phone.

"No."

"Then we will proceed as planned." Mikelsson hung up, rolled back onto the pillows, then he looked at the women on the love seat.

"Come here," the fat man ordered. "All three of you."

THE BLOOD-SOAKED MAN who had identified himself as Reynaldo Taboada took the Executioner's advice. Before the first shots had been fired, he was flat on the ground.

Bolan had been half a second ahead of the two men with the assault rifles. Now he held back the trigger of the Calico 950 and sent a full-auto stream of 9 mm semijacketed hollow-point rounds flying toward them in a lead wall of death. The two men reacted contradictorily and Bolan was reminded that there was never any explanation for the effect of gunfire.

The Executioner's first half-dozen bullets stitched the man wielding the M-16 from crotch to nose. He tumbled backward across the packed dirt like a circus clown performing somersaults. As he swung the Calico to the left, Bolan watched the man finally come to rest in a sitting position, slump to his side, catch his fall with an arm as he took his dying breath, then hit the ground as the arm gave out.

Bolan continued to hold the trigger back as he redirected his aim. The man with the Belgian FN-FAL wore a brown sport shirt and light blue slacks. The first 9 mm rounds to hit him struck his shoulder, ripping the shirt apart and sending swatches of cloth flying through the air. The Executioner walked the weapon on down the man's chest and watched the bullets tear new openings in the brown.

The drug runner's mouth opened in a silent "Oh!" Then he leaned forward and let the 7.62 mm rifle fall to the end of its sling. He stayed in that position for a half second as Bolan let up on the trigger. Then this man, who had been more than willing to transport death to others in the form of drugs, looked up at the Executioner, his expression pleading.

Bolan looked the man in the eye and pulled the trigger again.

The Executioner glanced down at the man on the ground. Taboada was frozen like a rock, his eyes staring up and looking for all the world as if he was dead. He had already been covered with blood so the Executioner couldn't use that as a guidepost to his present state. "Were you hit?" he asked.

"I...don't think so."

"Stay where you are," the Executioner ordered, then turned his attention to the airplane across the runway.

The pilot of the Payne Knight Twister SKT-125 hadn't let what had happened go unnoticed. Neither was he a fool. Deciding that discretion was indeed the better part of valor, and that a partially empty gas tank was preferable to immediate death, he had abandoned the refueling area and was now taxiing over the packed-earth landing strip preparing to take off again.

As the 125-hp Lycoming engine grew louder in his ears,

the Executioner twisted toward the plane. As it passed by he triggered the Calico once more, emptying the remainder of the 50-round drum magazine into the side of the aircraft. A series of 9 mm holes appeared across the body of the craft, but the Knight Twister absorbed the rounds with no vital damage. The Calico's bolt locked open, empty.

Ripping the drum off the 950, Bolan jerked the 100-round replacement magazine from under his left shoulder and snapped it into place atop the weapon. The Knight Twister had just left the ground at the end of the runway as he sent another dozen rounds its way. What, if anything, they struck, he couldn't know. The aircraft was out of range and rising in the air.

The Executioner moved back to where Taboada still lay. "What were they carrying?" he demanded.

"Heroin," the man told him.

"How much?"

"I don't know."

Bolan aimed the Calico at the man's head. "I'll only ask you once more," he said. "How much?"

The man on the ground looked up. But he was beyond terror now and had resigned himself to death. Maybe today. Maybe five, ten, or twenty years from now. But he knew he would be on borrowed time for the rest of his life. "I told you, I don't know," he said fatalistically. "I *do* know that they were leaving fifty kilos here." He took a deep breath, then sat up. "And they're on their way to Australia with the rest."

Bolan pulled the sat phone from his pocket and flipped it open, quickly connecting to Charlie Mott in the air. "You see what happened?" the Executioner asked.

"Yeah," Mott came back. "Had a good seat. High, but on the fifty-yard line."

"They're loaded down with H, Charlie," Bolan said. "You have visual on them?"

"I'm right on their tail."

"What's below you?" Bolan asked.

"Still over land. But unless the pilot changes course, in thirty seconds or so there'll be nothing beneath us but clear blue water."

Bolan looked up at the sky but by now both the Knight Twister and Mott's Learjet were out of sight. "Let him get out over the water then," the Executioner said. "Then you know what to do."

"Affirmative, Striker," Mott said in Bolan's ear. "You ought to be able to hear it from where you are."

Bolan glanced down at his wristwatch. Although it was hidden from view, he knew that the Learjet was equipped with a General Electric M-61 Gatling.

Forty-five seconds later the Executioner heard the distant explosion.

Mott's voice came back in his ear. "You still there, big guy?" the pilot asked.

"Still here," Bolan said.

"Well, they're not," Mott replied.

"So I heard. It's all clear now, Charlie. Come on in."

"On my way," Mott said.

Bolan looked down at Reynaldo, held the phone away from his head for a second and said, "Get on your feet."

The blood-soaked drug runner did as he'd been told.

Pressing the sat phone to his ear once more, the Executioner said, "Charlie, I'm going back for the other guys. You ought to be on the ground by the time I get back."

"I'll be waiting on you, then," Mott said.

The Executioner jabbed the muzzle of the Calico into Taboada's ribs, prodding him in the direction of the creek bed. "Let's go," he said. "And I've got a few questions for you on the way."

CHAPTER EIGHT

The Executioner let Taboada stop in the creek bed to wash his face in a puddle of the stagnant water. The man concentrated on the task like an obsessive-compulsive, his face dark, the skin drawn taut; a mask of terror. As Bolan had told him, if he was going to catch the virus, he already had. But ridding himself of the obvious reminder seemed to lift his spirits. At least slightly.

Bolan could understand the man's fear. Everyone died, one way or another. He, himself, lived with the possibility of death every day and had for his entire adult life. But there were some ways to shuffle off this mortal coil that were much better than others, and Taboada now stood a good chance of checking out slowly, after years of illness. It wasn't a death anyone would choose. Of course only suicides got to choose the way they died.

Taboada looked up at the Executioner. "It is no use," he said as he came up out of the puddle and twisted the tail of his shirt to wrench out the water. "I am already dead."

The Executioner stared at the frightened man. He was a drug peddler and who knew what else. As far as Bolan was concerned, he deserved death. But that didn't mean he had no compassion for what the man was going through. "Look at it this way," the Executioner said. "That virus may kill you eventually. But it's the only thing that kept you alive today."

Taboada frowned. "How could it have kept me—" He clamped his mouth shut without finishing the sentence as he suddenly realized what the Executioner had meant. If he hadn't gotten what he knew to be contaminated blood all over him at the onset of the firefight, and so obviously taken himself out of the action, Bolan would have shot him along with his friends.

The Executioner shifted the Calico's shoulder harness as he waved the man past him to begin the trek through the jungle. He gave the drug runner a ten-foot head start, then scrambled up the mud after him. "You don't even know if you've got it yet," he said as they reached the top of the embankment together. "Maybe you do. Maybe you don't. Either way, you're not going to know until you get a blood test. That's the reality of the situation. So accept that fact and learn to live with it."

Taboada walked ahead of him as they made their way back toward the jungle. The Executioner couldn't see his face. But he had a feeling the words were sinking in. So he went on. "I'll make you a deal. You help me and I'll let you live long enough to get checked out. Otherwise, the test won't make any difference."

The drug runner walked on without answering for a moment. Then a low, gruff and sarcastic, snort blew out of his nose. But Bolan could see that this chance of infection had had a significant emotional effect on the man. And once in a while bad men really did change and become good. Not often, just sometimes. Stony Man Farm's number-one pilot, Jack Grimaldi, was an example. He had flown airplanes for the Mob before he'd met Bolan and turned his life around.

The Executioner studied the other man's back as they re-traced his steps along the path. Most of the time, rehabilitat-ing criminals was more wishful thinking than fact. But on the rare occasions when a man did redirect his life away from evil and toward good, it was almost always after some harrowing event that had forced him to recognize his own mortality. Times when death looked him in the face and demanded that he take stock of the life he had lived and the things for which he had stood.

Taboada had been relatively clean before his friend's head blew up in his face. Now he was covered in mud, like every-one else who had crossed the creek that day, which reminded the Executioner that the man had to have come to the landing strip from some other direction. "How'd you get here?" he asked as they walked along.

At first the man pretended not to hear him. So the Execu-tioner took a quick step forward and jammed the Calico into his back. "When I ask you a question, I expect an answer," he said. "Keep what I said in mind. If you don't cooperate with me, it won't matter what bugs are in your blood."

"I came with the others," Taboada said over his shoulder as they walked.

Bolan jammed him with the machine pistol again, harder this time. "Did it ever occur to you that it would be easier to just shoot you and dump your body at the side of this trail than keep prodding you along like this." He paused for a second to let his words sink in, then said, "Don't lie to me. You were clean before your friend's head blew all over you. In fact, you didn't have any mud on you at all until we crossed the creek just now."

Reynaldo took a few more steps, then stopped. He opened his mouth to speak but no words came out. Tears fell from his eyes and suddenly his legs would no longer hold his weight.

He collapsed to his knees on the ground, clasped his hands together under his chin and cried, "Jesus Christ! Help me!"

The Executioner frowned at the man. He had assumed Taboada was Muslim since everyone else he had dealt with on Mindanao had been. But now he remembered that the island was primarily Christian and that the Muslims didn't become the majority until you traveled farther south into the Sulu Archipelago. And he wasn't dealing with Islamic terrorists at the moment—drug runners. He waited patiently for the man to gather his wits, then squatted in front of him.

"Look," Bolan said, "I don't know what else to tell you. What happens to us in life happens to us and we have to live with it. But if you ask me, you're borrowing trouble you don't even know that you have yet."

"From the other side," Taboada said, still looking down at the ground.

"What?" Bolan said. He had no idea what the man meant.

"You asked how I got to the landing strip. I came from the other side of the jungle."

Bolan stood, then reached down, took the man by the arm and hauled him up. "What's over there?" he asked.

"Nothing," Reynaldo said. "Just a village. My village."

They took up the jungle route again, passing the spot where Bolan had left the path to search out the drug runner guarding it. Taboada didn't seem to notice the tracks and probably hadn't known about the guard anyway since he'd come in from the other direction.

"So how come you weren't with the others?" the Executioner demanded.

The drug runner had started to speak when his foot caught a root growing up in the path and sent him tripping forward. He reached out instinctively to catch himself on a tree. Unfortunately the tree he picked had long white thorns growing out of the trunk that sliced through his fingers and the palms of both hands like razor blades.

The drug runner jumped back and held his hands out in front of him. The slashes from the thorns weren't deep, but bright red blood dripped from them. Which, to Taboada, was like a giant neon sign flashing AIDS! He threw back his head and screamed at the top of his lungs. Falling to his knees again, he crossed himself and then began to cry out in Tagalog. The Executioner couldn't understand the words, but he recognized the rhythm of the man's speech. It was the Lord's Prayer.

Behind him, Bolan could hear the sound of a Mott's Learjet coming down through the sky to land. They needed to get moving, to get back to Latham, Reverte and Mario Subing, then return to the landing strip. If Taboada was going to have a nervous breakdown over this he'd just have to wait until they had more time.

Hauling the man to his feet again, Bolan pushed him forward.

"I am dying," the drug runner said as he stumbled on along the path. "I will spend eternity in Hell."

That seemed a distinct possibility to the Executioner, but he didn't say so. They were nearing the clearing where the Buick and the flatbed truck were now parked. He recognized the area.

Taboada turned suddenly to face the Executioner, his face desperate with fear. "Please!" he screamed, dropping to his knees once more. "Give me a chance to redeem myself!"

"You want to redeem yourself?" Bolan said. "Talk to God. That's not my department."

The man was still on his knees, his arms raised, his bleeding palms outstretched. He sat back on his heels. "I am evil!" he shouted maniacally, then almost breathed, "I have killed men!"

"So have I," Bolan said. "Whether that's good or bad depends on who they were and why you did it." He stared down at the horror in the little man's eyes. If ever a man looked as if he wanted to change, Reynaldo Taboada was that man.

"My reasons were not good," the drug runner said, looking up. For a second he forgot about his bloody hands and wiped the tears from his face, smearing it with red streaks. "I must confess."

"I'm not a priest," Bolan said.

"Then I must find one," the man replied. "I must do only good for however long I have left. You must help me." His eyes fell to the ground in front of him. But a second later he looked up at the Executioner and said, "I know what you want. And I can help you."

Bolan took a deep breath and let it out. He had intended to briefly interrogate the drug runner, then turn him over to Mott and the blacksuits who were to pick up Mario Subing. He was too tied up right now to go after more drug dealers, but Mott could turn Taboada over to Phoenix Force once they were back in the U.S. and they could take over.

"Get up," Bolan said. "We'll talk while we walk the rest of the way in." He watched the man get slowly back to his feet again, turn and head down the path.

"So. What other drug deals can you tell me about?" he said as they started the final stretch to the Buick and flatbed.

Taboada reached down, ripping the tail off his shirt and wrapping it around his bleeding hands. "I do not know about any more drug shipments," he said. "This was my first time to deal in drugs. It was an unusual undertaking for my friends and me. Our group needed funds, and our leader knew one of the men from the drug cartel." He paused, coughing and hacking a few times, then continued down the path. "He was bringing ten kilos for us to sell. I was to take it back to our group on the other side of the jungle."

"I thought you said it was your village on the other side of the jungle," Bolan said.

"That was when I was still lying," Taboada said.

The Executioner shrugged, unseen by the man in front of him. He was a little disappointed. Taboada didn't sound as though he had the drug connections he had hoped for. But he would give the man to Phoenix Force anyway, and who knew where he might lead them? He seemed sincere enough and he might do more good than Bolan guessed at this point.

They rounded a bend in the jungle and came to the pile of leaves and vines covering the entrance to the path. Bolan directed the man in front of him to clear the way, then followed him out to the end of the road to the Buick and flatbed.

The Executioner stepped up alongside Taboada as they walked on to the vehicles, then stopped. He stuck two fingers under his teeth and sent a loud whistle flying through the air.

A moment later Latham and Reverte appeared with Mario Subing in tow.

"This group of yours you mentioned," the Executioner said off-handedly as the three men neared. "You said they don't usually sell drugs. What is it they do?"

"We...*they* have been known to kidnap people in the past," Taboada said.

That hardly surprised Bolan.

"Tourists, sometimes," the man went on, "especially if they look like their family might have money."

Bolan nodded. That was good enough for him. Kidnappers deserved to go down as much as drug dealers and Phoenix Force could take it from here. He waited silently as Latham and Reverte dragged Mario up to the vehicles, then turned his attention to the old man. It looked as though he still had a lot of fight left in him, and it wasn't going to be easy if they had to drag him all the way back to the landing strip.

Bolan was only half listening when Taboada said, "Right now, my group has kidnapped people who have no money."

The Executioner's eyes fell to the old man's wrists. It looked as though he had chewed halfway through the plastic restraints while Latham and Reverte weren't looking. In several places, the interior wire shone brightly through the outer surface. Bolan reminded himself to rebind the man's hands before they set off for the landing strip.

His mind was still on Mario when he said to Taboada, "Why would you kidnap people you knew didn't have money?"

"For political reasons," he replied. "The hostages are American missionaries."

Bolan turned to face the man. Suddenly, Reynaldo Taboada had the Executioner's full attention.

FOR THE THIRD TIME that day, Bolan trudged along the path from the dead-end road, where the Buick and flatbed were parked, to the landing strip. With Latham and Reverte still having to prod old Mario every step of the way, he had Taboada take the lead and followed the man where he could keep an eye on him. Although the drug runner seemed to have truly had a change of heart, it was far too soon to trust him. Besides, there was at least one aspect of his story that simply didn't make sense.

Taboada has just informed the Executioner that he had come in from a Tigers's campsite deeper in the jungle. He claimed to be a Tiger himself, a fairly recent enlistee. And he swore that Candido Subing himself had sent him to pick up the ten kilos of heroin that were to be used to help finance the terrorist cell. Bolan might have accepted that as at least possible, if not probable, had it not been for one major flaw in what he'd seen and heard from the man.

It was one flaw, but there were two ways to ask the question. What was a Christian doing in an Islamic extremist group? Or what was a Muslim doing crying out for Jesus to save him? Either way you looked at it, it didn't add up.

Bolan moved up close behind the man as they walked on through the jungle. "I've got a few questions for you," he said.

Taboada looked over his shoulder and said, "Go ahead."

"You say you're a member of the Tigers?"

Taboada nodded as he walked on ahead of Bolan.

"Then what was that little song and dance on your knees back there? You were asking Jesus to save you, and then you wanted to confess your sins. To me, that doesn't sound much like something you'd hear a follower of Islam say."

Taboada sighed audibly as they started up a steep incline in the jungle path. Bolan watched the back of the man's head as he followed, hearing the others close behind. "I was raised in a Christian orphanage on the island of Mindoro," the Filipino said. "I converted to Islam when I grew older." He shook his head back and forth as if even *he* was confused with the intricacies of his story. "It seems that my Catholic roots came out when I realized I had—might die." He stopped speaking and Bolan could hear him breathing hard.

Maybe, Bolan thought. And maybe not. He followed the man down the path. Taboada might be telling the truth. On the other hand, he might just be a good con man. He'd wait and see. Until that verdict was in, Bolan intended to keep a close watch on the little Filipino.

The Learjet was idling at the end of the landing strip when they stepped out of the jungle. Bolan and the drug runner led the way as they skidded down the muddy bank and crossed the creek. Charlie Mott, wearing a green-and-yellow California Angels cap, a white T-shirt and the pants to a navy-blue nylon jogging suit, was leaning against the side of the plane as they came up the embankment.

Three blacksuit operatives—all wearing shorts and T-shirts rather than the hot blacksuits themselves—surrounded Stony Man Farm's number-two pilot.

As Bolan and Taboada led the others up the bank, Mott grinned their way. "Looking good, Striker," he said. "Tell me. You send your laundry out or do it yourself?"

Bolan looked down at his mud-encrusted body and chuckled.

One of the blacksuits, a tall man with wide, powerful shoulders stretching his gray T-shirt stepped forward and looked past Bolan to Mario Subing. "This our guy?" he asked.

The Executioner nodded. "Put him on ice at the Farm for a few days. Somebody can fly him home after all of this is over." He stopped and wiped some of the mud from his face with the back of a wrist. "I just don't want him running around the countryside telling everybody everything he knows about us."

"Consider it done," the broad-shouldered man said. He stepped forward and took Mario's arm from Latham as the other two moved in to help.

But the old man had found his second wind and he lashed out with a foot, catching the big blacksuit in the shin. The man in the gray T-shirt jumped back and laughed. "Damn," he said. "That *hurt.*"

He grinned up at Bolan and added, "I see now why you told us to bring more guards."

With the help of the other two men from Stony Man Farm, they pulled and jerked a kicking and thrashing Mario Subing onto the Learjet.

The gear Bolan had requested had been unloaded and the Executioner looked it over now. Included in the shipment were two M-16 A-2 assault rifles, extra 9 mm ammunition for his Beretta and Calico, and several boxes of .44 Magnum rounds for the Desert Eagle. Also among the shopping list the Executioner had called in were a six-pack of extra magazines for Latham's Browning Hi-Power and a half dozen boxes of .40 S&W ammo.

Mott frowned at Reverte, then looked back to the Executioner. "You gonna need another long gun?" he asked. "I've got one in—"

Bolan shook his head and lifted the Calico slightly. "I'll stick with this," he said. "We can always trade off if we need to." He glanced at Reverte, who looked ever so slightly nervous. He probably didn't like not being center stage. "Give our CIA buddy some extra 1911 mags and all the .45s he thinks he can carry." He looked back down at the stack of equipment in front of him. "You have any more mags on board for the 16s?"

Mott nodded to one of the blacksuits who had stuck his head back out of the Learjet. The man disappeared for a moment, then returned with the gear.

"Anything else?" Mott asked. "Any messages to go back?"

"Yeah," the Executioner said. He nodded his head sideways and walked out onto the landing strip, out of earshot of the other men. Mott followed him. "I've got a bad feeling about Reverte. Don't ask me to explain it, I can't."

Mott frowned. "Something you want me to do?"

Bolan shook his head. "No. Just be aware of it if anything happens to me. Look at him hard."

The pilot nodded his head. "How about the other guy? The little one?" he said.

"Used to be a Tiger," the Executioner said. "Got religion."

Now it was Mott who shook his head. "You *do* like living on the edge, don't you, Striker?" he said. "Latham watching your back?"

The Executioner nodded. "Just let Hal know we've got two

potential problems inside the ranks," he said. "Any more word on what's going down in America?"

"If there is, Kurtzman hasn't told me about it," Mott said. "He'd call you first, I imagine."

Their conversation finished, the two men walked back to the plane.

Mott started to duck under the wing, then glanced out over the landing strip where the bodies of the drug runners still littered the field. "Hope I don't disturb any of your friends," he told Bolan over his shoulder. "They seem to be sleeping so peacefully."

A moment later the Learjet was in the sky on its way back to the U.S.

Bolan, Reverte and Latham geared up with guns and reloads, then dragged the rest of the equipment just inside the jungle and out of sight. The Executioner caught a moment when everyone but Latham was out of earshot and whispered to Latham, "Anything go on while I was gone?"

Latham knew exactly what he meant. He glanced quickly to where Reverte sat, thirty feet away, loading .45s into his magazines. "He made a couple of phone calls is all," he said.

"To who?" Bolan asked.

"One to headquarters back in Langley. Another to some chick."

"You're sure about the calls?" Bolan asked, squinting in the sunlight.

Latham shrugged. "That's what he told me."

The Executioner nodded and they prepared to leave.

Taboada had promised to guide them around the thick marshes on the other side of the landing strip on the same dry path he had used earlier in the day. If the Filipino could be believed, the hostages were less than ten miles from where they stood right now.

Bolan studied the back of the drug runner's head again as they crossed the clearing toward the jungle. Actually he didn't know exactly where the little Filipino might be leading them. Or what he might be leading them into. It all seemed just a little too convenient and it hadn't been his experience that things often came that easy.

On the other hand, if Taboada was making up his story as he went, he was darn good at it. According to him there were at least a dozen guards on the premises at all times. Candido Subing himself came and went. No one seemed to know where, and none had the courage to ask him. But the Tigers's leader had been scheduled to make an appearance today, and while he hadn't yet arrived when Taboada had left, the little Filipino thought there was a good chance he would be there when they arrived. Subing often stayed overnight.

The site itself, he had said, was a barn and farmhouse on an old banana plantation, and it would take roughly three hours to get there. If that proved true, they should arrive shortly before dusk.

Which was perfect as far as the Executioner was concerned. It would give him a chance to recon the area in daylight to see if the details matched the story Taboada was giving him.

As they stepped from the clearing onto another jungle path, the Executioner continued to watch the man who led the way. He had to remind himself yet again that sometimes leopards really did change their spots, and bad men changed their lives for the better. It was rare, and if you were a police officer or a soldier, you saw so many who didn't change that it was easy to start believing it never happened.

The bottom line was the man was either on the level or was dancing what cops called the Jesus Hustle. Many cons seemed only to get religion right before parole hearings, or at other times at which it might benefit them. Only time would tell about Taboada.

Bolan and the other men walked on, making their way up and down hills, crossing streams on rickety wooden jungle bridges and slipping and sliding at every turn. A light rain began after an hour or so but it was welcomed—it not only cooled the air, it washed some of the mud from their skin and clothes.

The path widened and narrowed, with Bolan walking next to Taboada when he could, dropping back behind to keep an eye on him when he couldn't. As they walked along side-by-side at one point, Bolan decided it was time to question the man a little further about his strange Christian-in-a-Muslim-camp situation to see if he could poke a few holes in the story. "Tell me how you got linked up with the Tigers in the first place," he said.

Taboada shrugged nervously. "When I turned eighteen I left the orphanage and went to Manila. But I could not find work and I remembered a friend from the orphanage. Angelo. Angelo had always said he had distant family in Davao."

Still walking abreast on the wider stretch, Bolan studied the man from the corner of his eye. Davao, he remembered from the map, was a city on the other side of Mindanao, a port town on the Davao Gulf.

"I found Angelo," Taboada said, "but he never found his family. I still wonder sometimes if it had not all been in his imagination." He sucked in a deep breath and let it out slowly. "Many orphans invent families to help them cope."

"So," the Executioner said as they started across a lone log stretched over a forty-foot drop. "What's this have to do with the Liberty Tigers?"

"Angelo and I found a job. We worked on the docks. And we fell in with a bad crowd, as I think you Americans say.

They were Moros, Muslim extremists. They talked of nothing but the coming jihads."

Bolan walked on. Jihads. Muslim holy wars. "So suddenly you decided to just change religions?" he asked. "Kind of like changing your shirt?"

"There was nothing sudden about it," the drug runner said as they walked. "Looking back on it now, I can see how gradual the change took place. A little bit at a time. Then, before I really knew what had happened, I was with the Tigers."

The Executioner knew that evil usually came one small step at a time. Criminals committed small crimes on the way to big ones. Cops ate free lunches before they started taking bribes. And religious fanatics—at least those who chose terrorism as a legitimate tool—didn't just wake up one morning and decide to kill innocent men, women and children. Such perversions of philosophy and ideology came in small bits and pieces.

Bolan watched his prisoner out of the corner of his eye as he asked the next question. "Was Angelo one of the men at the landing strip?"

Taboada shook his head. "No," he said. "I don't know where Angelo is. He went to America for a while. I saw him briefly when he first got back. He had married."

Bolan remembered the rumors about Subing's "big strike" in America. "Is Angelo with the Tigers, too?" he asked.

"Yes, but as far as I know, he is not involved with the missionaries."

The jungle path narrowed and Bolan dropped behind the man until it widened again. He waited until they were side by side again so ask, "Is Subing running some other deal right now, too?" It sounded like it. Taboada had said that the leader "came and went."

The little Filipino shrugged. "Probably. But I don't know

what it is. None of us—they—the other Tigers, do. Each of us knows only what we must know. Subing is the only one who sees the big... What is the expression?"

"The big picture?" Bolan said. "The only one who knows everything that's going on?"

Taboada just nodded.

Bolan didn't comment as they started up a steep incline. Regardless of whether or not he could always find the right slang expression, the man had an extremely good command of the English language. The Christian orphanage could account for that—if the story was true. But there were other ways he might have picked up his language skills, too.

One of them was training in a terrorist school.

The rain stopped and the sun came out again. As the sun began to fall quickly over their canopied path, Taboada finally stopped in his tracks. "We are close," he whispered.

The Executioner held up a hand and Latham and Reverte halted behind him.

They took off again, slower this time, and when they had gone another fifty yards Taboada stepped off the path and into the trees, waving behind him for them to follow. Bolan went second with Reverte next and Latham bringing up the rear. He led them deeper into the foliage, then dropped to one knee, reaching out and grasping a thick vine. Slowly he pulled the vine back out of the way.

Bolan looked through the opening. In the quickly fading sunlight he saw what appeared to have once been a medium-size plantation. Several acres of land had been cleared from the jungle and to his right stood row after row of banana trees. But the trees looked as if they hadn't been tended in some time.

A small house stood just to the side of the trees, the front door facing them. It looked as neglected as the orchard. The walls had been covered over with black tar shingles and the shutters on the windows—he could see one window on each side of the door and another on the side of the house within his field of vision—had cracked and fallen off long ago. Several small outbuildings, sheds really, surrounded the house with a large barn visible behind it.

Bolan hurried to memorize the layout before the fading sunlight disappeared altogether. The site was just far enough off the beaten path to be hidden. But not so far that the Tigers couldn't slip in and out for supplies. There were a mixture of odors floating toward him from the place, some strong and fresh, others lighter and lingering. His nose told him that even though the trees had been abandoned, there were still plenty of bananas growing wild. A faint whiff of molding hay met his nostrils, along with the even fainter smells of sheep and cattle. He could see no fresh tracks in the mud around a partially filled water trough, however, which meant the animals had been moved.

The Executioner's eyebrows lowered in concentration as he turned back to look at Taboada. The place looked deserted, but that didn't mean it was.

Bolan studied the man. The time had come for him to either take a chance with Taboada or to get rid of him and go forward on his own. Was he telling the truth? Was he sincere in his change of heart?

Or was Reynaldo Taboada leading them all into an ambush? The little Filipino wasn't stupid; he knew Bolan had come close to killing him. Had he made up this story just to buy time? Was his whole connection to the Tigers simply fiction, or was this actually one of their sites? If so, was there some way he could have warned the other terrorists that he was bringing men in for the kill? Some method so subtle that he hadn't noticed it?

Bolan could not be certain one way or the other. Perhaps

they had passed an unseen sentry who had then taken a short-cut back to warn the camp. Or maybe some kind of audible signal was used to announce a Tigers's arrival and if anyone showed up without using it they faced bullets. There were any number of ways, active or passive, that Taboada could have warned the plantation that he was coming in. And bringing trouble.

The Executioner moved closer and looked deeply into the man's eyes. "You're sure the missionaries are here?" he demanded.

Taboada looked straight back at him. "They were here when I set out early this morning for the landing strip. There was a rumor yesterday among the men that they might be moved soon." He shrugged. "But they were here when I left."

The Executioner frowned. "Is this where they've been all along? Since their capture?"

He nodded.

"Why are they talking about moving them now?" Bolan asked.

Taboada looked surprised. "You don't know?" he said.

"I wouldn't have asked you if I did."

"Because of you. Word has come to us that two Americans are looking for us. You were in Rio Hondo last night and the night before."

Bolan didn't bother answering. He already knew the word was out. He just hadn't known how far or fast it had traveled.

As the sun moved to the tree line, the Executioner continued the hard stare at the little Filipino. "You realize what's going to happen to you if you're lying, don't you?"

Taboada stared right back. His face took on a look of hurt. Whether lying or telling the truth, that face told Bolan that the change within his soul was so profound that he found it hard to believe anyone would question it.

The Executioner turned to face Latham and Reverte, who had squatted behind them. "We wait until dark," he whispered. "Then I'll head in and recon the place. Stay here and stay ready." He met Latham's eyes and nodded slightly toward Taboada.

Latham's head barely moved as he nodded back, showing he understood that he was to keep an eye on both their new acquaintances.

Turning back toward the plantation, the Executioner took a seat on the ground to await darkness. He had a bad feeling about the place. If there were five hostages in the barn as Taboada claimed, there should be at least some sign of activity. There should have been sentries in the jungle and outside guards closer around the buildings. What he had said about possibly moving the missionaries hadn't helped the Executioner's bad feeling one bit.

Bolan took a deep breath, let half of it out, then the rest. Regardless of what he might feel, he still had to check the place out. Even if the missionaries were no longer here, there might be some lead to wherever they had been taken.

Fifteen minutes later the sun had dropped behind the trees and once again the jungle was cast into darkness. Bolan looked up at the sky, seeing the Southern Cross clearly through the blackness. Shrugging out of the Calico shoulder rig, he handed it behind him to Latham. The weapon was more cumbersome than he wanted on this scouting trip and he drew the sound-suppressed Beretta.

The Executioner stayed hidden just inside the jungle line, slowly making his way around the clearing away from the orchard area. Just because he had seen no sentries didn't meant there weren't any, and he didn't like the idea of a bullet in the back while he conducted his soft probe of the grounds. Moving silently was nearly impossible in the dark, dense undergrowth, but he kept the noise down as best he could. He came across no guards and in the darkness he could not tell if there were telltale signs of recent activity. The night had blacked out any tracks, any discarded cigarette butts or food wrappers that might have been present.

The Executioner carried a small Surefire laser flashlight in his pocket, and more than once he considered pulling it out. But the Surefire's beam was so strong that even if he cupped his hand around the lamp, he feared it might be seen from the house or barn. So he went on, not knowing for sure whether men even occupied the grounds, but knowing that if they did, and they saw him before he saw them, he was dead.

Which meant that Latham, Reverte and Taboada would also die. And if they died, so did the missionaries.

When he finally stopped opposite of where he'd left the other three men, the Executioner found a dirt road. It had been invisible from the other side of the clearing, even before the sun had set. Wide enough for all but the largest trucks, it appeared to lead deeper into the jungle. But he suspected it connected somewhere close by with another road that would loop back to the highway.

Scanning carefully both ways, the Executioner darted across the road and back into the cover of the jungle. Reasonably certain that there would be no guards in the banana trees if there had been none guarding the house, he increased his pace, hurrying through the orchard and making his way back around toward the house and other rundown structures. When he had drawn abreast of the largest of the outbuildings—a ramshackle barn—he squatted again just inside the trees.

According to his prisoner, it was here that the hostages were kept.

Slowly the Executioner emerged from hiding yet again. He sprinted to the side of the barn. Through the rotting wood of the walls, he could hear something, but the noise was too low to make out. His feet sank into the mud surrounding the building as he made his way along the wall, stopping at the corner.

Lowering himself to his belly, Bolan hurriedly restored the mud-camou to his face from the wet earth on the ground. Then, inching forward, he peered up and around the corner.

The barn door was right where he'd suspected it would be, but it was closed and from his angle he couldn't tell if any light came through the cracks. Rising to his feet, he cast a quick look at the back of the house, twenty yards in front of him, then moved silently past the door to the other side of the barn.

On the opposite wall, he could see a large square hole in the second story. The door had rotted off long ago and no one had bothered to replace it. But it was from here that the odor of molding hay was strongest.

Bolan moved to a small outbuilding that looked like a toolshed. The door was closed and he saw no sign that anyone was inside. Quickly floating through the dark like a phantom, he checked the other outbuildings before sprinting to the front of the house.

The Executioner stopped at the front wall of the structure and pressing his back against the shingles. Slowly he edged his way from the door, hoping to catch a glimpse inside from the windows to know what he would face when he burst into the house.

Dropping to his knees as he neared the window, Bolan peered up over the crumbling sill through the glass. The room had looked dark from the trees, but the Executioner could see that was because at least a quarter inch of dirt covered the glass. Closer now, he could make out a dim, spreading light behind the grime. He dropped below the ledge again. There was a light on inside somewhere.

Bolan rose to his feet again and edged his back around the

corner of the house. The window on this side was dark—if there was a glow of any kind behind it there was too much dirt on the glass for it to be seen. He moved on to the rear of the small dwelling and found the back door. The top half was of glass. Clean glass. The only clean glass he'd come across so far. Through this window, he could clearly see inside to a semilit kitchen. What light it held drifted in from some other room in the house. Also, from somewhere deeper inside, came the sounds of voices.

Bolan hurried past the opening, dropping to all fours and scurrying around the corner to the other side wall. The glass in that window had been knocked out, and by the same secondary lighting he had used to see into the kitchen, he saw a twin bed mattress atop box springs on the floor. The mattress and a chest-of-drawers were the room's only furniture. Both were strewed with rumpled clothing and other odds and ends.

Returning to the front of the house, the Executioner risked a quick peek around the corner into the front door. Inside, he saw the same dim glow—some kind of light—and once again heard the sounds of voices. This time he also heard a laugh.

Bolan moved away from the house and began to make his way back to the other men. At least he now knew there were people in the house. He suspected there were others in the barn. But he could not be sure who they were.

Terrorists? Hostages? Or had Taboada made up this whole story? If so, the Executioner was about to run a full-blown SWAT operation on some poor down-on-his-luck Filipino banana farmer.

Stepping into the trees, the Executioner grabbed his prisoner by the collar and lifted him to his feet. His jaw set hard as he stuck his face an inch from the other man's. "You get one last chance," he growled in a low voice. "Tell me this was all a lie right now and I'll let you live. But if I have to find out on my own, I'll put one in your head. Right here." He placed the Beretta's sound suppressor on the bridge of Taboada's nose.

Taboada looked him square in the eye and said, "I have told the truth."

Bolan lowered the gun and turned to the others. "Then we've got some planning to do," he said.

THEY DIDN'T HAVE the manpower to hit the barn and house at the same time. So they would hit the barn first, Bolan had decided, since that was where the hostages were supposedly being kept. As soon as the missionaries were secured, they would move to the house. Some of the men, Taboada claimed, slept in the hayloft between shifts. Others in the house.

The Executioner slid the shoulder rig for the Calico back over his arm and let the weapon hang across his shirt. He double-checked both the Desert Eagle and the Beretta, then made sure the other men were armed.

In addition to his .40 S&W Browning Hi-Power, Latham had one of the M-16 A-2s Mott had delivered. The other black assault rifle was slung over Reverte's shoulder and the Colt Combat Commander was jammed into his pants. Somewhere on his body, Bolan assumed, the little .32 was also along for the ride.

Bolan glanced at the Filipino, the only unarmed man of the bunch. The situation demanded that the Executioner trust him, but only up to a point. His instincts said the man was on the level. But he knew he was only human and his instincts, while reliable 99 percent of the time, were still not totally infallible. If this happened to be one of those times within the remaining 1 percent, he was about to lead Latham and Reverte into a trap. The Executioner took one final look at the man, trying to see if he could read any more information on the man's face. He couldn't, so he made his decision.

It was calculated risk he couldn't afford to pass up.

Bolan had given an order of silence, so he used hand signals to wave the men to their assigned places. The barn had only two entrances-exits—the large sliding door in the front and the second-story hayloft window on one side. Bolan and Reverte crept from the trees, taking up positions at the side of the house where they could see the barn door. Latham hurried to cover behind the toolshed near the hayloft. He would watch that exit should anyone try to escape that way.

The plan was unusual in that the Executioner had ordered the other men not to fire unless it was absolutely necessary. They were there as backup only and Bolan himself would do his best to take out any terrorists with the sound-suppressed Calico, Beretta or his knife. The reason? After they raided the barn he wanted to double back to the house to clean out the terrorists inside. And if those men were alerted too soon by gunfire in the barn, they might escape or trap Bolan and Reverte inside.

The Executioner and Reverte bent low against the house as Taboada walked up to the barn and pounded on the door. He raised his voice slightly and called out in Tagalog.

Bolan looked to Reverte next to him. The Tagalog-speaking CIA man nodded his head—it was cool. At least it was cool if he could trust Reverte. He wasn't completely convinced of that yet, either. But he nodded back.

A few seconds later the door slid noisily open on its track. Light shot out of the barn into the night. The Executioner saw a man holding a lantern. He wore OD fatigue pants and a thin, white-ribbed undershirt. A red cloth was tied around his forehead and a pistol of some sort was hidden beneath the flap of a holster on his hip.

Hanging in front of him on a green webbed sling was an AK-47.

Bolan waited. Taboada's job was to get the door open, then do his best to sidetrack whoever opened it so that the door did not get closed. He was to try to keep the man engaged in conversation, walking him deeper into the barn to give the Executioner and Reverte time to sprint from hiding. According to the Filipino, there were usually six to eight guards on duty at any one time. The rest would be in the house or sleeping in the overhead hayloft.

The guard at the door muttered a few words, then stepped back and let his comrade into the barn. Faintly through the night air, the Executioner could hear Taboada speaking rapidly in Tagalog. But whatever he said didn't work because the man in the white tank top slid the door back into place.

Bolan had taken that possibility into consideration and now he crept from hiding next to the house and hurried to the barn. Behind him, he could hear Reverte's feet quietly hitting the ground as the CIA man followed. The Executioner reached out, grabbed the door and slowly tried to run it along the track. It moved a quarter inch, then halted with a soft click.

As the Executioner had feared, it had not only been shut, it was now locked. Bolan waited several seconds to make sure the click had not been heard, then led Reverte around the corner to the side of the barn.

Plan B was now officially in effect.

Latham had seen the problem and now stole out from behind the toolshed, meeting up with Bolan and Reverte directly beneath the hayloft opening. Without speaking, he and Reverte turned to face the rotting wood, then bent slightly at the waist. The Executioner moved behind them and climbed quickly onto their shoulders. Reaching up, he grasped the bottom of the opening and pulled himself up high enough to see into the barn.

Bolan hung suspended as his eyes adjusted to the brighter

inside lighting. Light from the lanterns below drifted up to the hayloft and once his pupils had contracted he could see better than he had outside. But the seconds it took for that to happen seemed like years and he knew that if any of the men were on the second story, awake and looking in his direction, he'd likely get a bullet in the face before his eyes had fine-tuned well enough to see it coming.

When his vision finally cleared, the Executioner saw that the second floor was deserted. Filthy striped mattresses were laid end to end and side by side, and dirty clothing, food remnants and other miscellaneous items further besmeared the area. Pulling hard with his arms and shoulders, Bolan hauled himself up and into the hayloft, then froze in place to listen.

From somewhere below, conversation drifted up to him, and though he couldn't translate the words in his mind, he recognized Taboada's voice. Whatever the man was saying, he didn't sound excited or stressed. Neither did the voices that answered him.

The loft covered the back half of the barn, so Bolan crawled quietly across the mattresses toward a ladder against the far wall. Stopping a few feet from the edge of the loft, he gripped the Calico in his right hand and crawled the rest of the way on one arm. Twisting, he took a seated position against the wall, staying in the shadows as he looked down the ladder at the front half of the ground floor. As he'd suspected, and as had been confirmed by the voices below, he saw nothing of value from this vantage point. Just the muddy floor beneath him and a table stacked with food items against the front wall of the barn.

The men—and hostages if any of them were still here— were beneath him at the back of the barn.

The Executioner paused, evaluating the situation. It wasn't particularly good. It would be impossible to creep down the ladder without being seen or heard. He could jump, but then he'd have to orient himself to the Tigers's terrorists while in the air. If there were more than three or four, or if they were scattered throughout the hostages, they were very likely to fill him full of holes before he'd be able to get them.

Bolan sat back against the wall, taking it all in, trying to find a solution to the problem that wouldn't get him, the hostages or Latham and Reverte killed. The one bright spot at this juncture was that Taboada didn't appear to have given them up. He might before the action started, but if he hadn't turned on them yet Bolan didn't think that was likely.

In the darkness, the Executioner smiled. It appeared that the man's change of heart was sincere. As far as Bolan was concerned, the little Filipino had proved himself. He was now officially an ex-Tiger.

Turning his mind back to the problem at hand, the Executioner stared down at the table at the front of the barn. He had hoped that some of the terrorists would be here—where he could open up with the multiround Calico on semiauto and, using the sound suppressor, pick them quickly off one by one.

No such luck.

The Executioner was still weighing his options when he heard movement below him. Taboada's head appeared, but the man didn't look up. He walked to the table against the wall at the front of the barn and began looking through a stack of food cans. Finally picking one, he lifted a can opener from the table, then turned around and leaned back against it as he went to work opening the can. For a brief second only his eyes looked up at the loft.

Bolan knew the man couldn't see him as he mouthed the word "four." Then, the can finally open, Taboada set the opener down and walked back beneath the Executioner, out of sight. But not before reaching up to scratch his head and placing four fingers atop his hair.

Bolan frowned in the darkness. The number was clear. Four. But did that mean four terrorists, four hostages or a combination that came out to four?

Deciding Taboada had to have meant terrorists, the Executioner made a final weapons check, then rose to his feet and prepared to jump. He could leap from the loft, twisting in the air to face the rear of the barn as he came down. And with any luck, he'd be able to take out one or two of the Tigers before his feet even hit the mud.

He was a half second from airborne when Taboada appeared again. He walked back to the table and set the opened can down again. Still facing away from the Executioner, he turned his head sideways to the left, held two fingers up in front of his face, then curled them back into his fist before shooting them out to the left again. As soon as he'd done that, he formed the age-old hand signal for gun, using his index finger for the barrel and his thumb as the hammer. His thumb fell twice, then he repeated the performance to the right, again keeping his fingers hidden behind his head so the men at the rear of the barn couldn't see them. When he had "shot" twice to the right and twice to the left, he turned and walked out of sight beneath the hayloft once more.

The Executioner took a deep breath. The message was now clear. As he'd guessed—four terrorists. Two to the left, the other two to the right. It would be up to the Executioner to identify their exact locations as he dropped to the ground. But now he at least knew in which directions to look.

If he had been right about Taboada. If the man actually had had a change of heart. And if the four terrorists, even now, weren't training their AK-47s toward the front of the barn and waiting for him to show himself.

But now wasn't the time to second guess his decision to trust the man. He had made his decision and he couldn't afford to look back. His gut reaction had been to trust the man, and so he would.

The Executioner's feet left the loft and he sailed out into the air.

CHAPTER NINE

He saw all four men while still in midair. And he saw the tw◀ hostages, as well.

Before his feet hit the ground the Executioner's brain ha◀ registered the entire scene in front of him and created a pla◀ for dealing with it. It was a psychological phenomena tha◀ sometimes occurred during life-threatening situations; an in◀ tense reaction to threat in which the mind shuts out all super◀ fluous details and focuses solely on the task at hand.

That task being to survive.

It was just as Taboada had indicated—two Tigers on th◀ right, two on the left, with a small wooden table roughly half◀ way between them. As warriors have done since time bega◀ during battle stress, the Executioner's brain registered ever◀ detail. On the table, next to the lantern illuminating the bar◀ was a black sat phone. One of the men on the left sat in◀ straight-backed wooden chair to the side of a table, a news◀ paper held up and open in front of his face. On the table it◀ self rested an old oil lamp, the flame flickering eerily behin◀ the smoky glass.

The first burst of fire from the Executioner's sound-sup◀

pressed Calico left the barrel as his feet hit the ground and he
felt them sink almost ankle-deep in mud. The 9 mm hollowpoint rounds shredded the newspaper the terrorist held in
front of him, drilling on through the news to splatter the man's
chest, throat and face. The terrorist flew up out of his chair
and struck the rotten wood of the wall, collapsing to the
muddy floor as newspaper-confetti fluttered in the air and settled over his body.

The Executioner swung the Calico back toward the left,
where the man who had opened the door for Taboada was
wiping down an AK-47 with an oily rag. The Tiger in the
ribbed undershirt had barely had time to look up since the
Executioner's appearance and now his hands froze on the So-
viet-made rifle.

Bolan triggered another burst of near-silent rounds. At
least one hit the rifle's action and the loud sound of the semijacketed slug meeting steel made far more noise than the
sound-suppressed explosion that had started the bullet along
its path. The AK-47 went spinning out of the gunner's hands
as more 9 mm slugs followed it.

But the man who had come to the door still sat frozen. He
showed no reaction at all and had it not been for the tiny red
spots that now popped out on the white undershirt, Bolan
might have thought he'd missed. For a second or two, the terrorist just looked back at the Executioner with hatred flood-
ing his eyes.

Bolan's mind continued to race with the superspeed that
came only during a duel with death, when the blood sent
chemicals to the brain that allowed it to think at a rate far beyond normal. At least five holes had appeared between the Tiger's belt buckle and collarbone, but the man still seemed to
have had no reaction to them. It happened sometimes, Bolan
realized as he brought the Calico down and prepared to fire

again. Round after round after round sometimes struck a ma
but for one reason or another hit no vital organs. Such me
usually died from their wounds. But it took too long for ther
to do so and, knowing they were about to die, they often di
the damage of the damned before death occurred.

But as Bolan started to trigger another burst of rounds, th
delayed effect of his earlier assault finally kicked in. The ma
in the ribbed undershirt suddenly opened his mouth and
gush of crimson blew out from his lungs. He slumped to th
mud and there was no longer any doubt as to the bullets doin
their job.

Bolan let up on the trigger and jerked the Calico to hi
right. By the time the first round of the next burst blew fro
the machine pistol, he had brought the gun around and aime
it at the closer man on the other side of the barn. His min
and body still moved with the speed of light. But the easy pa
was over now. Not only had the last two terrorists had tim
to react, they both stood directly behind two bound-an
hooded figures on the slippery ground.

It had been less than two seconds since the Executioner ha
jumped from the hayloft, but two seconds was like a centur
in a gunfight.

The man Bolan's Calico located first had drawn a SIC
Sauer P-220 from his belt. He got off one hurried shot befo
the Executioner's high-capacity machine pistol sought hi
out with a half dozen more rounds. The bullets hit along a ho
izontal line along his lower chest, threatening to saw him i
two. Another burst of autofire stitched him vertically from be
to nose, forming a series of dark red holes that quickly ble
out to make a straight line.

The terrorist froze where he stood, looking down at h
body in wonder before falling facedown in the mud.

Taboada had dived under the table next to the newspape

reading man the second the Executioner had opened fire. The
sat phone had fallen from the table as he'd squirmed beneath
it. So had the lantern, the glass shattering and the candle inside tumbling out. The little Filipino had grabbed the phone
and was grinding it down into the candle wick, the tiny flames
rising up from it. The fire didn't worry the Executioner. The
ground inside the barn was far too wet for the flames to reach
the wooden walls.

Bolan swung the Calico toward the final terrorist in the
barn. The last man standing wore what looked like old U.S.
Nam leaf camouflage pants and a black cutoff sweatshirt.
The muscles of a power-lifter—huge and strong, but without
much definition, extended from the chopped garment. He had
short black hair and narrow ferret eyes that looked like miniature berries, and they were focused on the sights of his AK-
47 that, in turn, was focused on the Executioner.

But Bolan had seen the strongman's movement as he had
finished up the man with the SIG-Sauer and a split second before the AK-47 could spit death he dived forward into the
mud. Wet, brown earth splashed upward to both of his sides,
with more mud bespattering his eyes and partially blinding
him. But part of his vision remained and he looked up over
the two blurry hooded hostages to see the beclouded outline
of the muscle man.

The terrorist's burst of 7.62 mm rifle rounds sailed over Bolan's head as he came to a halt in the mud. He aimed the Calico upward over the hooded figures in front of him at the
man-shaped haze and pulled the trigger.

Another long burst erupted from the Calico's barrel, the
hollowpoint rounds catching the cloudy target in the center
of the chest. The strongman went down fast. His rifle fell and
struck one of the hostages on the top of the hood. A grunt is-
ued forth from under the material. Then the Tiger's scream

of death drowned out the grunt as he toppled forward between the two hostages to fall on his face next to his comrades.

But the man's scream was the least of the Executioner's worries as he leaped back to his feet and clawed mud and grass from his eyes with his free hand. Maybe the men still in the house had heard the screams and maybe they hadn't. It didn't matter. He was sure they'd have heard the SIG-Sauer go off, as well as the AK-47.

The element of surprise regarding the terrorists in the house had just disappeared.

"What...what's happening?" asked a timid voice beneath one of the hoods. Bolan realized that the hostages had to be both confused and terrified. He needed to get to the house as quickly as possible. But with the enemy rounds already having gone off, a second or two longer here to comfort the imprisoned missionaries would make no difference.

"Hang in there, both of you," the Executioner said as he watched Taboada crawl out from beneath the table. "We're the good guys and we've come to rescue you. But we've got to get the men in the house first. Then we'll be back."

Taboada looked down at one of the fallen AK-47s, then looked up at the Executioner.

Bolan stared back at the former Tiger. There had been any number of ways the man could have set them up for death during the last five minutes. But the little Filipino hadn't even tried. He had done exactly what he'd promised and followed the Executioner's orders to the letter. He still had his doubts about the man—after all, he had been a terrorist. But if he was trusting Reverte to carry firearms, he might as well trust Taboada, too. But he would keep both of them closely scrutinized.

Still looking into the little Filipino's eyes, Bolan nodded at the AK-47.

Taboada reached down and grabbed the rifle, then began

again and pried the SIG-Sauer from the hand of the man who had wielded it.

"Let's go," the Executioner said, turning toward the front of the barn.

"Hey! Wait!" shouted one of the missionaries. "Aren't you going to at least untie us first?"

If anyone had ever deserved a better explanation of what was going on, it was the two men, bound and gagged, in front of the Executioner. The problem was that there was no time. "Sit tight—we'll be back," Bolan shouted over his shoulder as he slammed the sliding door along its track and darted out of the barn.

Bolan and Taboada met Latham and Reverte in front of the barn. Looking up at the men who had stayed outside, the Executioner whispered, "Cover the front! Don't go in until you hear fire!"

Latham and Reverte both nodded their understanding. It had been only fifteen seconds or so since the gunfire had sounded inside the barn and there had been only the lone pistol round, then the short burst of the rifle. The men in the house had to have heard the shots, but when he saw none of them emerging from the back door Bolan realized the noise could have been interpreted in a variety of ways. The men inside could have written them off as an accident, or someone practicing or just fooling around. Shots in the dark weren't always the precursor to serious trouble. And these men felt secure on their hidden plantation.

Bolan led Taboada to the rear of the tar-shingled house as Latham and Reverte split up and circled to the front on both sides. As he neared the back door, a man wearing an OD T-shirt and matching BDU pants stepped suddenly out of the door. The terrorist had another of the AK-47s strapped to his back on a sling and an unfiltered cigarette dangled from a cor-

ner of his mouth. A silver lighter was held to the end of the
smoke with one hand, his thumb on the wheel. His other hand
cupped the cigarette as he stared down at the flame.

Bolan ground to a halt ten feet away, reading the situation
instantly. The terrorists inside the house had heard the rounds
from the barn and while they didn't immediately expect the
worst they'd thought it merited checking out. So they had sent
this man, and this man so suspected he'd find some nonthreat-
ening answer to the gunfire that he was stopping to light up
before he ventured on.

But he heard the Executioner's pounding feet suddenly
stop and sensed human presence around him. His eyes, temporarily blinded by the flame of the cigarette lighter, squinted
up over his hands.

The Calico rose to spit lead at the flame at the end of the
cigarette. The 9 mm hollowpoint rounds sank deeply into the
Tiger's skull before passing through and exiting. They splattered the door frame inside which the terrorist stood with
blood and brain matter.

Bolan charged forward again, sweeping the man to the
side of the door with the Calico before stepping into the
kitchen. The same light he had seen earlier drifted in from another room to half illuminate the area. As soon as he was inside, he stopped and held up a hand. Taboada halted directly
behind him.

The Executioner stood still, listening. He had used the
sound-suppressed Calico again just now, and the weapon
made more of a slapping sound than what was usually associated with gunfire. But the Tigers inside the house were
likely to recognize the signature of a sound-suppressor. And
if they had heard those slaps just now it behooved the Executioner to find out before moving on. So he froze on the tile in
the middle of the kitchen, waiting, listening, unconsciously

noting the dirty dishes in the sink, the stench of stale garbage in paper sacks on the floor, the spilled wet coffee grounds on the cabinet around a coffeemaker.

From deeper in the house, he once again heard voices. But they sounded no more excited than they had earlier when he'd reconned the house. He couldn't tell how many men were in the room, or if they were all in the same room, or exactly where the other rooms in the house were arranged. But the house was not large enough to have a floor plan too complicated, and wherever the men might be they couldn't be far.

A doorway to his right led past a refrigerator door with mold growing out around the rubber seal, then into a short hallway. At the end of the hall, the Executioner saw the same bedroom he had seen through the dirty window glass earlier. He moved slowly, the ancient curled tile beneath his feet squeaking slightly with every step. When he reached the hallway, he saw two doors—one on each side. Both were closed but light stole out from under the door on his right. Leaning close, he pressed his ear against the wood and heard the faint sound of a slightly unbalanced toilet running. But he could hear nothing else so he turned to the door on his left. A utility room or a closet or pantry or shallow storage area of some type. There was not enough room behind it, and the outside wall, to be anything else, so there was no need of opening it and taking the chance of being heard.

Turning back, Bolan stepped out of the hall onto the ragged carpet in the bedroom. The voices were closer and louder now but they still sounded calm as they drifted to him from wherever they were toward him at the front of the house. The Executioner wished for a moment that he could understand the language. But wishing did no good, so he chased the irrelevant thought from his mind.

An open doorway on the other side of the bedroom led to

the front of the house and what looked like a living room. On the far side of the living room, slightly offset to the right, he could see the front entrance to the house. In his mind, he pictured Latham and Reverte just beyond that door, weapons ready, waiting to kick themselves inside as soon as they heard the first round go off.

Turning his attention back to the living room, Bolan studied what he could see within his ever-expanding field of vision as he slowly crept forward. The walls were covered with cheap imitation wood paneling and a threadbare blue-gray couch was the only item of furniture. Several political posters, featuring the silhouettes of armed men in BDUs, had been tacked to the walls. Slogans in Tagalog were printed across the paper, all of them ending in huge exclamation marks.

But the Executioner could see no humans in the living room and the voices didn't sound as if they were coming from there, either. The men sounded as though they had to be in some room that lay just beyond it, to the right.

Slowing, Bolan kept the Calico up and ready as he slid along the bedroom wall. Behind him, he could hear Taboada trying to keep his breathing low. By the time they reached the doorway he was certain that the voices came from somewhere to the right of the living room. And now he could make out the words, if not understand them. He stopped at the doorway and risked one eye around the corner. All he could see was another door leading off the side of the living room.

The Executioner felt a hand on his shoulder and turned. Taboada had cocked an ear that way, too, and now he looked up and whispered, "Like we did at the airstrip, they are playing cards. And they are talking about a football—what you would call soccer—game. They sent the man behind the house to check on the gunfire. They don't expect it to be any big problem."

Bolan nodded. He had guessed right. "How many? Can you tell?" he mouthed.

"Four. Maybe five."

The Executioner nodded silently in the semidarkness. Counting the men in the barn and the one he'd shot just outside the rear of the house, that was more than enough to continue guarding two hostages. He was about to peer around the corner again when the Filipino grabbed his arm.

"They are sending someone to check on the man who already went," he whispered quickly.

Bolan looked down at the Calico. The men seemed not to have heard the suppressed noise from outside the house. But here, maybe ten feet away, there was no way they would miss it. Letting the weapon fall to the end of the sling under his arm, he drew his Loner knife and waved his companion back toward the kitchen. The two men backtracked as quickly as they could without making any noise.

The Executioner had barely rounded the corner into the short hallway in front of the bathroom when he heard feet pounding from the living room into the bedroom. There was no place to hide and precious little room to maneuver. Unless he wanted to tip the rest of the Tigers off to their presence, he would have to take the man out quickly and quietly. Crouching slightly, he clasped the fingers of his right hand around the knife in an ice-pick grip, then extended his left arm slightly in front of him.

A tall man rounded the corner, his face looking down toward the floor. Before he could look up, the Executioner moved in, reaching up to cup his free hand over the hardman's mouth. Lowering a shoulder into the terrorist's chest, he drove the man back into the bedroom until his knees hit the edge of the mattress and box springs. The Tiger went down onto his back on the bed, the Executioner on top of him.

With his left hand still silencing the man, the Loner flew up in his right. Bolan brought the thick armor-piercing blade down with all his strength, sinking it deeply into the man's neck just above the collarbone. The reinforced point sliced down through the skin, severing the subclavian artery two and one half inches below the surface. The Executioner left the knife where it was as he rolled off of the man, at the same time rolling the Tiger over onto his side. Jerking the knife out again sent a jet steam of blood gushing out of the Tiger's upper chest to splatter against the wall and slosh down into the mattress.

The Executioner wiped the blade on the back of the man's shirt, then returned it to its sheath. As he stood, he saw Taboada staring half hypnotized at the blood still flowing from the man's upper chest.

Blood. In it, Taboada saw his own death.

It would take three and a half minutes, give or take a few seconds, for the man on the dirty mattress to completely bleed out and die. But he would lose consciousness in roughly two minutes. Bolan stood watch over him until he did.

Turning his attention back to the front of the house, the Executioner had to reach out and shake Taboada to bring the former Tiger back from his tortured thoughts. But when he did, he motioned for the man to follow him.

Bolan took a deep breath as he reached the door to the living room again. Latham and Reverte were still following orders—they had heard no gunfire yet so they were still outside, waiting. If the men were still playing cards, sitting around a table, then the best plan of attack at this point would be to simply flip the Calico onto full-auto, step into the room, and take them all out with however many rounds it took.

Which is exactly what the Executioner did.

Bolan stepped into the living room and moved to the door to his right. He paused for a second, heard someone say something and someone else shuffle a deck of cards, then stepped into the doorway, the Calico gripped with both hands.

Just before he fired, the Executioner's mind registered the fact that there were four men seated around a card table. All wore the same unofficial uniform the Liberty Tigers seemed to have adopted—part dress fatigues and part whatever-else-they-had. But one man in particular caught his attention as the Executioner pulled the trigger. He was bigger and broader than the Filipinos with whom he played cards.

And he had a full head of long blond hair.

A burst of 9 mm semijacketed hollowpoint rounds flew from the Calico like miniature angels of death, ripping through plastic-coated playing cards, money and bottles on the table. Shards of glass and pieces of paper flew through the air as other rounds drilled through chests, throats and faces. A mist of crimson rose around the table as the men made impotent grabs for weapons.

The whole ordeal lasted less than five seconds, but when it was over, the four terrorists lay dead on the floor.

Bolan kept the Calico up and ready as he rounded the table, stopping to double-check each body on the floor. The men's pockets and the rest of the house would be searched for clues before they left. But for now, he wanted to make sure that none of them "rose from the dead" to kill again as sometimes happened.

He was standing curiously over the big man with blond hair when he heard the rifle shots.

BOLAN BROUGHT the Calico up in time to see Taboada jerk slightly as he fired the AK-47. But whoever, or whatever, he was shooting at was out of sight in the living room.

The Executioner rushed out of the card room in time to see yet another terrorist clutch his chest and slump to the living-room floor. A Colt Government Model .45 slid out of his limp fingers.

"He must have been in the bathroom," the little Filipino said, turning back to the Executioner.

A second later Latham burst through the front door, followed by Reverte.

But there was nothing left to do.

The Executioner made a fast once-over of the house, then checked the pockets of the big man with the blond hair. He found nothing, and that in itself was enough to further whet his curiosity. Straightening, he turned to Latham. "You and Reynaldo check the rest of them," he told the man in the straw cowboy hat, indicating the bodies on the floor. "Then go through this place with a fine-tooth comb. We need to figure out where they took the other missionaries." His eyes fell one final time on the big blond man. German? Scandinavian? American, maybe? There was no way to know. But he sure wasn't Filipino and the Executioner couldn't help wondering what he was doing in this house with the Tigers.

Latham was frowning at the man, too. "Doesn't quite fit the profile, does he?" the Texan said. He had slung the M-16 A-2 back over his shoulder. He looked down at the bloody blond hair. "You suppose he was here on business? Arms dealer, maybe?"

Bolan shrugged. "There's a million possibilities. Pick your favorite."

"Maybe there's a money trail in here somewhere," Latham said as he dropped to his knees and began looking through the pockets of another man. "Maybe he's PIRA or something. They're all connected when they need to be."

Taboada looked a little confused by the statement, but Reverte nodded his understanding. And Bolan knew what the Texan had meant, as well. Terrorist groups the world over

even those with conflicting goals, had a way of banding together any time it was to their advantage. Bolan had seen cases
in which rival biker gangs—men who'd shoot each other on
sight under normal conditions—joined together in the meth-
amphetamine trade. He'd seen Communist groups work with
fascists, and Black Panthers in league with Ku Klux Klans-
men. Latham's suggestion that the big blond man might be
with the Provisional Irish Republican Army was a viable one.

Evil had a way of binding its followers to continue making life miserable for the good people of the world.

Bolan turned to Reverte. "Come on," he said. "We've got
some hostages to release."

Things were changing, and changing rapidly, the Executioner realized as he and Reverte left the house and jogged toward the barn. He had kept a close eye on Reverte since he'd
joined them, for some reason not quite trusting the CIA man.
But then Taboada had come along and become an even greater
security risk. So when the situation called for the men to split
up, he had taken the Filipino with him and left Latham to
watch over Reverte.

But now, after the signals he had given the Executioner in
the barn, Taboada seemed the more trustworthy of the pair.
Enough time had still not elapsed to fully trust the little Filipino so he still had two men over whom he needed to keep a
watchful eye. He couldn't be certain there was anything
wrong with either one of them. But he couldn't be certain either one of them was on the level, either.

The Executioner glanced at Reverte. There was something
the CIA man did that caught Bolan's attention on a subcon-
scious level. Something that...just didn't fit. What was it? The
Executioner didn't know. But whatever it was, Reverte bore
watching as closely as the Filipino. Bolan's instincts told him
it was better to be safe than sorry.

The hostages still sat in the mud, their hands and feet bound, the rough canvas feed sacks over their heads keeping them blind. "We're back," Bolan said. "And in case you got confused while we were gone, we're the good guys."

"Praise the Lord!" said the hooded man who had spoken to Bolan before. "And to change the old saying a little bit, Praise the Lord and I'm glad you had the ammunition!"

The Executioner smiled as he leaned down and pulled the sack off of the man's head. Reaching past him, he removed the other man's hood. The missionaries's eyes had grown used to the darkness and they now squinted even in the dim lighting afforded by the open-flame lanterns and oil lamps scattered around the barn. The Executioner glanced around the room as he let the men's eyes adjust. They had been lucky that the one on the table where Taboada had hidden had been the only ancient lighting device to break. Others were scattered around the barn, and many were close enough to the rotten wood of the walls that they might have ignited them.

Stepping around to the front of the men, Bolan withdrew his knife and quickly sliced through the restraints at the men's wrists, waists and ankles. "How long has it been since you've been on your feet and walking?" he asked.

The man who had spoken before grinned up at him as his eyes still tried to focus. "I lost track of the time quite a while back," he said. "But it's been a while." The Executioner looked to the other man, who simply nodded.

"Well, take it slow. Easy," he said. "You'll be weak and stiff. But we've got some walking to do." Reaching down, he lifted both men up to their feet. They stood, wobbling back and forth, finally taking hold of the wall behind them to steady themselves. The missionary who had remained silent still looked frightened but the man who had spoken was grinning as if he'd just won the lottery. He looked to be in his late thirties and he wore what were perhaps the filthiest pair of dungarees the Executioner had ever seen. They were so saturated with wet mud that they had turned brown, as had the shreds of a once-white T-shirt which still tried, but failed, to cover the man's chest. Even in the dim light of the lanterns Bolan could see the rash blanketing the missionary's skin through the holes in the shirt. Several of the areas, left untreated, had become infected, and puss oozed from the irritated skin. The rash could also be seen on the top of the man's bald head, looking angrily back at the Executioner from the center, and making its way below the curly black hair that circled his head above the ears. All in all, he didn't look as though he'd bathed at all during his ten months of captivity.

But the missionary's face was still beaming as his eyes adjusted to the light and he chuckled as he looked up at the Executioner. "Yeah, you look about like I figured you would," he said.

Bolan frowned, not knowing what he meant.

The missionary laughed out loud this time. "You *are* the Archangel Michael, aren't you?" he said.

The Executioner laughed with him. It was good to see a man go through so much and still come out the other side with a sense of humor. He was dirty, worn out, half starved and his nerves had to have been stretched about as far as they could go without snapping. But as Bolan looked at him now he could tell the man would probably be chomping at the bit to return to his missionary work within a week.

The other missionary's attitude didn't seem to have fared quite as well. He stood against the wall, his eyes flitting from one dead body on the barn floor to the next. He had still not spoken. But now he did. In a low, hoarse voice that sounded as if it hadn't been used in some time. "Was it necessary to kill them?" he asked, looking up at Bolan with an accusatory expression on his face.

Bolan let several seconds go by without answering. He reminded himself that some men never accepted reality, even when it hit them in the face. Finally he said, "No, it wasn't necessary to kill them. I could have let them kill you instead."

"Shut up, Tom," the bald missionary told the man, punching him lightly on the arm. "This guy comes in and saves our lives and you want to complain about the way he did it?" He turned back to Bolan. "Sorry about that. By the way, his name is Tom Fairbanks. I'm John Parks." He extended his hand.

Bolan shook it. "Cooper," he said.

"Well, you'll always be Michael to me," Parks said. He gave Fairbanks a dirty look and the other man stuck his hand reluctantly out. Bolan shook it, too.

The soldier stepped back and said, "Come on. Let's go outside." He needed to interview both men in the hope they might have intel on where Candido Subing had taken the other hostages. But the dead men on the floor would be a distraction. The house was out, too. There was even more blood strewed around there than there was in the barn. The Executioner picked up two of the lanterns and led the way to the door. Their talking would be done outside.

Reverte had remained quiet so far. But now he knew what step had to be next and his extroversion made him take center stage. "I'll conduct the interview," he said as if there would be no argument. "One of my specialties."

Bolan glanced at him out of the corner of his eye as he led the missionaries to the side of the toolshed behind the house. The CIA agent, he realized, would be even more of a distraction than the dead bodies littering the barn and house. "It's one of my specialties, too," he said. "I've got two specialties, actually."

"What's the other one?" Reverte asked.

"Slapping around smart-mouthed CIA agents who get too big for their britches and start thinking they're in charge."

Reverte got the message.

"Go see how they're doing in the house," Bolan said as they reached the side of the shed. "And send Taboada back here to me." He set the lanterns down to illuminate the area, and when he looked back up Reverte was still standing there. "Now," he said.

For a moment the Executioner thought he saw true hatred in the CIA man's eyes. Then again, it might have just been anger at the fact that Bolan was running the show—hard to tell in the flickering light from the lanterns. Whatever it was, Reverte turned and walked back to the house as he'd been ordered.

Bolan turned to the two missionaries who were still not steady on their feet. "If you guys need to sit down, do it," he said.

Fairbanks didn't hesitate and Parks wasn't far behind. Both men dropped to the ground. "I thought I'd never want to sit again as long as I lived," Parks said. "Day after day, week after week. Eating, sleeping…everything sitting." He snorted through his nose. "Now it seems it's all I *can* do." He was still smiling, though, which was a good sign.

Bolan waited for the Filipino to join them. He not only wanted Reverte out of the way, he wanted the former Tiger in on the interview in case he could put intel gained from the missionaries together with things he already knew. As he waited, the Executioner watched John Parks. And behind the good-natured smile he finally saw the pain. The missionary was exhibiting as much good spirit as he could muster. But it wasn't all genuine. Finally, Bolan dropped to one knee in front of him and said, "John, are you all right?"

The smile slowly faded from the man's face. He looked up at the Executioner kneeling over him and said, "No. I'm about as far from being all right as a man can get, to be honest. Now that the jubilance of being free has worn off a little, I'm forced to face reality. And there's a question I've got to ask you. A question I'm afraid to have answered."

Bolan nodded. "Whatever it is, you'll have to face it sooner or later," he said. "Might as well get it over with."

Parks looked down at the ground, then up again. "Are we the only hostages you've found?"

Suddenly, Bolan understood. He had read the CIA files concerning the missionaries held hostage during the flight to the Philippines and learned their names. Two of them had been husband and wife, and their last name was Parks. He hadn't snapped to that when John had introduced himself earlier, having too many other things on his mind.

The Executioner nodded. "I'm afraid so," he said, looking the man in the eye. "But we're not through yet, either."

Parks smiled again but a tear ran down his cheek. He nodded. "We've *got* to find her," he said. "*I've* got to find her." He paused and his voice choked for a moment. Then he went on. "She's the only thing on this earth that I care about."

"We'll find her," the Executioner said. "You've got my word on that." He knew he'd do everything he could to reunite the couple, as well as to free the other missionaries. And that included giving up his own life if it came to that.

Bolan stood. He was about to say more when he heard footsteps behind him and turned to see Taboada jogging their way. The missionaries saw him, too, and Parks stiffened. "What's *he* doing with you?"

Bolan realized that the missionary had to have caught glimpses of Taboada during the rare times their hoods had come off during the past ten months. He didn't have time to fully explain the complex situation in regard to the little Filipino, so he just said, "Don't worry. He's on our side."

Parks frowned. "What, like he was an undercover agent or something? Then why—"

Bolan waved a hand in front of his face to put the man off. "It's complicated," he said. "I'll explain it all to you when I can. For now, just trust me on it, okay?"

"Okay."

The Executioner looked deep into Parks's eyes as Taboada joined them. He hoped either Parks or Fairbanks could provide at least some shred of evidence that would point them toward the remaining hostages.

Because unless he found a new lead from them, or somewhere here in the house or barn, the Executioner knew there was very little chance he'd be able to keep his promise to John Parks.

THE AIR WAS STILL THICK with humidity, and heat still hung in the air as Bolan and Taboada took a seat next to the shed across from Tom Fairbanks and John Parks. The glass-covered candle flames in the lanterns flickered back and forth in the soft breezes, casting distorted and ever-changing shadows across the grounds. From the jungle that surrounded them came the sounds of insects, birds and night animals. Somewhere, hidden beyond the trees, the Executioner heard a raspy tap-tap-tapping—the mating call of the gecko.

Bolan glanced back toward the house where Latham and Reverte continued the search for leads on the other captive missionaries. Taking a deep breath, he turned back to the shadowy faces in front of him.

Both men were still in a state of half shock. Fairbanks, the Executioner would have guessed, had retreated inside himself after only a few days of captivity. He was no doubt a good man, intent on spreading the gospel and helping the natives of the Philippines. But he didn't strike Bolan as being particularly strong-willed. And it took every bit of will a man could muster to mentally survive the experience he'd gone through during the past several months.

Parks, on the other hand, impressed Bolan as a man of true determination. In addition to the Reverend James A. Worden—the man who had been so brutally murdered on videotape—Parks had probably been one of the leaders throughout the ordeal, lending his own courage and moral stability to the others, encouraging them during weak moments and keeping them united in the belief that rescue would eventually come. But Parks was on the edge now himself. And Bolan knew why.

Much of Parks's strength of character had no doubt come from his wife and their successful marriage. Some husbands and wives, the Executioner had noted over the years, truly did become one. And once that happened, they no longer functioned very well on their own. Now, John Parks and his wife were separated, and the man was like a twin engine plane flying on one engine. He had no idea where the woman he loved could be or whether or not she was even still alive.

So, the Executioner knew, he would be walking on eggshells during his interview with both of the men in front of him. He had to pump them for information and he had to do so as quickly as possible. But he couldn't confuse them or push them to an emotional point where they broke down. An interview such as he was about to conduct was, in some ways, the direct antithesis of a criminal interrogation. Not only could he not come on strong as he would with a criminal, he'd have to treat both men with kid gloves to keep from tipping them over the edge psychologically.

The Executioner cleared his throat. "Tom, John," he said, looking back and forth between them. "First, let me say I admire you for what you came here to do. And I admire you for what you've survived during the last several months."

"Thank you," Parks said. Fairbanks just nodded.

"What we've got to do now is find out anything you might know that could lead us to the other hostages." He looked directly at Parks now, for two reasons. First, his words would have special meaning for him because of his wife. And second, because Bolan's gut level instincts told him that, even with his extra burden of stress, John Parks would prove to be the more helpful of the two. "Tell me what you can about Candido Subing," the Executioner began. He wanted to start easy, with generalities, then slide gradually into more pointed questions after the two men were more relaxed.

"A few of the men called him Candy," Parks said, then went on to tell Bolan mostly things that he already knew. The Liberty Tigers were actually a fairly small outfit compared to some of the other Filipino-based terrorist groups, and once more Bolan had to take a step back when Parks told him he had kept hearing snatches of conversation about "something big in the U.S."

"Did you ever hear any details about that?" Bolan asked the man.

Both men shook their heads. "No," Parks said. "I don't think the other Tigers knew much about it themselves. But I guess Subing couldn't resist letting them at least know he was about to go play in the big leagues. He made sure everyone knew that he was the main player, too."

Bolan puzzled over the situation for a moment, as he'd done so many times since this mission had begun. Subing and his group simply didn't have the money or manpower to pull off something on the scale of the September 11 attacks. Selling ten kilos of heroin certainly wasn't going to do it. In fact the small drug deal Taboada had gone on only proved how small-time they really were.

No, the Executioner realized. If there was any truth to this "big strike" story, it meant the Tigers had teamed up with someone else who *did* have the bucks to carry through with a large-scale attack of some kind. But who would that be? Hamas? Al-Qaeda's worldwide network? The local MILF or Islamic Jihad? The problem with that theory was that those groups didn't need Subing at all. They could go it alone, and they certainly wouldn't put him in charge.

The Executioner let John Parks ramble on, doing his best to separate the wheat from the chaff, and decide which details might be pertinent and which superfluous. Each time the man ran out of words Bolan prompted him with new questions. As the missionary answered, the Executioner cast periodic glances to Taboada to see if anything Parks said was clicking with information the former Tiger had. Each time he did, the Filipino met his eyes, then gave him a tiny shake of the head.

Fairbanks sat silently, nodding now and then. Periodic agreement with a "Yeah" or "Uh-huh" was his only contribution.

Finally, Bolan said, "Think hard, John. Not just their words, either. Mannerisms, routines, anything. Especially on the day when they separated you and Rachael."

The Executioner turned to look at his companion. The little Filipino had already told him that Subing ran the Tigers on a need-to-know basis and everything John Parks had said seemed to confirm that fact. In addition, Taboada had been the newest recruit, and because of that even less privy to information that didn't concern him than the others.

Parks closed his eyes in the flickering light of the lanterns. "I'm trying," he said. "It's just so hard…I mean, I was so emotional. And while I speak Tagalog, they often used some other language. One of the dialects—"

Bolan turned to Taboada but addressed his words to Parks. "You know which language it was?" It was a long shot, but if the missionary could even remember the right sounds, Taboada or Latham or Reverte might be familiar with the words and be able to turn them into leads.

Parks opened his eyes and shrugged. Looking down at the ground in front of him, he said, "No. I didn't recognize it. Take your pick. Besides Tagalog, which they now call Pilipino to keep from offending the other tribes, there are almost a hundred different languages and dialects spoken here."

Taboada nodded his agreement. "Sometimes I could not even recognize the languages they used," he said.

"Think," Bolan told the missionary again. He remained quiet, letting the man concentrate, as an eerie quiet fell over the grounds of the old banana plantation. The Executioner was surprised when that stillness was broken not by Parks but by Fairbanks.

"They said Sulu," the missionary stated. His voice was still low and rough, trying to remember how to work after months of disuse. "I don't know what language they were speaking—one of the Moro dialects probably—but I caught Sulu several times that day."

Bolan turned his attention to the man. Fairbanks was short, maybe 5'5" at the most, and until recently the Executioner suspected he had run to fat. His khaki work pants were every bit as brown and stiff from mud as Parks's jeans. The remnants of material on his torso looked as though they had once been part of a striped polo shirt. Both garments hung off his body after ten months of bad nutrition and he looked like an anorexic scarecrow. Bolan remembered the man having to hold his pants up with one hand to keep them from falling when he'd staggered out of the barn.

"Go on," the Executioner said.

Fairbanks shook his head. "That's all. At least, that's all I can remember."

The Executioner ground his teeth together, fighting back the frustration that threatened to invade his soul. He'd need better directions than that if they expected to find the other hostages. The Sulu Archipelago was almost two hundred miles long. It consisted of more than five hundred islands stretched from Basilan—the island just south of Mindanao—all the way to Borneo.

Turning to look at Taboada in the flickering lamplight, Bolan said, "Any ideas?"

The Filipino shook his head. "Sulu is almost all Muslim, and while many do not agree with the acts of the Tigers, they would still shelter them from anyone they considered infidels."

The Executioner knew that meant they could be anywhere. But wherever the terrorists had taken the other hostages, he and his crew would need transportation to get there. Pulling out his sat phone, he flipped it open and dialed Stony Man Farm.

"Go ahead, Striker," Barbara Price said.

"Is Charlie back yet, Barb?" Bolan asked.

"Negative."

"Who's available? We're going to need transport."

"How about I reroute Jack?" Price countered. "He just started back from Saudi a few minutes ago."

"Fine," Bolan said. "Get him the coordinates on the same landing strip where Charlie landed earlier. We'll meet him there as soon as he can get there."

"Roger, Striker. Where will he be taking you?"

"The Sulu islands."

"Want to be more specific?"

"I would if I could. When I know, you'll know."

"Fair enough," Price said. "Let me get off and I'll get on it."

"'Bye, Barb."

The Executioner had barely disconnected when John Park reached over and grabbed his sleeve. "I thought of something," he said. "It sounds silly. But maybe it has some meaning."

"Go on," Bolan said.

"When they took Rachael away," he said. "I tried to get up. I tried to fight." As he spoke his voice began to rise in volume. "God knows how I tried!" he said. "But I couldn't...I couldn't...." He broke into tears, grabbing his face with both hands and squeezing the way Bolan suspected he would have squeezed Subing's throat, given the chance.

The Executioner reached out and put a hand on the man's shoulder. "Take your time," he said. "Settle down. Then tell me the rest."

Parks dropped his hands back to his lap and looked up, taking a deep breath. "I want to kill him," he said in a calm and controlled voice. "May the good Lord help me, I want to kill them all."

Bolan waited.

As soon as he'd composed himself fully Parks said, "Like I told you, this may be stupid. And it might not mean a thing. But when they were taking her away, and I was trying to get to my feet and go to her, one of the men hit me with his rifle. He was laughing and he said, 'Sit down. Weaving is for women anyway.' It didn't make sense to me. Maybe that's why I remember it now."

From the corner of his eye, Bolan saw the look of recognition come over Taboada's face. The former Tiger leaned closer. "I think I may know," he said. "Weaving?"

Parks nodded his head. His sobbing was over but his face was still a mask of grief. "He said, 'Weaving is for women anyway.'"

Taboada turned to the Executioner. "There is a place called the Yakan Weaving Village a few miles west of Zamboanga. Actually, it is just a few small booths where the Yakan sell their weavings and a few other things. Brassware, batiks, things like that."

Bolan frowned. "Why would they take hostages there? I there someplace they could be hidden?"

The Filipino shook his head. "None that I know of."

Bolan reached up and pinched the bridge of his nose, clos ing his eyes. Weaving. Sulu. He opened his eyes again an stared at Taboada. "The Yakans," he said. "That's one of th tribes in the Sulus, isn't it?"

"Yes."

The Executioner's jaw tightened as he concentrated. Ya kans. Sulu. Weaving. The Yakan Weaving Village—no, the hadn't gone there. This Filipino version of a shopping mal wasn't the answer. If he had gone to the trouble of separatin; them, Subing would spread the hostages out farther than tha

Bolan was still thinking when the back door to the hous banged open and Latham and Reverte came hurrying for ward. Latham held up a small pad of paper as he jogged to ward them. He was out of breath when he halted in front o the Executioner, but Bolan suspected it was more from excite ment than physical exertion.

Latham grabbed one of the lanterns and moved it in fron of Bolan, then plopped down cross-legged next to him. H held the notepad in front of the lantern.

Bolan looked down to see that the Texan had used an ol trick. He'd lightly rubbed a pencil lead across the blank pape on the top of the pad. What had been written before—on page that had then been torn off—showed up in white wher the writing instrument had pressed through the paper.

To the Executioner, it looked like an address and telephon number. At the bottom was the abbreviation "Bas."

"Basilan," Latham said, a smile taking over his face.

Bolan knew Basilan to be just south of them.

"That's the real home of the Yakans," Taboada said. "Th Weaving Village just sells the things that are made there."

Bolan was the first on his feet. "How far is it?" he asked Latham.

"About thirty minutes in a fast boat maybe."

Bolan pulled Fairbanks and Parks up off the ground. "We've got a little walking to do," he said. "Then there's a plane coming that will take you back to the U.S."

"I don't want to go back to the U.S.," Parks said. "I'm going with you."

Bolan looked down at the man. "John," he said, "I can appreciate you wanting to go find your wife—"

Parks interrupted. "If the next word you're about to say is *but,* don't bother. I *am* going."

Bolan sighed. "With all due respect, you'll just get in the way."

One of the most stubborn looks the Executioner had ever seen came over the missionary's face. "She's my wife," Parks said, "and I'm going after her."

Bolan turned to Latham. "Take Reverte and Reynaldo and get things gathered up," he said. "We move out in five minutes." As the three men hurried off to gather up guns and other equipment, he turned back to Parks. "Look, Reverend, or Pastor, or whatever—"

"It's John," Parks said. "Just John." His chin had started to stick out in defiance, and to the Executioner he looked a lot like an angry junior-high-school kid. He respected the man's dedication, his courage and his enthusiasm for getting his wife back, but he couldn't afford to have deadweight along, either.

"Okay, John," the Executioner said. "With all due respect, there's not much likelihood of finding your wife without shedding a good deal of blood."

Parks looked him in the eye. "I'm a Christian," he said, "but we're not all pacifists, you know." He waited a second, then

said, "The same Jesus who said, 'Turn the other cheek' also
said, 'He who has no sword, let him sell his coat and buy
one.'" The missionary took a deep breath, then finished with,
"What it boils down to is this, Mr. Cooper. If some of us
weren't the Christian soldiers the pacifist Christians would
never get a chance to practice their pacifism."

Bolan stared into the man's eyes, hoping they really were
the window to his soul, and doing his best to judge exactly
what this soul was made of. He certainly didn't begrudge the
man his desire to help find his own wife. Any man who
wouldn't want to help would be a coward. Parks had guts, and
the Executioner respected that. But there was a difference between having guts and having skill, or even possessing the will
to actually *do* the dirty work when it got to that point. And
this mission had already gotten there—it had been down and
dirty since he'd first landed and he saw no reason to think
things were going to change now.

"You're ready to kill people, are you?" Bolan asked. "You
ever done that before?"

For a moment Parks broke Bolan's gaze. Then his eyes returned to the Executioner's and he said, "No, sir. I've never
had to. But I could."

"It's not like you think," Bolan said.

"I'm sure it's not."

"It's not going to bother you?" Bolan said. "How do you
know that when it comes time to pull the trigger—when it's
either you or him, and there's no way around it, and you don't
have time to think about it—how do you know you won't stop
and think about it anyway? How do you know that won't
happen and you'll get yourself killed?"

"If I don't find Rachael, I don't care if I get killed."

"Great," Bolan said. "That's fine. But how do you know you
won't get *us* killed? It can work that way, too, if you hesitate."

"I won't hesitate."

Bolan tried one last time to talk the man out of it. "Think about the words I'm about to say next before you answer me, John. *Thou shalt not kill.*"

Parks stuck his chin out again and said, "I assume you're referring to that unfortunate interpretation of the sixth commandment in the King James and other versions of the Bible," he said. "If you'll go back to the original Hebrew and Greek, which I have, you'll find it actually says, 'Thou shalt not *murder.*'" He paused. "There's a big difference."

"Yes," he said. "So I've heard." Before he could say more Latham, Reverte and Taboada returned. In addition to the weapons they had brought into the fight, they had also procured several of the AK-47s and extra magazines used by the terrorists.

"You ever shot a gun before?" Bolan asked Parks.

"I've hunted deer," the missionary said. "And ducks, pigeons, quail."

"This is a little different," Bolan said. He reached out and took one of the AK-47s from Reverte. Checking to make sure it was on safe, he handed it stock-first to Parks. "Show me," he said.

The missionary took the weapon without reserve. But his face showed that he was unfamiliar with this type of military rifle. "Where's the safety?" he asked.

Bolan reached up and tapped the front of the receiver.

"This is one of those that you just pull the trigger once and it shoots until you let up, right?" Parks said, flipping the lever all the way down to full-auto.

"Or until you run out of ammo," Latham told him.

"Can you make it shoot one at a time?" the missionary asked.

"Pull the selector back up one click," the Executioner said. The barrel of the AK was aimed away from the men toward the house. Parks adjusted the selector and threw the stock to his shoulder. "See that shingle hanging off the side of the door?" he asked.

Bolan nodded toward a tar shingle that had come halfway off to stick out at an odd angle.

Parks pulled the trigger and the tar shingle jumped. "Not much kick to it," he said. "Nothing like my 30-06, anyway." He stared at the rifle in his hands and nodded. "Okay. I think I've got the hang of it now." He dropped the selector down to full-auto, aimed again, then cut loose with a long stream of automatic rounds. By the time he let up on the trigger, the shingle, and several more around it, had fallen to the ground.

"Not bad," Bolan said.

Parks put the safety back on and looked up at him again. "Then you're not going to try to stop me from going with you, Mr. Cooper?"

"Let's get started," Bolan said. "And it's Matt. Just Matt."

CHAPTER TEN

Dawn was breaking, and Jack Grimaldi was sitting on the ground next to another of the Stony Man Farm Learjets when Bolan and the other men stepped out of the jungle and onto the landing strip. The pilot wore a snub-nosed .357 Smith & Wesson Model 66 in a horizontal shoulder holster over a sweat-stained T-shirt. On his head was a suede Alaskan bush pilot's cap. He stood as the men approached.

"Took you long enough to get here, Striker," Grimaldi said with a grin as the Executioner led the way to the plane. "What'd you do? Stop for dinner or something?"

The Executioner smiled. There was enough light now to see the air strip and he noticed that the bodies of the dead drug runners were gone. "What did *you* do, Jack?" he asked. "A little housecleaning to keep yourself busy while you waited?" he said.

Grimaldi laughed. "You know me," he said. "Neat and tidy. A place for everything, and everything in its place. Their place is just out of sight in the jungle." He made a face of disgust. "They don't last long in this climate and it was getting pretty gross." He stopped talking for a moment and frowned in concern. "I didn't think, was there still something you wanted from them? I know where—"

Bolan shook his head. "Had all of them I want." He turned to Fairbanks and Parks, who were right behind him. Latham, Reverte and Taboada brought up the rear. "Jack," he said, "this is Tom Fairbanks and John Parks. Two of the missionaries." Both men stuck out their hands and Grimaldi shook them. "Tom will be going back with you."

Grimaldi raised an eyebrow at Parks. "Not you?" he said.

"My wife's still missing. I stay."

Grimaldi looked questioningly at the Executioner, who nodded.

"So where do I take the rest of you?" the pilot asked.

"Since I called in last night things have changed a little," Bolan said. "We're heading for Isabela on the west coast of Basilan, just south of here."

"Yeah, Basilan." Grimaldi nodded. "I know the place."

"The only airport the island's likely to have is the commercial one, and I don't want to draw a lot of attention." He stopped and turned to Latham. "I assume there's a boat line or two running back and forth, isn't there?"

Latham nodded. "Two. Basilan Lines or AS Express—take your pick."

Grimaldi took off his cap and used it to wipe sweat from his brow. "How far is it by boat?" he asked.

"Half hour or so," Latham said.

The pilot put his cap back on. "That makes it maybe ten minutes air time, and that's mostly take off and landing. Tell you what. Hop aboard and I'll fly you down there. Like I said, I know that island and I'm pretty sure there's a spot along the coast where I can set her down and let you out."

Bolan hesitated. "We do that, Jack, and we're going to draw more attention than we would at the airport," he said.

Grimaldi shook his head. "Not if we work it right. I can set her down, let you out and take off again."

The Executioner grinned. "The old 'rich kids' entry?" he said. It was an unorthodox infiltration procedure he and Grimaldi had used several times in the past. It had always worked like a charm in small communities with limited technology.

"The very one," Grimaldi said. "Let's hit the air."

The Executioner followed Grimaldi up onto the plane and the other men followed him. They buckled themselves into their seats for the takeoff, then took turns cleaning up as best they could at the lavatory in the rear of the cabin. Bolan changed into a clean version of what he'd had on before—khaki pants, white T-shirt and another light blue chambray shirt. Again, he left the tails out and the shirt unbuttoned to provide quick access to the Beretta and Desert Eagle. The other men also found clean clothes in the lockers along the wall.

While the others were still busy in the back of the plane, the Executioner leaned into Grimaldi. "Anything new on whatever the big deal is that's supposed to go down in the U.S.?" he asked.

Grimaldi shook his head. "Not really. Aaron said there's a distinct slowdown in internet and phone chatter, as a matter of fact. Maybe it's all just been talk."

"Or maybe they have more secure communication than usual," Bolan said.

Grimaldi turned to frown at him. "The Tigers?" he asked. "These guys don't strike me as being able to pull anything big off. This missionary thing's already more than I'd have guessed they were capable of."

"Me, too, Jack," Bolan said. "That's why I'm convinced that they're in it all with some other group. Somebody with money and know-how."

Stony Man Farm's ace pilot nodded and turned back to the

control panel. He had overestimated the flight time, and roughly eight minutes from the time they'd taken off they were entering Basilan air space. Voices, first in Tagalog, then in English, came onto the radio demanding they identify themselves.

Bolan sat next to Grimaldi and Latham was right behind the Executioner. The Texan leaned forward and frowned. "Aren't you going to answer them?" he asked, staring at the radio.

"Not yet," Grimaldi said simply. "Relax. They don't have anything that can shoot us down, and they sure don't have anything fast enough to catch us. We'll find that stretch of beach I mentioned, I'll touch down and let you out, and be gone again before they're even sure we were here." He smiled.

Grimaldi guided the plane along the coast as the radio continued to demand identity, flight plans and other information. The Stony Man pilot pretended not to hear. They finally flew over the village of Maluso toward the south end of the island, then turned back north again. Through the windshield Bolan could see another small island in the distance. "What's that?" he asked Latham.

"Pilas Island," the Texan told him.

"Lots of mountains on this little spot of land," Grimaldi said as they cut out over the ocean and left Basilan air space again.

"See that place you were looking for?" Bolan asked.

"Yeah." Grimaldi nodded. "But it's not as long as I remembered it being. They've built up part of it since I was here."

"Can you still land?"

"Oh, yeah," Grimaldi said. "It'll be tight, and rough, but it can be done."

"Then let's do it," Bolan said.

He turned to Latham again. "Make sure everyone but Fairbanks is armed," he said. "But no weapons showing. As soon as we get out we've got to make a run for cover. Then, as soon as the heat dies down, we'll blend in with the populace as if we've been here for weeks."

"Then we're not taking the long arms?" Latham asked.

Bolan paused, his eyes rising to the lockers bolted along the wall in the passenger area. "You have any CARs with you, Jack?" he asked.

Grimaldi nodded. "Should be five or six back there."

Turning back to Latham, the Executioner said, "Trade in the 16s and the AKs for the CAR-15s with the collapsible stocks. And grab each man a backpack they'll fit into."

Latham got up and left to follow orders.

A few minutes later the Learjet was approaching the island from the same direction it had before. The only difference was that this time they were only a few hundred feet off the ground as they flew over Isabela and the voice from the radio tower went even crazier when the Learjet ignored their transmissions.

Which didn't seem to faze Jack Grimaldi in the least.

The plane continued to drop through the air as it raced toward the sand along the coast. "Ladies and gentlemen," Grimaldi said in a mock-official voice as they made their final approach to the sand. "The captain has turned on the seat belt sign—please return to your seats and fasten your seat belts."

Latham, having just finished overseeing the issue of weapons and ammunition, hurried back to the seat behind Bolan.

The tires hit the beach and the plane began to fishtail along the coast, throwing sand up and over both wings. One front tire hit a large rock, and the Lear went airborne again for a moment, then Grimaldi wrestled it back down onto the beach and fought to slow the aircraft. "Hang on to your chewin' gum, ladies," he said.

Bolan had been through far worse landings with the Stony Man pilot and Latham seemed to be taking it fine right behind him. But both Taboada and Reverte looked as if they might throw up everything they had eaten in their entire lives. Parks eyes were closed, whether in prayer or fear or a combination of both, Bolan didn't know. But Fairbanks wasn't praying unless he did so with his eyes as wide as dinner plates and his hands trying to break the armrests off the seats.

Ahead, an outcropping loomed up, which marked the end of the makeshift runway. They were still racing along the sand, only half in control, and finally even Latham began to show a little concern. Then, at the last moment, Grimaldi skidded the plane to a halt amid a hailstorm of wet sand and ocean spray. He took off his headphones and turned in his seat. "Ladies and gentlemen," the ace pilot said, "welcome to Basilan. Please remember to check beneath the seat in front of you, and in the overhead compartments before deplaning. And I'd like to thank you again for flying with us."

The island of Basilan, just south of Mindanao, was the home of the Yakan tribe. Originally a people of the lowlands along the sea who practiced animism, some of the Yakans creature-worship had survived the invasion of Islam during the fourteenth century. Their coastal lifestyle, however, hadn't And as the years went by, and more and more foreign settlers claimed the shoreline, the Yakans had been pushed farther and farther inland, up into the mountains of the interior. They became primarily subsistence farmers growing corn, rice, cassava and other crops, and what little contact they had with the invaders on the coast centered around their weaving trade.

Bolan led the way into Isabela with Reverte and Taboada at his heels. They had scrambled away from the beach as fast as they could deplane and unload their equipment, knowing that Basilan officials would be on their way to investigate the unauthorized landing. The Executioner and his four companions had been almost a quarter mile away, having taken cover in the foothills of the mountains, when Grimaldi had taken off from the beach once more.

Bolan realized they had created more excitement about their arrival this way than they would have had they simply come by boat. But it was the government that would be excited now—not the Liberty Tigers's spies he suspected would be watching the dock area. To further separate them from the strange antics of the Learjet, Grimaldi would finish what they called the "rich kids entry" by finally breaking his radio silence. As he flew away, he'd inform the tower that he'd just won a thousand-dollar bet from one of his fraternity brothers on board by pulling off the landing. Then he'd make a few rude comments in reference to Basilan security to complete the ruse.

Grimaldi and Tom Fairbanks would be halfway back across the Pacific Ocean before Isabela even got any chase planes into the air.

Bolan had split the party into two groups to further avoid suspicion. Taking Reverte and Taboada with him, he had ordered Latham to leave the rocks thirty minutes later with Parks. Now, as he led the two men into the city of Basilan, he saw that the authorities weren't likely to put much effort into investigating the mysterious Learjet landing. From the looks of things they already had their hands full right here in town.

"It's the festival of Lami-Lamihan," Taboada told the Executioner when he asked. They walked along the edge of the city, following the docks, passing more of the stilt houses such as the one Mario Subing had inhabited in Rio Hondo. "And this is the small celebration. The big one is in Lamitan on the other side of the island.

Bolan nodded as they walked along. Taboada had at least a working knowledge of the island and when asked he had suggested the city's old mosque as a place to meet up with

the other two men. The Executioner let a hard smile come over
his face as he saw the building in the distance. It seemed that
every city and village in the Philippines, regardless of size,
had what they called the "old mosque."

Everywhere he looked, Bolan saw masses of colors. Men,
women and children flocked along the streets dressed in pic-
turesque native attire. They passed a small park where men
dressed as nineteenth-century Sulu warriors danced a ram-
bunctious mock battle with swords, highly decorated war gir-
dles, tunics and brightly woven pants. Equally ornamented
spiked helmets covered their heads. Their blades slashed the
air and their feet kept time to the music coming from stringed
instruments just off the dance area. The atmosphere of the city
was Casbah-like, and it was hard to believe it really was the
twenty-first century.

The trio walked on, passing stand after stand that sold not
only the Yakans's intricate geometric-patterned weavings but
other native crafts, souvenirs, food and beverages. They
stopped as a parade of men dressed similarly to the dancers
passed, then walked on along the shore, passing a colony of
Badjao—or sea gypsy—houses.

Bolan stopped outside the mosque. The other two men fell
in at his sides. All around them, the festival continued as they
waited for Latham and Parks to arrive.

On his back, the Executioner wore a very touristy-looking
backpack. But the contents were anything but that which the
average tourist would carry. Hiding beneath the canvas was
the Calico with both the 50- and 100-round magazines re-
filled. Extra ammo for both the Desert Eagle and Beretta had
been stuffed into the backpack's side pockets.

Bolan leaned up against the handrail separating them from
the water. Taboada and Reverte did the same at his sides.
Caucasians stood out like a lima bean in a bowl of black-eyed

peas on this small island and their cover stories had changed to fit the new surroundings. As soon as Latham and Parks arrived they would join Bolan as American businessmen taking a side trip from Manila. Taboada would play the part of their native guide who had brought them down to see the festival, and Reverte, with his dark looks and command of the language, would be portraying his cousin who was along as added muscle—insurance against robbers, kidnappers and murderers. Such arrangements were common on this island where shootings and other skirmishes between the government and Yakan rebel factions were practically a daily affair.

Far ahead in the crowd, the Executioner finally saw Latham and Parks making their way through the throngs of people. The two men were dressed similarly to Bolan with Latham substituting a khaki shirt for the Executioner's chambray and wearing blue jeans rather than cargo pants. Parks wore jeans, as well, with a baggy cutoff sweatshirt covering the S&W Model 640 .357 Magnum pistol Grimaldi had given him.

Latham and Parks were still a half a block away when the Executioner saw two uniformed police officers cut through the crowd and reach up, grabbing the men by the collars. They hustled them off to the side, to a green bench beneath a tree, away from the crowd. The uniformed men could only be described as tiny compared to the Americans. But they roughly pushed both Latham and Parks to sitting positions on the bench.

It had all happened so quickly that John Parks looked as if he had just awakened from a dream. Bolan saw a dead-pan expression on Latham's face, the result of good training and experience.

Reverte stepped in at the Executioner's side. "We'd better get out of here before they get us, too," he said.

"Wait," Bolan said.

"Are you crazy?" Reverte said. "There's no point in all of

us getting busted. Maybe we can figure out a way to get them out of jail later. But for now—I'm cuttin' out." He turned away from the Executioner and started to take a step.

Bolan reached out and grabbed the man's arm, jerking him back. "I said *wait,*" he ordered. "This is nothing but routine hassle."

And it did look that way to the Executioner. It looked like two diminutive men wearing badges who were resentful of bigger men, and especially bigger Americans. He suspected they'd do their best to frighten Latham and Parks, hoist their own egos up a couple of notches in the process, then let them go. It would be best if they could get out of this mess without the cops putting them together with him, Taboada, and Reverte. On the other hand, he didn't intend to let them get carted off to jail if things looked as though they were headed that way.

Taboada stepped up to Bolan's other side as the police officers strutted back and forth in front of the two men, stopping long enough to fire questions at them, then walking away before they got an answer. It was an age-old tactic used by cops the world over to intimidate foreigners. Get them good and scared first, then ask your questions.

After two minutes of strutting and yelling, the cops finally stood still. Both Latham and Parks reached into their pockets and pulled out their passports. The officers kept their hands on their pistol grips as the IDs were produced. Then they carefully scrutinized the pictures, looking back and forth from the passports to the men on the bench several times, then trading documents and starting all over. Only when both cops suddenly produced handcuffs did the Executioner decide to intervene.

Turning to Taboada, he said, "You know how to play it?"

"As if we just lost them?"

"Yeah. Let's go."

Bolan let Taboada lead the way. He and Reverte followed. As they neared the bench, the Filipino said, "Gentlemen! I thought we had lost you!" Though he couldn't see it, the Executioner suspected the former Tiger had a big smile on his face.

The police officers turned to face them as they stopped in front of the bench. Both spoke English. "And who are you?" demanded one with black horn-rimmed glasses. He stood about 5'2" in height.

"I am helping these men see the sights," Taboada said. "We were separated when the parade came through."

"You are a guide?" asked the other cop, a tiny man who would have done well to break the five-foot barrier on the height chart.

Taboada hesitated, then said, "Oh, no. Not an official guide. Just a friend."

Bolan approved the words silently in his head. If Taboada had said he was a guide, they would demand to see his license, and although there were probably two dozen unlicenced guides within spitting distance right now, it was something the cops could always pull out of their hats if they wanted to cause them problems.

"Let me see your license!" ordered the shorter of the two short men.

Taboada smiled broadly again. "My *friend* license?" he asked. "I was not aware being a friend required a license."

The little man back-handed the former Tiger across the mouth, splitting his lip. Blood ran down his chin.

Bolan stepped forward, slumping as best he could to make himself seem smaller. He had seen men like these two the world over, and it didn't matter what the color of their skin might be or what country they were from. They were angry that they hadn't grown taller and would take that anger out on any tall man they encountered if given the opportunity.

But slumping had its limits, and still the Executioner towered over the two men like Gulliver in the land of the Lilliputians. "Excuse me, Officers," he said politely. "We didn't know he needed a license, and I don't believe he knew, either."

The man with the horn-rimmed spectacles had dropped his hand to a long wooden baton on his gun belt as soon as he saw Bolan. But before he could pull the stick the Executioner had reached into his pocket and pulled out his roll of bills. "We're Yankees and not real smart," he said with a smile. "Can we pay the licensing fee directly to you?"

The cops's eyes fell to the money and their brains switched from tall and short to rich and poor. Bolan flicked a pair of one thousand peso bills off the roll and extended them to the man with the glasses. "I'm not sure how much the license costs," he said.

"Twice that," the cop said, snatching the money from the Executioner's hand and sliding it into the front pocket of his pants. "You give the other half to my partner."

Bolan handed the cop another pair of thousand peso bills.

When the little man reached up to take the bills he paused, for the first time noticing the blood on the back of his hand. It had come from Taboada's lips when he'd backhanded the former Tiger, and now he dropped it to his side and took the money with his other hand. He pocketed the bills but then turned back to stare toughly at Taboada. Without another word the cops turned and melted into the crowds.

BOLAN WATCHED THE COPS fade into the distance.

When he was certain the cops wouldn't return, he pulled out of his pocket the piece of scratch pad they had found in the plantation house. Looking down at the white lettering under the thin coat of pencil lead, he read the top line: Just below that he saw that the same hand had signed the note with a single initial: *A.*

Gathering the men around him at the edge of the crowd, Bolan said, "We've got to find Alano Street."

Latham reached into his back pocket and pulled out another folded piece of paper. It shone with some kind of preservative treatment as he unfolded it, and said, "I picked up a map of the island a minute ago. Guy at one of the stands was selling them." He handed the map to Bolan.

The Executioner found Alano on the legend to the side of the page, then used the coordinates beside it to find the street. It looked to be only a few blocks from where they stood in front of the old mosque. "Let's go," he said, and took off through the crowd.

The people gradually thinned out as they reached the edge of the festival. Latham hurried up next to Bolan on the cracked concrete sidewalk and said, "You don't figure they've actually got the hostages at this address, do you? I mean, they couldn't be that stupid to leave the address lying around, would they?"

Bolan held the paper up in front of him as they walked. "They didn't leave the address lying around," he said. "You stenciled it out of the next page, remember?"

They reached a corner, dropped down off the sidewalk to the street and moved on. "Yeah," Latham said. "But I mean, this just doesn't seem like a convenient place to hide hostages." He glanced around him. "In town, I mean, when there are so many remote and deserted sites open to them in these islands."

Bolan nodded. "I agree," he said. "I doubt we're going to find any hooded missionaries at this address. But it's all we've got to go on." He stopped as they reached a street the map promised would be Alano, and the other men stopped behind them. "But I'll be happy just to find someone there whose first initial is *A*, or any other letter for that matter, who can point us toward them." He turned to Parks, Reverte and Taboada behind him. The Filipino was walking next to Parks and the former Tiger and missionary seemed to be deep in conversation. "If all five of us walk up to the door together it's going to look like a SWAT operation," he said. "You three—Parks, Latham and Reverte. Stay here. Reynaldo and I'll go check things out first."

The Executioner had seen a number on one of the cross streets they had passed and knew Number 47 should be in the middle of the block to their right. He walked at a moderate pace along the sidewalk past small stores and shops—some permanent, others handcarts that would be whisked away at the close of the day. The area was relatively quiet. The action today was down at the festival.

The numerals four and seven were easy to see on what looked like an abandoned storefront on the other side of the street. But the windows were dark and covered with dust. Bolan said, "Keep walking," out of the side of his mouth and the two men walked on to the corner.

"I couldn't see anything," Taboada said.

"I did. On the side of the building." Bolan crossed the street to the other side and they walked back toward the darkened windows. "A staircase between the buildings leads up to the second floor." A few seconds later they passed the store front again. Bolan kept his eyes forward in case anyone was watching but studied the steps in his peripheral vision. They were old and made of iron and covered in rust. Like the windows, each step was covered in dirt, except for the middle where feet went up and down.

The store might have been abandoned, but whatever was on the second floor was still being used.

The Executioner led the way back to the other men and told them what he'd seen. "I'm going back," he said, then looked at Latham, Reverte and Parks. He would take one of the men with him up the steps. The other three could follow thirty seconds behind and cover outside windows and any other exits on the other side of the building. Latham was the man he'd have chosen to go with him under normal conditions. But both Taboada and Reverte needed to be carefully watched, and someone needed to look after Parks to make sure the well-meaning missionary didn't get himself killed.

Bolan watched Reverte out of the corner of his eye. Whatever it was the man did that bugged him, he was still doing it. And no matter how repentant and contrite Taboada might be acting, he didn't dare let himself forget that the man had been a Tiger himself only a day earlier. Billy Reverte might not be the only good actor in the Executioner's troupe.

The Executioner looked down at Taboada. "Ready?"

"Ready."

"Bring up the rear," Bolan told Latham. "Cover the downstairs and don't come up until I call for you." He paused. "Check to see if there's a window on the other side and post somebody there if there is."

Latham nodded.

Bolan and Taboada took off again, crossing the street and walking casually toward Number 47. When they reached the darkened glass, the Executioner cut to the side of the store and stepped up onto the first step. The ancient iron screamed in protest under his weight, so there would be no sneaking up the stairs. If there was to be any surprise at all on his side now, he would have to create it himself with speed.

The Executioner took the rest of the stairs three at a time and reached the second story of the building in three leaps. He had left the Calico in his backpack to avoid attracting attention on the street, but now the Beretta leaped into his hand. Behind him, he heard Taboada's feet pounding the iron.

An old wooden door, the upper half glass, stood at the top of the steps. The window was as dark as the ones below and Bolan started to press his face to the glass to peer inside. But the warning system in his brain told him to stop. And he listened to it, taking a quick half step to the side as the glass exploded where his face had been.

The bullet whizzed past as the window collapsed in front of him. The roar was low but distinct behind the door.

Bolan kicked the door with his foot, sending it flying back on its hinges. He crouched low as he charged through the opening into the dark room, his brain registering a light somewhere further back in the building. As his eyes tried to adjust to the darker environment, he saw a blurry shadow in the corner of what looked like an apartment living room. Another shot rang out, brushing past his arm. The shadow suddenly lit up with the muzzle-flash.

The Executioner aimed slightly to his left of the flash, guessing that the man behind the weapon was right-handed. And strangely, as he pulled the trigger, he thought of Reverte. The CIA man was left-handed he suddenly realized, and that had been what bothered him. Each time the CIA agent used his left hand instead of his right, the Executioner got the feeling something was wrong. But why? Being left-handed was no big deal. Why did the simple fact that Reverte favored his left over his right send warning signals to the Executioner's brain?

Now wasn't the time to try to figure it out. But this sudden awareness reminded Bolan that the man shooting at him now might be a southpaw, as well. He swung the Beretta to the other side of the muzzle-flash and fired again.

At least one of his shots hit its target and the Executioner heard a grunt on the other side of the room. The dark form behind the muzzle-flash collapsed and a thud sounded as it hit the floor.

Bolan's vision was in something of a state of shock—first by the darkness, then by the sudden burst of flame from the other gun. His pupils didn't know whether to dilate or to contract, and the result was nearly temporary blindness. But as they did for blind men the world over, his other senses suddenly went to double-time in an attempt to take up the slack.

A sound to his left. A footstep on a wooden floor? Yes. Down a hall? Probably. The thin, hollow sound made it sound like it. The Executioner turned that way, the Beretta in front of him. But good people as well as bad made footsteps and he refused to fire until he knew at whom he was firing.

A whiff of body odor floated through the air. A man in need of a bath. A pair of clicking sounds now snapped at his ears. They were clicks Bolan had heard more than once over the years and there were no other sounds exactly like them in the world.

The clicks were made when someone cocked both hammers on a double-barreled shotgun.

Bolan closed his eyes. More light—even brighter than that which had temporarily blinded him—was about to flash, and there was no sense in slowing down his eye's adjustment further. Aiming instinctively at the noise, he pulled the trigger again.

A trio of 9 mm rounds jumped from the Beretta 93-R. They had to have hit home. The Executioner heard the stagger of feet on the wood, then the blast of a shotgun roaring through the air.

As soon as the gun had fired, the Executioner opened his eyes again. He found that most of his sight had returned. He could see another dark blob—man-shaped—on the floor down a hallway. A double-barreled shotgun lay on the floor in front of the man. One of the shotgun's hammers was still cocked. The other rested against the firing pin. White dust and pieces of plaster rained from above, and when he looked up his vision had cleared enough to see the huge 12-gauge hole in the ceiling. His 3-round burst from the Beretta had struck the shotgunner dead-center in the chest, causing him to jerk the gun upward toward the ceiling. It had gone off almost directly over his head.

Bolan heard a footstep behind him and turned around. Taboada. "Are you okay?" he asked the man.

"Yes," the Filipino replied.

"How's your eyesight?"

"It's okay. I wasn't through the door yet when the shot went off in the front room."

"Then come on." The Executioner moved slowly forward, the Beretta still in front of him. He passed a kitchen area, sweeping the machine pistol across it before turning back to the hall. By the time he reached the body on the floor his eyes were working perfectly again. He reached down, lifted the shotgun and lowered the cocked hammer. Jamming a finger into the neck of the man on the floor, he felt no pulse. So he dropped the scattergun back to the floor, out of his way.

Bolan hoped this wasn't the man who had signed the note *A*. But the gold-and-onyx initial ring on the corpse's right hand displayed that letter in Old English, and he didn't like his odds that it wasn't.

There was only one other door out of the hallway, and it was closed. But what little light there was in the apartment had come from under its threshold.

"Cover the front," Bolan whispered over his shoulder. He moved on to the closed door, silently pressing his ear to the wood. On the other side, he could hear someone in the room trying hard not to breathe. Behind him, he heard Taboada doing the same thing. He reached out slowly and twisted the knob. Locked.

Quietly stepping back with his left foot, Bolan brought his right up to his knee, then shot it forward in a front thrust kick. His heel struck just below the knob and the strength of the kick ripped the door all the way off its hinges. It flew back into the room as if it were a sail caught by the wind. The Executioner leaped into the room with the Beretta gripped in both hands. A lamp next to the bed had been the source of the light and in its glow he saw the source of the restrained breathing.

Seated on the edge of the bed, an olive-skinned baby wrapped in a light blue blanket pressed to her breast, was a blond-haired woman in a nightgown.

IN THE HALLWAY, Bolan heard the now-familiar gait of Taboada's feet on the floor. Then the footsteps paused, and a second later the former Tiger screamed out some kind of lament in Tagalog.

Bolan turned to look back through the doorway. Taboada was kneeling next to the man who had wielded the shotgun. Tears dripped from his eyes as he cradled the man's head in his arms.

The Executioner could never have explained how he knew. Maybe it was just several pieces of evidence suddenly gelling in his mind—the note at the plantation signed with the letter *A,* the initial ring on the man's hand and the memory of Taboada telling him about his friend from the orphanage who had also linked up with Subing. But however it came to him, Bolan suddenly knew that the *A* stood for Angelo.

Taboada looked up at him. With one eye on the former Tiger and the other on the woman with the baby, the Executioner tightened his grip on the Beretta. The former Tiger was showing signs that he might be trustworthy, but now Bolan had just killed his best friend. Would the turn he'd made in life stand up to that?

Reynaldo looked back down at the dead man in his arms, then waved the Executioner on. Bolan stepped back into the bedroom, quickly checking the open closet and under the bed to make sure no surprises waited for him in either place. Confident that the room was secure, he hurried back to the doorway as Taboada stood.

Bolan studied the man's face as the former Tiger walked forward. It was a mask of grief, but the Executioner saw no desire for revenge in the man's eyes. Instead his head dropped toward the floor as if it had been held by a string that was suddenly cut.

"Angelo," Bolan said.

His gaze on the floor, Taboada just nodded.

"Is he dead?" came the voice of the woman on the bed.

Bolan had stood sideways in the door so he could watch her as well as the hallway. He nodded. But in addition to her light yellow hair, the woman's voice betrayed a hint of Scandinavian accent, and the Executioner was reminded of the big blond-haired man who had been with the Tigers at the plantation. Both he and this woman were as out of place in the Philippines as a bottle of vodka at an Alcoholics Anonymous meeting.

Taboada stepped past the Executioner into the room. His face was still wet with tears when he said, "He was my best friend. From the orphanage."

The blond woman was taken aback. "Reynaldo?" she asked.

Now it was Taboada who was taken by surprise again. "Zona?"

The woman looked at Bolan. "I am...was...Angelo's wife."

The Executioner stared into the woman's eyes. They were vacant—not stoned or high or drunk, just listless.

Taboada stared at the bed. "This is Angelo's son?" he asked, still astounded.

Nodding looked as if it took Zona's last ounce of strength. "Yes."

Again, she turned to the Executioner to explain further. "Reynaldo and I only met once," she said. "Before I realized I had been sentenced to a life in Hell."

She had spoken enough now that the Executioner recognized her accent as Swedish. She looked past both men, trying to see into the hallway. Bolan knew that the angle at which she sat, her husband's body wouldn't be visible. "He is dead?" Zona asked again. It seemed as if she was having a hard time believing it.

"He is," Bolan said.

"Good," she said with the same inflection someone might have when asking for the time of day. She pulled the baby away from her chest and placed him gently on the bed before pulling her nightgown back up over her breast.

Bolan looked over at Taboada. He still saw no signs that the former Tiger held the Executioner responsible for Angelo's death. "Go tell the others to come upstairs," he told the man, and the Filipino turned to leave.

The soldier holstered the Beretta and took a seat next to the woman on the bed. "You don't seem too upset about your husband."

Zona gave him a tired, forced half-smile. "Should I be?" she said. "When I have been kept prisoner in this godforsaken Third World country since we married? Forced to use twelfth-century plumbing and treated like property?" She picked up the baby again and hugged it to her. "Had it not been for this little one I would have killed myself long ago." She hugged the baby harder, then looked up into Bolan's eyes. "You have freed us both. I shall be eternally grateful to you." She stood. "But now, I am ready to leave before I wake up and find it has all been a dream."

Bolan reached out and gently took her arm. "Please," he said. "Not so fast. If you're eternally grateful to me I'll let you prove it."

Zona sighed wearily. "Let me put the baby down," she said. She set the child on the bed and started to take off her nightgown.

The Executioner reached out and grabbed her arm again. "You took that the wrong way."

Zona's eyebrows furrowed.

Looking at her closer now, the Executioner could see the fear behind the uncaring attitude she was using to try to hide it. He suspected that Zona had been abused beyond words. Her automatic assumption that he expected sex as a gratuity, and even more her immediate resignation to giving it to him, was proof.

"Do you want to tell me your story or do you want me to tell you?" Bolan asked.

The blond woman frowned. "How would you know my story?"

"I don't know the details," the Executioner said. "But here it is in a nutshell—you went to the U.S. to go to college. While you were there you met this Angelo. You fell in love and got married. You were both planning to stay in America, but Angelo wanted to come home for a visit and let you meet the family."

Zona had nodded after each sentence. "And once we were here," she started to finish for the Executioner.

But Bolan completed the story on his own. "You were here for good."

"Exactly."

Bolan looked at the blond hair. It was dull, dirty, lifeless, but he suspected at one time it had shone. Assuming she was roughly the same age as Angelo, and assuming Angelo was roughly the same age as Reynaldo, her skin had wrinkled far beyond her years. Earlier he had noted the listlessness in her pale blue eyes but now he also saw an austerity, a self-imposed meltdown of the ability to feel emotion because every emotion she had was too painful.

In his heart, the Executioner hurt for her. She had been helpless. And she had been used.

But what was even worse was the fact that she was going to have to be used again. This time, by him. He hated to do it, and he would be as gentle as possible. But he could see no other way to stay on the trail of the hostages and physical survival had to outweigh a little more emotional discomfort.

"Zona," Bolan said, "I wish I could just let you go, but I can't. Not yet anyway." He turned to look at her again and saw that she was still not convinced this was not leading to some kind of sexual overture. "But I promise you this—as soon as I don't need your help anymore, I'll buy you and your son a first-class ticket back to Stockholm or anyplace else you want to go."

Still wary, Zona said, "What is it you want?"

"The Liberty Tigers," the Executioner said. "What can you tell me about them?"

Zona shrugged. "No more than everyone else knows," she said hesitantly. "Probably not as much as you know yourself if you're asking that question."

"Your husband was a member?" Bolan asked.

Zona had already taken a seat next to him and now she crossed her legs. The baby had fallen asleep, and she laid him out behind them on the bed again, first making sure he was wrapped well in the blue blanket. "He didn't tell me such things," she said. "At least not after we came here from America. When we were there, before we married, he told me everything. Or at least I thought he did."

Bolan remained silent as the woman stopped talking. He

watched her eyes redden and the skin around them swelled slightly, taking on a puffy look. But she was beyond tears.

"He was a different person in the United States," Zona went on. "He was kind. Gentle. That changed as soon as we got here." Her eyes were still dry but she rubbed the back of her hand across the lids anyway, as if it was a habit that had developed back in the days when she could still cry, could still feel. "I fell in love with the man who was in America with me. He was a liar. I was a fool."

Bolan could tell how fragile she was and let her ramble on. He was no psychiatrist but, as John Parks and Tom Fairbanks had been when he'd first rescued them, she looked to be a half step away from a nervous breakdown if he pushed too hard, too fast. But time was passing and he wanted to get back to the subject at hand. "Okay," he said. "He didn't tell you what he was up to. Tell me what he did for a living."

"He said he sold weavings," Zona said. "But I never saw any sign of it." She snorted.

"He did strange things. Mysterious things he wouldn't talk about. He came and went at all hours. Sometimes when he came home he was so excited he couldn't sleep. Once I found blood on his shirt. But I didn't ask him about it. I just did my best to wash it out. If I asked questions, he—" She stopped talking suddenly and a tear finally crept into the corner of her eye as the emotional wall she had built around her heart began to lower. The lone tear called the Executioner's attention to that eye, and it was only then that he noticed the lingering pale blue and gray around the socket.

A week ago she'd had a fairly bad shiner.

Bolan glanced out into the hall as he heard footsteps coming up the steps. Nonchalantly he reached up and began to scratch his chest, putting his hand within inches of the Beretta. One of the interesting aspects of this mission had been trying to determine who you could trust and who you couldn't. He had almost gotten to the point where he felt he could rely on Taboada, and then he'd been forced to shoot the former Tiger's childhood friend, which made it a whole new ball game.

Latham led Reverte, Parks and Taboada into the room, and the four men started to look around for seats. Bolan shook his head at Parks, Latham and Reverte, but gave the Filipino a nod to stay. All five men at once would intimidate the Swedish woman. But Taboada had a direct link to her through her husband. And besides, the Executioner wanted a chance to read the former Tiger's reaction to his friend's death a little better, too. The thought of catching a bullet in the back the first time the little Filipino got the chance hadn't left his mind yet.

Taboada found the only chair in the room and sat facing the bed. The other three men went back out into the living room. The Executioner resumed the interview. "You know why we're here?" he asked Zona.

The new widow shook her head.

"The hostages. The missionaries. We're looking for them."

Zona lowered her eyebrows. "Everyone said they were someplace on Mindanao."

"They were," Bolan said. "They've been separated. We think at least some of them may be here. On Basilan."

Zona stared at him, her green eyes clearing. Now the Executioner could see that at one time, before the harsh life on this island had taken its toll, she had been a knockout. With any luck maybe she could be again someday. Maybe she would still find a husband who loved her, and who would make a good father to the baby.

"You think the missionaries are here?" she asked.

Bolan pulled out the paper with the pencil tracing and showed it to her. "We found this in a house with two of the missionaries," he said.

Zona stared at the page. "That's this address," she said, frowning. "And that's Angelo's handwriting." She looked up and her eyes widened in confusion. "But why would he give them this address? The missionaries have never been here."

"My guess is that Angelo just gave it to them so they could contact him," Bolan said. "I imagine he found some other place—some better place—to take the hostages. You said he came and went. Was he on Mindanao a few days ago?"

"I don't know," Zona said. "He was gone. He could have been."

"It would have been day before yesterday," the Executioner said.

Zona shrugged, and for the first time Bolan noticed how thin she was. In the U.S. or any other major nation, he'd have guessed she suffered from anorexia nervosa. But here, kept against her will as if she were a common criminal or a pet who no longer caught her owner's fancy, he suspected she was just half starved. "I told you," she said. "I don't know. He came and went as he pleased. He was gone for a few days. That was one of them." She paused. "He left Francisco to keep an eye on me. You could ask him."

"The other man who was here?" Bolan asked.

Zona nodded.

"He's in the living room," the Executioner said. "I don't think he's going to say much of anything."

Zona might have been suffering from malnutrition but her brain was coming back and she understood what Bolan meant. "Good," she said. "I had to fight off his advances whenever Angelo was gone."

Taboada hadn't said anything since the others had left the room. But now he said, "Angelo put up with that? The Angelo I knew would have killed—"

"Angelo never knew," Zona said. "But he was no longer the

Angelo you knew, either. Trust me when I say that if I had told him he would have beaten me. He would have said I led Francisco on."

Bolan glanced at Taboada. The former Tiger lowered his eyes. Each new thing the Executioner heard about this Angelo made him a little bit happier that he'd killed the man. The world—especially Zona's world—was going to be a better place from now on.

"Zona," Bolan said, "think hard on this next question. It's important. If you needed a place to hide out on this island, and needed to keep maybe three white-faced Americans hidden at the same time, where would you go?"

The Swedish woman's response was immediate. "I don't know," she said. "I was hardly ever allowed to leave this room, let alone roam the island."

Bolan took in a deep breath. "Try to think," he said again. "Think of any places Angelo might have mentioned—"

"I told you," Zona said. "He told me nothing. Unless he wanted sex. Then he told me that."

"Something you might have overheard him tell Francisco, then," the Executioner pressed. "Or something he might have mentioned to somebody else." He paused. "Maybe it didn't seem important to you at the time. But it could be now."

Zona closed her eyes. Behind her, the baby stirred.

The Executioner glanced at the child, happy that in a few days—maybe even in a few hours—both mother and son would be flying to Sweden.

Finally, Zona opened her eyes again. "I don't know if this will make any sense at all," she said. "It's just something I overheard from the living room when I was changing the baby one day. For some reason it struck me as strange. Maybe just because I'd never heard the voice of the man Angelo was talking to before."

248   FALSE FRONT

"Tell us," Bolan said.

She did.

The Executioner felt himself tense. "You didn't see the man your husband was talking to?"

"No, but Angelo said his name several times. I remember that, too, because it seemed like such a sissy name for a man."

"What was it," Bolan asked.

"Candy," Angelo's widow said.

The Executioner pulled out his sat phone. They were going to need another plane.

CHAPTER ELEVEN

The Executioner led the way out of the jungle toward the drug plane landing strip again. A light breeze drifted across the clearing, bringing with it the pungent odor of decaying bodies, and then Bolan remembered that Grimaldi had tossed the dead drug dealers into the foliage the day before.

For what seemed like the hundredth time during the past two days, the Executioner made his way down the creek bank that separated the path from the landing zone. It hadn't rained since they'd left, and while the creek area would still be called muddy by most standards, it wasn't nearly the slippery slide it had been the day before.

Bolan crossed the creek bed, hearing the rest of his party begin the downward slope behind him. As soon as Zona had told him about the conversation she'd overheard between her husband and the man called "Candy," he had contacted Jack Grimaldi, on standby in Manila.

The Executioner hurried up the other creek bank to the landing strip. After Grimaldi's unauthorized landing on Basilan, he hadn't wanted to chance a Stony Man plane coming to the Isabela airport, so they'd taken the ferry back to Mindanao. The only interesting thing about the boat ride had been when Latham had cornered him to tell him that as soon as he and Taboada had headed up the steps at Angelo and Zona's apartment, the CIA man had pulled out his sat phone and called Langley again. "Progress report," Reverte had told the Texan before scurrying off under the building to be by himself.

That was possible, Bolan knew. But it seemed strange that the man only called in when the Executioner was out of earshot. It might just be that the man was trying to make sure he got the credit for the operation when it was over. But to the Executioner, it seemed there had to be something else going on. "I want to check that phone," he'd told Latham. "We need to—"

"Already have." The Texan grinned. He'd looked over his shoulder to make sure Reverte couldn't see him and then reached into his pocket, pulling out the man's sat phone. "My old man was a Texas Ranger," he'd said proudly, then, in a voice almost as proud, added, "But Grandpa Latham was a pickpocket in Baltimore."

Bolan had quickly checked the phone's call memory and found it had been erased. Aaron Kurtzman could probably find a way to bring up the numbers if he could have gotten the thing back to Stony Man Farm, but he couldn't. So Reverte's sat phone had gone over the side of the ferry into the water.

As Bolan reached the end of the landing strip, he heard the distant roar of a Learjet descending through the sky. A moment later, the plane came into view. He herded Latham, Reverte, Taboada, John Parks, Zona and her baby to the side of the isolated runway. As they waited for Grimaldi to touch down, he watched the Swedish woman adjust the blue blanket around the child. "Shh, Edward," Zona whispered to the boy in her arms. "Quiet now. Go back to sleep."

A few minutes later the jet's tires hit the packed-earth runway and the plane taxied toward them. Bolan ushered the rest of the party on board, then dropped into the seat next to the pilot.

"Where to this time, Sarge?" Grimaldi asked.

Bolan spoke as Jack began to turn the Learjet around for takeoff. "You know Bongao?" he asked.

"Sulus. In the Tawi-Tawi group? It's the main island, right?"

"Right," Bolan said. "You familiar with it?"

They had completed the U-turn and now the Learjet was picking up speed. "Just from the map," Grimaldi said.

"Then you'd better look at the map, because that's where we're headed."

He turned in his seat, addressing the men and woman crowded into the seats behind him. "As soon as we're in the air, you can take turns at the lavatory," he said. "But it's a short flight so everybody make it quick." Without waiting for an answer he turned back around. As the jet left the ground, he closed his eyes.

Bolan had learned over the years that flight time might be his only chance for rest during the course of a mission and had taught himself to take advantage of it. Ten seconds after the jet left the ground, he was asleep. He didn't know how long he was out when he came to again. But he knew what had awakened him without having to turn around. He had heard the same noise before, earlier, in the jungle between the Rio Hondo mosque and the stilt house where Mario Subing lived.

The Executioner twisted in his seat to see Latham sitting directly behind him. The Texan's snores weren't only loud enough to awaken him, they'd have driven a rock into consciousness. Taboada and Reverte were staring at the man. John Parks was trying not to laugh and Zona had cupped her hands protectively over Edward's ears.

Even Grimaldi, with his headset on, could hear the snoring. He glanced to his side at Bolan, then said, "Hey, forget about your 'Shock and Awe' bombings. Next time the U.S. gets in a war, let's just send him. We could have saved the U.S. millions by just renting him a hotel room in downtown Baghdad."

The Learjet hit an air pocket and bounced up and down. Latham came to with a jerk and the straw cowboy hat that he'd pulled down over his face went tumbling into his lap. He blinked twice, looked around at all of the faces staring at him, and said, "What?"

Bolan turned back to the front. Below, he could see a large landmass. To his right were the blue waters of the Sulu Sea and on the other side of the island the waves from the Celebes Sea lapped toward shore. The Sulu Archipelago was divided into two provinces with the major island in each serving as its capital. They were passing over Jolo Island at the moment and would soon see Tawi-Tawi, the long narrow strip of land where Bongao was located.

The Executioner turned back to the front. Zona had only heard bits and pieces of the conversation between her husband and "Candy," whom Bolan had to assume was Subing. She had heard them talking about Mount Bongao, a mountainous outcrop located just outside the village. From what she had gathered there was a hiking trail that led to the summit where a royal Muslim cemetery was located. Candy had told her husband it was roughly halfway up and to the right or left. He was to look for a red rock.

Then, as if they had suddenly realized they might be overheard, Zona had told the Executioner that their voices had dropped to whispers.

"We've got ten minutes," Grimaldi said, breaking into the Executioner's thoughts.

The soldier closed his eyes again, but this time it wasn't to sleep. His face tightened as he replayed for the hundredth time what Zona had told him. "It is roughly halfway up," Subing had said. Well, what was it? It was on the right hand side of the trail, and taken in context, it sounded as if this red rock was near *it* but was not *it* itself.

So what would he be looking for? Something hidden under the rock? Directions to where the hostages were, perhaps? Bolan's eyes shut tighter in concentration. Then there was the most upsetting question of all—did any of this even have anything to do with the hostages in the first place? The imprisoned missionaries had to be the prime topic of conversation between Zona's husband and Candido Subing. But it didn't have to be the only thing they talked about and he could be setting off right now on a wild-goose chase.

The Executioner opened his eyes as the plane began to descend. The fact of the matter was that the only reason he was following this lead was that it was the only one he had. He twisted in his seat again and looked at the woman behind him who had her face buried in the blue blanket. She was whispering to the baby. Should he take them with him? Something might jog her memory if they ran dry at this red rock. On the other hand, she and little Edward might die, too.

Was it worth the risk? the Executioner wondered. Did he even have the right to make such a decision for her and her child?

"Good God, Sarge!" Grimaldi said, again breaking into the Executioner's thoughts. "I do believe that's a real live tarmac down there. I'm not sure I can even remember how to land on a strip that's not dirt or grass or sand."

Bolan didn't answer as the wheels hit the runway and glided smoothly to a halt. A man wearing ancient U.S. Navy bell-bottom jeans—the belt line was almost up to his armpits—ragged athletic shoes and a light blue shirt with a shining silver badge walked forward carrying a clipboard.

"Reynaldo," the Executioner said, "you come with me.

The rest of you stay on board until I call you." He opened the door and dropped down out of the jet.

The man with the clipboard stopped ten feet from the plane and stood there importantly, making the Executioner walk the rest of the way to him. Bolan heard Taboada's footsteps behind him.

Bolan gave the man—a Custom's official, he assumed, though the badge was so badly cast he couldn't read it, and the man wore no shoulder patches or other hints to his title— a friendly smile. "Hello," he said. "English?"

The man with the bright shiny badge shook his head, but was smiling, too. The Executioner read the situation quickly and turned to his companion. "Tell him we got off course. Tell him our pilot's incompetent."

Taboada spoke in Tagalog and the Customs man answered.

"He says there is usually a fine for such mistakes," he told the Executioner.

It was what Bolan had expected and he nodded. "Tell him we'd be happy to pay the fine, and that we'd like to refuel while we're here." He paused. "And tell him we'd like to rest for a few hours before taking off again. We'd also like to pay the fine right here if that's possible, and for his trouble—and directions to the nearest decent restaurant—we'd be happy to give him a finder's fee."

Moments later, Taboada turned back to Bolan. "He says it will be quite expensive."

Bolan shrugged and reached into his pocket. He pulled out his roll of thousand-peso bills, peeled five of them off, hesitated, then added one more. "Will this cover it all?" he asked.

Taboada translated and the man answered. "It will cover the fine and his fee," the former Tiger said, "but he is worried about your plane while you rest. There has been much trouble out of the rebels this far south. MILF and IJ both."

The Executioner knew what the man was after—more money to watch the plane. He didn't mind that, but he wanted to get this over with and get on with the job.

The Customs official mistook his hesitancy in answering for an unwillingness to part with more money. He was speaking directly to Taboada, and the former Tiger translated his words as, "He hopes no one destroys your airplane while you are away."

The Executioner smiled as the man did his best to squeeze the very last drop of blood out of the turnip. "Tell him I'll double the money to him when I get back if the plane is okay, the tank's filled and my pilot's ready to take off."

Another translation. A nod of the head above the shining silver badge and then the bills were quickly taken from the Executioner's hand and stuffed into a pants' pocket.

Bolan turned back to the plane. Opening the door he stood on the tarmac and started to speak but Grimaldi beat him to the punch. "Tsk, tsk. I *heard* that. 'Our pilot's incompetent.' I'll remind you of that next time I have to pull your fat out of the fire."

The Executioner chuckled as the rest of the passengers in the Learjet began to deplane. "Best I could come up with considering that about half of this crew has no papers," he said. Then, getting back to the point he added, "Jack, refuel this bird and keep her warmed up. I don't know when we'll be back. But when we are, we may need to get out of here in a hurry."

"Gotcha."

Bolan turned to Zona, who had just let Latham help her and the baby out of the plane. He still hadn't decided whether to take her with him on the mountain hiking trail or not. But it seemed Zona had decided for herself.

"This man," she said, nodding toward Grimaldi. "He can take care of a baby?"

The door to the passenger's side of the plane was still open and the Executioner looked up to see the ace pilot's face suddenly grow pale. "Sarge, I can't—" the pilot started to say.

"He can't *wait*," the Executioner said, grinning up at the pilot. "He loves children." He saw that Grimaldi's mouth had frozen in an open position.

Turning back to Zona, he said, "Just show him where the diapers are while I get everyone ready."

The Executioner moved to the side door and began to help the other men pull their backpacks out of the cargo area. As he did, he heard Zona explaining to Grimaldi that Edward could drink from a baby bottle, too.

SHE HAD FELT SOMETHING come over her several hours ago. She might have been asleep and dreaming, she wasn't sure. But while she could not explain it, Rachael Parks knew that something in her was different. A feeling. Or maybe more a knowledge. No, neither feeling nor knowledge fully explained it. It was both, and more, but while she couldn't put it into words—even in her mind—Rachael knew that her husband was all right.

She caught herself smiling behind the hood. Not one of her forced smiles, which she hoped would lead to the real thing, but a genuine smile of happiness. John was all right. Of course, what "all right" meant, exactly, she didn't know. She just had this hazy, cloudy, semiformed surreal picture floating through her mind that told her all was okay with John. Sometimes this idea, this thought, this knowledge tried to take a more substantive shape in her brain, and that's when she wondered if it hadn't come to her first in a dream. Maybe these fleeting glimpses of more concrete data were the bits and pieces that often come back after dreaming. When they came, Rachael pictured John being rescued by a band of angels, led by a grim-faced and determined Archangel Michael.

At other times Rachael wondered if this knowledge that John was okay might not mean he was dead. If that was the case then he had gone on to be with the Lord, and that meant he was all right, too. In fact, if John was in Heaven right now it meant that he was infinitely better off than she was; better off than anyone still walking the face of this planet.

Either way, there was a new peace in Rachael's heart and soul because "okay" meant "okay" both on Earth and in Heaven.

She closed her eyes behind the hood and silently mouthed, "Thank you, Lord."

Rachael heard the soft sobs coming from the woman next to her and whispered, "Kim?"

At first the other woman didn't answer. Then a timid voice said, "Yes."

"Are you all right?" Rachael asked.

Kim Tate snickered slightly, sobbed once more, then cleared her throat. Her voice cracked slightly as she whispered back, "Never been better, Rachael."

For a moment the words froze Rachael where she sat—if it was possible to be more frozen than she already was with her hands and feet still bound. What Kim had said was the epitome of dark humor, and Rachael had never heard her respond like that before. Then, softly, she heard Kim begin to laugh. So Rachael began to giggle, too. She knew it was crazy, but she couldn't help it. Here they were, after months of captivity, tied hand and foot all of the time, and kept in the dark with hoods over their heads, and Kim says she's never been better.

Rachael tried to stifle her giggles but they grew louder with the effort and she wondered if this sudden incongruous glee was another mental survival tool. But that thought seemed funny, too, and she decided that if she felt like having a good laugh she was just going to have it. "Hey, Kim," she whispered between twitters.

"What?" Kim asked.

"Think on the bright side," Rachael said. "Heaven is going to seem even better to us than most people."

And with that, the giggling of both women suddenly became riotous laughter. Rachael knew that they both might have just broken the bonds with sanity for good and that the laughter was hysterical; wailing in disguise. She also knew it might bring them a beating from their captors. But she no longer cared. She was having fun for the first time in what…ten months? Eleven months? Twenty years? She didn't know. But she'd had all of the fear and mournfulness she could take. She was in God's hands now and whatever happened to her was okay.

Suddenly the hood was ripped from her head and Rachael looked up, squinting into the light to see Candido Subing himself glaring down at her. The terrorist leaned down, close to her face and screamed the only word in English she'd ever heard him use.

"Silence!"

The way he said the word seemed now like the funniest thing Rachael had ever heard and instead of quieting down she threw back her head and cackled even louder. Next to her she could see that Kim's hood had been taken off, as well, and her fellow missionary thought it was pretty funny, too.

"Silence!" Kim shouted back at the man above them at the top of her lungs. Then she broke into hysterics again herself.

Subing pulled the sword sheathed on his belt. It was an ugly thing, Rachael had always thought. Long, like a kitchen knife she had once had, pointed at the end for sticking into people, she supposed. But now she looked at it and her eyes happened upon the handle where it stuck out from the end of his hand. It was made of wood, carved into a crude horse's head, and it suddenly made her think of the plastic toy horse her little brother had loved so dearly when they were kids.

"Horsey" her brother had called the toy—of course David had never been the most creative child. That thought brought another smile to her face because she loved her brother and she now remembered that he was never without Horsey and had cried when he'd been forced to leave it at home when they went to Sunday school. Candido Subing reminded her of David in that way—he was never without his little horsey sword, and she suspected he would cry if he couldn't wear it around all of the time. In her mind Rachael suddenly saw Subing, still looking like an adult but dressed as a little boy in a striped T-shirt and diaper, sitting cross-legged on the floor and playing with his horsey sword. And now the smile that had crept across her face exploded into laughter again, even as Subing raised the blade over his head and his eyes bored angry holes through her with the intensity of a laser beam.

Kim had to have seen the horsey on the sword, too, because she stopped laughing long enough to say, "Getty up! Getty up!" before breaking out into uncontrollable mirth again herself.

Rachel couldn't even stop laughing when the sword reached its full height, and she was sure that within the next second or two Subing would bring it down and cut off her head. Suddenly the whole situation just seemed too stupid to take seriously. Little men keeping them prisoner, demanding things from governments they should know they would never get, and playing with their horseys.

As the two women continued to cackle in their mind-cleansing, emotion-purifying, stress-purging release, Rachael watched the hatred in Candido Subing's eyes change to confusion. He had never seen them behave like this before. In the past, his threats had always produced fear. But now their uncontrollable laughter was telling him to go ahead and kill them if he wanted, that he had already taken everything else away from them so he might as well take their lives, too. Rachael could see on the terrorist's bewildered face that the leader of the Liberty Tigers had just realized he had nothing left with which to bargain, and she threw her head back, offering him her throat if he wanted it, as tears of joy ran down her cheeks. She laughed. And she heard Kim laugh with her. Both women laughed and laughed, and they didn't even stop when Candido Subing lowered the sword, turned around and stomped away.

He thinks we've finally lost our minds, Rachael thought as she did her best to curb her giddiness. Finally, after what seemed like hours but had probably been less than a minute, both Rachael's and Kim's laughter began to fade. As she regained control, Rachael became aware of the fact that, in addition to Subing, all of the other terrorists in the room had been staring at the two of them, too. Somehow, the laughing jag had unsettled them, and instead of the Tigers being feared, the missionary woman now saw that it was the Tigers who were afraid.

Rachael Parks felt something come over her again now that the outburst was over. It was a comforting feeling of peace, of love, and she was reminded of why she had come to the Philippines in the first place. She was a missionary, and God had sent her to spread the word to men just like those who stood in front of her in awe right now.

The laughter was over, but Rachael knew she was still smiling as she looked at the nearest terrorist and said in Tagalog, "You can kill us both if you want. Jesus will even forgive murder if you only ask Him to."

IT WAS QUITE AN ENTOURAGE he had picked up along the way on this mission, Bolan thought as he got out of the first of the two twenty-year-old Datsun taxis that had driven them to the hiking trail. He had one man who was not only a former terrorist but a former member of the very same outfit the Executioner was pursuing. He also had a CIA agent who had taken Shakespeare literally when the bard had said the whole world was a stage, and whose left-handedness kept ringing incomprehensible warning bells in the back of his brain. To that he could add a well-meaning minister who had never seen combat and the wife of a dead terrorist he had killed. Of the entire company Charlie Latham was the only one he knew he could both trust and count on when the bullets began to fly.

Bolan paid both cabdrivers. Across the road from the entrance to the hiking trail was a small building with public rest rooms and what looked like a curio shop. A 1940-looking telephone booth stood against the wall and Bolan glanced through the glass and noticed that some vandal had torn off the receiver and stolen it. A pretty minor crime in a country where kidnapping and murder were daily events.

The Executioner turned to where the others had stopped at the entrance to the hiking trail. A sign just to their side read in both Tagalog and English Mt. Bongao, 314 m. Business appeared to be slow at this out-of-the-way tourist trap and he could see only two other hikers. A late-middle-aged man and woman—American if the man's Oklahoma Sooners baseball cap and the woman's Penn State T-shirt were any indication— were adjusting their belt packs and getting ready to start the hike.

Bolan stopped in front of the others and looked them over carefully. "Everybody ready?" he asked the group.

"We all going?" Reverte asked innocently. But the fact that he had chosen to ask at all added fuel to Bolan's suspicion of the man.

"Yeah," Bolan said. "Why? You have something else you'd rather be doing?"

If the CIA man was covering himself rather than just acting honestly, he was good at it. Before he answered his eyes flickered to Parks, then back to Bolan. The message he was trying to convey was clear—John Parks might be more hindrance than help. But whether or not that had been the sincere meaning behind his question was up for grabs.

Reverte shook his head. "No, just wondering." He glanced to Parks once more.

"Then let's go," the Executioner said. "Keep your guns out of sight unless we need them." He turned toward the trail, which rose steeply at first, then leveled off considerably as it curved around the mountain. "Until then, we're still just tourists who got off course in our plane and we've decided to see the local attraction while we're here."

Bolan led the way up the well-worn trail, his boots pounding against earth that had been packed down by thousands, if not tens of thousands, of other feet. There were prints to follow but they meant nothing. Every sole tread imaginable had imprinted itself into the dirt at one time or another, which meant you couldn't differentiate a terrorist boot from a visiting Catholic nun's shoe.

Even though the trail was not difficult, the Executioner kept a moderate pace as he led the way. Latham was fit, and Taboada and Reverte also seemed to be. But Parks hadn't walked much for the past ten months and Zona didn't look as though she'd spent much time outside of the pathetic little room in which he'd found her kept prisoner. Even though the older couple seemed to have no trouble while they were still in sight, Bolan didn't want to get fifty yards into the trek and have the weaker members of his party gasping for air or trying to work out muscle cramps.

The Executioner rounded a curve and caught a brief glimpse of red in the distance. But it was moving, and the thought that it might be the red rock passed quickly out of his mind. A closer look told him it was the older man's red baseball cap. It disappeared around another bend in the trail as Bolan led them on. He nodded grimly to himself, slowing the pace even more to get distance between his group and the couple ahead. He wanted them well ahead and out of the way, when they found the red rock.

Birds took off in the trees overhead as they walked along the pathway. Bolan saw several of the fowl that had given the mountain its name. *Bangow* was a Tasaug word meaning heron. But the mountain seemed more full of monkeys than birds and simians of all sizes, shapes and colors scampered through the trees, chattering at Bolan and the others as if they were some invading army of occupation. From somewhere in the back of his mind, the Executioner pulled out a memory of one of the many legends concerning the creation of the islands. In an Atlas-like tradition it seemed that a weary giant had dropped a rocky ball of earth from his shoulders after which it had shattered and formed the 1900-kilometer chain.

A thin coat of sweat broke on the Executioner's brow as he continued to climb. But as they rose farther above sea level, the humidity began to drop and soon it had evaporated. They were near the southern end of the archipelago, in an area with no clearly defined wet and dry season. Monsoons seemed to come and go as they pleased, with an occasional typhoon thrown in for good measure. But today they were lucky and, while the day was hot, they stayed dry.

Bolan shifted his backpack as he walked, tightening the belt around his waist, then loosening it, as well as periodically adjusting the shoulder straps to redistribute the weight. Behind him, he hoped the others were doing the same. By his estimate they would be walking for more than half an hour on the uphill slope before they came to the area where the red rock was supposed to be. What they'd find then was anybody's guess. But he had at least two members of his party who were not combatants and he didn't need them exhausted and nursing sore backs, too.

The forest to both sides of the trail was thick with bright yellow narras—the national flower of the islands. But orchids of all colors lined their path, as well, creating a vivid atmosphere of beauty that sharply contrasted to the Executioner's mission. If looks were all that mattered, anyone walking along the trail might mistakenly think they'd found the Garden of Eden and never know that somewhere along this path lay a rock that linked the beauty to kidnapping, torture, murder and terrorism.

A Sulu hornbill seemed to jump out of a tree as Bolan passed beneath to wing its way up through the narrow passage between the trees directly above them. The Executioner's eyes followed the bird's flight and a dull rusty blob of color suddenly passed through his sight path. He jerked his head back toward the color. Ahead on the trail he could see a reddish outcropping through a break in the trees along the side of the mountain.

Bolan turned around to find that Latham was right behind him. Reverte came next with Zona, Taboada and John Parks bringing up the rear. The former hostage and his former guard seemed to have formed a bond and it looked as though they were engaged in another deep discussion.

Latham pulled out his tobacco can and took a dip as he looked past the Executioner. Bolan saw in the Texan's eyes that he had spotted the red rock too. "Stay here with them," the Executioner said. "John and Zona both look like they could use a rest. I'll go on ahead and look around."

The Texan stuck the round tin back into his pocket, took the straw Stetson and bandanna off his head and nodded.

Bolan walked forward slowly, his eyes on the outcropping head. When he reached it, he saw that it grew out over the rail and he had to lower his head to pass under it. He studied he face of the mountain from both sides but saw nothing out f the ordinary. The wall of rock was solid—no cracks or cavties or hollows or any other place something could be hidden. There were definitely no caves in the immediate vicinity nd on the other side of the trail was nothing but a drop-off f at least two hundred feet.

The sudden sound of movement above him sent the Exeutioner's hand flying inside his shirttail to come to rest on he Desert Eagle. But before he drew he looked up toward the ource of the noise and saw a brown-faced monkey looking lown at him from a ledge at the top of the red rock. No more han twenty feet over his head, the little animal made a few oises Bolan could only assume were monkey curses, then isappeared behind the ledge once more.

Bolan let his hand drift away from the big .44 and stepped ack from the mountainside. His eyes moved from right to eft, then back again several times. But he saw nothing of inerest, no steps, no fissures that might be used to haul oneself p over the side. Still, the monkey had gotten there somehow. And if he could do it, so could a terrorist.

The Executioner glanced at his watch. They had been on he trail slightly less than thirty minutes and he had to assume hat while they were walking slower than he would have on is own, they couldn't be much slower than the average hiker. hey had to be roughly halfway up the mountain and unless e missed his guess this outcropping was the red rock of vhich Subing and Angelo had spoken. He thought back to vhat Zona had overheard them say. "It" was halfway up the nountain. They should "look for the red rock."

Turning away from the outcropping, Bolan leaned his

backpack against the wall of rusty red. He knew that what
ever he was looking for was halfway up the trail. The red roc
wasn't necessarily the "it" for which he was looking. So "it"
might be farther along the trail. The red rock was only a land
mark.

Bolan glanced back in the direction from which he'd come
Latham and the others were out of sight on the other side o
the outcropping now. Zona and John could use a longer rest
so he'd leave them and the rest of the team where they wer
for now and go on up a little farther to see what he could find

The strong scent of danao fruit trees filled his nostrils a
the Executioner walked on. The trail moved out away from
the mountain wall and the hemplike abaca began to appear be
tween him and the rock. Bolan's eyes skirted back and fort
as he walked, across the trail, down the slope, back across th
pathway and through the bright colorful flowers, green leave
and vines between him and the side of the mountain.

He had gone no more than a hundred feet past the red roc
when something caught his attention. He stopped in his tracks
Looking to the flora between the trail and the mountainsid
he saw nothing but more of the same vegetation he'd see
since leaving the red rock. He took two steps back to wher
he'd been when whatever it was had caught his eye and a smil
came over his face.

Bolan stepped to the edge of the trail and dropped to on
knee. Reaching down, he lifted a freshly cut vine. The en
where the green stem had been cut was slightly lighter i
color; it had been whacked off with a machete or at least
blade of some kind. Moisture still formed at the cut.

The Executioner remembered the hidden landing strip o
Mindanao as he reached out to grab more of the vines. Th
drug dealers—in league with the Tigers—had used severe
plant life to hide the entrances to both the road leading int

the jungle and the footpath to the airstrip. So he wasn't surprised when he lifted the vines to find they had all been recently cut.

Quickly, the Executioner dug his way into the stack of green and found himself standing in front of a cleft in the mountainside. Barely wide enough for a man to squeeze through at the bottom, it opened wider as it rose and at the top he could see the blue sky above Tawi-Tawi. He glanced over his shoulder toward the hiking trail, now hidden behind him by the greenery, then turned to the mountain again.

Bolan guessed that this pathway led up to the ledge where he'd seen the monkey. That would explain Zona's husband telling Subing to look for the red rock. The red rock was where they were going, not how they got there from the trail. He glanced back toward where he'd left the others once more, frowning. There would be rough climbing ahead, far more physically demanding than the simple hike up the mountain trail. Zona and John Parks simply weren't up to it. Latham and Reverte and Taboada could probably handle it, but could they do so without making noise and alerting whoever they found hidden up in the rocks?

The Executioner didn't know, but he saw no reason to take the chance. On the other hand, he couldn't just leave them where they were with no explanation. Sooner or later, at least one of them would come looking for him. And if they spotted the obscured path off the trail as he'd done, they might even try to follow it, too.

Quickly, Bolan retraced his steps from the mountain to the trail, then jogged along the pathway, ducking under the red outcropping once more and slowing to a walk. He found Latham, Reverte and the others all seated along the side of the trail.

"Find anything?" Reverte wanted to know immediately.

Bolan looked into the CIA man's eyes, trying to see past

them to his soul, doing his best to read whatever thoughts Reverte had hidden in his brain. It wasn't just being left-handed that bothered him about the man. Just as the red rock led to the trail, Reverte's left hand led to something else within the man that shouldn't be there. The Executioner could feel it, but he didn't know what it was.

Bolan stopped and stood in front of them. "No," he said. "But I want to look a little farther." Now it was he who glanced at Parks and Zona to tell Reverte they were the reason he was going on alone. "The rest of you just stay put and rest. I'll be back for you." He turned to leave.

Reverte leaped to his feet. "I'll go with you," he said. "I'm rested."

The Executioner stopped and turned to face the CIA man. "Stay here," he said. "I need you to help watch over everybody."

Reverte's arms spread wide as if he were finishing up a song on stage at Carnegie Hall. "Are you kidding?" he said in his thick Brooklyn accent. "Latham and Reynaldo can watch over those two. Hell, the only other people we've even seen are those old—"

"I don't understand you, Reverte," the Executioner said. "First, you sound like you want to stay down at the bottom. Now, you want to go with me." He paused, took a step closer to the man. Then, looking down, he said, "Stay here like I told you to."

The CIA agent stared back at him for a second, then broke eye contact. "Yeah, okay," he said as he turned around. "Whatever you think's best. I mean, we're all in this together, right?"

Bolan didn't answer, but with Reverte's back now to him he looked over at Latham.

Latham shot a glance at the CIA agent, then nodded. Yes, he'd still keep an eye on the man.

The Executioner kept his pace moderate until he was out

of sight beneath the outcropping again, then broke into a jog to the entrance to the hidden pathway. He dug his way through the cut foliage again, this time doing his best to put the leaves, vines and flowers back in place behind him. He not only didn't want Reverte deciding to take off on his own and finding the spot, he couldn't be sure that whoever had cached the path was inside the mountain now. They could be out somewhere, then come along the trail behind him, see that this route had been found and creep up on him from the rear.

Reaching the cleft in the rock, Bolan stepped up into the narrow space. Using his arms as much as his legs, he started to squeeze through the opening but his backpack frame jammed into the wall. Stepping back down, he shrugged out of the pack, unzipped the top and took out the Calico rig. The backpack went under a pile of the weeds that had been already cut.

The Executioner followed the fissure upward, looking for signs of other human presence as he went. The cleft sloped upward at nearly a forty-five-degree angle, and by the time he reached the top his arms and back were screaming. He didn't know exactly who he might find when he got wherever he was going, but he knew they'd have to be strong and in good shape.

Finally, Bolan reached the top. He risked a quick look above the fissure and found himself on a ledge overlooking the city of Bongao. Sparse trees and other shrubbery had grown up through cracks in the mountain and, looking to his right, he could see the red rock ledge on which the monkey had stood. More monkeys scampered about the flat area in the boulders. Several looked his way, but none seemed startled at his presence.

Which was significant. It meant they were used to seeing humans come up through the rocks as he'd just done.

The Executioner hauled himself on up out of the crevice,

took a second to catch his breath and let the lactic acid buildup
in his arms and legs recede. He had clipped the barrel of the
Calico and the 100-round drum magazine worn opposite the
machine pistol to his belt for the climb, and now freed them
both for quicker access. As he made a quick 360-degree scan
of his surroundings, only one thing caught his interest. Approximately ten yards away, caught in the twigs of a scrub
bush, a shiny silver object fluttered back and forth in the
wispy mountain breeze.

Bolan rose to his feet, his right hand falling to the Calico's
pistol grip. He was out in the open, and knew it, and as he
walked toward the silver object he half expected to catch a bullet. But there was nothing else to do at this point. The other
half of the Executioner told him that had someone been
watching him the bullet would have already come.

There was no need to reach down to grasp the silver paper
to know what it was. The lining from a pack of cigarettes.
Bolan looked out away from the bush, his eyes making gradually increasing circles until they caught the tan filter of a cigarette. He moved cautiously forward, bent at his knees, and
lifted it to his nose.

The paper around the stubbed butt was still dry, which
meant it had been dropped here this day. He had no idea
when the last rain had hit the mountain but the early morning dew would have been absorbed had it been here overnight.
Looking back down at the spot where he'd found what was
left of the cigarette, he saw where a boot heel had ground it
into the rock.

More boot tracks led the Executioner deeper into the heart
of the mountain, toward a small grove of stunted trees. Other
foliage surrounded the clump, and here the men who had hidden the entrance below had seen no reason to cut greenery to
conceal another crevice in the rocks. Slowly, carefully, his bat-

tle senses coming on full alert, Bolan moved smoothly through the trees and into the cavity.

The tunnel between the boulders led straight rather than up and the Executioner lifted the Calico to waist level. He looked down, making sure the sound suppressor was threaded tightly in place, then stepped in between the rocks. Here he saw more signs of human presence. As the crevice through which he had crawled earlier, there was barely enough room at the bottom for a man to walk. But someone had built a platform three feet off the ground to make the trip easier.

Bolan stepped up onto the aged wood, freezing for a moment when he heard it creak. He brought the Calico to shoulder level, reaching out and grasping the front grip with his left hand and looking over the barrel toward the end of the tunnel. When he neither saw nor heard any response to his noise, he walked slowly on across the platform. Each step produced another squeak in the timeworn wood. But again, he knew that if anyone was watching or listening they would have heard him and reacted by now.

Near the end of the passageway Bolan stopped, pressing his back up against the rock wall on his right. He leaned forward and looked out onto another open area where the rocky formation dipped down to create a flat plateau. A mountain breeze whispered across the clearing, fluttering the leaves on the trees before whistling past him back through the passageway. But above the soft sounds, he heard a human voice.

The Executioner leaned out farther, eyes and ears straining to see and hear. He could see no one in the clearing, and while there were plenty of boulders and thickets behind which a man might hide, none looked big enough to hide two or more. And unless whoever it was had lost his mind and was talking to himself, there had to be at least one other person listening.

Bolan closed his eyes for a moment, zeroing his brain into the sounds. Whoever was speaking was doing so in one of the tribal dialects. The voice rose in volume and now the Executioner could tell the general direction from which it came. Across the clearing, perhaps twenty-five yards away, he saw what looked at first like a dark shadow, low on the side of the mountain. The sun was in his eyes from the angle at which he stood and he couldn't be sure, but it looked like the entrance into a cave.

The voice quit speaking and another began to drone on. While he had no idea what the man might be talking about, the tone held the excited, zealot passion found only in religious extremists and petty dictators. What the speaker was actually doing sounded like a pep talk of some kind, which led the Executioner to believe there were more than two men in the cave.

Bolan zeroed back in on the cave entrance, shielding his eyes against the sun and squinting at the dark spot on the rock. The opening was low—anyone interested in going into the cave would have to drop to all fours and go in on hands and knees. An almost impossible route to transverse quickly or without being seen. But near foolproof when it came to defending the area from attack once you were inside.

Stepping back into the passageway between the rocks, Bolan ran the situation down in his mind. Somehow he had to get inside the cave. And if the men inside were Liberty Tigers, he had to get in without taking two dozen rounds from AK-47s while he was still on all fours.

That wasn't going to be easy.

The Executioner was still trying to devise a plan when one was suddenly handed to him on a silver platter. First, he heard the voices in the cave stop talking. Then the sound of something sliding along the ground met his ears. He stepped back to the edge of the rocks and peered around the edge.

One of the men, wearing a long full beard beneath a turban, a woven white pullover shirt and camouflage BDU pants came crawling out of the entrance. He got to his feet, brushed off his knees, stomped his sandals on the ground a couple of times, then began making his way into the grove of trees in the center of the clearing. If he had a rifle he had left it inside the cave. But he wore a thick leather gun belt buckled over the tail of his shirt and what looked like a French 9 mm Mab PA-15 in the holster. His hands began to unbutton the fly on his BDUs as he walked.

The Executioner pulled the Beretta from under his arm, lifted it to eye level, then steadied his arm against the rock wall at his side. The shot was not long—fifteen yards at most—but only a fool didn't take advantage of a makeshift bench rest when one was available. As the man began to urinate, Bolan lined up the front and rear sights of the Beretta 93-R on his forehead and flipped the fire selector to single shot.

He let the man finish and begin buttoning his pants before he pulled the trigger.

CHAPTER TWELVE

Lars Mikelsson glanced around his opulent office, admiring the elaborate furniture and expensive carpet. Two of the walls were covered with original oils and watercolors by some of Europe and Scandinavia's most widely celebrated contemporary artists. The other two walls held plaques and certificates of achievement commemorating his monetary contributions and work in civic affairs around the Stockholm area. He loved this office. It reminded him of how far he had come. Yes, this was the office of a highly successful man.

Mikelsson shoved himself back from the desk and heard the wheels on his chair scream in protest. Although he had become a millionaire many times over in legitimate business, it had eventually begun to bore him.

He would have been hard-pressed to think of any business he hadn't dabbled in at one time or another. At various times he had been in Sweden's forestry, hydroelectric power, automobile, aircraft and heavy machinery businesses. His companies had mined iron ore in the country's northwest region and lead, gold, zinc, copper and silver in other parts of the country. These businesses had brought him great wealth, more han he could ever spend. But he had found no satisfaction in hem. If there was one thing he had learned during close to sixty years on the planet, it was that no amount of money could satisfy him. When he had secured his first hundred million kroner, he'd wanted five-hundred million more, and when he had the five-hundred million more, even that was not enough. There was no such thing as enough money in legitimate business and he had been in his late forties before he'd figured out what had been missing in his life.

Excitement.

Food was exciting, and women were usually exciting although he'd found them less so in the past few years. But the real thrill of living came from taking a chance with his wealth. Not at the blackjack tables of Monte Carlo or Las Vegas or in horse races or sporting events. The only thing that had ever really stimulated him was the risk that came from breaking the law. Big laws, little laws, felonies and misdemeanors— they all had their place. Of course it was always more fun to break big laws but he had found that he even derived a certain degree of satisfaction out of jaywalking, exceeding the speed limit and ignoring no-parking zones. Big or small, it was his way of reminding himself, and the world, that he was no longer poor. There was nothing his money could not buy him out of, and he had proved that several times over in the days when he'd financed drug deals. He was wealthy beyond the imagination and it allowed him to snub his nose at laws and enforcement officers by simply buying cops, prosecutors and judges when necessary.

Mikelsson smiled to himself. The money he made in his criminal ventures had never been the goal—he already had money. Money was simply the way he kept score.

He glanced at the phone, then at his wristwatch. Subing was beginning to make him nervous. He was a madman, a re-

ligious fanatic, a loose cannon to say the least. He always had
been, but these Americans who seemed determined to find his
hostages now had the little brown man at his wits end. Had it
not been for Mikelsson's own agent in the Philippines and the
incredible stroke of situational luck the man had fallen into,
the fat man would be tempted to call the whole American deal
off and look for someone else to carry out the strike. If not
for his man reporting to him periodically, following each step
the Americans took and keeping him advised so he could
keep Subing one step ahead, the little brown idiot would have
gone to visit his uncle and been killed or captured.

The fat man sighed. Now Subing had returned from Israel
to find that his banana plantation had been raided, two of the
missionaries freed and all of his men killed. The Tigers's
leader had been livid, swearing to kill whoever was responsible with something called the "death of a thousand cuts."

It had been all Mikelsson could do to keep from laughing.
He knew who was responsible. His man was traveling with
the Americans. But he couldn't tell the little Filipino about
that, so he had listened as if in shock and shown the appropriate amount of sympathy. The truth was, he couldn't have
cared less whether the American missionaries lived or died.
He had financed their kidnapping for one reason and one reason only—to see if Subing still had enough sense left in his
Islam-riddled brain to carry out the strike he had planned for
the United States. He needed a man who believed in this jihad
nonsense so strongly that he would give up his life for the
cause. But he also needed a man who was still logical enough
to follow orders.

Mikelsson's mind traveled back over the past fifteen years.
He had financed millions of dollars in cocaine and heroin
deals, and the return on his money had been good. It hadn't
equaled what he made in his legitimate enterprises, but that

hadn't been the point. He had dealt drugs simply for the rush. That same rush had come when he'd smuggled guns from Belgium to drug cartels and terrorists in Latin America. But nothing equaled the adrenaline jolt he got from setting up what was about to be the biggest suicide bombing the world had ever seen.

The fat man sat back in his chair. The idea had come to him during the first business quarter following the bombing in Oklahoma City in 1995. Sales of firearms, he'd noticed—always a good business in southwest U.S. "cowboy" country—had practically tripled. The sale of home security systems, devices to discourage automobile theft and all other items related to personal security had skyrocketed, as well. But what had caught his eye the most was the big jump in what both federal and state governments were now willing to spend on defense equipment. He regretted not being in any such businesses at the time; he hadn't made a kroner from that disaster.

It was that regret that had brought the plan together in his mind. First, he bought all of the companies he could that supplied various governments with articles of war and counterterrorism. When he couldn't purchase a company outright, he bought all available stock. Step two was to make sure the terrorist organizations around the world were well-funded and supplied. It was simple, actually—nothing more than the law of supply and demand. With one hand, he sold ammunition, small arms, high-tech weapons systems, aircraft and other items to legitimate governments the world over. And with the other hand he made sure they kept needing such items by helping groups like the Liberty Tigers. His first big score had been during the months after the World Trade Center and Pentagon attacks. But after what he was planning with Candido Subing, the profits after September 11, 2001, were going to seem like pocket change.

The phone rang. Knowing who it had to be, he said, "*Salaam.*"

"*Salaam,*" Subing said on the other end.

"So," Mikelsson said. "Have you found out yet what happened at the banana plantation?"

"Not yet," Subing said. "But I will. I am on my way to check on the other two sites. Thank Allah that I moved the minions of Satan when I did!"

"Yes," the fat man said. "Allah had you do that just in the nick of time, didn't he?" The sarcasm flew high over the other man's head. Mikelsson's own man in the Philippines had warned him of the new American mission to free the missionaries, and he had casually suggested to Subing that they be separated.

"But I am ready to go to America at any time," Subing said quickly.

Mikelsson laughed. "Good," he said. "Very good."

"Everything is ready? In America?" Subing asked anxiously.

"Almost," the fat man said. "The ship is still quarantined for inspection. But that will be taken care of shortly."

"Should I leave now?" Subing asked excitedly.

Mikelsson hesitated a moment. If Subing stayed in the Philippines and went on trying to find out who had attacked the plantation, he might well run into these Americans. If that happened, the little Filipino would be killed. According to his man who was traveling with them, two of the Americans—and one in particular—were very good at what they did. If they killed Subing, Mikelsson would be back to square one looking for a sucker willing to blow himself up.

"Yes, I believe you should," Mikelsson said into the phone. "You have the airline tickets and the new passport?"

Subing's voice rose slightly with his excitement. "They had arrived when I returned."

"You will go through Canada," the fat man said. "Draw no attention to yourself and call me when you arrive in New York." He stopped to take a breath, then added, "What you are doing will bring great glory to you, and Allah." With the little brown man it was impossible to lay it on too thick.

"Praise Allah!" Subing practically screamed into the phone. "And we will talk when I arrive in New York!"

"Allah be praised!" the fat man said back, then hung up and bent forward over his desk, laughing. His eyes watered and his heart raced, and for a moment he couldn't catch his breath. When he had control of himself again, he checked his watch.

The man he needed to talk to next would be asleep, but he didn't care. U.S. Customs Agent Randall Williams was getting paid enough to wake up if the fat man wanted him to. He lifted the phone to his ear once more, dialed the country code, then the number in New York City.

"Hello?" said a sleepy voice on the other side of the Atlantic.

"Yes, and hello to you," Mikelsson replied.

The voice was suddenly more awake. "Yes, sir!" Williams said.

"Where do we stand?" the fat man asked bluntly.

"I got delayed a bit." A second later he added, "I told you about the supervisor coming on board. He was up my ass all day yesterday."

Up his ass, Mikelsson thought. The Americans and their penchant for sexual profanities always irritated him. "I am not interested in your personal problems," he said. "I will ask my question once more. Where do we stand?"

"I passed it this afternoon," Williams said. "I've got your…TV here at home with me. Er, I hate to bring this up, sir, but this one cut things really close. I've got a pension to think about. A family. If I get caught…" He let the sentence trail off but the meaning was clear. He wanted more money.

Mikelsson shook his head and smiled to himself. Little Customs Agent Williams was begging for more money again. "I will add one thousand dollars to the wire transfer," he said. He caught himself almost laughing into the phone. He had spent more than that on last night's dinner and entertainment.

"Thank you, sir," Williams said.

"You have not opened the box, I hope," the fat man said. "Those antiquities are very valuable. If even one of them gets broken—"

"No, sir, of course I didn't open the box," Williams said quickly. "You told me not to, and I didn't."

Mikelsson smiled again. The real reason the man hadn't opened the box was that he feared it might contain drugs. How little he knew. "Very well. There will be a man contacting you with instructions tomorrow. His name is Candido."

"Good, sir," Williams said. "The sooner I get rid of these things the happier—"

Mikelsson hung up and pushed back against his chair. He struggled to his feet, crossed the room and opened the door. His secretary looked up for a moment, smiled, then went back to her computer. Mikelsson nodded, left the office and walked down the hall to the elevator still thinking about Williams. The Customs man was a fool, but a useful fool. He was being paid six thousand—no, make that seven thousand dollars now— to deliver a box labeled to be a twenty-four-inch Sony television to Subing once the Filipino arrived in New York. Williams had been told this special box contained illegal antiquities from Egypt. He would suspect that it really held drugs, but he could still lie to himself if he didn't have to open the box and see them. What he would never suspect was that the contents of the box was worth far more than any pharaoh's treasure or drug shipment. In the long run, it would create not millions but billions of dollars in sales. Of course to make hose billions would require taking a few million American ives, but business was business, and the suicide bombings he inanced in Israel, Iraq and other areas around the world were .o small they had become boring.

Americans liked things big just like he did. So, Mikelsson hought as he waited on the elevator, it was only appropriate hat they host the world's first nuclear suicide bombing.

As the elevator dropped toward the ground floor, the fat nan chuckled again. The funniest part of it all was that Candido Subing *knew* he was going to be disintegrated along vith at least eight million other people and he not only didn't nind, he was looking forward to it.

The fat man got off the elevator and started toward the delcatessen across the street, still laughing. He had never in his ife seen a fool so eager to die.

THE EXECUTIONER'S 9 mm hollowpoint round blasted from the varrel of the Beretta and entered the side of the terrorist's head ust above the ear. Still traveling at over 1200 feet per second it such close range, it drilled through the skin, skull and brain, hen reversed that order as it exited.

The man who had been buttoning up his trousers fell sidevays against the trunk of the tree next to which he had stood, ebounded and collapsed to the ground.

Bolan wasted no time. Leaping off the wooden platform vetween the rocks, he sprinted across the mountain clearing o the trees. Dropping to one knee next to the dead man, he rained the 93-R on the low opening into the cave. The sound uppressor had done its job, but it still made noise—a noise hat these men would likely recognize and would be much out of place in this lonely mountain retreat.

When no one appeared at the cave entrance, the Executioner urned his attention to the man on the ground. The woven white shirt tucked under his gun belt showed spots of blood but Bolan doubted that would be noticed during the second o two that he needed the shirt. Unbuckling the gun belt from around the man's waist, he quickly unbuttoned the garmen and pulled the dead arms out of the sleeves. The Executioner' blue chambray shirt was dropped next to the body as he slippe into the white top. It was far too small around the chest, an he was forced to leave the top three buttons undone.

Bolan looked down at the three-color desert tan pants th Tiger had worn. They weren't that different in overall hue tha the khaki cargo jeans he had on and, once again, he would b using this camouflage for only a second or two while h crawled into the cave. The pants would be the last thing see as he entered on all fours anyway and he would more tha likely fire his first shot as soon as he was inside. After that i wouldn't matter if he had on the uniform of a British Roya Guardsman at Buckingham Palace.

What worried him more than the pants was his head. I would be the first thing the other terrorists saw as he crawle into the cave and, while his hair was as dark as that of the ma he'd just shot, the Tiger had worn a white turban. It was fa more red than white now after the bullet had passed throug it, and even if the Executioner put it on it was likely to attrac fast attention.

Bolan hesitated only a moment making his decision. H would go without the turban. What he lacked in camouflag he would have to make up with speed and accuracy.

Racing out of the trees to the side of the cave opening, th Executioner dropped to his knees and waited. Inside, he coul distinctly hear the voices now. And as he'd suspected fron across the clearing, they were speaking some language un known to him. It wasn't Tagalog. He had heard enough of tha by now to recognize the difference.

Whatever they were saying, the voices didn't sound excited. It was too soon for the man lying in the trees to be missed, and Bolan took advantage of that fact and waited. Listening closely, he picked up on three distinct voices carrying on the conversation. That meant there were at least three more terrorists inside the cave. There could be any number more who didn't happen to feel talkative at the moment.

There was only one way to find out.

The Executioner holstered his weapons; he would need both hands free as he crawled into the cave.

Bolan took a deep breath, then dropped to all fours. Slowly he peered around the edge of the opening. There was light inside—candles, lanterns, lamps of some kind—but it was considerably darker than where he was now. The Executioner closed his eyes for a count of sixty to let his pupils adjust, then opened them and crawled forward.

A shallow, tunnellike stretch of ten feet or so separated the inside of the cave from the outside. The Executioner crawled toward what he could see was a large cavern at the end. It was brighter in the cavern than the entranceway and he was thankful for that—while his eyes had adjusted to a certain degree, his vision was still partial in the low light.

The voices inside continued to speak in calm tones as Bolan neared the end of the tunnel. As he moved closer, the arm of another woven white shirt appeared. He couldn't see the man to whom it belonged, but the hand on the end of the arm held a china teacup. It disappeared from the Executioner's vision as the man took a drink, then returned to sight as the hand set it down in a saucer.

Bolan reached the end of the tunnel and suddenly saw the rest of the man attached to the arm. He was reclining on the rocky floor on his side, drinking tea. Four more men, similarly dressed, sat around him, forming a circle. The man facing the cave exit glanced over as the Executioner's head appeared, then returned to the conversation. But a second later, his eyes shot back to the exit in a classic double-take.

But by then the Executioner had drawn both the Desert Eagle and the Beretta, and before the terrorist could sound the alarm, a 3-round burst had drilled into his chest just below his breastbone.

The Beretta was quiet, but the blood that flew from the Tiger's back and chest caught the attention of the others. They all turned Bolan's way. Expressions of shock, confusion and fear passed over their faces as they realized that the man coming into the cave wasn't the one who had gone out. During the two to three seconds it took them to react, the Executioner put another burst of 9 mm rounds into a terrorist with a long, droopy mustache and a .44 Magnum slug through the face of another wearing a kaeffiyeh. The Desert Eagle roared like thunder from Hell within the close confines of the cave and one of the men instinctively raised his hands to cup both ears.

The Executioner aimed between the hands and three more hollowpoint rounds coughed from the 93-R to obliterate the terrorist's features.

Bolan had swung the Desert Eagle to one of the men remaining in the circle when another explosion from the side caught his attention. What felt like a bee buzzed past his ear. But the Executioner had experienced such buzzes too many times over the years to confuse them with insects. He turned to his right and saw a terrorist holding a Glock of some caliber in a classic two-handed grip. The recoil of the weapon had brought it up over the man's head and before he could return it to a firing position another 240-grain jacketed hollowpoint round had roared from the Desert Eagle and blown out a portion of his back.

Two men who had been in the tea-drinking circle still lived.

and both took advantage of the distraction to jump behind large stalagmites growing out of the floor of the cavern. One man hid behind one of the thick rock structures to Bolan's left, the other to his right. The last glimpse the Executioner had of both was of the men pulling weapons from their belts.

Bolan saw now that the cave was at least forty feet deep and roughly the same in width. The ceiling varied at different points, rising high—up to thirty or more feet—in some places, dipping down to less than three at others. Some of the stalactites had grown down to join with their brothers on the ground, forming thick pillars throughout the cave. The cavern looked like something out of *Grimm's Fairy Tales* or some fantasy novel. The overall effect was that of an evil otherworldly atmosphere.

The Executioner pulled the Desert Eagle's trigger four times in a row, the blasts almost deafening as they bounced back and forth against the rock walls. The deep-penetrating .44 Magnum rounds splintered the stalagmite behind which the man to his right had hidden and suddenly the gunner stood in plain sight—almost naked to the world. But in reality he wore the same camouflage trousers the terrorist outside had worn, and a similar muslin pullover shirt below an OD baseball cap.

In his hand was a huge single-action Ruger revolver. Cocked.

Bolan fired again as soon as the terrorist came into view and the .44 ripped through the man's ribs and exploded his heart. The Ruger flew through the air, still cocked, and bounced across the cave floor, finally coming to rest not three feet from where the Executioner stood.

But the man behind the stone pillar to Bolan's left opened up with what looked like a Heckler & Koch P-7. Bolan caught a glimpse of the squeeze-cocker mechanism on the front of

the grip as he dived to the floor and rolled behind a stalagmite. The terrorist's trigger finger was heavy with nerves and
he fired at least ten rounds semiauto before giving it a rest.

Bolan leaned around the side of the stalagmite and fired
another 3-round burst from the Beretta. The rounds struck the
rock formation in front of the Tiger and sent wet chips of stone
flying through the air. Ducking back to cover, the Executioner dumped the partially spent magazine from the 93-R and
replaced it with a fresh clip. When the Beretta was up and running again, he did the same with the Desert Eagle.

Silence now fell over the cavern as the remaining Tiger
stayed out of sight behind the rock. Bolan heard some kind
of commotion from deep in the cave and turned his attention
that way. Low, almost inaudible, he could hear the sounds of
someone scraping against the rock.

More terrorists? Maybe. He would keep one eye and ear
aimed that way.

The Mexican standoff continued silently for another minute or so, then Bolan leaned around the side of his cover and
triggered another four rounds from the .44. But either this stalagmite was more sturdy or he had luckily found the weak
points in the earlier one. While four white-edge holes appeared in the rock, the stalagmite stood firm.

Not so the man behind it. Suddenly he called out in a
thickly accented voice in whatever language they had spoken
earlier.

"Try English," the Executioner shouted back.

Now the man called out in what Bolan recognized as Tagalog but couldn't understand.

"No better," Bolan yelled back. He cocked one eye around
the side of the rock.

No verbal response came this time. But the man behind the
rock had worn a turban similar to the terrorist who now lay dead

outside in the trees, and now he extended the white flag around the side of the stalagmite, waving it frantically up and down.

Bolan called out in Spanish and the man answered excitedly. "Sí! Español!"

"Throw your gun and any other weapons out first," the Executioner called in Spanish. "Then come out yourself. Keep your hands high and wide. You understand?"

"Sí, sí!" the terrorist shouted. A moment later a SIG-Sauer pistol fell out from behind the stalagmite. A second later a kris knife followed.

"Anything else?" Bolan demanded.

"No!" the terrorist shouted. "Please! I surrender!"

"Then show yourself," the Executioner yelled.

The man came out still holding the unwrapped turban from his head. He was bald on top but had a kinky, wiry stubble over his ears.

"Throw the turban down and show me your hands!" Bolan yelled at him. At the same time he dropped the Desert Eagle's sights on the man's chest.

A look of surprise and confusion spread across the terrorist's face. Rather than do as commanded, he kept walking forward and returned to the language the Executioner didn't understand.

Bolan pulled the trigger, and the semijacketed hollowpoint round tore through the man's chest and out his back, taking a trail of blood and organ tissue with it all the way to the opposite wall of the cavern.

The Tiger dropped where he stood, his knees buckling under him. He fell to his side, still gripping the turban.

The Executioner stood and walked out from behind the pillar of stone. He holstered the Desert Eagle but kept the Beretta ready in his left hand. He still wasn't sure what had made the noise at the back of the cavern. He stopped next to the body on the ground just long enough to reach down and grab the .32-caliber Davis derringer from behind the turban in the man's hand. As he had known it would be, the hammer was cocked.

Bolan noticed a pool of water in the middle cavern, which he hadn't seen earlier. Hidden behind several more rocky growths from the floor, he passed it on his way to the rear of the cave and dropped the derringer into the water. The scraping sound could be heard louder now and he raised the 93-R in his hands as he tracked toward the noise.

Reaching the back of the cave, Bolan saw a small hole in the wall at the far right-hand corner of the room. Approximately four feet off the ground, it was just big enough for a man to crawl into and hide. He walked slowly toward the dark aperture, the Beretta up and ready. But when he reached the hole he looked inside, then holstered the weapon.

The man's head was at the other end of the tiny hole but Bolan could see the sack hood covering his face. The hostage was tied with rope at the ankles and wrists, and the sound he had heard was that of the hostage rubbing the rope back and forth against the rocks to his side.

Bolan couldn't imagine what had to have gone through his mind during the gunfight just now. He could see nothing and would have had no idea what was going on.

"Hey," Bolan called. "I'm a friendly. I'm going to pull you out, so sit tight." He grabbed the man by his ankles and dragged him from the hole. As soon as he had the missionary standing against the rocky wall, he reached up and lifted the sack-hood off his face.

The missionary blinked twice and then his reaction was similar to that of John Parks when Bolan had rescued him. Staring up into the Executioner's eyes, he smiled as if he'd just won the lottery. Then those same eyes dropped to the Executioner's shoulders and he said, "You know, I half expected wings."

"ARE THERE ANY OTHER hostages here?" the Executioner asked.

The man who had just introduced himself as Dr. Roger Ewton shook his head sadly. He had been brought to this hideaway on the mountain by himself.

As the Executioner used the Loner to cut the ropes from his wrists, Ewton's face suddenly wrinkled in pain.

"What is it?" Bolan asked.

"Cramps," the missionary said. "Calves, hips—been getting them for several days now."

The Executioner dropped to one knee to sever the rope at the man's ankles. "The muscles have atrophied," he said. "And you're electrolytes are probably all low. It may get better as you loosen up. We'll take things slow."

Ewton nodded his understanding.

But by the time they had crawled out of the tunnel leading to the exit, with the Executioner half dragging the man, he suspected the missionary's maladies might stem from something more serious. He helped Ewton stagger across the clearing to the trees where the dead terrorist still lay. Dropping the blood-stained garment over the man's face, the Executioner leaned Ewton against a tree and slid back into his blue chambray shirt. He had hoped that the missionary would "find his legs" as they warmed up. But if anything, Ewton was having even more trouble now. He needed help as they walked to the wooden platform at the bottom of the V formed by the rocks, and when the former hostage was unable to lift either leg high enough to take the short step mounting the platform required, Bolan's suspicions were confirmed.

The Executioner had seen the symptoms before. Roger Ewton was severely dehydrated. Probably suffering from heat exhaustion. While he was able to shuffle along if Bolan held him upright, the nerves in his legs that signaled the muscle to lift the leg had shut down. They simply ignored the order given them by the brain no matter how hard Ewton tried to step up.

Bolan looked at the man and noted the tight skin on his face. His neck looked thin, too. The bottom line, the man was seriously sick and in dire need of medical care. But before they even thought about that, the Executioner had another problem to solve. How was he going to get Ewton down off the mountain to the hiking trail when he'd had trouble getting up it by himself?

Ewton continued to try to lift his legs, growing a little more angry at himself with each attempt, and finally cutting loose with a string of colorful words the Executioner suspected he hadn't learned in divinity school. He turned to Bolan with fire in his eyes and said, "Pardon me for that. But this is frustrating." He paused and gradually the anger in his eyes became an ironic smile. "But if you noticed, I didn't use the Lord's name in vain once during that whole little tantrum."

The Executioner chuckled. "Believe it or not, I've heard such words before," he said. He liked Roger Ewton—liked his attitude. He had spunk; he was a fighter and survivor and he'd recover just fine if Bolan could get him to medical help within a reasonable length of time. "I'm going to carry you," he said, then turned his back to the man.

Right before he turned, the Executioner saw the look of embarrassment on the missionary's face. No man liked thinking he couldn't take care of himself, but sometimes you just flat couldn't do it on your own. "Get on my back," the Executioner said, facing away from the man. "This is no different than if you'd been shot in both legs. No shame to it. And you'd do the same for me."

He couldn't see Ewton's reaction, but a second later he felt the man's hands on his shoulders.

Bolan squatted, reached back and grabbed the man's legs, then pulled them up and around his waist. Turning to the wooden platform, he stepped up and walked across. But the Executioner's mind was racing ahead as he made his way between the rocks. Ewton wasn't heavy, but he was cumbersome and awkward, and getting through the crevice to the hiking trail was going to be all but impossible. One shift in the man's weight could throw Bolan off balance as he made his way down the rocks with the man on his back. It could be a thirty- to forty-foot fall. Ewton could wind up with a few broken bones to add to his problems. And while that might be a reasonable risk if they were being chased, or even if the man was in good health, it wasn't now—not with the missionary's immune system beaten to the point where a common cold might be the final straw that killed him.

When they reached the end of the platform, the Executioner stepped off onto the ground and set Roger Ewton down behind him. A sudden thought occurred to him: there might be an easier route off the mountain than the way he'd come up. Turning to face Ewton, he said, "How'd they get you up here?"

Ewton pointed across the clearing to the crevice Bolan had climbed up.

The Executioner frowned. "You were able to climb that thing?" He didn't know what kind of shape the man had been in a few days ago but his physical problems had to have begun a while ago. Besides, even a strong and healthy man had to struggle on such a climb.

The missionary shook his head. "They pulled me up," he said. "They have—had this rope system thingy they used." Before Bolan could ask the next logical question, Ewton shook his head. "No, I don't know where it is. I didn't see it in the cave."

The Executioner took a deep breath. So much for finding an easy way off the mountain. Pointing to the edge of the wooden platform he said, "Have a seat. I'm going down to where I left my pack. I've got rope in it." Without another word, he turned and walked across the clearing to the crevice.

Climbing down was often harder than going up, and Bolan found this was no exception. The problem now wasn't pulling himself upward, it was trying to keep from falling. By the time he reached the bottom, he could feel the strain in his arms, legs and back.

The backpack was right where he'd left it under the cut brush. He knelt, then jerked it out and unzipped the main compartment. He had pulled the rope out and was about to turn back to the crevice when he heard something.

Slowly, Bolan set the rope on the ground and pulled the Beretta from his shoulder rig. He thumbed the safety to the 3-round-burst mode.

The Executioner waited. Just as slowly as he had moved, just as carefully, he heard someone digging their way through the cut foliage in front of him. And the slowness and sureness made it a certainty that whoever it was knew he wasn't alone just as the Executioner knew he wasn't.

Long seconds became slow minutes. But the man stalking through the greenery knew how to do it, and he was doing it right.

He just wasn't doing it as well as the Executioner.

When he sensed the man was within a yard or so, Bolan rose to his feet and crashed suddenly through the thick foliage. Vines and branches parted in front of him and a split second later the shape of a head appeared in the dark shadows. The Executioner jammed the Beretta forward at the dark face.

But at the same time the dark shadowy figure pushed a gun forward, too. Bolan's left hand shot up, sweeping the gun to the side as he drove the barrel of the 93-R on into the other man's face and made to pull back on the trigger.

The Beretta had been worked over by Stony Man Farm's armorer to have a three-pound, single-action pull. And there could not have been more than a pound and a half of that left when Bolan noticed the red dot dancing through the thick undergrowth—right in front of where he had pushed the other man's gun. And at the same time, his brain registered the fact that the dark head-shape also wore a cowboy hat.

Charlie Latham's face was still dark in the shadows. But as Bolan backed up and Latham followed him on out into the sunlight, the man with the Beretta could see that the Texan's face had turned a pasty white.

Latham shoved his .40 Browning back into his belt and looked up at the Executioner. "Well," the Texan said, his hands shaking lightly. "Haven't had that much fun since the pigs ate my little brother." He shook his head back and forth several times as if to clear it.

"What are you doing here?" Bolan asked. As the only member of the party he fully trusted, he was mildly annoyed that Latham hadn't stayed where he'd ordered him to keep an eye on the others.

"Hey," the Texan said, sensing his irritation. "You were gone one hell of a long time. And we heard what sounded— at least to *me*—like shots." He looked up into the gaping crevice. "Sounded like they came from up there. Somewhere. Long ways away."

The Executioner nodded. The .44 Magnum pistol had to have been heard even from within the cave.

"That you doing the shooting?" Latham asked.

Bolan nodded. "Most of it, anyway."

"Okay. You find anybody?"

"One hostage," Bolan said.

Latham turned back toward the hiking trail. "I'll go get the others," he said. "You can brief us on whatever plan you've got as we—"

Bolan reached out and grabbed the man by the shoulder before he could get away. "We don't need the others," he said. "I've already got him out."

Latham frowned, reached up and scratched the side of his face. "You already got him out?"

"Yeah."

"How many of them were there?"

"Five," Bolan said, then remembered the man he'd shot before going into the cave. "Six in all." He looked up into the giant fissure in the rocks and said, "The missionary's up top. I could use your help getting him down." He grabbed the rope off the ground and began uncoiling it.

"Six bad asses, by yourself," Latham said. "A guy could get to feeling fairly useless when you're around. Gimme the rope." He reached out and snatched it away. "Least you can do is let me show you what an ol' boy from just north of the Rio Grande can get up to."

Bolan watched as Latham knotted the rope into a lasso. There was just enough room for him to get it spinning, then he tossed it upward and over chunk of rock shooting up off the edge. Handing the other end of the rope to the Executioner, he swept the straw hat off his head and held it over his heart. "Now, do me a favor, will you?"

"What's that?" Bolan asked.

"Tell me you couldn't have lassoed that rock the first time like I did. You don't even have to mean it. Just say it so I can go home when this is over feeling more useful than tits on a boar hog."

Bolan kept his grin to a minimum as he turned and grasped the rope with both hands. "I could never have done it," he said, and began pulling himself up. "Not in a million years." He could see the Texan's shadow on the rock as he began to climb. Behind him, he heard Latham say, "Well, that's mighty kinda ya, pahdnuh," and then the shadow put the hat back on its head.

As soon as he reached the top, the Executioner looked across the clearing. Dr. Roger Ewton still sat where he'd left him and he raised a weak hand in a wave. Bolan waved back, then held the rope steady as Latham climbed up. Together, they hurried over to the missionary.

"I'm feeling considerably better," Ewton said, standing. But almost as soon as he was on his feet his legs began to give out on him again. Bolan and Latham each caught an arm. With the man between them, they helped him back to the downward route.

Bolan wrapped the rope around the missionary's waist and up over his arms. Hooking an arm though the slack, he began to lower them both over the side. Latham stayed up top, steadying the rope. When they were halfway down he began his own descent using his body weight as a counterbalance.

Roger Ewton had done none of the work but the poor man was so exhausted he could barely stand when they reached the bottom. Latham helped him up onto Bolan's back again, and they made their way to the trail, under the red rock overhead and back to the spot where the others should have been waiting. Zona, John Parks and Taboada were.

Reverte was nowhere to be seen.

After allowing Parks and Ewton a brief reunion, and letting Parks tell the other man that Fairbanks, too, had been rescued and was on his way back to the States, Bolan said, "Where's Reverte?"

"Took off shortly after Latham left to look for you," Parks said. "Somehow he lost his sat phone and he was going down to use the booth at the bottom of the trail."

Latham turned quickly to Bolan. "He was bitching about his phone before that, trying to find it." He gave the Executioner a look. "But I didn't hear anything about him going back down the mountain before I left."

The Executioner turned to Taboada. The little Filipino shrugged. "I did not know he had lost the phone at all," he said. "If I had known, he could have used mine."

"Yours?" Bolan said. "Where did you get a sat phone?" He hadn't found one on the man when he'd searched him. Could he have missed it somehow? If Taboada did indeed have communication, there had been plenty of moments during which he could have slipped away long enough to make a quick call without Bolan knowing it.

The little Filipino reached into his backpack and pulled out a black compact phone. "This one," he said, his eyes a combination of innocence mixed with confusion at the Executioner's harsh tone of voice. "It was in the barn at the plantation. On the table I hid under. You remember?" He stopped for a second, looking even more innocent than ever. "I thought it might be of use to us, so I picked it up." He shrugged. "I had forgotten I even had it until now."

Bolan stared at the man, trying to decide if he was telling the truth or just a good actor like Reverte. If he was lying, why would he volunteer that he had a phone now? Maybe he thought that since the subject had come up, sat phones would be on Bolan's mind. If that was the case, he might think if he got his story in first, it was more likely to be believed.

The Executioner started to take the phone, which was a cell-satellite phone, then stopped. If Taboada had made any tip-off calls to Subing or anyone else, he would have erased the Caller-ID memory. Even if the memory was still intact, he had the perfect alibi. All recorded numbers could be blamed on the phone's previous owners—the Tigers who had been at the plantation.

The Executioner looked back to Latham and saw that the Texan had picked up on the new problem, too. Actually, it was just an old problem that kept getting reinforced.

They had two men they couldn't fully trust.

"Gather up your gear," Bolan said. "Then we're going to it for a short talk before we head back down." As the others began stuffing items they had taken from their packs into the carriers, the Executioner's thoughts returned to Reverte. His phone had gone into the waters of the Sulu Sea, but what was interesting was that when he'd finally realized it was lost, Reverte hadn't even asked to borrow Bolan's sat phone. And it was also interesting that even though he knew the phone was missing before Latham left, he had waited until both Bolan and the Texan were gone to take off for the phone booth below.

The Executioner remembered that phone booth and what condition the instrument itself had been in. But he said nothing more on the subject. When it looked as though everyone had gathered up their things, he said, "Everybody, take a seat for a minute." When they had formed a circle on the ground, he went on. "Dr. Ewton—"

Ewton cut him off. "I'd say anybody who saved my life deserves to call me by my first name," he said.

"Okay, Roger," the Executioner said. "We're going to get you some medical help just as quick as we can. I've seen men in the shape you're in and while you're not in any immediate danger, you're going to need some IVs and some tests run. But for a little while at least, can you put up with the discomfort you're in and give us some help?"

"Of course," Ewton said bluntly.

"Then tell me, do you have any idea at all where the remaining two missionaries—the women—might be?"

Ewton shook his head. "No. The good Lord knows, I wish I did."

Bolan nodded. Men unaccustomed to warfare or polic
work often knew more than they realized. "Start from the tim
they separated you at the plantation and tell—"

Parks interrupted and said, "The barn, Roger. It was on
banana plantation." He turned to Bolan. "I didn't know wher
it was either until you showed up. The hoods."

The Executioner nodded. "Tell me every step you took be
tween there and here," he said. "Were the women with yo
when you left?"

"Not when we left," Ewton said. "We were all put into sep
arate vehicles. But then we were together again on the docks

"What docks?"

"The docks wherever the boats were," Ewton said. "W
were still hooded, of course, but I could tell we were by th
sea even before they put us in the boats. By the smell."

"You were all put in the same boat?" Bolan asked.

"No. We all waited together in some kind of building o
the docks. They took our hoods off and let us talk." He shoo
his head. "You don't know how important something like tha
is—how much it, well, seems like you've won a prize o
something—until you've been held like we were."

"Was there anything in the building you can remember?
Bolan asked. "Anything that might identify it?"

Ewton shook his head. "It was a small building. At least
got that feeling—it might just have been that the room wa
small. It had concrete walls—very dirty—and smelled o
fish." He paused, caught his breath, then went on. "There wa
one window. I sat against the wall on the floor directly acros
from it. All I could see from that angle was sky."

The Executioner repressed a sigh. This was getting ther
nowhere. "What happened when they took you out?"

"They put our hoods on again first. Then they led us ou
and down into boats. The women were…" Ewton let his voic

rail off, and looked at John Parks. The missionary appeared to be trying to decide if he should say what he had started to say. Apparently he decided it was important. "The women were crying," he said. "That's how I knew they were in the boat next to me."

Parks looked away from the others and Bolan couldn't tell by his expression whether he wanted to cry himself or strangle the animals responsible for his wife's tears.

Bolan looked to Taboada. "Zamboanga would be the closest docks to the plantation, wouldn't they?" he asked.

The Filipino nodded.

"No," Ewton said. "I don't think it was Zamboanga," he said.

"Why not?"

"Because wherever we went wasn't close at all. After we got off the jungle roads onto the highway, we drove for maybe two hours. I could tell we were on the highway because, bumpy as it is, the jungle roads are even worse."

The Executioner turned to Taboada again. The former Tiger shrugged his shoulders. Bolan pictured a map of Mindanao in his head. If they'd been on the asphalt highway, they had to have gone either north or south. If it had been south, they would have ended up in Zamboanga. He supposed they could have driven around enough to confuse Ewton and the women, then gone to the docks there. But he didn't think that likely. There would have been little point in confusing hostages whose brains were already about as scrambled as they could get.

"Did the boats stay together when you left?" Bolan asked the man.

"For a little while, yes," Ewton said.

The Executioner could see that the trip down from the mountain, and the conversation, were quickly tiring the man. His eyelids were dropping. But he was still doing his best to help.

"I got the feeling that we were together only long enough

to get out of the port. Then the boat I was in went one way—south, I guess, as it turns out I'm down here on Tawi-Tawi now—and they went the other. I could hear the motor—" he glanced again at Parks "—and the crying get fainter and fainter until it was gone."

Footsteps sounded on the trail next to where they sat and the Executioner looked up to see the middle-aged couple on their way back down the mountain. All weapons had been hidden in the backpacks or under clothes, and the man and woman smiled as they went by but said nothing. When they were out of earshot again, Bolan tried a different angle. "Were they speaking a language you could understand?" he asked.

"Tagalog sometimes," Ewton said. "Other times one of the tribal dialects I'm not familiar with."

"What you could understand?" the Executioner said. "Anything they say stand out in your mind?" He paused a second then said, "It doesn't have to be something earth-shaking, Roger. Just anything at all they said." He glanced to Zona and Taboada. "They might pick up on it."

"They talked about us, of course. Things like 'Get him in the boat!' and 'Tell her to quit crying.' Things like that."

"What else?" Bolan asked. He couldn't help but think there was something in the back of Ewton's memory that would lead them to the remaining two hostages. If so, the Executioner would have to bring it out of the man. He was a fine man, and a good missionary, Bolan was sure. But he was playing in somebody else's ballpark when it came to the treachery of which other men were capable.

"There was one man who seemed to be the butt of their jokes," Ewton said. "They called him some nickname in the tribal language. I doubt I could pronounce it even if I could remember it. But when they switched to Tagalog, I took i from context that it meant something like hypochondriac. They joked about him always worrying about his health."

Out of the corner of his eye, Bolan saw Taboada grimace slightly. This line of conversation had brought back to mind his exposure to the HIV virus.

The Executioner was beginning to think he was kicking a dead horse. If Ewton had heard anything that might lead them to the women, it could take days, if not weeks, to get it out of him. And Bolan might never push the right button to jog his memory.

Ewton looked down at the ground as if he'd failed a test. "I'm sorry," he said. "I—I wish so much I could help."

Bolan nodded. "You've done all you could. Now it's time we got some help for you." He rose to his feet and the others took that as their cue to get up, too. "We'll head back. We can pick Reverte up on the way." Latham and Taboada helped Ewton to his feet and this time it was Latham who took the missionary on his back. The former hostage looked as though he might die of embarrassment before his weakened physical condition got a chance to kill him. A feeble smile crept across his face and he said, "Maybe it's me who's the hypochondriac."

"No, I think your problems are about as real as they come," Latham said over his shoulder as they started down the path off the mountain.

"That's what the other men told the Tiger who always worried about his health," Ewton said. He laughed without mirth. "They teased him unmercifully. Said he wouldn't get better until they got where they were going and saw the mangkuk-ukus—or something like that."

Taboada, who had been walking next to Latham and Ewton, suddenly grabbed Latham's arm, stopping all three of them in their tracks. Bolan, Zona and Parks heard them grind to a halt behind them and turned around.

"What did you say?" Taboada demanded.

Ewton, still on Latham's back, shrugged. "Just that the other Tigers teased the one man all the time. Kidded him—"

"No," the Filipino said, shaking his head violently. "About him getting better when they got where they were going. When he saw the...what did you say?"

"Mangakuks or mangookoos, something like that. It was a word I wasn't familiar with."

Reynaldo was clearly excited. "Could it have been *mangkukulum?*"

Ewton was slightly taken aback by such firmness in the man who had remained silent for most of the conversation. He hesitated for a moment, then finally said, "Yes, it could. In fact, I'm pretty sure that was it." He tried to pronounce the word but failed again.

Taboada turned to Bolan. "*Mangkukulum* are healers," he said. "What you might think of as witch doctors." He was growing more excited by the minute.

"So what's that mean?" the Executioner asked him.

"It means," he said, grinning broadly, "that they've taken the women to Siquijor. It's a small island just north of Minandao. South of Negros and Bohol. The island is famous for its *mangkukulum.* Magic healers."

Zona had stayed as quiet throughout the earlier conversation as Taboada. But now she spoke up in her Scandinavian accent and said, "Are you sure they have gone to Siquijor?"

The Filipino lost a slight bit of his confidence but still seemed sure. "No one could be certain," he said. "But if they took the women off by boat, then Siquijor is not far from where they were. It all fits what the other men said."

"Good." Zona beamed with one of the first smiles she had

given the men since they'd found her in the scum-ridden apartment in Isabela. "Because if you're sure they went to Siquijor, I can tell you *exactly* where they've taken the women."

CHAPTER THIRTEEN

They could tell they were nearing the port by the smell of fresh fish in the air. It overrode the odor of the salt sea and filled the Executioner's nostrils with hope that they were finally about to locate the remaining two missionaries.

Bolan stood near the front of the Delta Fast Ferries boat and looked out over the waves toward Siquijor Town, the capital of Siquijor Island. He glanced back over his shoulder to see Latham, Taboada, Parks, Reverte and Zona seated along the port side of the transport boat. Little Edward's face was hidden inside the blanket his mother had wrapped around him and she hugged the boy to her chest.

The Executioner turned back to the bow of the boat. They had met Reverte heading back up the mountain trail on their way down. Bolan had casually asked him if he'd been able to reach his CIA superiors at Langley. The man had half surprised the Executioner by being honest, and telling him the phone by the rest rooms was out of order—someone had cut the cord and stolen the receiver, which left three possibilities in regard to the dramatic CIA agent's mysterious disappearance.

First, he might be on the level about everything. Maybe this thing about him being left-handed—and for some unfathomable reason not being supposed to be left-handed—was all in the Executioner's mind.

Another possibility was that Reverte had gone on some errand that had nothing to do with the phone, noticed it was inoperative and told Bolan the truth because it didn't matter. Even liars told the truth when it was to their advantage. But if that was the case, what was that other errand? What could the man have possibly done on Tawi-Tawi?

The last contingency was that he'd talked the lone curio salesman in the shop into letting him use the phone inside. But the Executioner had ducked into that very shop when they'd reached the bottom of the hiking trail and the others had stopped to use the public rest rooms. There was no other phone inside.

The Delta Fast Ferries boat cut its engine as they entered the port and they began to drift into the docks. Jack Grimaldi had been waiting for them when they'd returned to the Tawi-Tawi airport, and had been all too ready to turn Edward back over to his mother. From there, they had flown to Dumaguete on the island of Negros, and taken the ferry on its forty-five minute cruise to Siquijor. All but Dr. Roger Ewton, who Bolan had insisted fly back to Manila with Grimaldi for medical treatment. The Stony Man pilot would meet them on Negros when they had finished up in Siquijor.

Bolan was the first off the ferry when it reached the dock. He helped Zona up and over the side and onto the wooden planks. The rest of the men followed, carrying their backpacks. "He doing all right?" the Executioner asked Zona, looking down at the baby.

Zona smiled. "He's fine. Do not worry, he is strong. Half-Viking, you know."

Bolan laughed. He hated having to bring a mother and

child along, but Zona had insisted that she would never be able to explain how to get where they were going without coming along to show them. So the Executioner had satisfied himself by making her promise that she wouldn't argue when he finally told her that she and Edward could go no further.

As he led the party up into Siquijor Town from the docks, Bolan was surprised to see that the fish he'd smelled for the last several miles were being sold out of a modern marketplace. The building would have looked right at home in port cities like New York, San Francisco, Galveston or New Orleans. It stood out strangely, surrounded by the quaint old buildings around it. The Executioner led the way past a coral-stone church and saw the date 1783 etched into the stone. A bell tower that looked as if it belonged in a fortress rose from the church, and a climbing vine known locally as Santo Papa coiled around it like a boa constrictor.

As they walked past dozens of shops selling everything from seashells to fruit, vegetables and crude wooden carvings, Bolan began to understand something Taboada had told him on the ferry—the island of Siquijor had an eerie atmosphere about it. For every shop and stall selling something else, there seemed to be at least two that specialized in healing herbs, aphrodisiacs, hallucinogenic plants and other mind-altering and god-seeing substances. Many of the men selling their wares were dressed in mysterious combinations of modern and ancient clothing, and several of them stared hard at Bolan and his entourage as they passed. Whether it was because they looked different than the average tourists or the *mangkuku-lum* were sampling too much of their own medicines, the Executioner couldn't tell.

Taboada caught up to Bolan and began to walk abreast with him. "I thought about seeing if they could treat me," he said in a slightly shaky voice. "You know. The blood."

When the Executioner didn't respond he said, "I am being ridiculous, I know. I do not even believe in them. But I am...feeling desperate, I suppose."

Bolan nodded as they walked on. "I can understand that," he said. "But you don't even know if you contracted the virus yet, Reynaldo. In another day or two, we'll get you to a modern medical facility someplace."

Taboada bit his bottom lip. For a moment he said nothing. When he spoke again he changed the subject. "They originated in the mountains around San Antonio," the former Tiger said. "The *mangkukulum,* I mean." He waved his hand around him. "Now they are everywhere—all over the island. Most of them are fakes. Charlietowns, I think you call them."

The Executioner smiled. "Charlatans."

They left the busy port area and Zona took the lead. Since Angelo had brought her to this island before, Bolan had asked her about lodging and she led them toward a sign that read Calalinan Beach Garden Mini-Hotel & Restaurant. Bolan went into the lobby while the others waited outside, paid 450 pesos for a room facing the beach, and came back out.

He handed the key to Zona. "This is for you," he said. "I expect you to keep your promise. When I tell you to go back, you take Edward and come back here. We'll meet with you here when we're finished."

Zona nodded. She had already gone the extra mile for them and he wasn't about to put her and the baby at any more risk than he absolutely had to.

Across the street from the Calalinan, the Executioner saw a rental agency. Old cars, motorcycles, scooters and bicycles stood in the lot next to the one-story building. But it was what the Executioner saw sticking out around the corner from the back of the shop that caught his eye. It was the perfect vehicle for what he had in mind. Gaudy as it might be, it would be

a regular sight, and therefore low profile on the small island
Plus, it was big enough to take all of them together and Zona
would be able to drive it back later when they cut her loose.

Bolan left the others outside again and walked into the
shop. Inside, he saw row after row of other equipment for rent.
Power saws, lawn mowers, post-hole diggers—the swarthy
man with curly black hair behind the counter seemed to have
a bit of everything as he puffed away on a white meerschaum
pipe shaped like an Arab wearing a turban.

"I'd like to rent the jeepney out back," the Executioner said.

The man sucked in on the pipe and let the smoke come out
as he answered. "Don't rent it," he said. His accent was German. "Tours at one and five."

The Executioner reached into his pocket and pulled out the
money roll again. The German's eyes lit up as Bolan rolled
ten thousand peso bills off the top and dropped them on the
counter. "Cancel the tours for today," he said.

The man behind the counter swept up the money and it disappeared into the pocket of his dirty brown slacks. He didn't
even ask the Executioner's name, probably hoping the vehicle was never returned and that he could collect insurance in
addition to the money Bolan had paid him—an amount
around twice as much as the aged bag of bolts was worth.
"The key is in it," he said.

Bolan exited the front and the others followed him around
the side of the building.

"What in the world is that?" John Parks asked.

Latham laughed out loud. "It's a jeepney, John."

When World War II ended, several U.S. Army Jeeps had
been left in the Philippines, many of which had been converted into tourist vehicles by enterprising locals. But none
were left with their original drab green or gray colors. The one
the Executioner had just rented had been painted a bright yel-

low and two wooden benches had been installed in the back
with enough sitting room for at least a dozen people. The jeepney's body was covered with stickers, badges and hand-
painted flowers that looked as though they'd been added
during the "flower power" sixties. Bells and horns were
mounted in every conceivable place, and here and there,
pieces of chrome had been tacked on to further brighten the
vehicle. A Hawaiian hula dancer shook her grass skirt and hips
on the dashboard and giant dice, a baby shoe and what looked
like a raccoon's tail, hung from the rearview mirror.

Bolan dropped behind the wheel with Latham taking shotgun. The rest of the group climbed into the back. The Executioner twisted the key and the engine sputtered to life. Along
with it, came the blaring sounds of some Filipino pop band.
For a moment the voices screamed in musical Tagalog, then
the Executioner located the tape deck beneath the front seat
and pulled out the ancient 8-track.

A moment later they were leaving Siquijor on the coastal
highway that circled the small island. The village of Canda-
bay Sur appeared less than two miles later and another mile past
that they turned left onto an intersecting road that led inland.

As soon as Taboada had said Siquijor, Zona had felt certain that the remaining two hostages had to be in one of the
limestone caves in the mountainous interior of the island.
Several of them like Cantabon Cave, Cang Anhao, and others were open to the public with guided tours conducted daily.
But other caves had yet to be fully explored and there were
many of which even most of the island natives were unaware.
Zona had visited one with Angelo when they'd first come to
the Philippines—before she had learned that he had no intentions of letting her leave again. They'd had a picnic and
made love within the cavern, and she suspected it was there
that the women would be found.

It had sounded logical to the Executioner, as well. Since it had been Angelo who seemed to have set up the site on Tawi-Tawi, it might very well have been he who had scouted this hiding place, as well. And since it had been a cave in which Bolan had found Roger Ewton, it seemed likely that Angelo might pick a cave on this island, too.

Three miles later, they passed through the village of Cantabon and saw signs pointing them on toward the cave of the same name. But Zona directed the Executioner to turn left onto a short road that led to Mount Bandilaan just east of town. He pulled the jeepney to a halt at the end of the road and killed the engine.

In front of them stood some of the craggiest-looking terrain anywhere in the world.

Bolan got out, then leaned into the back where Zona sat with Edward. "This is as far as you go," he said. "Just give me directions and take the jeepney back to the hotel. We'll meet you there later."

Zona shook her head. "You will never find it," she said. "Even Angelo had a hard time and he said he had been there before."

The Executioner stepped back, took a deep breath and looked out to the side of the mountain. As he tried to decide whether to take Zona and Edward with them, he noticed a long, flat area—big enough to land one of the Stony Man Learjets. Good information to file in the back of his brain.

Bolan turned back and looked down at the baby in the woman's arms. The child was asleep. He was about to tell Zona that she was going back now whether she liked it or not, when the woman said, "You worry too much. Believe me, I will not put my boy at risk. I would rather die first." A tiny smile curled her lips for a moment, and then she added, "And to be truthful, I would rather you died than either of us."

Bolan couldn't help but laugh.

"There are two rather tricky areas, " Zona said. "When I get you past them, I will come back with Edward and go back to the room."

Bolan nodded and helped her out of the vehicle.

While the town could be seen from where they stood, they were far enough away that no one would notice them checking their weapons. The Executioner ordered a complete examination of all guns, long and short. When everyone had nodded that they were ready, he led the way up a short path onto the mountain. The path ended after fifty feet and they began to make their way up and over the boulders toward a small plateau on the side of the mountain. Bolan went first, with Taboada and Latham climbing on both sides of Zona, making sure she didn't slip with the baby. Parks and Reverte brought up the rear. When they reached the plateau, the Executioner saw three deep crevices in the rocky wall.

"The one to the left," Zona said, and they entered the opening. Bolan turned, pressed the button on his Sure-Fire flashlight, and the interior of the cave lit up as if the noonday sun had just entered. They walked over a light trickling stream of water, Latham and Taboada again helping Zona. Several dark passages appeared, shooting off to the sides into unknown areas of the mountain. Each time they passed one the Executioner glanced to the woman. But each time he did she shook her head.

Another hundred feet or so and Zona said, "Stop."

Bolan turned to see her frowning in thought. "Shine your light over there, please," she said, pointing to the wall of the passage. The Executioner followed her direction and she walked forward, looking closely at the rock. Finally she shook her head. "This is not it."

They moved on another few feet and Zona had him repeat

the process. Again she shook her head and they took several
more steps. Bolan shot the light at the wall and Zona walked
forward. "Yes!" she said. "This is it!" Waving him forward
she said, "Come, look!"

The Executioner stepped forward and saw faint speckles
of red and blue on the limestone. He couldn't make out exactly what it was, but there was no doubt that at one time it
had been a contemporary work of art. That time, however, had
been thousands of years ago.

"THERE ARE MANY CAVE paintings throughout these mountains," Zona said. "But come on. We take the third turn past
this point." Still excited, she held Edward with one arm and
grabbed the Executioner's hand with the other, hurrying him
forward. Bolan shone the laser flashlight down the tunnel and
they walked on as the footsteps of the others sounded haunt-
ingly behind them in the hollow passageway. When they came
to the third passage shooting off from the main tunnel, Bolan
stopped. "This the one?" he asked.

"Yes," Zona breathed. "We are getting close."

"Keep me in sight but stay back behind me, all of you," the
Executioner said. "I'll take a look and if it's safe I'll wave you
forward." He turned to the Swedish woman. "As soon as I
know for sure where we're headed, I want you to turn back.
And this time, no argument, okay?"

Zona nodded.

Bolan had to bend to enter the side passage that shot off at
a forty-five-degree angle from the main tunnel. Twenty feet
later, it bent back deeper into the heart of the mountain again.
But when he turned, he could see exterior light drifting in from
further down.

The Executioner killed the flashlight and walked the rest
of the way along the passage. At the end, he could see where

opened into what looked like a small, high-mountain val-
y. He stopped just inside the exit and looked out. Short,
ubby, yet stubborn little trees did their best to grow up from
e fissures in the rock foundation beneath them. Without
rning he waved the others forward.

Zona stopped next to him and wrapped Edward tighter in
s blanket. Then her eyes rose and she pointed across the val-
y. "Look," she said.

Bolan followed her finger and saw several more openings
the mountainside. "Count four from the right, and that is
," Zona said. "Count now. They disappear when you reach
e other side."

The Executioner knew what she meant. While the en-
ances to the caves wouldn't actually disappear, the light and
adows would blur and camouflage them when they got too
ose. He counted, then fixed the spot in his eyes.

"When you reach that tree," Zona said, pointing to one of
e short scraggly growths he had already seen, "run your
and along the wall. Pass the first three entrances you feel
ur hand go into and take the fourth. Otherwise you will
iss it."

Bolan nodded. "What do we find after we go in?" he asked.

"The passage is straight for a long way," Zona said. "And
rk. Angelo and I used a flashlight."

"Could you have seen a flashlight coming?" Bolan asked.
After you were in the cavern, I mean?"

"I don't think so," Zona said. "But maybe. Anyway, you
o about fifty feet, then you must start climbing up through
e rocks. Only one person at a time. The cavern is up above
e passage into the mountain."

"How big is the cavern?" the Executioner asked.

Zona frowned in thought. "I am just trying to think of how
tell you," she said. Her eyebrows furrowed for a moment

longer then she said, "You know the wooden floors where the play basketball?" she said.

Bolan nodded.

"About two of them. And there are those things that han down from the top, and the ones like them that grow up fror the bottom. I do not know the English words for them."

"Stalactites and stalagmites," Bolan told her.

"Yes." Zona smiled. "When I was little, my grandfathe told me trolls lived in them."

The Executioner smiled as he looked at the young woma who had been so mistreated. "Thank you," he said. "Now. G back to the hotel."

He looked to Latham. "And I want you to go with her make sure she's okay."

The Texan frowned, then glanced at Taboada and Revert "Uh, look, Matt…" he started to say.

Bolan had no doubt as to what was bothering the mar Latham knew he was the only one of the bunch who could b fully trusted. But that was exactly why Bolan was sending th man back with the woman and baby. "Go on," the Execution ordered. "We'll scout it out and wait for you to get back be fore we go in. Meet you on the other side."

Latham stared at him for a moment then finally said, "Okay

Zona reached up and hugged the Executioner. "I will wait fe you at the room," she said. "And I was joking when I said wanted you to die instead of Edward and me. I was making—

"A joke," Bolan finished for her. "I know what you mean Now, go."

Latham and Zona started back into the mountain usin Latham's flashlight. Bolan led the rest of the men across th valley toward the cave entrance, and what he felt in his gi was the last leg of the search for the missionaries and the me who had kidnapped them.

The missionary women he would rescue.
The men, the Executioner planned to kill.

BOLAN SHRUGGED OUT of his backpack and leaned it up against the rock wall of the tunnel. Unzipping the top compartment, he reached inside and pulled out four stun grenades. He had needed them on Tawi-Tawi and hadn't had them. He hadn't made the same mistake a second time, adding them to his pack when they'd returned to the cache of gear just off the landing strip on Minandao. Dropping two grenades into the left-leg pocket of his cargo pants, two more into the right, he looked at Parks, Reverte and Taboada. "You ready?" he said.

All three men nodded.

"Okay," Bolan said. "Keep it quiet. We'll make our way on over, find the place, then wait for Latham to get back. He knows the way now and it shouldn't take him long." The Executioner turned and stepped out of the passageway.

Bolan hadn't felt he had any choice when he'd picked Latham to escort Zona and her baby back to the jeepney. He refused to leave the helpless woman and child in the hands of either Reverte or Taboada, neither of whom he could still fully trust. And John Parks was a great guy, and, the Executioner suspected a terrific minister. But he wouldn't make much of a bodyguard if they encountered trouble.

There was another reason, however, that Bolan had sent Latham with the woman. They were nearing the end of the game now and if either Reverte or Taboada were going to try something, this had to be where it happened. Someone had been leaking information about them ever since Bolan had arrived in the Philippines. Sometimes those leaks had gotten to the appropriate parties in time to ruin his plans—like in Rio Hondo. Other times the intel was late—like at the plantation and on Tawi-Tawi. But a leak was here, somewhere, and it had

to either be Taboada or Reverte. Reverte had had a sat phone
during most of the mission and Bolan had no idea if the calls
he'd made to "Langley" had really gone back to CIA headquarters. The Filipino, as it turned out, had a sat phone, too,
and although he had been with the group ever since Bolan had
spared his life on the landing strip, there would have been any
number of opportunities for him to sneak out of earshot long
enough to make a quick call.

The Executioner led the way, mindful of the footfalls behind him. He watched the men's shadows as he walked. Both
carried CAR-15s slung over their shoulders assault-style. But
if either planned to gun him down from the rear, he would see
their movement and hit the ground shooting. He considered
both men further as he walked. Taboada had had several
chances to set him up or try to kill him, but hadn't. Reverte,
the Executioner suddenly realized, had not actually fired a
round since he'd joined them. He had stayed outside the plantation barn to guard the hayloft exit, then gone with Latham
around the front of the house while Bolan and Taboada took
out the men inside. On Tawi-Tawi, the Executioner had been
alone during all of the shooting in the cave, with the others
resting back on the hiking trail.

Why, Bolan wondered as he neared the other side of the
valley, hadn't whichever one of them was the traitor already
tried to kill him and Latham? Whoever it was leaking the information to Subing seemed perfectly content to let their
brother terrorists get killed and the hostages set free. It didn't
make sense. Unless…

The missing piece to the jigsaw puzzle suddenly fell into
place, hitting Bolan between the eyes like a club. It didn't
make sense for the traitor to let their brother terrorists get
killed unless the Tigers getting killed were not brother terrorists. If Taboada, or Reverte, actually worked for this myste-

rious other group whose existence the Executioner had suspected all along—this group the Liberty Tigers had to have
to finance a major terrorist strike in the U.S.—then the deaths
of individual Tiger terrorists probably meant nothing to him.
This mystery group's top priority would be the strike in America, and they probably didn't give a plug nickel about the missionaries, the Tigers or anything else that went on in the
Philippines.

Candido Subing and his group, Bolan suddenly realized,
were nothing more than pawns on the chessboard of a more
powerful terrorist entity.

Bolan reached the rocky mountain wall on the other side
of the valley and stopped. He had been tempted several times
during the mission to just grab both Reverte and Taboada and
beat the truth out of them, and for a fleeting second he was
tempted again now. But the Executioner had known all along
that anything gained through such measures was unreliable.
Contrary to what some people thought, beaten men didn't necessarily tell the truth. Beaten men said whatever they thought
would end the beating.

The Executioner reached out, letting his fingers trail along
the rock until he felt them slip off—into an opening. Zona had
been only partially correct, he realized as he looked toward
his hand. He could barely make out the shadowy cave entrance. But it would have been easy to miss had he not been
looking for it. He took two more steps and felt the rock again,
then a second later his hand sank into another hole. He went
on to the third dark entrance, then stopped. They would wait
for Latham here.

Bolan turned to the Filipino and Reverte. One of them was
working for another terrorist organization, or at least another
party that could finance a large-scale terrorist strike in the
United States. And, somehow, he had been keeping Subing

one step ahead of them—not because he was with the Tigers
on the kidnappings, but because Subing himself was to play
some major part in whatever was about to go down in the U.S.
Bolan watched both men in his peripheral vision. One was a
traitor, and while he didn't care about the rest of the Tigers
he wanted to keep Candido Subing alive and well. That was
the only way any of this made sense.

"Hey," Reverte suddenly whispered. "How about dividing
up the stun grenades? Might come in handy."

The Executioner eyed the man. He had intended to hand
out the grenades anyway, with one for each man once Latham
returned. He might as well get two of them distributed now.
Reaching into his pocket, he pulled out one of the new designs
the Stony Man Farm armorer had come up with and looked
down at it. They were round, roughly the size and shape of a
baseball. Light and easy to throw. Looking up at Taboada,
Bolan lobbed a grenade through the air to him. The little Filipino had his right hand on the rifle, steadying it, and reached
up with his left to make the catch.

The Executioner's next toss was to Reverte, and it was the
exact moment that the CIA man caught his stun grenade that
a second epiphany hit the Executioner. Suddenly what had
bothered him about Reverte all along—and it did have to do
with his left-handedness—became crystal-clear.

In a smooth, natural motion, Reverte reached out and
caught the grenade. But he did so with his *right* hand. Since
he was left-handed, that was natural. Southpaws caught with
their right and threw with their left.

What wasn't natural was what Kurtzman had told the Executioner about Reverte's baseball days at Northwestern University. His CIA file had said he was a catcher, and there
simply weren't any left-handed catchers—at least, not past the
peewee leagues. Southpaws behind the plate were severely

obstructed by the men in the batter's box when runners tried to steal and they had to throw to the bases; any team that had a left-handed catcher might as well let an opposing player who reached first go automatically to third.

"Nice catch," the Executioner said, smiling at the CIA man. "I'd almost forgotten. They told me you were a baseball player when I checked you out."

Reverte smiled, then bowed in keeping with the ongoing drama in everything he did. "Oh, yeah," he said. "Loved the old round ball. Northwestern."

"What position again?" Bolan asked

"Catcher," Reverte said, still smiling.

Bolan kept smiling, too. The man had memorized the part he was playing well. But that was exactly what he was doing—playing a part.

The Executioner didn't know who it was standing next to Taboada, but it wasn't CIA Agent William Reverte.

THIRTY MINUTES LATER Latham had returned. "I had to wait and make her leave," he said, breathing heavily after running most of the way back. "She wanted to wait in the jeepney for us." He paused for another breath. "I couldn't swear she didn't come back after I left."

Bolan nodded. He had done all he could do. "You ready?" he asked.

The Texan leaned over and grabbed his knees. "Give me a minute to catch my breath, then we go," he said.

The men waited. Sixty seconds later, the former Delta Force man straightened and nodded. "Let's go."

Bolan looked the men over. "I'll lead," he said. "I want Reynaldo and Reverte next. Then you, John. Follow us, and keep to cover as much as you can. Latham, bring up the rear."

All four men nodded.

Bolan moved on, his fingers tracing the rock until he came to the fourth cave entrance. It was low, but not as low as the one he had crawled into on Mount Bongao. He was able to bend his knees and back and walk in a crouched position. Ten feet inside all light disappeared and he could see nothing but darkness. He didn't want to risk the flashlight unless he had to, so he made his way very much as he had found the entrance on the outside—letting his left hand guide him along the rock.

The Executioner figured Zona couldn't have been more than about ten feet short in her estimate about when they would have to begin their climb. As he moved slowly forward, his shins finally hit something hard and he stopped. Dropping to his knees, the Executioner pulled out the laser flashlight, cupped both hands around it and held it at his feet. He tapped the button on the butt and in the second it was on, he saw everything he needed to know.

Over the centuries, nature herself had cut steps into the mountain's interior; he saw them in front of him now. Some of them long and shallow, others short and steep, but they all led up toward a hole in the rock. There were perhaps twenty of these irregular stairs and they would have to climb them in total darkness.

Except for the men in Bolan's party, no humans had seen the short flash of light. But a flock of bats did, and they suddenly took to the air, flying over Bolan's and the other men's heads in a flurry of beating wings. Replacing the laser light, Bolan moved on as soon as they were gone, slowly feeling his way up the steps. It was long, tense, nerve-racking work, the kind that could make mighty men finally scream in frustration. He was used to such tension and suspected Latham would be fine, too. But Reverte, Taboada and Parks worried him. Reverte and the Filipino for more reasons than one.

Finally, Bolan reached the top step and felt the rock around

he hole. He reached up, took a solid grip and pulled himself
up, higher inside the mountain. Total blackness still sur-
ounded him and he had no idea which way to go from there.
Leaning back toward the hole, he whispered, "Wait."

The Executioner produced the flashlight again. He didn't
know if it would be seen when he turned it on, but he knew
he would never know which way to go if he didn't. Tapping
the button, he noted a passageway between boulders leading
into a dead end to his right. To his left, it twisted out of sight
after fifteen feet or so.

Holding the flashlight behind him so the other men could
see, the Executioner walked on toward the bend in the passageway. When he reached the corner, he peered around the
rock and saw the faintest of lights coming from somewhere
deeper in the mountain. And heard the faintest of voices, as well.

Bolan turned back, leaving on the flashlight until the other
men had joined him. All were trying not to breathe hard, but
the adrenaline running through their veins was making it
nearly impossible. Using hand signals, the Executioner signed
that they would turn the corner, then follow him. He killed the
light and felt his way around the curve.

As he moved nearer to the faint light ahead, Bolan could
smell the scent of burning lamp oil. And as he walked on, the
light grew brighter and he could make out the rocky walls on
both sides of him. Finally they came to the last bend in the
passage before the cavern and Bolan stopped.

By now the ambient light was enough that the men could
see each other. The soldier put his hand up, signaling the others to wait, then edged an eye around the rock. Again, Zona
had been fairly accurate. The cavern could have just held a
double basketball gymnasium. But the resemblance to a gym
stopped there.

The Executioner's first surprise was a huge, industrial-size, gasoline-powered rock-saw standing just inside the entrance. How they had gotten it into the cavern, he didn't know unless it had been disassembled, brought in, then put back together. In any case, why they had brought it became evident when he looked on into the cave. The Tigers had to have planned to use this hideout long after the hostages had either been released or killed, because they had done a good amount of remodeling since Zona had been here. Many of the stalagmites had been sawn off at waist level and below, turning them into crude tables and chairs scattered haphazardly throughout the cavern. To Bolan's right, on the other side of the wall behind which he still hid, was a long series of wooden tables that had to have been built inside the cave after the lumber was carried in. Closest to the doorway where the Executioner stood was a table upon which clothing had been folded—camouflage fatigues, T-shirts, boots and other gear. Next came a table that reminded him of the one in the banana plantation barn; it held several rows of canned food. Water was stored in two-liter plastic bottles just beyond the food and the last table appeared to be scattered with a variety of guns, other weapons and boxes of ammunition.

But it was what Bolan saw against the far wall that caught his attention most. What looked like some kind of wooden crate or cage rested on a separate wooden platform. Inside he could just make out the shape of two hooded figures.

Bolan counted perhaps a dozen men in the cavern, lounging around or going about simple tasks such as loading magazines. Most were seated, but a few leaned against the walls talking. He ducked back around the corner as one of the men seated at one of the stalag-tables eating something from a can glanced up. He didn't know if he'd been seen. Regardless, it was time to act. The men inside were as unaware of any threat right now as they were ever going to be.

"There's only room for two of us to enter at once," Bolan whispered as the men gathered around him just outside the cavern. "Latham, you and I'll go first. We'll toss our grenades toward the back, then take cover as far inside as we can get. Reynaldo and Reverte come next. The place is big and the stun grenades are going to lose a lot of their effect. So keep that in mind." The Executioner hesitated a moment, then looked to John Parks. "Somebody needs to cover the exit, John," he said. "That's you. Stay here and shoot anybody who tries to get out."

Parks started to speak, then nodded. He was a brave man, but he knew his limitations, too, and knew his wife had a better chance of being rescued if he let the pros handle this end of the mission.

The Executioner looked to Latham. "On three," he said. "One...two..."

Bolan and Latham burst into the cavern shoulder to shoulder, heaving their grenades and then diving forward for cover. Latham headed right past the clothing table and the Executioner rolled past the huge rock saw to the rear of a stalagmite that had been cut into a seat. Both men covered their ears but felt the concussion as the stunners went off on the other side of the cavern.

Several of the Tigers in the room had looked up and stared, not believing their eyes. Then the stun grenades exploded and the few men toward the rear of the cavern fell to the ground. The grenades had less effect on the men closer to the front. Still, they were surprised at what was suddenly happening and froze in place.

The first rounds of the battle coughed out of the Calico in a sound-suppressed, 3-round burst. They drew first blood when they peppered the chest of the terrorist who had been eating from the can. He jerked in spasms, then fell forward over the makeshift table.

From the other side wall of the cave, Latham opened up with a 3-round burst of 5.56 mm NATO rounds from his CAR-15. In the corner of his eye, Bolan saw Reverte and Taboada come barreling into the cavern and fly to cover behind more of the stalagmite stumps. The Executioner watched as a Tiger with a long wispy beard, carrying a box toward the front of the cavern, suddenly rollicked in a dance of death. Reverte followed Latham, cutting loose with his own CAR, and Taboada dived behind the power saw just behind the Executioner.

Bolan rose over the rocklike stump, fired another 3-round burst from the Calico and dropped a terrorist who was running toward the weapons table. Return fire finally came as the hardmen awakened from their temporary shock and the effect of the stun grenades. AK-47s appeared and return fire flew toward the invaders.

The Executioner rolled out from behind cover and kept moving as he crossed the floor to another of the sawed-off stalagmites. He fired as he rolled, a full-auto blast from the Calico scattering across the cavern. Two of his rounds caught a turbaned Tiger in the throat and face. Two more took another terrorist in the chest. The final three blew into the groin and lower abdomen of a Tiger wearing green jungle cammies. All three men had hit the ground by the time the Executioner rolled to a halt.

Out of the corner of his eye, Bolan could see Taboada carefully picking his targets, firing semiauto with the CAR-15. Good, Bolan thought. The man had already proved he didn't panic, and he wasn't wasting ammo, either. And the Executioner no longer needed to worry about the little Filipino shooting him in the back.

It was Reverte he would have to keep his eyes on during the firefight.

Bolan glanced across the cavern toward where Latham

and Reverte had taken cover. He could hear their CARs exploding but both men had disappeared.

More full-auto fire from the AK-47s pounded into the new stalagmite in front of the Executioner and he felt the vibrations against his body. He leaned around the side of the stalagmite, firing the Calico one-handed at a flash of green he had suddenly seen. He didn't know who it was, or whether the green had been a shirt or pants. He just knew none of his men was wearing green and by that process of elimination the color became a target.

It turned out to be a BDU shirt on a clean-shaven Tiger in his late twenties. But the green blouse quickly darkened as it soaked up blood in the wake of the Executioner's 3-round burst. With a wild, crazed, violent screech, a tall man with a full beard, dressed in a long flowing caftan, suddenly leaped to the top of one of the tables. With another shriek he jumped down and sprinted straight for the Executioner, firing his AK-47 on the run. But his rounds were as wild as his screams and the Executioner dropped him with a triple-tap of 9 mm hollowpoint rounds.

Latham and Reverte were still invisible behind cover, but Bolan could hear the boom of their CAR-15s at work across the room. They were firing, which meant they were still alive. Whether they were hitting anything, he couldn't tell. The Executioner dropped a man who leaned out from cover too far, then glanced over his shoulder at Taboada. The little Filipino had his weapon on full-auto and was cutting loose on a terrorist near the back of the cave.

A small Filipino with a Czech Skorpion suddenly popped up not ten feet from the Executioner. He had been on the floor behind a short stalagmite and was so tiny Bolan had assumed no one was hiding there. Only Bolan's split-second reflexes saved him from the 7.62 mm rounds blasted his way. Dropping below the assault, he tapped the trigger of the Calico and spit three hollowpoint slugs to the little man's throat and face.

Another terrorist, deciding he'd had enough, rose from hiding and raced for the doorway. Bolan twisted at the waist and snapped off another short burst of fire. The runner wore the odd combination of blue jeans, T-shirt and kaffiyeh and groaned as the rounds took him across the backs of the thighs. The Executioner started to fire again as the man reached the opening, but before he could pull the trigger he heard a full-auto burst of 5.56 mm rounds from outside the cavern. The terrorist stumbled backward into the cave and toppled to the ground. John Parks stepped into the doorway, a wisp of smoke rising from the barrel of his rifle.

Bolan turned his attention back to a terrorist wearing a Day-Glow orange sport shirt with BDU pants. The man might as well have had "Shoot me!" painted on his chest. The Executioner dropped the Calico's front sight on the orange and pulled the trigger.

But as he did, a full-auto volley of fire suddenly passed within a hairbreath of his head, warming the skin on the side of his face and making his ears ring. Even before the man in the orange shirt had fallen, Bolan turned in the direction from which the shots had come.

And saw the scowling face of William "Billy" Reverte rising up behind another of the shortened stalagmites across the room.

Bolan turned the Calico his way and cut loose with his own autofire. Reverte ducked back, but at least one of the Executioner's rounds had to have hit because he heard the man groan.

Reverte stayed hidden. Keeping one eye cocked toward the traitorous actor, Bolan turned most of his attention back to a Tiger who was making his way from cover to cover at the back of the cavern. He stood directly in front of the wooden cage where the missionary women sat, huddled together in terror.

Bolan checked his angle of fire, making sure it would rise above the hooded heads, and held the trigger back again. Another burst caught the hardman center-chest.

In his peripheral vision the Executioner saw Reverte appear again across the cavern. He was swinging the Calico back that way when Taboada suddenly rose to his feet next to him. Reverte adjusted his aim toward the little Filipino and the two men fired as one.

Reverte jerked back and forth twice, then fell to the floor. Bolan glanced to his side and saw the Filipino still standing.

Throughout the firefight, rounds had ricocheted around the cavern like maddened wasps, bouncing off the rock walls, the sawed-off stalagmites and the stalactites that grew down from the ceiling. But now, the gunfire suddenly died, and after a few more ricochets around the room, the last of the lead, and the noise, fell away.

Across the room, Latham rose and began making the rounds of the dead terrorists. Bolan and Taboada walked toward Reverte, who lay on his back, his chest heaving up and down. John Parks entered the room, reminding the Executioner why they had come in the first place. "Keep an eye on him," the Executioner told Taboada. He nodded toward Reverte, then looked back to the little Filipino.

Only then did he notice the blood soaking Taboada's shirt and the pain on his face.

The Executioner reached out to help the little Filipino, but he jerked away. "No!" he screamed. "Do not touch me!" Then, more quietly, he said, "The…blood."

Parks had arrived by then and Bolan took him by the arm. "This way," he said, and hurried toward the rear of the cavern where he'd seen the wooden stand and crate. As the Executioner and the missionary neared, it looked more like an animal cage than a crate. But the figures inside were human. And female.

John Parks reached down through the top of the wooden structure and pulled the hood off of the nearer woman. He leaned forward, kissed her on the cheek, then jerked the other hood away.

This woman, he was still kissing when the Executioner moved back to where Reverte lay.

Taboada was swaying back and forth on his feet, both hands pressed to his bloody shirt. "Let me do something," Bolan said.

The Filipino shook his head. "There is nothing you can do," he said. "Besides…it is better this way."

The Executioner stared into the man's eyes. Then, slowly, he nodded.

Turning his attention to Reverte, Bolan looked down at the man who was gasping for air, blood spewing from his lips with every breath. "You aren't Reverte, and you aren't with the CIA," Bolan said. "What's your real name?"

"None…of your…business…" the man breathed. The fake Brooklynese was gone now, replaced by an accent the Executioner couldn't quite place. Saudi, maybe. Or Yemeni.

"You're dying," the Executioner stated flatly. "Tell the truth for once. How'd you get Reverte's CIA credentials?" he asked.

The face of the man on the ground contorted in pain. "I killed…him," he spewed.

The Executioner stared into the dying eyes and thought of the picture on the CIA card. There were any number of explanations for it from replacing the real picture with one of his own to simply looking enough like the man to get by. That didn't matter now, though. But there were other things that did.

"How'd you learn everything?" Bolan demanded. "The details about Reverte? Northwestern baseball. Drama. About our mission?"

"He…told…me," the dying man said. An evil grin momentarily replaced the grimace. "Not…willingly…at first."

Bolan continued to stare at the man, fighting the urge to
ll him now. Whoever he was, he had tortured an American
lA agent. He deserved to die and he would. But rather than
d his life now, the Executioner needed to make the most of
e minutes and seconds the man had left; to get all the infor-
ation from him he possibly could because the Subing situ-
ion didn't end with freeing the missionaries.

"Why didn't you try to kill me before now?" Bolan asked.

The dying man laughed, and the laugh became a choking
ugh that sent more blood flying from his lips. Bolan thought
would end then, but suddenly he was under control again.
ou and…your…friend," he gasped. Bolan knew he meant
atham. "Always…together."

Bolan nodded to himself, remembering the subtle ways this
an had tried to separate him and Latham. Like on Mount
ongao, when he didn't think all of them should go up the
il together. Then later, when he'd tried to accompany Bolan
the scouting mission that led to the cave and Roger Ewton.
it, as the Executioner had already surmised, he had been in
particular hurry to kill them. His job was simply to make
re they didn't get Candido Subing, and he didn't care how
any other Tigers died if it kept the Executioner away from
eir leader.

A few feet away, Taboada sat on one of the cold hard seats.
ne hand still held his chest. When Bolan turned toward him,
held the other arm out, palm up, to keep the Executioner away.

"You aren't a Tiger," Bolan said, turning back to the man
the cavern floor. "Who are you with? Who are you work-
g for?"

The evil smile curled the lips of the man on the ground
ain. "You…will never…know." He spit the words out.

"What have you got planned in America?" Bolan asked.
e could see the man's time was drawing short. If nothing

else, he would bleed out in a few more seconds. "What's Sul
ing going to do in the United States?"

"That…I *will* tell…" the dying man said. "Because yo
will…never find…him in time." He paused, took in a dee
breath, then breathed out one faint and final word. "Nuke
he said.

Latham had finished checking the bodies and had walke
up as the man uttered the word. "Oh, hell," the Texan said.

John Parks had cut both of the women loose and was help
ing them to walk toward where the others were gathered i
the middle of the cavern floor.

The Executioner looked back down at the man who ha
called himself Reverte just in time to see him take his la
breath. Then he looked back to Taboada and saw that the li
tle Filipino had done the same.

CHAPTER FOURTEEN

Jack Grimaldi pushed the Learjet through the air at top speed as Bolan pressed the phone to his ear. "Okay, Bear," he told Kurtzman. "It was a long shot but worth trying. See if you can get a hit on Interpol or any of the European agencies."

"Call you back," Kurtzman said quickly, and hung up. The Executioner didn't take his briskness as an offense. There simply wasn't any time for amenities at the moment.

Somewhere in the United States of America, a suicide bomber armed with a nuclear bomb was about to kill millions of people.

The Executioner sat back against his seat, every cell in his body screaming to go into action. Waiting was always the hardest part of any mission. But in many ways, that ability to be patient when inaction was called for, was what separated the real warriors from the also-rans.

Bolan closed his eyes. The best way to identify the man who had impersonated CIA Agent William Reverte, he had known, would be fingerprints. So, lacking ink and an official fingerprint card, he had used the man's own blood to roll a complete set of finger and palm prints from the corpse. The prints had gone onto a blank piece of paper Latham had found in the cavern which had then been faxed to Stony Man Farm the second they had gotten on the plane with Grimaldi. Kurtzman had run them through AFIS—America's Advanced Fingerprint Identification System—but had come up with no matches. Whoever it was beginning to rot away on the floor in the cavern on Siquijor had no record in the U.S.

The Executioner thought back to the whirlwind events of the past few hours. As Latham had suspected she would, Zona had returned with the jeepney to wait on them. But by then the Executioner had already called Grimaldi and told him about the open stretch of land next to the mountain. Both Zona and Grimaldi were there when he, Latham and the three missionaries had come out of the cave. But the Executioner had another surprise waiting for him, as well. Charlie Mott and two blacksuits had just dropped off a still-angry-and-fighting Mario Subing on Minandao, then island-hopped to Siquijor and landed next to Grimaldi. He had taken John and Rachael Parks, Kim Tate and Zona and little Edward with him. They would fly back to the U.S, with a short stop on the way to return the mother and child to Sweden.

Bolan turned to see Latham behind him. The man was as tightly wound and ready for action as he was. But he was a professional, too, and was controlling it.

The sat phone rang and Bolan thumbed the on button and held it to his ear. "Yeah, Bear?"

"No record in Europe or Interpol," Aaron "The Bear" Kurtzman said. "That's the bad news."

"It take it there's some good?" the Executioner said.

"That's a big 10-4," Stony Man Farm's computer genius said, and Bolan could almost see the familiar smile on the man's face as he spoke. "You remember telling me about the big blond-haired guy back at the banana plantation?"

"I do."

"I got to thinking about that, and took another long shot—ran the prints through all the Scandinavian countries. Got a hit in both Sweden and Finland." He paused. "Your man is Hashem Ali Mohammed," he said. "Saudi mercenary. He's been loosely associated with several Mideast terrorist groups over the years but only on a contract basis. He's not in it for anybody's cause except his own."

Bolan nodded to himself. He knew Kurtzman had to have more, and waited.

"Swedish Intelligence has a file on him," the computer man went on. "He's—I guess *was* is the proper tense—employed by a company called Northern Lights Security, International."

"And that's what?" Bolan asked. Latham had leaned forward in his seat and the soldier could feel the man just over his shoulder.

"They sell security equipment to governmental agencies all over the world," Kurtzman came back. "We aren't talking burglar alarms here. More like explosive detection devices, some of the most sophisticated metal detectors for airports, that sort of thing. Subsidiary of something called Mikelsson Enterprises," Kurtzman said.

"Have you checked Mikelsson out yet?" the Executioner asked.

"Running it now. Thought I'd update you while I waited."

"Thanks, Bear. Call me back when you have something else." Bolan killed the sat phone again and leaned back, closing his eyes.

"We're about ten minutes out of NYC," Grimaldi suddenly said, breaking into the Executioner's thoughts.

Bolan opened his eyes just as the phone rang again.

"We may have hit the jackpot," Kurtzman said. "Mikelsson Enterprises is a guy named Lars Mikelsson. Besides security he's into the automobile and aircraft industries, mining, you name it. He deals heavy arms to half the governments of the world, including our own. In fact, I think he may *own* half of the world."

Bolan knew the man was exaggerating but he got the point. "Any intel on him?" he asked.

"Yep," said the man from Stony Man Farm. "No record, but Swedish Intelligence has a file on him, too. He's suspected of doing business with the bad guys as well as the good. But nothing anybody can prove." Kurtzman paused and Bolan heard him suck in a breath. "I got to wondering how he might get a nuke into the U.S. if he had one. So I dug a little deeper."

The Learjet had been cleared for landing and was descending through the air toward the runway when the Executioner said, "Let's cut to the chase, Bear. Bottom line?"

"Along with everything else, he owns a fleet of cargo ships," Kurtzman said. "And one of them just sailed out of port from New York."

Bolan could feel his blood racing as what was happening began to take shape. Before he could say anything, Kurtzman went on. "The ship was delayed for a day," he said. "Got red-flagged for a thorough search."

"They find anything?" the Executioner asked, feeling himself frown. If Customs had found the nuke, it seemed a little too good to be true.

"Just some minor stuff," Kurtzman said. "Not what you're looking for."

Bolan's eyebrows fell lower on his forehead. Something didn't smell right. There was more to this than met the eyes. "Bear," he said, "find out who was in charge of searching the ship."

"Already have," said Kurtzman. "Officer named Williams. Randall Williams."

Bolan felt his fingers grip the phone tighter. "Okay," he said. "Bear, we've got to do a lot of things fast." He paused, forming a list in his mind, then said, "Check with Immigration and see if a Candido Subing entered the U.S. during the past two days. It'll come up negative because he'll have used some other name, but check just the same. Then have your computer team start checking on everyone who matches the profile who flew in from the islands."

"That'll take some time to narrow down," Kurtzman said.

"I know. So I want to tackle this thing from the other end at the same time," said the Executioner. "Have an N.Y.P.D. chopper waiting for us when we get to the end of the runway. And have this Williams character in the U.S. Customs office waiting when we get there. Have Hal get the President to call ahead and make things happen. I'm not going to have time to argue with a bunch of Customs bureaucrats."

"Chopper's already waiting," Kurtzman said. "I took the liberty. And I'll have Hal give the Man a call. Anything else?"

"Yeah. Contact Charlie Mott and tell him to stay in Stockholm when he arrives. Tell him to put up the Parks and Kim Tate in a four-star hotel and give them a well-deserved vacation compliments of the government. But I want Charlie to locate this Lars Mikelsson for me, and find out everything he can about the man."

"You got that, too," Kurtzman said, and disconnected the line.

Bolan and Latham had both changed into sport coats and slacks they had found in the lockers aboard the plane, and as soon as Grimaldi rolled them to a halt they deplaned and sprinted across the runway. A blue helicopter with the letters NYPD painted in white on the side was ready to take off, and they ducked under the whirling blades and climbed on board.

The pilot had evidently been told to take orders and ask no questions because he just nodded when Bolan told him where to take them. A few minutes later they were setting down twenty feet from the U.S. Customs office just off the shipping docks.

Bolan led the way inside where the chief Customs inspector was waiting. A burly, red-faced man, he crossed his arms over his chest and said, "You want to tell me what all this is about?"

"When we have time," Bolan said, "I'll be happy to. Where's Williams?"

"In my office," the chief said, looking toward the back wall.

Bolan and Latham didn't wait for introductions. They hurried past the man and through the opening. The Executioner closed the door behind him, almost hitting the chief inspector in the face.

Williams sat in a chair in front of the desk, looking frightened. "I don't know what this is all about," he tried to say.

"Shut up," the Executioner said, standing over the man. "Answer my questions and don't say another word. We don't have time for it."

Williams nodded.

"You passed something you shouldn't have yesterday," he said. "Don't deny it. Just tell us who you gave it to and where."

Williams made one last stab at innocence. "I really don't know—"

Bolan slapped the man across the face. "Listen to me," he said. "I don't know what you were told you were helping smuggle, but it's not what you thought. What you did was help get a nuclear bomb into the country."

Williams's bottom lip dropped almost to the floor as the blood drained from his face, leaving his skin ghastly pale. "I didn't know—"

"Who, where and when?" he demanded.

"I didn't know the guy," he said. "I thought it was antiquities. Egyptian—" When he saw Bolan's hand rising again, he said, "It was in a TV box with a shipment of TVs. I just took

to a room and gave it to a guy at the Howard Johnson on
ight Avenue. Between Fifty-first and Fifty-second."

"What room number?"

"It was 304," Williams told him.

Bolan opened the door to find the Customs supervisor
vaiting, still red-faced and angry. "Take this clown into cus-
)dy," he ordered as he and Latham raced toward the door
gain. "Explanation will be forthcoming."

A moment later the N.Y.P.D. chopper was rising in the air
gain. Bolan gave the pilot the directions and it took only a
ew minutes before they were descending again into the heart
f New York's theater district. Cars screeched to a halt, and
ie people along the sidewalks ducked into available door-
vays as the helicopter set down in the middle of 8th Avenue.

Bolan and Latham sprinted into the lobby, racing past the
pen mouths of both residents and motor lodge employees to-
vard a red sign that read Stairs. Pushing through the door, they
)ok the steps three at a time to the second floor. Another sign
n the wall, with an arrow, pointed them toward rooms 302
irough 324, and they rounded the corner to the second room
1 that hall.

Bolan pulled the Desert Eagle from under his sport coat
nd lifted a foot. To his side, he saw Latham's Browning Hi-
'ower. A second later, the steel trim around the door cracked
nd broke and the door swung inward. Latham followed him
ito the room, the red dot from the Crimson Trace laser site
n his Browning dancing along the floor.

The room was empty. So was the bathroom and the closet.

But sitting on the bed, open and empty, was a cardboard
ox that read Sony.

WE'RE GOING TO HAVE to let the locals in on this, Hal," the
Executioner said into the phone. "They're looking for a short

man of Filipino descent. He'll either be wearing a backpac
or carrying a large suitcase or trunk."

On the other end of the line, Hal Brognola said, "He cou
be anywhere."

"That's right," Bolan said. "Regular bombs, they try
find the spot where they'll do the most damage." He paus
and took a breath. "This one, it doesn't matter. Any place w
get the job done."

"I'd start evacuation if it would do any good," Brognola sai

"It won't, Hal. There's no time. If we don't find Subing b
fore he detonates, all of New York and half of Newark will I
history." He stared at the empty television box, trying to thir
of any way that the search might be narrowed down. "Sinc
he can set it off anyplace," he told Brognola, "he may go fc
symbolism. Tell the cops to pay special attention to Amer
can monuments. Big-name businesses. Churches and syr
gogues, too."

"I'm on it," Brognola said.

Bolan and Latham had already started walking out of tl
empty motel room and now sprinted back down the steps
the lobby. The chopper was still waiting for them in the mic
dle of the street and they rose into the air once more. Bola
looked down at the streets below, watching the people g
about their daily routines. None of them knew they were or
step from total vaporization.

The chopper flew low over the streets, with the Execution
and Latham both scanning the sidewalks. From their vantaç
point, they could see black-and-white police cruisers conve
ging on the theater district. Several large vans appeared, ar
men from the N.Y.P.D. Emergency Squad jumped out wea
ing blue baseball caps and matching coveralls. But the searc
seemed futile. There were no doubt thousands of men who f
Subing's description in the area.

The chopper's police-band radio scanner was busy with
traffic, both concerning the search and the regular calls.
Bolan listened with one ear as he continued to scan the streets
below. Under the circumstances, it seemed ludicrous that
citizens were still calling in with complaints about noisy
neighbors and even burglaries and robberies. The Executioner had to remind himself that they had no idea what was
going on.

Then, as he focused on a young man walking down the
street with a backpack, a snatch of radio traffic suddenly
caught the Executioner's attention. Amid the static and other
messages, he heard the words acting strangely and praying.

Turning to the pilot he said, "Did you get that?"

"What?" the chopper pilot asked.

"Something about someone acting strangely and praying,"
Bolan said.

The pilot shook his head. "No, but we can find out," he
said. He reached forward to the programmable radio mounted
in front of him, entered a different frequency and lifted the
microphone. "Air 17 to base," he said. "Come in, base."

A moment later he was answered by a female voice.

"Base, 10-9 on the traffic concerning prayer and acting
strange," he said.

The dispatcher's voice came back. "It was Midtown," the
woman said. "Some guy in the stairwell of Bloomingdale's."

Bolan grabbed the mike. "Any more details?" he asked.

"Let me check." The voice on the other end became silent
for a moment and static coughed out of the receiver. Then the
dispatcher came back and said, "Evidently, he's kneeling on
one of the stairwell landings there, and praying loudly. A
car's already been dispatched to check it out. No big deal.
They'll end up taking him to Bellevue."

Bolan reminded himself again that even the cops didn't

know all of what was going on. All they knew was that there was some kind of emergency and they were looking for a Filipino with a backpack or suitcase. Never in her wildest dreams had this dispatcher imagined a nuke going off in Midtown Manhattan. "What else?" the Executioner demanded.

"That's about it," the dispatcher said, her voice sounding irritated. "The caller said he was wearing a pack of some kind, muttering, 'Allah' this and 'Allah' that.'"

"Call off the responding unit," Bolan told the woman. "And tell Bloomingdale's security to stay away, too. Keep everybody away from this guy and out of the stairwells."

"I can't—"

"Yes, you can!" the Executioner boomed into the microphone. "And you will! If you'd like the President of the United States to call you, that can be arranged. But until then, get on the horn and get it done."

"Roger," the voice said weakly.

The pilot heard the transmission as well as the Executioner and Latham, and by now he had picked up on the severity, if not the details, of what was happening. "Bloomingdale's," he said. "I can set us down on the roof."

Bolan watched the ground below as they crossed out of the theater district into Midtown. A few seconds later the struts hit the asphalt on Bloomingdale's roof, and he and Latham dived from the chopper and raced toward a door in the center of the building. It was locked. But a round from the Beretta opened it as quickly as a key.

The Executioner stepped into the semilit stairwell. Latham followed. Somewhere below, he could hear the eerie murmur of a voice chanting out loud. Quickly but silently, the two men began to descend the steps. As each flight came and went, the voice below became more clear. Bolan couldn't understand

he language but recognized it as Arabic. And here and there,
here were enough "Allahs" and "Mohammeds" to convince
him it was indeed a prayer.

When they had reached the eighth floor, Bolan stuck his
head over the rail and saw a prostrate man kneeling in front
of the steps just below. Candido Subing's face was on the cold
concrete of the landing, his arms outstretched in front of him
as he said his—and New York City's—final prayer. Next to
him was a brown canvas backpack and on the first step leading up to where Bolan and Latham had stopped, he saw a rec-
angular instrument that resembled a television remote
control.

Bolan lined the Beretta's sights on the electronic detona-
or. Then, the possibility that the bullet might activate the im-
pulse to the nuke crossed his mind and he shifted the barrel
oward Subing's head. But before he could line up the sights
again, the Filipino suddenly jerked his head off the floor and
ooked straight up at the Executioner.

With a scream of anger, hatred and insanity, Subing
snatched the detonator from the step in front of him and
lucked back behind the stairs.

As he bolted down the steps after the man, Bolan heard the
loor to the seventh floor opening.

The backpack was still on the concrete as the Executioner
eached the bottom of the steps. But it didn't matter. Subing
had the remote detonator and could touch off the nuke from
anywhere within reasonable distance. Leaping over the bomb
hat was about to erase New York City from the map, Bolan
saw that the door was swinging shut and dived through the
opening.

Several shocked voices could be heard as the Executioner
it the ground on his shoulder, then rolled to his feet. He
ound himself in the ladies' wear department, with startled

women standing around racks of dresses, sweaters and skirts
They were all staring away from him toward a man sprinting
down the aisle.

Candido Subing's hands pumped back and forth in time
with his legs and in his right hand Bolan could see the remote
detonator.

The Executioner ground to a halt in the middle of the aisle.
He raised the Beretta to eye level, dropping the sights on the
back of the running man's head. The women who had been
speechless now saw the gun and several screamed. Bolan
barely heard them as he moved the Beretta's sights slightly
up and down in time with the bobbing of Subing's head.

The terrorist had the detonator in his hand, a finger or
thumb no doubt on the button. Only one thing would keep that
finger from contracting in death spasms and detonating the
nuclear weapon in the stairwell.

That one thing was a perfect brain stem shot that suddenly
and completely, shut down Subing's central nervous system.

The fleeing terrorist was a good twenty-five yards away, and
getting farther by the second. Bolan took a deep breath, let half
of it out and squeezed the trigger. The Beretta coughed once
and blood, brain matter and a host of other cranial fluid blew
out of Candido Subing's face ahead of him. The man flew forward onto his stomach, sliding through his own blood on the
slippery tile. More shrieks and screeches rose from the confused and petrified women who had watched the drama unfold.

The Executioner held the Beretta where it was, and waited.
Subing had either pressed the button, or he hadn't. But either
way, whatever happened now was beyond Bolan's control.

Five seconds ticked by and the women continued to
scream. Several had begun to cry, and one was even calling
out for the man with the gun to be arrested. The Executioner

let out the rest of his breath, walked forward and knelt next to the body of the man on the floor.

Holstering the Beretta, he took the remote control device out of the limp fingers.

LARS MIKELSSON had been angry at first, but word had leaked out among his governmental clients that New York had been one step away from a nuclear disaster, and that had worked almost as well as if the bomb had actually gone off. He was getting calls from all over the world, and it looked as though his new nuclear detection device—a handheld apparatus that looked vaguely like a metal detector, was going to become a must-have piece of equipment for every nation that could afford one. It could penetrate any cover a nuclear bomb, or nuclear components, were put into; iron, steel, anything, and he already had shifts of men in his manufacturing lab working around the clock, trying to fill the orders. And no one suspected he had had anything at all to do with the fiasco that had ended at Bloomingdale's in New York City.

Yes, Lars Mikelsson thought, he had won once again.

The phone on his desk buzzed and he lifted the receiver to his ear. "Yes?" he said.

"Your two o'clock appointment is here, Mr. Mikelsson," his secretary told him.

The fat man looked at his watch. They were five minutes early. Slightly annoyed, he said, "Very well, send them in," and cradled the phone.

The door to his office opened and his secretary stepped back to admit two men. Both were large and looked fit, but the one wearing the navy-blue suit was obviously the leader, and he came in first. The smile on his face looked hard. In fact, the whole face looked hard, as if this man had seen it all dur-

ing his lifetime but been tough enough to live it out. That didn't
surprise Mikelsson. He was used to dealing with such men.

The other man wore a light tan Western-cut suit, a turquoise
bolo tie and a spotless white cowboy hat. He followed the
taller man in to the chairs in front of Mikelsson's desk.

The fat man struggled to his feet and stuck a pudgy hand
across the desk toward the two Americans. Both shook his
hand, then sat down.

Mikelsson decided a little small talk might break the ice
between him and these new customers, so he looked at the
man in the cowboy hat. "I have always loved your American
Western films," he said, smiling. "Bang! Bang! The good
guys always win." He was surprised when it was the other man
who answered.

"Yes," the big man in the blue suit said. "You can count on
that." His smile still looked hard.

Turning his attention back to the cowboy, the fat man said,
"A beautiful hat."

The cowboy looked up at the brim in front of his eyes and
smiled. "Stetson," he said. "You wouldn't believe where I
found it, either."

"Oh?" said the fat man.

"New York City, of all places."

"Yes." Mikelsson nodded. "One does not think of New York
as a place for cowboys." He decided it was time to get down
to business. "So," he said, "you are looking for small arms,
no?"

The bigger of the two men nodded. "We were," he said.
"But we're also interested in one of your new products, as
well. Some nuclear detection device, I understand?"

"Ah, yes. They are back-ordered at the moment, I am sorry
to tell you. After the close call you Americans had…" He held
both pudgy hands out, palms up, and shrugged.

"Well," the taller man said, "I can understand that. If we'd ad a few of your new detectors when that nuke first showed p in port, we'd have found it then, wouldn't we?"

"Oh, most certainly," the fat man said. "It can detect the resence of uranium and other—" He cut his own words off uddenly, realizing what the man had just said. No one but he new the nuclear bomb had come in by ship and been in port. he Americans were still trying to trace the origin of the eapon.

Looking back at the two men, Mikelsson saw that their niles were gone.

"You had quite a little game going, didn't you, Mikelsson?" aid the man in the blue suit. "Create problems that need to e solved, then sell the solutions." He shook his head back and rth, and the fat man suddenly felt an emotion he had not experienced in many years. Fear. He waited, wondering if he ould sneak his hand to the phone on his desk and tap the nergency button that would call in his personal security experts from the offices down the hall.

"Subing was your fall guy," said the big man who had now sen to his feet and looked bigger than ever. "The missionies, they were nothing but a way for you to find a misled regious zealot willing to die for his cause." He looked down the fat man and shook his head in disgust. "He didn't know was really *your* cause, did he?"

The fat man knew he should say something. But when he pened his mouth to deny any knowledge of what was being id, no words would come out.

The cowboy had risen from his chair now, too, and stepped rward. Both of them towered over the desk and looked to ars Mikelsson like avenging angels sent from an angry god.

"Anything you'd like to say before you die?" asked the man the blue suit.

The fat man tried to speak again, but all that came out we[re] a few blustering, unintelligible syllables and a good deal [of] saliva.

Both men suddenly had guns in their hands, and the fat ma[n] saw a tiny red dot dancing on his shirt below his jowls. H[e] knew what it was. One of his own companies manufacture[d] such devices.

"No?" asked the man in the blue suit. "I guess there's re[e]ally nothing to say anyway." His gun didn't have a laser sigh[t]ing device, but the lighting in the office was such that the f[at] man could look down the barrel and see a hollowpoint bull[et] staring him in the eyes.

Lars Mikelsson saw the man with the bolo tie tighten h[is] finger on the trigger. He never heard the shot that ended his lif[e.]

Mack Bolan and Charlie Latham holstered their guns b[e]neath their jackets, then turned to leave.

FULL
BLAST

The President's fail-safe option when America is threatened is
an elite group of cybernetics specialists and battle-hardened
commandos who operate off the books and under governmental
radar. This ultra-clandestine force called Stony Man has defeated
terror on many fronts. Now, they're dealing with an escalating crisis
from outside the country—and a far bigger one from within....

From within the ranks of America's protectors and defenders, a
conspiracy to overthrow the U.S. government appears unstoppable.

STONY
MAN ®

*Available
June 2005
at your favorite
retailer!*

GOLD
EAGLE ®

GSM77

TAKE 'EM FREE

2 action-packed novels plus a mystery bonus

NO RISK

NO OBLIGATION TO BUY

James Axler
Outlanders

CHILDREN OF
THE SERPENT

After 4,000 years the kings return to claim their kingdom: Earth.

He is a being of inhuman evil, a melding of dragon, myth and machine.
He is Lord Enlil, ruler of the Overlords. As the barons evolve into
creatures infinitely more dangerous than the egomaniacs who ruled
from the safety of their towers, Tiamat, safeguarding the ancient race,
is now the key to the fruition of their plan. Kane and the Cerberus
exiles, pledged to free humanity from millennia of manipulation, face
a desperate—perhaps impossible—task: stop Enlil and the Overlords
from reaching the mother ship...and claiming Earth as theirs.

Available May 2005 at your favorite retailer.

Or order your copy now by sending your name, address, zip or postal code, along with
a check or money order (please do not send cash) for $6.50 for each book ordered
($7.99 in Canada), plus 75¢ postage and handling ($1.00 in Canada), payable to Gold
Eagle Books, to:

In the U.S.	In Canada
Gold Eagle Books	Gold Eagle Books
3010 Walden Avenue	P.O. Box 636
P.O. Box 9077	Fort Erie, Ontario
Buffalo, NY 14269-9077	L2A 5X3

Please specify book title with your order.
Canadian residents add applicable federal and provincial taxes.

GOLD
EAGLE

GOUT33